The Children of Lovely Lane

SS

The Children of Lovely Lane

Nadine Dorries

W F HOWES LTD

This large print edition published in 2017 by
W F Howes Ltd
Unit 5, St George's House, Rearsby Business Park,
Gaddesby Lane, Rearsby, Leicester LE7 4YH

1 3 5 7 9 10 8 6 4 2

First published in the United Kingdom in 2016
by Head of Zeus, Ltd

A CIP catalogue record for this book is available
from the British Library

ISBN 978 1 51005 766 1

Typeset by Palimpsest Book Production Limited,
Falkirk, Stirlingshire

Printed and bound by
T J International in the UK
Printforce Nederland b.v. in the Netherlands
Ligare in Australia

MIX
Paper from
responsible sources
FSC
www.fsc.org   FSC® C013056

For my own children. My three ferociously bright, independent, strong, kind, beautiful daughters, Philippa, Jennifer and Cassandra.

CHAPTER 1

Emily Haycock's hand trembled slightly as she read the letter that, unknown to her, Dr Gaskell had placed on her desk only half an hour earlier. The envelope, crisp, blue and distinctive, had called out to her before she'd even had time to remove her cloak. It was the first thing her eyes had alighted upon as she opened her office door. As the director of nursing at St Angelus, Sister Haycock lived in rooms on the first floor, above the main entrance TO the hospital. She no longer wore a uniform but was reluctant to abandon her thick, lined cape, which could be thrown over her shoulder in seconds. Emily was always in a hurry.

I shall have to retire someday, Emily, and I feel it may be sooner rather than later. I would like to leave knowing that St Angelus is in good hands. The right hands. The new NHS has presented us with many difficult challenges and I have no doubt there will be many more. The hospital must embrace this new and rapidly changing world and nothing would please me more than to see you established in the role of assistant matron. You would then be ready to take the helm when Matron reaches a similar conclusion to mine regarding her own tenure of her prestigious and long-held post. It is time for a new generation to take care of our patients and everyone who works at St Angelus.

Lowering herself into her chair, Emily let out the long breath she hadn't realized she was holding. Liverpool born and bred and just the wrong side of thirty, Emily had worked her way up through the nursing ranks of St Angelus. Over the years she had earned respect for standing up to Matron and was liked by all, even, rather begrudgingly, by Matron herself. She and Matron had got off to a bad start, but once Matron had been reassured that Emily did not covet her job – not for the time being, anyway – she had softened towards the now not so young woman.

Dr Gaskell was the most senior physician in the hospital and Emily had no idea that he watched over her, nor that it was because of him that she'd been taken on at St Angelus in the first place. He had treated Emily's mother for TB many years earlier and had never forgotten the earnest young girl with the worried expression and wide eyes who'd asked him, 'Is Mam going to get better soon?' When Mrs Haycock had later failed to turn up for her X-ray and transfer across the water to a sanatorium, he had made enquiries and was told that his patient had been one of the many casualties of the direct hit on George Street during the worst night of bombing Liverpool suffered in the war. The only surviving members of the Haycock family were the young Emily he remembered and her stepfather.

The next time Dr Gaskell saw Emily was on the day of her interview at the hospital. He recognized the name and then the face of his late patient's daughter. As she sat before the appointments committee, of which he was the chairman, something touched him. He could sense her vulnerability. He could only imagine what she had lived through and he was determined that St Angelus would do right by this obviously very capable young woman. It was his casting vote that had swung the position for her. It was a rare and sweet moment of satisfaction for him and he felt he had honoured a duty to his patient by proxy. He had, after all, been able to help. It was not a conscious act, but from that moment on he had become Emily's guardian angel.

Having become a ward sister, Emily was now responsible for the nurses' training throughout their three years at the hospital. She loved her job. She had passed up the opportunity to apply for the post of assistant matron herself in other hospitals in Liverpool, preferring to remain at the hospital she had known as a child, which sat between the Dock Road and Lovely Lane.

Emily kept Dr Gaskell's letter in her handbag

and when no one was looking she slipped it out and reread it many times. In her heart, she knew it was what she should do. It was what she wanted more than anything: the next and last step towards achieving her dream of becoming the matron of St Angelus. But she also wanted to take her current group of nurses all the way to finals and until that day arrived, she would stick with them. It was her obligation. It was too soon to become assistant matron. There was also the unspoken stigma, one she was as yet not ready to face or embrace, that all matrons were spinsters. Once a matron, never a wife. Tucked away deep inside her heart was the hope, small and fading, that one day she might meet someone she could love and marry. She was still young enough, but only just. She could still have a baby, but she would have to be quick, and there was no hint of either happening any time soon. The day she felt strong enough to abandon her dream would be the day she would say to herself, that's it, you are officially a spinster of this parish for ever more. Only then would she take the next step up the nursing-hierarchy ladder.

Weeks later, she finally shared the contents of the letter with Biddy. Biddy Kennedy was the housekeeper in the school of nursing and had assumed the role of mother, mentor and friend to Emily the day she became aware that all three posts were vacant.

'Well, if the board has now advertised the job,

why would ye not be applying for it?' Biddy asked her as she busied herself polishing the telephone on Emily's desk.

Emily had been reading the application forms for the new intake of student nurses and was about to start on her notes for the next lecture. The words *The Lymphatic System* had been sitting at the top of a piece of foolscap paper for the past two days, taunting her, waiting. But there was no point trying to concentrate when Biddy was in the room.

'You know what, Biddy, I think the January '52 intake were the best this hospital has had since I took up my post at the school,' she said, looking up from her papers and sitting back in the chair. 'I've had nothing but good reports about Nurse Tanner. She's so highly thought of, Matron is placing her on casualty next. Who would have thought that, eh, after such a rocky start?'

'Don't avoid the question,' chided Biddy with a smile. 'We all know you have a soft spot for Nurse Tanner and the nurses down at Lovely Lane. Anyone would think they were your own children. They've done their first year, they know their way around now and, believe me, not one of them will give you thanks for holding your career back while theirs moves forward.'

Emily laid down her pen. Here we go, she thought. I'm in for a grilling. There was no way to escape an interrogation led by Biddy and so she gave her her full attention.

'I know all of that, Biddy, but I'm attached to

this group. I stuck my neck out with this lot. You do realize that Dana Brogan is the first nurse from the west of Ireland to be put on to the SRN training and not the SEN, don't you? And that Nurse Tanner is the first nurse to work in this hospital with a full Dock Road Scouse accent? That's all my doing. Those girls are my responsibility. I can't desert them.'

Biddy raised an eyebrow but didn't interrupt.

'I've only been in this job for a few years and I can't leave until I can really show that I've made a significant difference. It's going to take another two, at least. The day I see nurses Tanner, Brogan, Baker and Harper all lined up and ready for me to pin a St Angelus hospital badge on to their uniforms is the day I can start to think about it. They will be the proof that I have done something useful.'

'That's as maybe. I hope it keeps fine for you and it isn't a decision you will live to regret. Imagine if the new assistant matron is even more of a scold than Matron – we all know how long it's taken to get her to be civil to you.'

Emily sat on the board of appointments which scrutinized the applications of every single person wanting a job on the medical team at St Angelus, from student nurse to consultant. Dr Gaskell chaired the board. Once he'd realized that Emily would not be applying for the role of assistant matron herself, he'd asked her to do the first sift and draw up a shortlist.

'Well, we have tried to get the right sort of applicant,' she said. 'Someone who isn't stuck in the pre-war days of the 1930s. A modern assistant matron is what this hospital needs. Someone who is kind and clever. Who cares about the patients and the nurses alike. Who wants to embrace all the new changes and who is committed to lifting the ban on married nurses being able to work. Which, as we know, is just plain discrimination and has to stop. That's the woman we are after, Biddy.'

Biddy picked up the pen pot and polished the already gleaming desk with gusto. Setting the pens back down, she grinned at Emily. 'You do know you have just described yourself, don't you?' she said.

Emily deliberately ignored both her question and the look she gave her. 'I've got a new technique to make sure we get just the right person,' she said. 'I was in charge of the first sift of applicants. I don't know how Matron agreed to that, but she did. The candidates were all much the same: same background, same experience, almost all military-trained, ex-members of the Queen Alexandra army nursing corps. That's the thing, the war is still having a big impact. So I only chose the applicants who had nice-sounding names.' She sounded rather pleased with herself.

Biddy stood upright, her brow furrowed as she looked at Emily with incredulity. She slowly replaced the handset of the telephone she had

7

been cleaning on to the cradle. The bell pinged in protest as she gave the handset a final flick with the duster.

'So, let me get this right. Your involvement so far means that the new assistant matron will have a nice name,' said Biddy, her voice tinged with disbelief.

She crossed the room to give the windowsill a final wipe over and slipped her polishing rag into her apron pocket. She stood and faced Emily straight on. She could see, out of the corner of her eye, hurrying through the back gate of the hospital, the contingent of nurses arriving from Lovely Lane to begin their day on their new ward placements. The pink uniforms were a sight for sore eyes against the soot-blackened red brick of the hospital building. Pammy Tanner was leading from the front, as always, chatting away, laughing, her starched cap on her head bobbing, looking danger-ously close to collapsing in the morning mist.

'Here come your girls,' she said to Emily, with an almost imperceptible nod of the head. 'A Scouser through and through, that Nurse Tanner. Always uses ten words when one will do. She can never keep still either, talks with her hands. Have you noticed?'

For a second Biddy was distracted by the clean morning freshness of the young nurses. Nine hours later, they would stagger down the steps, exhausted, the journey back to the Lovely Lane nurses' home taking twice as long as the morning journey in.

She watched the girls disappear as they mounted the steps into the main hospital building then turned her attention back to Emily. 'If you'd chosen your student nurses by how nice their names sounded, Nurse Tanner and Nurse Brogan wouldn't be here now, would they?'

'Well, what else did I have to go on?' Emily exclaimed. 'There was nothing to pick between any of them. Only having spinsters working in hospitals means that by the time they're forty their résumés read like facsimiles of each others.' They all become one big blur.'

Biddy shook her head in amazement. 'Well, let's hope that doesn't come back and bite you on your skinny little arse, miss,' she said, chuckling.

'It will do no such thing. They have all been QAs. All served in the military. All worked in field hospitals. All unmarried. All held a sister's post for between eight and ten years.'

Emily was only half offended. Her relationship with Biddy was special, but now that Biddy had put into words her less than scientific sifting process, it sounded utterly ridiculous, even to her. She was beginning to feel more than a little challenged. She decided to change the subject. 'Now, a cup of tea and a bacon sandwich would go down nicely. And later, I'm bagging a slice of that chocolate Victoria sandwich that I smelt being made in the kitchen yesterday. That would not go amiss and neither would a little less of your cheek.' Food was always safe ground where Biddy was concerned.

'I can smell the bacon,' said Biddy. 'Fancy that, we have chocolate in the kitchen. It's the first time since 1940, cook told me. Thirteen years ago. Can you imagine that? That was when the supplies ran out.'

'I knew we had chocolate,' said Emily. 'My nose can sniff it a mile off. Do you know, I swear that when cook took the lid off that tin yesterday, I could smell it all the way up in the classroom.'

'You should have seen Tom, the porter's lad who delivered it,' said Biddy. 'Drooling, he was. Put a smile on everyone's face, it has. Right, a cup of tea and a bacon sandwich on its way, Sister.' A subtle readjustment of the special relationship had just taken place, signalled by the fact that Biddy had just referred to Emily as Sister. Before the day was out, it would be back to skinny arse.

Biddy tipped up the coal scuttle on her way out of the room and threw a shovelful on the fire. Closing the office door, she left Emily to her own devices and smiled as she made her way down the stairs and into the kitchen.

'What are you grinning about?' Madge Jones from switchboard was leaning against the sink holding a cuppa, watching the small Chinese cook bake the best sponge she had ever seen.

'It's funny how popular our kitchen has become since the chocolate arrived,' said Biddy as she greeted Madge with a smile. In the hierarchy of non-medical hospital staff, Madge was somewhere up at the top, alongside the head porter, Dessie

Horton. Like Dessie, she had a job that no one else could have done without having a nervous breakdown.

'I've just come to smell it, Biddy,' said Madge. 'But don't think yourself too special. The tins are arriving in all the kitchens today – I can go anywhere to smell chocolate, you know.'

Both women laughed.

'What's the news then?' asked Biddy as she began to assemble a tea tray and butter two slices of thick white bread.

Madge moved closer so that none of the kitchen staff could hear. 'Well, there was an interesting phone call I stayed on the line to listen to. You know I don't do that very often, of course – confidentiality and all that.'

Madge took a breath and a pull on her ciggie while Biddy nodded furiously. Her expression gave not a hint of what she was thinking: yes you do, you bleedin' liar, you listen in on conversations all day long. But Biddy couldn't say that. Madge was very useful to the group, but she was a tricky one; she had an air of self-importance and no one dared challenge her.

Stubbing out her ciggie in the ashtray balanced in her hand, Madge continued. 'Anyway, it was Dr Gaskell. He was talking to one of the other doctors on the regional TB board, the one in Manchester. I heard him say that he was upset your Miss Haycock didn't put herself forward for the post of assistant matron. Said he'd written a

11

letter to her as good as letting her know that if she applied for the job, it was hers. Said he's going to ask her to reconsider.' She cast a nervous glance towards the cook and tapped the side of her nose.

They had a pact, Madge and Biddy. Not a word of what Madge said went outside of their little group. Knowledge and secrecy, they were well aware, equalled power.

'Well, he's going to be disappointed. She's not applying for the job,' said Biddy in a very matter-of-fact tone, 'because she wants to keep an eye on Nurse Tanner and she thinks none of them will get through without her. She's a guardian angel to that nurse and she won't stop until she's qualified and there is nothing me or Dr Gaskell or anyone else for that matter can say that will alter anything. She's a stubborn madam and that's the way it is.'

'It's not a job she needs anyway, Biddy; it's love she wants.'

Biddy moved to the griddle and, using a long fork, speared three slices of dripping bacon and laid them on to the bread.

'Do you think I don't know that? But she doesn't meet anyone, ever. She is devoted to her work, day and night. The only break she has is when she visits her stepfather in the old soldiers' home on the Dock Road. What life is that for her? She can't find love in a home full of injured and elderly veterans. She needs to meet a man her own age, and until she does, Cupid's bow has no chance of finding that skinny little arse upstairs. None.'

'Bet you don't say that to her face, do you!' Madge was rinsing out her cup under the tap and gave Biddy a sideways grin.

'Oh, I certainly do. We understand each other. I sometimes think I'm all she has. There's no one else that I've seen.'

'Oh, get out of here! What about the new consultant on gynae, Dr Gaskell's son?'

Mr Oliver Gaskell had been on gynae for over six months, but five more years would have to pass before Madge, who had worked at the hospital since before the war, ceased referring to him as 'the new consultant'.

'Oh, I had big hopes for him,' said Biddy. 'He seemed very keen. But no, she won't even let me mention anything to do with romance. Clams up, she does, and if I even speak his name, she changes the subject quick, so she does.'

Biddy had no idea that Emily had indeed considered the prospect of Oliver Gaskell; they'd even been out on a date. But after she'd discovered him slow dancing with Nurse Tanner at the doctors' ball and kissing her hair as he held her a little too close, all notions of a blossoming romance were banished. No one was given a second chance with Emily, and now her protégée, Pammy Tanner, was besotted with him. In her heart, Emily knew he had never really been for her.

Madge folded her arms across her red knitted

twinset and studied her freshly painted bright red nails. Her dyed blonde hair bobbed under her chin. Not for the first time, Biddy thought how good she looked for a woman of fifty. Unlike her, Madge was no slave to her curlers and bunions; she was always very well turned out. She loved bright colours, seamed stockings, stilettos and every new lipstick colour that came into Woolworths. But the description 'common' would never be applied to someone who was as clever as Madge and held down a job that no one else could do.

'Well, I think I know someone who is more than a little sweet on her,' said Madge as she turned her attention away from her nails and towards Biddy.

'Who's that then?' said Biddy, suddenly very interested in what Madge had to say. 'Anyone I know?'

'Oh, I would say that was the case all right. It's Dessie. Never stops talking about her, any chance he gets. You test him. Ask him what's the weather going to be like this afternoon and he'll find a way to mention her name even then.'

Biddy smiled. Madge spoke with a smart telephone voice and everyone admired it. Her sharp vowels and clipped diction conveyed knowledge and superiority, with the hint of a Welsh accent in the background. The Irish in Liverpool got along with the Chinese better than the Welsh and that was a fact. But then, as Biddy often said to her

14

friend Elsie, they weren't all bad, the Welsh, just the ones who were prejudiced against the Irish.

Biddy folded her arms across her ample chest and looked thoughtful. 'Dessie, well, that is one man that has never crossed my mind.' Dessie was a good friend of hers.

'No, he wouldn't, would he. You are a bit too close to Dessie, that's why. You can't see what's under your very nose. Fancied her for years. Now, if you ask me, she will never have even considered him – she's known him for too long. That's where you come in, I reckon. Cast a spell, make a love potion, put them in the same room. Something, anything to make her see Dessie in a different light, not as the head porter she works with at the hospital but as, you know . . .'

'Know what?' Biddy furrowed her brow.

'Oh, Biddy, as a man who she would want to . . . Oh, Jesus, Biddy, get into bed with, between the sheets, you know, show her a good time like.'

Biddy spluttered by way of response. A crumb of chocolate cake had fallen on to the table from cook's oven tray and she'd popped it into her mouth. Now she almost choked on it. Tears sprang to her eyes as she looked at Madge. 'Oh, help me! I've just realized how much like a daughter she is! The very thought of Dessie and my boss – get out of here! Haven't you got a switchboard to operate or something?'

Madge smiled as she clip-clopped out of the kitchen door on her strappy stilettos. But before

15

she left, she turned back to Biddy. 'Think about it. Two lonely people. Two lovely people, Biddy. You know it makes sense.'

Emily had frowned at the closed door as she listened to Biddy's footsteps descending the wooden stairs to the kitchen. She was disappointed with herself for how she'd handled the task of selecting candidates. She didn't want to let Dr Gaskell down and yet she knew she already had by not applying for the post herself.

A seagull swooped upwards from the Mersey, squawked, landed on the ledge outside her window and bumped its head on the glass, making her jump. The fire in the grate burst into flames and crackled as the coal settled into place.

'You stupid bird,' she said to the seagull as it turned and gazed into her room. It looked at the papers on her desk and then up at her face and back to the papers. It made her smile. She picked up her pen and one of the assessment sheets waiting to be marked. Within seconds, she had placed it back on the blotter.

'Let's hope that doesn't come back and bite you on your skinny little arse, miss.' Biddy's words repeated in her ear. They had hit a nerve. For the first time, Emily was concerned. Although she would never admit it, Biddy had an uncanny knack of always being right.

Emily had no idea that Matron had been very unhappy about Dr Gaskell giving her the responsibility of drawing up the shortlist of candidates. For Dr Gaskell, persuading Matron to agree to a new assistant had been a battle all of its own. He had needed to call on his fading charm and had deliberately dropped into Matron's rooms to talk about the new appointment some weeks earlier. There hadn't been an assistant matron since the war, since Sister April. That was 1941, twelve years ago. Sister April had left to work in the QAs, on transfer to the field hospitals, and hadn't been heard of since. Some thought that Matron had been waiting. Hoping. Sure that one day Miss April would return up the steps and in through the main doors of St Angelus and surprise them all. But there had been not a single word. Letters to her family had been returned unopened. Phone calls went unanswered.

When 1947 had arrived and there was still no news of Sister April, it was obvious to everyone that Matron was fretting. 'I shall make enquiries,' Dr Gaskell had said. He'd been chairman of the board for longer than anyone, even Matron, could remember. 'I still have plenty of medical contacts in the army, Matron. With a name like Sister April, someone is bound to know where she is.'

But his enquiries had fallen on barren ground and now the time had come to appoint a new assistant matron. He had broached the subject gently with Matron. 'St Angelus is growing almost faster than we can keep up. Who would have thought that so many reckless young men would be driving around in cars and on motorbikes. Two boys dead in casualty last night alone.'

Matron had sighed. 'I'm not opposing the idea,' she said. 'It's just that, Sister April, well, I had expected her to return. She loved St Angelus.' Her voice trailed off and she turned away, embarrassed, as tears filled her eyes.

'I know, Matron, but it has been a very, very long time.'

Matron could not deny it. It had indeed been a very long time, for them all. The after-effects of the war were fading every day. People were caught up in the excitement of what peace had to offer, not least in the hope that it would bring increased prosperity. For many, remembering was almost too painful. Everyone in Liverpool had lost someone or knew someone who had suffered during the darkest years.

'And it's not just the motorbikes and cars. The new wave of demobbing is keeping our maternity department full to the gunnels. The bedding down of the NHS is pushing everyone to the limit. You are exhausted. You work twelve-hour days seven days a week. You run her a very close second, but you aren't Florence Nightingale, you know.'

Dr Gaskell smiled. Matron relented.

'You're right. I haven't seen my mother in almost six months. I need to take the train to Lytham St Annes to visit her in the home. She's almost ninety now. I must do it soon.'

'Well then, I think you've just made that decision for yourself. An assistant matron we must have. I have asked Sister Haycock to deal with the initial applications, to shortlist down to eight. There, I've said it, and now you will give me a hundred reasons why you think I'm wrong. That's the way we've been running this hospital for years, isn't it?'

His smile and self-deprecating manner failed; they made no impact whatsoever.

'But, Dr Gaskell,' Matron protested, 'it is I who'll be working most closely with the assistant matron. It needs to be someone we find agreeable, someone I know that I can work with.'

'Someone like me, you mean?' Dr Gaskell raised his bushy white eyebrows inquisitively.

Again, Matron chose not to rise to his bait.

'She will be allocated some of the very important tasks that I simply no longer have the time to carry out, and there is the question of trust in her competency. I cannot hand over half my work to someone unless I can be absolutely certain that the job will be done properly. It is I, not the board, who will need to work with her every day. She will take on so many of the new changes . . .'

'And that, Matron, is exactly why we need to deploy the skills of Sister Haycock.' He didn't mention that he was secretly very disappointed that Emily had not jumped at the chance to fill the post herself. 'Come along now. You and I, we are of the old school. This new generation of doctors and nurses who served during wartime have already been tried and tested. They came back and picked up their careers exactly where they left off. They are a new breed altogether. They have different ideas to us, more in keeping with this new world everyone keeps talking about.'

They had moved into Matron's sitting room and both sat down in front of the fire that the Matron's housekeeper, Elsie O'Brien, had stoked up ready for Dr Gaskell's visit. As someone who had dedicated his life to the treatment of TB, Dr Gaskell abhorred a cold room, and they had been sitting in front of the same fire for more years than either of them would care to remember. The place was silent, except for the ticking of the longcase clock, which had once belonged to Matron's mother.

Matron was sitting on the edge of her seat, legs tucked beneath her, hands clasped in her lap, staring into the leaping flames. Dr Gaskell had known her since she was quite a young woman, but as he glanced at her profile he noticed for the first time that she had aged significantly and he didn't know when this had happened. Was it when Sister April had left for the QAs, during the war? Or when she had fallen in love with Sister Antrobus, who could not have been more unlike Sister April? That love had been horribly abused. Sister Antrobus had been exposed as a hard-hearted woman who would stop at nothing to get her way. A woman with a powerful personality and plenty of ambition who had let Matron down so badly and shamed her in front of the entire hospital. When Sister Antrobus was finally thwarted by Nurse Tanner, she'd been removed from gynae and transferred to casualty, a move that Matron had said meant she would no longer have to spend too long with any one patient.

Matron was all too aware that she'd been the subject of hospital gossip for weeks, but she had borne her ignominy with her frilled cap held high. It was possibly then that she'd aged so much, thought Dr Gaskell. A broken heart too far, a dignity crushed under the weight of whispers. His own heart suddenly felt very heavy. He was probably the only person in St Angelus who'd been aware that Matron was in love with Sister April. He had probably known even before she did. He was a man in love with his own wife. A woman he cherished and adored. A woman who had borne him a son, who supported his TB work, who never complained about the hours he worked, and she was never out of his thoughts. He'd seen the same affection he had for his own beloved wife in Matron's eyes, when she'd worked with Assistant Matron April. He'd also seen Matron's desolation on the day Sister April had walked out through the gates. He'd watched her heart break and he ached in sympathy, knowing that her feelings were socially taboo. Never to be spoken of; to be endured in agony and silence. What strength she must have had for all of these years, he thought. And then to fall for Sister Antrobus and lose face.

Dr Gaskell softened his tone to one that he was

more used to deploying at the bedside. 'Come along now,' he said. 'We are of a different era. The NHS, it will change everything. It is hard for us to understand, but, you know, what little power we have left here will also disappear one day. I've asked Sister Haycock to oversee the process for the good of St Angelus, and for you, Margaret. And if I'm entirely honest, for myself too. We have to move with the times.'

Matron looked up sharply. The last time Dr Gaskell had called her by her Christian name was to tell her that there was no news of Sister April.

'We will still be on the interviewing panel and we still have a vote each, even if the trustees from the Liverpool District Hospitals Board outnumber us now. Best let Sister Haycock take charge of the applicants. She has a more objective view of who and what will be required. Now, do you still keep a bottle of sherry in that sideboard?'

Matron smiled. Dr Gaskell never failed to get his own way with her. He was the only doctor in the hospital she truly looked up to. As she handed him his glass of sherry, she blinked as she took in the lined face and white hair. Although he never declared his age, it was widely agreed that he must have passed his seventieth birthday some time ago. 'How much longer do we two have left here?' she said as she sat back in her seat.

'I have no idea, but I'm confident that when the time comes, we will know. And with a bit of luck, that will be on the same day, and we can

22

leave together. This place will go on, you know. It's a fact of life that as we get older, our contribution becomes diminished by those who are younger and have more energy.'

'When did you become so worldly wise?' said Matron. There was a hint of irritation in her voice, but it quickly disappeared as she acknowledged that he was right. 'I find I'm fighting battles that I don't really need to fight,' she said. 'It never used to be that way. It's as if I want to fight them, to validate my authority. Such a waste of energy.'

Dr Gaskell tried to change the subject. 'How's your mother?'

Matron's mother was in one of the best nursing homes in Lytham St Annes. It was more like a luxury hotel and Matron had sold the family home to pay for it. Securing the best care was a way of assuaging her guilt at having dedicated her life to looking after others but not her own mother. She still had her savings and some money left over from the house sale, but when the day came for her to retire, she would have nowhere to go and no one to go to. Dr Gaskell had a wife and a family. The future would be very different for him, she thought.

As they sipped their sherry in front of the fire, Matron hoped that the day she'd have to face retirement, poverty and loneliness would never arrive.

Down in the yard, Dessie Horton called to the porter's lad hurrying towards the school of nursing with a metal bucket in his hand. He was spilling coal across the cobbles as he went. 'Where are you off to with that, Tom?' he asked.

'It's for Biddy, Dessie. She needs more coal in Sister Haycock's office over at the school. I'm taking it now.'

'Don't worry, Tom, I have it.'

Tom laid the bucket down on the cobbles, pushed his cap back, scratched his head and looked up at Dessie. 'But, that's my job, Dessie.'

'I know, lad, but I want you to run back to the lodge now. Jake has a list of wards needing oxygen bottles. Much more important than the coal.'

Satisfied that he hadn't upset or offended Dessie, Tom ran off in the direction of the lodge. Like all Dessie's lads, he was as loyal to him as the day was long. Dessie, a widower in his early forties and with no children of his own, treated every one of his lads as if they were the sons he'd never had, and they responded with unwavering respect and affection.

Emily looked up as she heard the office door being gently opened. 'Oh, hello, Dessie. There's a surprise. Where's Tom, he's not ill, is he?'

'No, not at all. Jake needs him, we have a run on oxygen bottles. Seems every ward as well as casualty is busy today. It's the smog, Matron says, giving everyone a bad chest.'

Emily turned and looked out of her window at the dark grey sky and the yellow tinge to the air. 'The smog has been really awful. What's going

24

on, Dessie? They say the winter is going to be bad this year, lots of snow coming.'

For a short moment, Dessie couldn't answer. He knew it was getting worse. He used to watch her from afar, as she walked through the gates to the school of nursing. She was so blissfully unaware of the impact she had on every man she spoke to. Even Dessie's assistant, Jake, happily married to Martha, melted under the blue and penetrating gaze of Sister Haycock. She was fêted by the nurses, a hero in their eyes. Always standing up for them, fighting their battles, championing their causes along with a few of her own. She was fiery and passionate but also lonely and vulnerable. When he saw her heading out at night to visit her broken stepfather, Alf, his heart crunched. Dessie knew her story. They all did. Her entire family – mother and brothers – blown up in the George Street bomb. Only Alf had survived, because he'd run out of the house to look for Emily.

Having given Dessie her polite attention, she was already looking back down at the papers on her desk. Dessie went to speak but then changed his mind and tipped the coal into the scuttle at the side of her fire. Straightening his back, he stole one last glance. His heart was pounding as it now always did in her presence. He had deliberately contrived to come to her rooms; he hadn't cared whether or not she would be there. To share the sweet air she'd breathed would have been enough.

She smiled at something that was written on the paper she was reading and tutted as she picked up her fountain pen from the desk. She began to write and was oblivious to Dessie as he took a moment to gaze upon the woman who was rarely out of his thoughts.

It was her hair, always neatly swept up but with curls that defied her kirby grips and set themselves free before lunch. It was in her small steps, her vulnerability, her smile, the way she wrapped herself inside the nurse's cape she refused to abandon. There wasn't a man alive who didn't want to be that cape. To protect her tiny birdlike form and to fold his arms around her. He watched her write, then backed towards the door and closed it with a light touch so as not to disturb her. He looked up once more through the panes of glass above the brass handle. She had failed to notice him leave, but Dessie didn't care. It was enough that she had known his name, thanked him for the coal, looked him in the eye. He could survive on that for a week or more.

Dessie, you have it bad, he said to himself as he took the wooden stairs down two at a time.

He didn't notice Biddy, who was standing on the mezzanine with a tray in her hand. A smile crossed her face as, head down and with the empty bucket in his hand, he skipped past her.

'Was that coal for Sister Haycock's office?' she asked.

Dessie stopped mid flight. 'It was, Biddy. I put

26

some on the fire and the bucket's full to over-flowing. She will be nice and warm now.'

'Right, well, we need some in the schoolroom too. There's twenty-two nurses in there near shivering to death.'

'Right enough, Biddy. I'll send Tom up with some.'

Biddy grinned. 'Oh, right, so you won't be doing it yourself then?' But she was too late; the outer door had clattered shut. 'Well, well,' she muttered. 'It looks like Madge was right.'

Emily had walked over to the window and pulled up the sash. The seagull trotted along to the far end of the wide red sandstone sill and eyed her suspiciously. Emily had taken half a stale arrowroot biscuit and laid it on the ledge.

'There you go, you daft bird,' she said. 'That's for you.' The gull looked at the biscuit and then back up at Emily. 'Eat it at your leisure,' she said, 'but be quick, before the rain comes.'

Bringing her head back in, she caught sight of Dessie rushing across the yard. She saw one of the lads rush up to him and take the empty coal bucket out of his hand and noticed the affectionate way Dessie slipped the lad's cap backwards on his head and then pushed it back into place. She heard the lad exclaim, 'Aw, Dessie!' and laugh.

Shivering, she pulled down the sash and watched as Dessie made his way to the porter's lodge.

Biddy came back into the room and set down the tray on her desk. 'Well, that's a good fire. I've brought my cup up, going to steal one out of your

27

pot,' she said to Emily, whose back was turned as she continued to stare out of the window.

Carrying Emily's cup over to her, Biddy saw Dessie about to turn the corner. Glancing at Emily, she could see that she was watching him too.

'What happened to Dessie's wife?' Emily asked.

Biddy decided to lie, to give her the story Dessie had been told. But this was going to be difficult; the least said, the better. 'It was the bomb on the dock. The same night.'

Emily looked sideways at Biddy as she took the cup and saucer. There were no further words needed. She knew exactly what Biddy meant. Dessie had lost his wife on the same night Emily had lost her family. They had both suffered and like everyone else in Liverpool who had lost people in the war, they did so in silence.

'I'm surprised he isn't with anyone, you know, engaged or something? He's such a lovely man. I'd have thought some smart and clever woman would have snapped him up by now.'

'Dessie, no. He grieved for a long time, but he's over it now. All he cares about are the lads and their families. A bit of a hero is our Dessie, down on the Dock Road.'

Emily nodded – she knew this – and turned towards her desk. Too late, she realized that Biddy had moved closer to the window.

'Holy Mother of God!' Biddy screamed. 'Would you believe this, the bird's brought us a biscuit all the way up here to the window.'

CHAPTER 2

Amy Curran's house was stuffed full of everything money could buy. Too many chairs. Too many side tables covered with fringed cloths and ornate lamps. Pictures and crucifixes adorned every wall and there was barely an inch of windowsill not covered in ornaments. Compared with their neighbours, Amy's parents were wealthy. Her father worked at McConaghy's, the jute and scrap-metal processing plant owned by his sister-in-law and her husband. He had been there from the start, done most of the work to establish the business and therefore enjoyed five per cent of the profits.

'Five flaming per cent. They wouldn't have a business if it weren't for me,' he complained to his wife every morning, about ten minutes before he was due to put on his cap and donkey jacket, pick up his sandwiches, which were always wrapped in greaseproof paper and tied up in damp muslin, and cycle the two miles to work. 'McConaghy's is what it is because of the hard work I put in. Keeping the traders sweet, buying them a pint of Guinness on a Friday night. Your sister and her husband, they don't know their arses from their elbows. Two people keep that place going: me on the floor and little Lily Lancashire in the office.'

This was a daily lamentation and Amy could mimic her father word for word. She had no idea what he was complaining about.

'I can't eat. My stomach's bad this morning,' her mother would reply as she laid his breakfast before him.

He always completely ignored her, supped his tea and continued. 'Lily knows every penny that comes in and out, and she's as honest as the day is long. That poor kid, she comes to work in rags and do they offer to give her a pay rise? Do they hell.'

'I think I'm going to go back to the doctor's today, I'm going to tell him it's bad. I need a new cough bottle as well, this one's not working,' his wife would reply. Two people holding two conversations over breakfast, each in their own world.

Amy often heard her father complain about his five per cent, but she thought it must still amount to quite a lot. It was enough to allow her mother to take her into town every Saturday morning and buy her a new outfit. Amy was the best-dressed girl around and she knew it. She had everything. A dressing table heaving under its collection of nail varnish and lipstick. Shoes in boxes that were stacked almost to the ceiling, and a brand-new fox-fur throw that sat in pride of place on a hanger on the outside of her wardrobe door. Amy loved her possessions and she lived for her Wednesday appointment at the hairdresser's and manicurist. She drew gasps of envy as she walked down the avenue towards home. Often her arms were laden with brown-paper bags and boxes adorned with the names of the best shops in town. On the day she turned twenty-one, she would do the same walk with her mother's mink coat swinging around her legs.

Amy had one friend, Dodo, who worked as a clerk in the casualty department at St Angelus Hospital. She'd been christened Doreen, but that was not a name Amy liked, so Amy decided to change it to Dodo. As an only child, Amy was used to getting everything she wanted. She had reached the age of eighteen without ever being told no, and changing Doreen's name was no different: it was as if Doreen were one of the many china dolls Amy had been given as a child. And if there was ever a hint of resistance, Amy knew how to make life difficult.

'Look, if you want to be friends with me, you can, but I cannot abide that name. Doreen? It's a terrible name. How are we ever going to pick up a fella in town with that name? It sounds like one of my mam's friends from the mothers' union.'

Doreen had looked disheartened. She quite liked her name. 'I can't change my name, Amy, you eejit. I'm Doreen O'Prey and I always will be.'

'Here, have this, Dodo.' Amy held out half a bottle of pink, gloopy nail varnish to a grateful Doreen.

Doreen's face lit up. No one in her house had ever owned a bottle of nail varnish.

'And, Dodo, I think it's about time you and me started to go out in town a bit. For bloody fuck's sake, we're both eighteen and virgins. That's not normal.'

Doreen almost dropped the nail varnish. 'Amy, hush, you can't talk like that. You will have to go to confession now.'

'No I bloody won't,' said Amy, who was trying out the swear word for the first time and quite liked the daring sound of it. They were in her bedroom and she began to laugh hysterically. 'Bloody, fuck! There, don't you love it!'

Doreen looked like she was about to faint.

'Oh, all right, Dodo, keep your knickers on. I'll stop. Look, all you have to do is wear some of my nice clothes – you can't have them, mind – and come into town with me. That way, you can bag yourself a nice fella and not a docker like all the other girls around here. You don't have to do the sex, but me, I can't wait. I want to know what all the fuss is about. It's not the Grapes Inn for me and you, Dodo. We have a bit of class. We're going out on the town.'

Despite some mild resistance, Amy persuaded her father to have a word with Dodo's father about her and Amy going into town together. 'Daddy, I'm dying here with Mam, she never stops going on about how sick she is. The only time she wants to talk to me is when it's about her rheumatism. Please, Da.'

He was putty in her hands. Whenever he got the chance to escape from the hypochondria for a night out himself, he grabbed it. Putting on his cap, he made his way to Dodo's door to explain to her father what a good idea it was that the girls should have a Saturday night out. He would make sure that they were safe and that all the costs were covered.

And so it was that Doreen became Dodo when she was with Amy, because, as Dodo, she was occasionally given a cast-off coat to keep, something with a ripped lining, or a pair of shoes with a broken heel that she could have as her own if she got them mended. And they did go into town and Doreen began to think that Amy really knew what she was talking about because on her first night she met a lovely man from Middlesbrough who was a travelling salesman. She fell for him the minute he walked over to her with a Cherry B in one hand and a cigarette in the other.

Doreen had never touched a drink in her life and it was the first time she had smoked. 'I don't know what to do,' she said coyly when he lit it for her and placed it in her fingers.

'Learn, and do it bloody fast, Dodo,' hissed Amy, to Doreen's embarrassment.

Doreen wondered why Amy didn't keep her comments for the man called Ben who was heaping his attention on Amy. She pulled and spluttered on her first drag and wanted to die as Amy laughed out loud and said to the two men, 'Would you

33

look at the cut of her! She knows nothing. Don't spill that Cherry B down my dress, Dodo, you can't afford to get it cleaned if you do.'

Doreen wanted to die with shame, wanted the floor to open up and swallow her. It was always the same with Amy. She wished she had the courage to tell Amy to stuff the dress and to walk out and go home, but with her dad unable to work as a result of his war injuries, she gave every penny of her wages to her mam and if she was ever to have any kind of night out, this was it.

Amy knew Doreen had no money and so she paid for the bus into town and the first drinks at the bar of the Grand, and Dodo was grateful. It was something she was not allowed to forget.

'What do you sell?' Doreen asked her admirer, moving the laughter away from Amy's unkind barbs.

'Vacuum cleaners,' said the man as he filled her glass. 'Stick with me, Dodo, and there won't be a time-saving device you won't have heard of. I get them all first hand, straight from America.'

Dodo, who had never actually seen a vacuum cleaner, was suitably impressed. Maybe Amy was right. A different life could be waiting for her.

By the fourth Saturday evening, the novelty of discovering smoky bars and music had worn off for Amy, but the novelty of the man who bought her drinks had not. She knew only that his name was Ben; he'd never told her what his surname was or where he lived, but she answered those questions herself when he went off to the gents while they were all in the bar of the Adelphi. She slipped her hand into his jacket pocket and pulled out his wallet. It was all there and in a flash she committed his name and address to memory. She admired the wad of ten-pound notes, then deftly tucked the wallet back in its place.

Doreen leant over to talk to her. 'I don't think I'll be coming next week, Amy. This Bob chap, he's not that nice and, to be honest, I'm bored with his talk of vacuum cleaners and steam irons. You will have to find someone else to come with you next week. I'm going to go up the bingo with me mam and her mates.' It had taken Dodo all day to build up the courage to tell Amy. Her throat was dry and her hands were shaking with the effort of it.

Amy turned on Doreen and her voice was so loaded with venom, it made Doreen's eyes sting with tears. 'Well, do that then, but don't come crying to me when you haven't got a decent dress to put on. Go up the bingo in your rags and tags, but don't come knocking on my door, you useless article.'

Doreen's throat thickened and she had no words to reply. Instead, she flew to the door and waited for the man she was relieved she would soon be rid of. Bob. Doreen had promised he could take her home on the bus and how could she refuse? Now that Amy had turned so nasty, she didn't have the bus fare anyway. If she had, she would have made her own way home; she would have run to the next bus stop and been rid of them all.

Doreen closed her eyes. She didn't care if she walked around in rags. All of this going out with Amy, all this seeing men and going to bars and swearing, it just wasn't her. It wasn't Doreen. She'd had enough. She might be poor, but she wasn't so daft that she couldn't see that it was a path to ill repute. Doreen was a good girl. Her family respected her. Her da was proud of her, getting taken on at the hospital. It was her da's friend Dessie who had seen to that. They had fought in the war together and as soon as her father had had to give in to his weakened chest and accept that he was an invalid, Dessie had come to the house to see what he could do. Doreen had found it hard at first. She'd started at the bottom, but now she was working in casualty, checking in the patients, and she loved it. People even knocked at the door to her house and brought their ailments with them. It dawned on her that she was a better person now than the one Amy was becoming and she would not take the same path.

Amy watched her run to the door of the Adelphi and stood and waited for her to change her mind and run back. But she didn't so much as turn around; she just stood there with her back to Amy. Well, sod off then, Dodo, Amy said to herself as she drained her Babycham. She would be back, of that she was sure. And Amy had other things to think about. Her parents had gone off to Abersoch for their annual holiday that morning, leaving her behind, and she was enjoying being free. Out in her red coat and shoes, she was like a bird with brightly coloured plumage and a daring vivacity to match.

Ben had come back from the gents and was now striding towards her, zipping up his fly as he walked. He was always much more smartly dressed than Bob. He definitely had money, she was sure of it.

'Where's the Dodo?' he asked as he lit a cigarette.

'She's buggering off early. Bob is taking her home on the bus, she said.'

'She's still a bit of a child. Not like you, eh, Amy? You're all woman.' Ben leant forward and, just before he kissed her ear, blew his smoke in her face.

'My parents are away. Would you like to come back to mine?' she whispered.

As he lifted his head from her neck, his eyes lit up. 'Would I? I would. I think that sounds like a very good idea.'

On previous Saturdays, Ben had walked Amy to the bus stop. On the first night he'd kissed her. On the second, he'd slipped his hand inside her bra and Amy had been wild with the daring and the excitement of it. As he kissed her neck and throat he'd whispered, 'Lift up your skirt, Amy,' but she hadn't had the time as the bright lights of the approaching bus they had failed to hear were already illuminating the bus stop.

Amy wanted Ben to go further as soon as possible. She knew this was wrong and that if her father walked past and saw her, he would all but die with the shock, but she didn't care. She was bored. She had to have something she wanted that couldn't be bought. She was bored with clothes and shoes and bags, and now she was bored with Dodo. The girl whose name she had changed.

'Maybe if I let Ben go all the way, he'll want to marry me,' she'd said to Doreen that afternoon.

'No one does that until after they're married,' a shocked Doreen had replied.

That morning, when it was finally time for her parents to depart for their annual Abersoch holiday, Amy couldn't push them out of the door fast enough. They were driving themselves in the new car, bought with the five per cent.

'My gall bladder is playing up something rotten,' her mother had complained. 'I don't feel right being so far from St Angelus when I'm feeling this unwell. What if it bursts or something and I need the hospital?'

Amy's mother had been complaining about her gall bladder ever since the GP, in a desperate attempt to hang some kind of label on her mother's many aches and pains, had mentioned this organ, famous for being at the root of all pain in women who were fair, fat and over fifty.

'Can it burst?' asked her husband, concerned.

'No, of course it can't, Da,' said Amy as she closed the car boot on her mother's new leather

case. 'I asked Dodo, she said it was impossible.'
Amy had done no such thing but had prepared
for every obstacle her mother might try and put
in the way of her father having the holiday he
worked for all year long. 'Anyway, isn't there a
hospital in Abersoch?'

'I don't know if there is a hospital.' Her mother's
voice was filled with alarm. 'Did we check?'

Her husband lifted the cap from his head, pushed
his hair back and waited for a second before he
spoke again. His wife was the worst type of hypo-
chondriac and had suffered from every ailment
known to man, and some that weren't.
Miraculously, she never felt ill on Wednesdays,
which was the day for the hairdresser's, or
Saturdays, which was her shopping day. On every
other weekday there was a possibility that her sister
might ask her to call into the processing plant and
help him earn his five per cent. It had been
mentioned on a number of occasions since Amy
had turned fourteen. That was the day she developed her first mysterious illness and they had come
thick and fast ever since.

'I am very sure there is a hospital and a doctor
and that once we get to Abersoch the sea air will
make you feel much better.'

Amy's mother looked at her husband with mild
disdain. 'You care nothing for how I feel,' she
grumbled as Amy propelled her into the passenger
seat then slammed the door shut after her.

'Are you sure you're going to be OK, queen?'

asked her father, before he opened the driver's door. Amy was the apple of his eye. The one his heart adored, and he spoilt her something rotten. She could say or do no wrong.

'Look, Da.' Amy pointed to Dodo running down the street towards them. 'Dodo will be staying with me. We're going to have a pyjama party and do our hair and watch the TV tonight. We haven't bought a TV for it to just sit there in the corner of the room, you know.'

Neither Amy nor her parents knew anyone else who had a TV. The day Amy had asked for it, it had been delivered.

Her father kissed Amy again on the top of her head and with a grin slipped into the car and started the engine. Amy knew he couldn't wait to reach Abersoch and have fourteen whole days away from the processing plant and Mrs McConaghy, the sister-in-law he had never been allowed to address by her first name. She pictured him taking himself down to the long beach and finding a bench far from her mother's nagging tongue where he could listen to the sea and rediscover his natural calm.

Amy and Dodo stood and waved the car off down the avenue. As soon as it had turned the corner, Amy said, 'Right, we've only got six hours to get ready. Get a move on.'

The afternoon involved a lot of messing about with hair and make-up as well as the trying on of almost every outfit in Amy's wardrobe.

'Shouldn't we tidy up, Amy?' asked Dodo.

'Dodo, you know we have a lady who does. She'll be in on Monday – leave it for her, else she'll have nothing to do. Our house is too tidy anyway.'

Dodo looked around the room, concerned. She had never seen such a mess. It crossed her mind that now Amy's parents had left, Amy was turning a little wild. Her eyes were bright and she could barely contain her excitement.

'I'm going to bring Ben back here tonight, Dodo,' Amy said as she sat at the dressing table and brushed her hair a hundred times.

'What, to this mess?' Dodo looked around her. 'Amy, do you know what you're doing? I mean, what do you know about the man? You've only met him three times.'

'I know that, but he's a gentleman. Come on, Dodo, if you had a little more class about you, you would like him too. Trust you to get yourself a vacuum-cleaner salesman. That's very common, you know, and he's probably married. Mind you, that's very exciting, isn't it? What do you think it's like to be kissed by a married man, Dodo? Let the fella kiss you tonight and then tell me. I'll give you an eyeliner pencil if you do.'

Dodo was holding the hairbrush and she felt as though she wanted to smash Amy over the head with it. 'No, I will not. I'm not that type of girl, Amy, and nor should you be.'

Amy laughed. 'Dodo, you are so old-fashioned,

but I don't care. I'm out to have my fun. Babycham all the way for me tonight and then I'm going to get Ben back here and it will be the best night of my life.'

And now here she was, excitedly shrugging on her red coat as she made her way out of the Adelphi, all set to put into action her plan for her night of passion. Ben ran down the short flight of steps in front of the bar and asked the doorman to hail a cab. 'No need for the bus tonight, Amy. I'm going to treat my lady special.'

Amy grinned. She felt special. She was wearing her fox-fur stole and new hat and she knew she looked sophisticated and much older than her eighteen years. She wondered whether she should tell Ben she was a virgin, but she decided against it. He might think she was a child, be turned off by her lack of womanly ways. No, she would keep going to the last second and perhaps he might not even need to know at all.

'It's a shame your friend Dodo had to leave so early.'

Amy was momentarily confused. 'Oh, Dodo, she's just a baby. If she isn't home by ten her ma and da would kick off. It's not like that for me, though. I'm my own woman, Ben.' Amy blew her cigarette smoke into Ben's face for effect. She thought it worked. Tonight, she was Rita Hayworth, only prettier.

When they reached the house, Amy didn't even have time to switch the light on in the hall. Her keys fell to the monogrammed coir doormat as Ben kicked the front door shut with his foot and immediately began undoing the buttons on her coat. He took the fox-fur stole from her shoulders and threw it on to the stairs, where it landed on the new Axminster carpet with a dejected thud.

'Careful,' said Amy as she caught her breath. Ben was everywhere. He was in a hurry. This wasn't how she wanted it to happen. She felt his hands down her blouse, heard a button pop and his fingers were skimming the edge of her silk French knickers. She had no idea what to do or where to put her hands. 'Ben!' she said. 'Ben, can we go in the kitchen, to the sofa. Do you want a drink? My da has whisky in the press.'

For a brief moment, Ben let her go. He looked over her shoulder and down the hallway, weighing up her words. 'Where is it?' he asked, his voice now altered, strange to Amy, guttural and impatient.

Amy wanted to play it coy, but failed. Instead, she stumbled slightly and opened the door to the kitchen. Within seconds, she was lying on the sofa, Ben on top of her. She couldn't think fast enough.

His weight was pressing down on her and she found it difficult to breathe. She was aware that from the waist down she was now naked because Ben's well-practised hands had removed most of her clothes.

'I'm a virgin,' she spluttered. She hadn't meant to say that, but she could think of nothing else to say that would give her time. She wanted to hold

43

him back while she caught her breath and gave her mind the chance to properly grasp what was happening.

Outside she heard a scream. Was it a scream? She struggled on to her elbow, but he pushed her back. 'Where are you off to, miss?' His smile was more of a leer and his breath smelt strongly of whisky and smoke. The scream came again. It sounded like Dodo. Was it Dodo?

'Ben, did you hear that?' She had never in all of her life heard a scream like that. It was coming from the entry that ran down the back of the houses. She wanted to push herself up, to open the door and check, but it was too late, his lips were harsh and clamped over her mouth again. She felt her body stiffen in response. This wasn't going how she had planned.

She wondered what was missing. Was it supposed to be like this? She had imagined her first time to be different.

He moved, and she gasped and managed to speak. 'Ben, wait.'

He raised his head and looked down at her. 'What?' he said gruffly. 'What's wrong?'

'I want to,' she whispered. 'I do. It's just that I never have before.'

'Look, it will be fine. It won't hurt. I love you, Amy, I really do. You're an amazing woman. Really beautiful. There isn't a woman as beautiful as you in all of Liverpool, you know that, don't you?'

Amy softened. He had called her a woman. He

44

loved her. She was beautiful. This was more like it. And then, without another second's delay, he pushed himself hard inside her and she yelped in pain.

It hurt a lot. He was impatient, his fingers sharp. Her leg pained as he pushed it to one side. He failed to hear her ask him to hold on for a second while she accommodated the pain, became used to the sensation, and before she knew it, he was pushing and his hip bones pierced her side and the weight of his thighs pained her. But it was too late to speak: he was gone, lost somewhere in the mission of his own desire and then he let out a sound like an animal and stopped. It was over in seconds and her first thought was, was that it? She turned her face and looked at his profile, eyes staring, half grinning, breathing hard, and she felt repulsed, and then her heart stopped in terror. She heard the front door slam.

'I told you I was sick, but you wouldn't believe me. Do you think I vomited that soup back up deliberately? That hotel was the worst place I have ever stayed in my life, and that's saying something, given our honeymoon. I wouldn't let my new suitcase stay in that room, never mind us. What a carry-on. What on earth . . .? Is that our Amy's stole?'

Ben was gone. In a flash he withdrew, dragged up his trousers and, seeing the kitchen door, slipped the bolt across and ran out through the back door. But not before the room was flooded with light and his naked rear end had been spotted

45

by Amy's father, who, after a slight delay while his mind absorbed the horror of the sight before him, gave chase.

Amy did some quick thinking. 'He broke in, Mam,' she said as she gathered her clothes and made herself decent. 'He broke in.'

'Really? Through the bolted kitchen door? Really? Decided to throw your clothes around the hallway first, did he?' Her mother's voice was as cold as ice and Amy knew that her life was about to change.

Ben scaled the fence and, even with his trousers round his knees, was too young and too fast for Amy's father, who was shouting so loud, he woke the whole neighbourhood. He didn't catch Ben, but he did find Doreen, lying in the entry, her head bleeding.

And so, on one night, Amy lost her virginity, her reputation, her best and only friend, her parents' trust, and Ben. But unbeknown to her, she had gained something far more problematic than the anger of her parents and, as it would transpire, dangerous too.

Doreen thought she must be at work. Her eyes were closed and she was confused. She was lying on her back. What in God's name was she doing, lying down at work? She struggled to raise herself up and almost made it. The sound of hurrying footsteps came closer and there were whispers, in what sounded like Matron's voice.

'Do her parents know?'

'Yes, they accompanied her here. They're in the waiting area with the police. She was found just a few yards from the house.'

That was Night Sister, Doreen thought.

'Hello . . .' She tried to speak.

Doreen didn't work on nights, so what was she doing at St Angelus now? She only ever spoke to Night Sister when she did the handover in the mornings. And why was Matron here on casualty? Matron always telephoned her to let her know she was coming; they got along well together, Doreen and Matron. She knew Matron was tough with the nurses, but she didn't need to be tough with Doreen. Dessie had introduced her to Matron and Matron had helped Doreen to work her way up into the clerk's post on casualty. Ever since, she'd spent every day making sure that Matron and Dessie would never be disappointed with her. She wanted them to know that they had made the right choice.

'We called you, Matron, I hope you don't mind. I thought that with her being a member of staff, you would want to know.'

'Can you hear me, Doreen?'

Doreen tried to reply, but her throat was swollen and her mouth appeared to be full of something and the metallic smell and taste was making her sick. It was blood. Someone must be bleeding a great deal. It was a smell she had become used to, working on casualty. But this smell, today, it was strong and it was making her ill.

She leant up and retched.

'It's OK, my dear, I have you.'

Arms across her back, supporting her. Whose arms? She tried to look down at the arms to see who they belonged to. Her eyes cracked open just in time to see the white enamel kidney dish as she vomited and heard a clinking sound.

'Count those teeth, Nurse.' It was Matron. Whose teeth?

'We need to get her to theatre.' That was Night Sister again.

Doreen attempted to open her eyes, but they were stuck together and try as she might, they just would not part. The dull, heavy, so heavy, pain across the front of her face made her want to cry out.

'I came as soon as I could. What are her obs? Count those teeth, Nurse, just so we know. Mind you, we'll be able to see how many are missing.' That was definitely Dr Mackintosh. Dr Mackintosh was there and he wanted to count someone's teeth.

'I'm not happy with the vomiting. When did it start? Let's get her into X-ray.'

'She's been raped, Doctor. She's got a large perineal tear. She's lost a great deal of blood and her arm's broken. But it's the head injury that seems to be the big problem. Looks like it's been banged against the wall.' Night Sister again. Should she not be going home now?

'Look at her eyes. I can barely open them to check her pupil reaction. He must have been very heavy with his fists, the poor, poor girl. What did she do to deserve this?' Matron was nice. She was obviously very worried about some poor, poor girl.

Just before she blacked out again, Doreen heard someone crying and it sounded like Matron. But it couldn't be Matron.

'Nurse, quickly, please. I need this young lady on to the ward and tell the police they can come back in the morning and I will give them a full report. Right now, I'm more concerned with her head injuries and keeping her alive. This is going to be a long, long night.' And then, 'She is one of ours, Doctor. She is part of the St Angelus family. Do your very best.'

Who was? Who was Matron talking about?

Doreen attempted to lift her head. The phone was ringing, she needed to answer it, but instead she closed her eyes and slipped into the darkness.

CHAPTER 3

If there was one thing Lily Lancashire hated more than anything else in the whole world, it was the sound of children playing.

Home for Lily was Clare Cottages, situated on the bank of the River Mersey on the Old Dock Road. She thought that the person who had named the ugly, four-storey, soot-blackened red-brick tenement buildings had either been drunk or cruel, giving the cottages such a pretty name. 'We only agreed to move here because it sounded so nice,' she often heard the neighbours say. 'What a joke. Someone in the corpy was 'avin' a right laugh there.'

'The corpy' was the Liverpool Corporation, the landlord of Clare Cottages. It was the corpy that had decided to move the bombed-out residents of Scotland Road, where there had been up to four large families to every house, to the already overcrowded Clare Cottages.

Those who complained about the condition of Clare Cottages were the ones who took pride in their homes, who washed their net curtains and scrubbed the step, who borrowed dolly blue for their laundry from each other when they'd run out. Lily's mother, much to Lily's shame, was not one of those women. Her mother never jumped out of bed on a bright and breezy day, eager to get the nets on the line, never helped other women on the same landing to bounce a pram full of wet washing down the steps to the courtyard, was never one to pop in and out of their neighbours' homes.

Lily wished her mam could be more like Mrs McGuffy, who installed herself in the courtyard as self-appointed guardian of the washing lines. 'I'll watch the nets don't blow off,' Mrs McGuffy would shout when the weather was fine. 'You just send our Billy down with the chair and me fags. Me bleedin' leg ulcers will only let me do those stairs once a day.' And there she would sit, all day long, surrounded by a plume of blue smoke, her face turned to the sun, the hot metal of her curlers burning into her scalp, the black tar on the top of the bin sheds melting. As soon as the nets were dry, she'd round up the cottage kids and instruct them to return the curtains, sun-bleached and folded, to whichever home they'd been sent from, and to bring out the next batch for the lines and a fresh cuppa for herself. There was always a chipped and brown-stained cup on top of the metal bin beside her and when she finished the tea, she used the dregs to extinguish the last of her cigarette. Mrs McGuffy was a demon for cleanliness and objected to anyone throwing a ciggie butt on to the concrete floor of the washing yard, even if it was

51

in the middle of the worst housing in Liverpool. 'Chuck that stub down the sink, would you, love, before you fill the cup up,' she would say to whichever kid she sent for a refill. The kids didn't always remember, but it didn't matter, the tea was so strong and sweet, she drank it anyway.

There were two distinct types of families in Clare Cottages. There were those with mothers like Mrs McGuffy, who scrubbed children and steps with equal vigour and regularity. They cleaned windows, baked biscuits, visited the wash house on the same day every week and took their children to the public bath house on Saturday nights, ready for church on Sunday. Such families were free from lice and scurvy. Their children did not stagger around on rail-thin legs or rub at weeping eyes. Their hair was not lank through lack of food and their skin was not permanently darkened as a result of ingrained dirt. They were rarely cold.

Families such as Lily's, on the other hand, had parents who shunned Mass at St Chad's, preferring to worship at the bar in the Red Admiral public house. They lived in homes where there was no routine of orderliness or cleanliness. Where a trip to the public bath house came rarely, usually when a visit from the welfare inspector loomed or the lice had become too numerous to bear; homes where food came, not always, but usually once a day. No one asked these mothers for a loan of the dolly blue. The nets and bedding in these homes were the colour of a miserable winter sky.

The so-called cottages were cramped, small, damp and squalid. They'd been built to house Liverpool's second influx of the Irish poor and unemployed who'd arrived to build the new roads; talk that there would soon be new council estates constructed meant that half of Dublin had rucked up looking for work. There were homes on four floors, reached via many flights of steps and a long, dark landing that ran outside every kitchen window. Each home had a fire grate in the lounge, running water in the kitchen and a coal bunker next to the front door. There was a toilet on every half landing, shared by ten families. The central concrete yard provided space for the bins, washing lines and a refuge for the children, who spent hours there, out of their mothers' hair and beyond the reach of their fathers' belts.

'Are youse coming out to play?' was the cry that echoed down the landings as the children knocked on doors as they ran. They would spill out into the courtyard, to congregate in the narrow lane along the front, to kick a football, if a child who owned one had surfaced, or to play Ollies with glass marbles and Jacks as they squatted in the dirt.

Girls as young as four would push prams up and down the landings. Up and down. Up and down. Halting only to tend to the trouserless and nappy-less toddlers following in their wake. They were mothers themselves, even before their first day at school. Clare Cottages spewed smoke, children and opportunities lost.

The ceaseless, nameless whoops and yelps and the relentless thud of balls bouncing, feet running, babies crying and prams bouncing up and down the stairs rebounded straight back in through Lily's bedroom window. And she hated it. 'God, please, give me quiet,' was her most frequently uttered prayer as she lay in her room in the middle of the noisy world that was Clare Cottages.

There were times when, late at night as she tried to sleep, Lily would lie on the horsehair and straw mattress she shared with her little brother Joe and her sister Katie and attempt to count how many children lived in Clare Cottages and contributed to the noise. She reached almost a hundred and it felt like she could hear every one. The number was growing by the day, evidenced by the number of times she'd spotted the midwife's bicycle parked at the bottom of the stairwell or on the half landing. Before she'd started to work at McConaghy's, Lily had often been called on to help out. A half-dressed toddler would turn up at her front door with a note asking, *Can I borrow your Lily for half an hour? The midwife's here.* The note was never from one of the homes where the mother hung clean nets. And it never was for just half an hour.

It sometimes felt that because the nuns at school had draped the label 'Clever for five' around her neck, she had overnight become responsible for every child in Liverpool, when she had not long learnt to read herself. Sister Therese had been

54

forever at her mother's front door. 'Mrs Lancashire, the child has a gift. Let us send her to board at the Convent of the Holy Martyrs out in the country in Hunt's Cross. I'm thinking that Lily could even become a teacher herself one day. She has a real gift with numbers and the like. You are a Catholic woman, are you not?'

But Lily's mother was having none of it. 'I am that, Sister, but I married an Englishman, as you well know, and he won't hear a word of it. And besides, who will help me with the kids if she goes?'

Sister Therese became exasperated. 'I will help you. Let us nurture her God-given talent. The Lord may have a calling for her. She would one day earn her own money, good money, and sure she wouldn't forget her own mother when she did.'

Lily knew Sister Therese was whispering her silent prayers, sure that God would deliver as she waited for her mother's response.

But her mother's reply was swift and unambiguous. 'Her calling's here,' she said, 'helping me with the kids. And besides, it would take years before she earned any money worth speaking of.'

Her mother hadn't just meant her own kids, she'd meant all of the kids who lived in homes whose mothers preferred the public house to the wash house. And from that day on, until Lily had started work at the processing plant, mothers who lived on their landing had begun to offload their offspring into the care of the young girl who had, as even her own mother said, a very old head.

'Just mind our kids while I go to the bingo, will yer, Lily,' was a common request. Or it might be the doctor's, the shops, Mass, the pub or the welfare. Or even, 'Lily, I've been caught short, the old man's on nights and the bucket's full – quick!', and then a screaming baby would be thrust into Lily's arms as its mother ran to the toilet on the half landing. It didn't matter what the reason was: the clever and serious Lily spent her childhood being a glorified babysitter and she resented it deeply.

Now, on this cold winter's morning in 1953, she needed to get ready for work. She slipped out from under the pile of old army blankets covering her and her little brother, Joe, and clambered across her sleeping siblings to kneel at the head of the bed, underneath the window.

Her younger sister Katie stirred.

'Sshh, Katie, five more minutes,' she whispered.

Katie's thumb headed for her mouth and her heavy lids closed again. She gave a sleepy smile as Lily tucked the blanket around her.

At seventeen years old, it felt to Lily as though her two younger siblings had been her sole responsibility for almost all of her life. She slept on the outside of the mattress so that if either of them needed the pot during the night, or if they were ill and had to vomit, she was conveniently positioned to help. Joe was always in the middle, between Lily and Katie, who lay next to the wall. Katie complained often about this.

'Lily, swap with me,' she would say in the night. 'The wall is freezing and it keeps waking me up.'

'The wall can't wake you,' Lily would reply.

'It does, Lily. I roll over and me leg touches it and it's as cold as ice. Please . . .' she'd whine. There were times when Katie drove Lily to the point of exasperation and she had to suppress her irritation that her little sister couldn't do more to help.

Lily had long, thick, chestnut-coloured hair, whereas Katie's was short, thin and mousey. Lily's eyes shone inquisitively and were the same colour as her hair. Katie's were a pale blue. Lily's face was bright and alert, but, given that she rarely smiled, often sad. Katie was kind, trusting and incapable of resentment. She could also never think anything through far enough to reach a conclusion. A weak and sickly girl, Katie mostly just did as she was told. For as long as she could stay awake. The fact that they had different fathers was apparent in their wildly differing appearances. Lily could barely remember her own father. He'd left when her mother's drinking had begun. Lily knew her mam had sat at the bedroom window for a very long time, waiting for him to return, but he never had. The kindly if impatient man had left Lily to suffer at the hands of his replacement, a bad-tempered stepfather, who had no compunction about using his fists on his stepdaughter.

Clambering across the mattress, Lily listened for a moment to Joe. His breathing had become much worse lately and at only three years old he was beginning to struggle with the frequency of his attacks. Careful not to disturb him, because he needed every second of his sleep, Lily reached the iced-up curtainless window. She peered at it and gasped. Overnight, snow had fallen, deep and silent, and the inside of the window was covered in the most beautiful and intricate tendrils of ice crystals she had ever seen. They were so thick, they cast an eerie grey haze over the bedroom. There was nothing in Lily's life that could be described as beautiful, and yet, on this cold and icy morning, she had opened her eyes and there it was. Silence in her life. Beauty on her window. A smile on her face.

'Are you going to bleedin' work, or what?'

Lily's mother burst into the bedroom and slammed the door against the wall with such force, it felt to Lily as though her bones had rattled with the shock. She'd been so busy tracing the ice patterns with the frozen tip of her index finger that she'd failed to hear her mother's slippered feet crossing the bare floorboards from the direction of her own room.

'Get up, now!' her mother barked.

The other sound Lily hated was that of her mother's voice.

'Come on, ger up, we need your money this week more than ever. Your da has nothing left. Nothin'. The bastard's drunk the bleeding lot. Doesn't think of any of us, or that his kids need food in their mouths. Took the money out of the bread bin last night before I could catch him. Tell your boss and 'is stingy bleedin' wife you need your pay packet on time this week or your mam will be down at your fancy office to deal with him. You got that, queen?'

Oh, the hypocrisy of her, thought Lily as she listened to her mother, her speech still slurred from her own night out drinking with the other cottage women who frequented the pub. Last night they'd congregated at the dockers' club, where someone who'd been quicker to the bread bin than Lily's mother had stood the drinks.

But this was Lily's mother trying to be nice. This was her on a good day. At least she's got a bad head, thought Lily. Too bad to lash out. She wanted and needed Lily's money, and having to wait until the evening, when the brown-paper pay packet would be placed on the kitchen table, was a huge inconvenience. She had hardly any fags or food to keep her going.

'Yes, Mam,' whispered Lily. Her breath hung in the air in a white cloud and her teeth began to chatter as she trembled with the cold. Lifting her hands, she started to untie the knots in the rags at the bottom of each of her long plaits. She tried hard to look as presentable as she could for work.

The bedroom door banged shut as her mother shuffled into the kitchen to take her morning pee in the enamel bucket that sat under the kitchen sink.

Leaning forward, Lily placed her hands on the

wall either side of the small window and exhaled loudly, breathing on the glass and watching in wonder as the thinnest part in the middle of the ice almost melted. She breathed hard, again and again, willing it to clear as the sound of her mother's urine hitting the sides of the metal pail and her mutterings faded into the distance. Using the nail of her thumb, she scraped away a hole big enough to see through and gasped. Clare Cottages and everything she could see of the smog-blackened neighbourhood looked beautiful. Soot-stained grime had transformed overnight into pristine white. The roof of the wash house at the end of the road appeared almost magical.

St Chad's school playground to the side of the cottages was the whitest, an as yet untouched blanket. Glistening pillows sat on top of the chimneystacks and bin lids, but what was most exciting was that it was peaceful. All was quiet. The filth and the dirt and even the roofs of the redundant corrugated-metal air-raid shelters down in the concrete square were covered in soft white folds of virgin snow and Lily wanted to cry with joy at the beauty of it.

As she turned her gaze up towards the grey and heavy sky, she wondered if it was the cold and the threat of yet more snow to come that had given her the sweetest of all gifts. She had awoken to the sound of nothing. The streets were empty. There were no children thundering along the land-ings, racing up and down the connecting stairs or congregating on the corner of the lane. It was soundless and it was bliss. Sitting back on her heels, Lily listened to the silence and smiled a rare and sweet smile.

'Fecking hell, Lily, get up!' Her mother's voice boomed out yet again from the doorway, where she stood tucking her vest into her knickers and rearranging her skirt before she shuffled away in her freshly dampened slippers.

Katie and Joe stirred.

Lily heard the front door open and the sound of a metal shovel scraping along the concrete floor of the coal house. The cold had driven her mother out to fetch the coal herself. A rare occurrence. Lily held her breath as a thought seized and froze her. Oh no. Will she find it? Will she break it? Will she go mad that I hid it? She bit her lip and waited.

'Do I have to get up now as well, Lily?' whispered Katie, her thumb hanging in mid air, ready to slip back into her mouth should the answer be no.

The coal-shed door banged shut. Her mother shuffled back indoors. The front door slammed. Lily breathed again. She was safe. Her secret stash had not been found. She heard her mother throw the coal on to the small fire, the only source of heat in the house. It pounded against the chimney wall as it clattered and fell into the grate.

Normally at this time the docks' klaxon would ring out and, before it had finished, the landings would spring into life. Doors would bang open and shut and the air would be filled with the jokes, curses and complaints of men making their way to the docks and work; men who were far more industrious and sober than Lily's stepfather.

He was always late, swearing loudly as her mother roused him. He was never allowed to sleep off his hangover, unless of course he did it in the bin sheds, which, on occasion and much to Lily's shame, he had been known to. 'Get out of that fecking bed and down those stairs into work,' was her mother's own daily klaxon. The only woman Lily's stepfather never raised his fists to was his wife. Instead, it was Lily who bore the brunt of his anger and frustration with his drunken wife and Lily who had the bruises to show for it.

She would hold her breath and wait for the thud she knew was her stepfather being dragged out of his bed and on to the floor. Her mother's temper at his taking the money from the bread bin, failing to turn up to work the previous day, or any one of the many things that made her angry with him when she wasn't drunk herself, gave the woman enormous strength.

This morning she could hear her parents arguing. The familiar words floated into her room and woke her siblings.

'You fecking cow bitch.'

Within minutes, their own front door would bang violently as he was ejected, barely dressed and without tea or ceremony, out into the snow to take his place in the pen, ready to join a gang down at the docks. Only today there were no ships.

The klaxon hadn't rung. The smog on the river was too thick even for the tugs and the ships waited out at the bar. But they had both been too stupefied to notice.

Lily frowned. Her blissful moment of privacy had finished almost before she had realized it was hers.

'Lily.' Joe's little voice was nothing more than a whisper. At such a young age, he had learnt the most important survival trick: to be invisible in the Lancashire house.

Lily smiled. 'Yes, love,' she said as she shuffled across the top of the blankets towards him. Scooping him up, she lifted him out of the bed and stood him at the window. 'Look at that, Joe,' she said. 'It's been snowing.'

The patch of ice Lily had cleared was already beginning to ice over again.

'Can we play a game in the snow, Lily?' Joe's eyes were bright and hopeful and Lily's heart sank.

'I can't, Joe, I have to go to work, but I'll tell Katie she has to play with you when she gets up, or one of the girls on the landing.'

Joe's smile vanished. They both knew that Katie would give Joe ten minutes, but he couldn't run as fast as the others, or keep up with their games, and they would quickly forget. Katie forgot most things.

Lily bent down and kissed Joe's brow. She didn't like the telltale rattle in his breathing. His exhalations were noticeably much longer than his inhalations and the wheeze on the tail end whistled ominously. His overly bright pink cheeks felt warm to the touch in the frozen room. Lily said a silent prayer that today the wheezing wouldn't last for too long as she sat Joe on the pot and hurried Katie along.

'Katie, come on, love, I'm a bit late. Give us a hand and get yourself ready. I've got milk and pobs for you this morning.' She helped Katie drag her legs out of the bed and began to dress.

When they had finished on the pots, they would be emptied into the metal bucket. Lily's next job would be to carry the bucket down to the toilet on the half landing and tip it away. She prayed that there would be no queue today and that she could be quick. As soon as she returned home from work, she would do the same thing over again.

No one ever got fed until she arrived back home. Often there would be no sign of her mother, who had long since taken to joining her stepfather down at the pub. Sometimes her mother forgot that there was no food in the cupboard and Lily had to take from the rent money in the bread bin and run down to the corner shop and wait until it was closing and beg.

'Could I have the cut-offs from the meat blade?' she would ask as her face burnt red with shame. 'Would there be any veggies you are throwing out tonight I can have?'

Lily truly disliked the corner shop. Its smell was so pungent, of potatoes on the verge of rotting, that it caught in the back of her throat. It was a place of shame to Lily, and she knew the less than friendly owner gossiped with the women. She avoided it as much as she could.

When there was no rent money, in desperation she would knock on the convent door for Sister Therese, who was the only person, along with Father Brennan, that her parents feared and who Lily could turn to for help.

'There's no money for the tea and little Joe won't stop crying, Sister.' Lily said it as it was to Sister Therese. There was almost nothing to hide from the woman who had done more for little Joe and her sister than their own mother had.

'Holy Mother of God.' The reply was always the same. 'Come into the kitchen with me.' Sister Therese would load Lily's covered basket with whatever was on the convent kitchen table and send Lily back home with enough to feed them all. The following day her parents would be full of recriminations and shame when Sister Therese arrived at the door.

'You try my patience to the end, Mrs Lancashire. You need to take better care of your children, and the burden you put on poor Lily here, it is too much,' Sister Therese would remonstrate. 'I don't want to do it, but you will be forcing me down to the welfare office with your behaviour soon, so you will.'

For a day or two, sometimes longer, Lily and the kids would feel the benefit. Lily would return home from work to a hot pan of scouse, ready for them all, and a happy Joe. 'Here you are, luv, here's your tea,' her mam would say as soon as she got through the door. As though they were words she uttered on a regular basis. A reformed mother, trying her hardest to be nice.

Her stepfather would miss a night or sometimes even two down at the pub and would sit Joe on his knee and, for a while, Lily dared to hope that things were improving. That there could be a future for her that didn't involve being a crutch for her parents and the only person who stood between her siblings and the children's home on Menlove Avenue or over in the convent itself.

Lily studied Joe carefully as she fastened her thick stockings. He had been known to slip off the pot, spilling the contents all over the floorboards. Without a mirror, she used the almost toothless comb to calm her hair and then skilfully wound it into a bun as Katie now plonked herself on the pot and, slipping her thumb back in her mouth, appeared to fall asleep.

'Katie, wake up,' said Lily. 'Come on, please, not today. I have to leave early. It'll take me for ever to get to work in this.'

Lily dressed in seconds. It was so bitterly cold, she'd wanted to keep her threadbare flannelette nightshirt on under her office clothes. She possessed two winter work outfits and it was only the most enormous row at home that had enabled this to happen.

'Are you shivering, Lily?' whispered Joe through his wheeze.

'I am, it's freezing. Come on, you. Enough. Let's get you back under the blankets. Don't you get out of the bed until the fire is going. I'll go and warm some milk. Stay there, do you hear me?'

Joe burrowed down under the blanket with a grin, glad to be back in the warmth.

Lily opened the bedroom door and the blue smoke from the last of her mother's cigarettes filled the air. The kettle whistled a welcome as she stepped into the kitchen.

'Make the tea,' barked her mother. 'Use the leaves from last night.'

Lily poured the boiling water and slipped out to the coal house, returning with a bottle of sterilized milk.

'Where the hell did that come from?' said her mother, casting a cursory glance as Lily poured the entire contents into the pan she had cleaned the night before.

'Save me some for me tea,' her mother said through a haze of cigarette smoke.

'Oh, I'm sorry, Mam,' said Lily as she shook the last drops into the pan. 'I didn't hear.'

Her mother narrowed her eyes and inhaled deeply.

Lily had heard her full well and she knew it. She'd bought the milk for Joe and Katie on her way home from work the previous evening and hidden it behind a coal sack. As far as she was concerned, it was for them. Not her mother, who lived her life sustained by nothing more than Guinness. She breathed a sigh of relief to discover that the bread she'd hidden at the back of the cupboard was still there. She crumbled it into the bowls.

'A right Mary goodwife you think you are, don't you,' sneered her mother as the kids came in and picked up their bowls and took the spoons Lily held out to them.

'Your stepfather has gone out to do a day's work with nothing in his stomach. I didn't know we had owt. It should have been him what had the milk.'

Lily knew her stepfather would be back through the door within minutes, once he realized no one else was heading to the docks that morning. Taking nothing for herself and also off to do a day's work, she lifted her coat from the nail on the back of the door, slipped it on and began fastening the buttons. The coat smelt strongly of cigarette smoke and refried lard.

'I'm off to work now, Mam. I'll be back at six thirty as usual. Shall I call into the shop for food with my pay, before I come home?'

'No, you will not. Bring it straight here. They can have a pie from the van when I've counted it.'

Lily made a mental note to collect the pies herself and pretend she had misunderstood. The kids would have nothing after their breakfast until she retuned home. Not unless Mrs McGuffy next door gave them a biscuit or two, as she often did.

Fastening a headscarf under her chin, Lily bent down to kiss Joe. 'You stay in here in front of the fire today, Joe. 'Tis too cold for you to go outside. Come straight home from school, Katie. Get back to Joe, don't dawdle. Do you hear me?'

'The state of you in yer fancy coat,' sneered her mother as she dragged on her cigarette. 'I could get a few bob for that, if the notion took me.' It was a second-hand coat, acquired by Sister Therese for her star pupil. 'Think you're something in that, don't you, eh? You know what they say, don't you? Eh, you, miss.' Lily's mother stopped speaking just for a moment, to pass wind loudly. 'Ah, that's better,' she said as she shifted in her seat and pulled on her cigarette. 'First ciggie of the day, always gets me going.' And as though nothing had happened, she continued, 'They say pride comes before a fall and that'll be you one day, miss. Flat on your face, you will be. You watch my words, And me, I can't wait. Someone needs to teach you a lesson, Miss La-de-da Lily.'

Lily stepped out on to the landing, inhaled the bracingly sharp icy air and closed the door gently behind her. Her own mother was jealous of her, she thought. She resented her. She hated her, even. Yes, that was it, she really hated her.

Far more than Lily hated the sound of children playing. And that was a lot.

CHAPTER 4

Sister Therese had found Lily her job. When she'd appealed to Mr and Mrs McConaghy she'd known exactly what she was doing and what buttons to press to achieve the desired result. It was a technique she had deployed time and time again and not a day passed without her giving thanks for good old Catholic guilt and the premise that all sinners were forgiven every indiscretion the moment they left the confessional. If they did exactly as the priest had instructed.

Sister Therese and Father Brennan had a deal. 'Oh, 'tis a great deal,' she often said to him. She would tell him what penance she needed to be pressed upon whichever financially flourishing tradesman happened to be sitting in the confessional, and he would oblige. No one ran a community as efficiently as Sister Therese.

Mr and Mrs McConaghy owned a business that was growing in profitability year on year. Their processing plant took raw jute from the docks and spun it into rope and, using a furnace and smelter, spun raw metal into brass wire. The plant was staffed by the steady flow of Irish labour that arrived in Liverpool; the men came straight from the Emerald Isle, through the dock gates and down into the hot bowels of the processing plant.

The McConaghys attended St Chad's once a day and twice on Sundays but had performed barely a single charitable act in their lives. They both knew it and felt it and their guilt grew as fast and as large as the company bank balance. This guilt was obvious to Sister Therese. It was as clear to see as the nervous tremble on their lips when they blessed themselves and bent a knee to the Holy Mother before they slipped into their pew. Sister Therese had observed similar behaviour many times among the better-off. They were conflicted. They veered between adoring the vast amounts of money they made in their processing plant and fearing that, if they didn't take the right steps, their paths to heaven would be forever blocked by an impenetrable wall of fifty-pound notes. They were seeking a way to avoid eternal damnation.

Father Brennan had already hinted at how their respective paths could be made clear. 'Share the proceeds of your wealth,' he had whispered through the mesh. He had instilled the fear of God into them and they'd both broken out in a cold sweat. 'It is easier to pass a camel through the eye of a needle than for a rich man to enter the kingdom of heaven,' he'd continued, driving the point home. It was then up to Sister Therese to show them how.

This she did by offering up a girl she described as 'the most clever and gifted I have ever taught, a competitor to Einstein himself, so good is she at her figures'. And then she'd landed the killer blow. 'As virtuous as any daughter would have been, had the good Lord seen fit to bless you with your own.' They were done for.

'She's only half Irish, that I will admit,' Sister Therese said. 'Her mother is from Dublin – and not from the best area. But she is a grand girl of great religion and honesty and the good Lord, well now, he would just love the person who gave a poor girl like Lily a job in a nice warm office. Without a doubt, that is his very favourite type. Father Brennan and I have discussed this on many an occasion.'

The double-act of Father Brennan and Sister Therese had triumphed yet again and they celebrated with a glass of Irish whiskey.

'Make sure you negotiate a good deal for the girl,' Father Brennan had said. 'They are neither of them filled with the milk of human kindness. And childlessness has left her a bitter woman, though she dotes on that niece of hers, Amy. The one that never comes to Mass.'

Sister Therese filled up Father Brennan's glass. The supply of Irish whiskey at the priest's house grew weekly as one or another Irish returnee to Liverpool dropped off an offering. It was not unusual for Father Brennan's housekeeper to open the front door to six bottles of milk and one of whiskey. No one, no matter how hungry, dared to steal from the priest's house.

'Sure, but there is a reason why the good Lord left them childless and I'm thinking that they could be just the people to help Lily out. They both need salvation. Greed will be their eternal undoing before too long and I have just the way of letting them know that.' She always spoke faster after a drink, and Father Brennan, being slightly deaf, had to follow her lips to understand what she was saying.

He drank his whiskey and smiled. 'That you do. There is no one quite like you, Sister Therese, for getting her own way. Be careful though. Someone needs to look after that tiny little fella, Joe. Both parents were in the Red Admiral the whole day yesterday. Sheila behind the bar told me as much at Mass. She said someone needs to be keeping an eye on the children and that Joe is not as good as he should be. He has the worst chest in Clare Cottages, apparently. But I told her not to be worrying and that we could manage it ourselves. We can, can't we, Sister? All those children have been christened as Catholic, have they now?'

'They have, Father.'

'In that case, we don't want the Corporation interfering, do we? We'd have no control over where the wee ones were put should they take them into care. 'Tis into our own home they must go should that happen. But there's time for that yet. Let's see what can be done. Have no fear of using the McConaghys. They will be grateful to have been diverted off the road to hell.'

Sister Therese tipped up her glass and emptied it. She had never actually liked the taste of whiskey, but she did like the warm feeling that burnt beneath her breast and the sudden flush in her cheeks. And once she'd finished the first glass, she found herself looking forward to the second.

Father Brennan emptied his own glass as his speech began to slur. 'Grand. You know, I wish the good Lord would give me the power to close down the Red Admiral. If I could, I would, and that's a fact. Alcohol has ruined the families around here. 'Tis the most wicked evil of all.'

''Tis that, Father,' Sister Therese replied as her forlorn gaze rested on her empty glass.

Not a day went by when Mrs McConaghy didn't wonder why she and Mr McConaghy had not been blessed with a child. In her heart, she suspected that it could be because they earned so much money and coveting was a terrible sin. She also knew that pride was a sin and she spent a lot of her non-working hours on her knees at the side of her bed, praying for forgiveness.

Sister Therese had caught them in the church straight out of confession. 'A hundred Hail Marys and be guided by Sister Therese,' Father Brennan had said, and there she was, Sister Therese, standing by the church door. There was no way to escape her even if Mrs McConaghy had wanted to, and sure, was it not a coincidence that she was there by the door, straight after the father had spoken to her?

The following day, Sister Therese walked up the steps of the processing plant and into the office. 'Well, would you be looking at all this now,' she said, almost before she was through the door. 'The size of the place and all those people down those stairs, by the big furnace. Do they all work for you? Do they?'

Half an hour later they were sitting in front of the office fire, heads bent towards each other, as Sister Therese discussed the terms of Lily's employment.

'God himself has put Lily on the path to your own door. I would be saying that was his very idea now. Would you not agree?'

Mr and Mrs McConaghy nodded. It wouldn't do to contradict the wisdom of a nun.

'Imagine that? Ye see, there are people God really wants to have in heaven with him. Oh, no, is that custard slice for me? You shouldn't have.'

Sister Therese played them both like a finely tuned fiddle. Their lack of children set against the success of their business was the gossip of the workforce, and they knew it. By the time she'd tucked into a chocolate éclair as well as the custard slice and had downed a second pot of tea, the McConaghys felt rinsed with relief. Absolution had arrived on their doorstep. The process had been entirely painless. And it was cost neutral.

'We will pay her a fair day's pay for a fair day's work, Sister. You don't have to worry about that,' said Mrs McConaghy, making sure that everything was well understood.

'Oh, saints above, I don't worry. 'Tis not I that worries. I am just a messenger for Father Brennan, 'tis he who is worried. Sure, I know you will. And I know you, Mrs McConaghy – Lily will have a lovely cake each morning, like the one you gave me, will she not?'

Mrs McConaghy was speechless; she simply nodded her head.

'And, as well as her pay, I know I can count on you to give the girl a good lunch too.'

Again, Mrs McConaghy nodded dumbly.

'Imagine, she will have a grand time in here.' Sister Therese looked around the office. 'And will she be sitting here now, in this nice chair in front of the fire?' She'd jumped out of her seat and had her hands on the back of Mrs McConaghy's tattered but beloved leather swivel chair. The problem with Sister Therese was that she never knew when she had won, when to call it a day and cut and run. She couldn't stop herself.

Mrs McConaghy took a protective step towards the chair and began to cut her off. She could see that if this progressed, Sister Therese would have them handing the business itself over to this gifted waif. 'Well, actually, Sister . . .' She didn't make it past three words before Sister Therese continued, a little louder.

'Do you know what I am going to do, Mrs McConaghy? I am going to bring Father Brennan down here himself, to show him what wonderful generous people ye have been and to ask him to offer up a prayer for your own reward in heaven and urge the good Lord to press the business into even greater prosperity. If that is at all possible now.' She dropped her voice to a conspiratorial whisper. 'He has a direct line, Father Brennan, as ye well know, straight to the Lord Almighty himself. 'Tis as clear as that phone on your desk, so it is.'

Both Mr and Mrs McConaghy, equally perplexed, turned to look at the black Bakelite telephone on Mrs McConaghy's desk, viewing it now in an entirely new light.

'Would you be agreeable to that now?'

'How could we not be?' asked Mrs McConaghy. 'We would love to see the father visit, wouldn't we?' She nudged her husband.

'Oh, aye, of course we would.'

In the weeks that followed, Sister Therese often commented to the other nuns at St Chad's that Mrs McConaghy had been true to her word and that with the help of the Lord, she and Father Brennan had achieved a grand result.

For his part, Mr McConaghy often commented to Mrs McConaghy that they'd been thoroughly charmed by a wily nun and that if he didn't know better, he'd have said she'd cast a spell over them.

Whatever the explanation, it was the

McConaghys' fear of the telephone that they had understood sat on Father Brennan's desk – the one that didn't connect to the exchange but rather had its own line all the way to heaven and the good Lord – that ensured they did for Lily exactly as they'd promised Sister Therese they would.

Two days after Sister Therese's visit, a thin and terrified Lily stepped through their office door on the arm of the persuasive sister. And from that day on, the McConaghys set about providing Lily with a sound training in bookkeeping, regular pay, a mid-morning fancy and a free lunch. Mrs McConaghy kept her swivel chair, however.

Lily slipped most of the food she was given into the basket that she kept under the desk at her feet. At the end of her first week there, with her first pay packet, she bought a bright pink floral-patterned plastic birdcage cover from the market for threepence. She slit this across the middle, slipped it over the handle of her basket and tucked the elasticated edge around the woven rim. No one knew that, apart from her battered purse and a handkerchief, she carried nothing in the basket to work. But the journey home was a different matter. Every cake and treat put on her desk by Mrs McConaghy found its way into the basket and back home to Joe and her sister.

The plastic birdcage cover was now three years old and Lily had become an old hand at her job. As the months and years had gone by, Mrs McConaghy had handed over more and more responsibility to Lily and did less and less herself. This was reflected in the size of Mrs McConaghy's ever-expanding waistline. She had also grown increasingly fond of her young employee, becoming noticeably warmer hearted in the process.

'Do you know, Lily, you are as thorough at the bookkeeping as I ever was myself,' she had commented one day when Lily had been asked to stay behind for an extra hour to sort out the men's pay.

Lily made no reply. Much of her time in the first weeks in the office had been spent correcting Mrs McConaghy's mistakes, not that she would ever have said so. The fact was, as she knew herself, she was practically running the business. Everything ran to order. Payments in, payments out. Hours clocked, wages paid. Goods measured in, bankers' drafts out. Lily took pride in how, under her management, the business ran like clockwork.

She also noticed how Mrs McConaghy bristled when anyone commented on how good she was. 'What a find that girl was. You must be beside yourself with all that time on your hands now,' a trader delivering a wagon of jute had said only the previous morning. And she positively hated it when the comments were made to Lily as they left the office. 'This place would grind to a halt if you weren't here, queen.' When that happened, Mrs McConaghy would harrumph ungraciously, scrape the legs of her chair on the floorboards, throw looks like daggers over her shoulder, and then become all thoughtful. But her grumpiness did not affect her treatment of Lily.

Lily always took care to make a fuss of Mrs McConaghy when this happened. She'd make her tea and run to Sayers for an Eccles cake, anything to put a smile on her face. But she never complained. Mrs McConaghy was as nice as pie to her most of the time, and she said as much to Sister Therese every time she asked.

'Are they treating you well? Are they?' Sister Therese, always suspicious of those who had to be dragged into offering a poor form of charity, would look intently into Lily's eyes as she waited for an answer.

Lily didn't dare hesitate for a second too long. If she did, she knew that Sister Therese would be down at the plant, checking up on her. 'They are, Sister. Mrs McConaghy, she's very good to me. She's used to me now, and me to her. It all runs very smoothly.'

She smiled a rare smile because she was absolutely correct. Things at work could not have been better. It was home that remained the stubborn problem and there was the constant nagging worry that, day on day, little Joe's breathing was getting worse. His rib cage stuck out like a bird's and yet every time she took him to the doctor's, the man always said the same thing. 'The boy is crying out for his mother. That wheeze, it's a psychological illness. The day your mother gets herself out of the pub and looks after him herself will be the day it stops.'

Lily would scoop Joe into her arms and call into the chemist's for another bottle of camphor oil. How could she explain to the doctor that she was the only mother Joe knew? The only one he wanted. She felt desolate when the doctor dismissed them. Helpless and sick with worry that no one anywhere wanted to do anything to help little Joe.

CHAPTER 5

I wonder when someone is going to offer me a cup of tea, thought Miss Ava Van Gilder as she folded her gloves in her lap for the hundredth time. This wooden chair is hard, my journey has been long, cold and uncomfortable, and yet no one appears to be the slightest bit concerned.

She shifted her handbag further up her lap, sniffed disapprovingly to no one but herself and straightened her back ready to respond when she was called in for her interview. To pounce. To dazzle and impress. To ensure she left St Angelus with the job she so desperately needed, because there was no going back to whence she'd come.

Her morning had not been a good one. Her train into Lime Street had been delayed due to the sudden snow and Liverpool had appeared like a ghost town as she'd steamed into the city from the Crosby bed and breakfast she'd booked into the night before. She had enough money to last for two more weeks and she desperately needed this job and the accommodation that came with it. But, more than anything, she needed to keep her past a secret. I'm jolly glad my interview is the last one of the day, she thought. Wouldn't have done to be late. Never been late for anything in my life. Not about to start now.

The corridor outside the boardroom of the St Angelus hospital, in which she now sat, made her train carriage seem luxurious in comparison. It was cavernous and silent. The walls were covered in dark, bottle-green tiles from halfway up to the arched ceilings. The tiles had been polished until they gleamed and the walls below were painted in a dark cream gloss stained brown by nicotine that had stubbornly defied even the fiercest application of elbow grease.

Miss Van Gilder sat like a bird on a perch staring at the cage floor. Her thin frame and beaked nose trembled from time to time. Directly in front of her stood the two large wooden doors that led into the hospital boardroom. The sound of murmured voices slipped out from under the gap at the bottom of the door and wafted tantalizingly towards her. She heard a laugh.

Laughter? Her hawk-like features crinkled as she peered over the top of her glasses, as if to stare harder at the door. How odd that they are laughing, she thought. Her bony wing nubs that passed for shoulders relaxed and a puzzled frown crossed her face. It was the candidate before her who was being interviewed, that much she knew, and she was suddenly overcome with the urge to know exactly what they were talking about. That interview has lasted far too long, she thought. I've been sitting here for over three quarters of an hour. She threw a sniff of disapproval in the direction of the doors.

The ceiling above her soared upwards into a large, ornate dome. She'd noticed its clock as she'd walked up the main hospital steps and now she heard it strike three. Her interview had been scheduled for two thirty. I'm not sure I want to work in a hospital with such a laissez-faire attitude towards timekeeping, she thought. But as she bristled with disapproval, she remembered with a jolt that she had no choice. She had run clean out of choices.

A set of footsteps echoed on the parquet flooring in the unseen distance. She could not see from whom or where they came and as they approached and grew louder, a shiver of fear ran down her spine. 'They have found me,' she whispered out loud, clutching at the handle of her handbag. Her feet shifted quickly under the chair, poised and ready to jump. Her knuckles shone white and her short breaths came faster as her gaze focused on the sound of the footsteps. A film of perspiration broke out on her top lip and she quickly wiped it away with the back of her glove as she licked her dry lips and almost started praying.

Sitting there on the small wooden chair below the vast dome, she felt like a minute specimen in a vast bell jar waiting to be experimented on. The fading sun threw down a shaft of watery light and lit the floor around her.

I'm doomed, she thought. I'm done for. The footsteps became louder and firmer and she was sure they'd speeded up. Her eyes almost filled with tears, but not quite. Tears were strangers to Miss Van Gilder. Her heart began beating faster and louder in her chest and she thought whoever it was that was coming for her must be able to hear it too.

'Fancy a cup of tea, dear?'

The owner of the footsteps came into view. They turned the corner and walked purposefully along the high-ceilinged corridor towards her.

'I said, would you like a cup of tea, dear?' It was Elsie O'Brien, the housekeeper for Matron's apartment, which was just off the administration corridor and overlooked the main entrance to the hospital. This time her tone was a little impatient.

Miss Van Gilder exhaled slowly.

'You must have walked all the way from Lime Street,' Elsie said. 'There's no trams running because of the weather, so they say. Have you travelled far?' Elsie patiently awaited a response.

She was disappointed. There was no reply other than, 'Black, no sugar. Thank you. Most welcome.'

Miss Van Gilder had managed to slow her breathing back down to normal. She felt her pulse steady. The blood retuned to her cheeks as quickly as it had drained away. She was exhausted.

'You look a bit peaky. Are you feeling all right, dear?' Elsie peered at her face, curious, confused.

Ava Van Gilder wanted to snap at the insignificant woman who called her 'dear'. To demand to know who she thought she was talking to. But this was not the time. Be calm, be charming, most charming, Ava reminded herself. At least until you know you've secured the job. You must. You do need this job. Charming.

'You don't have to, you know,' said Elsie, never one to give up.

'Don't have to what?' Too late; she had snapped.

But Elsie was unfazed. 'The sugar and the milk. We've got loads of sugar here for general use now the sugar rationing is over for hospitals. I can put a couple of spoons in, if you fancy. I'm like you with the black, though. It was all we had during the war. The dairy house at the end of George Street was bombed. The cow went west, along with the rest of the street. Don't even like milk any more now, I got so used to having the tea without. I do like a milk stout though, every now and then. Do you?'

Elsie smiled, revealing the badly fitting false teeth she wore only for work. Removed within seconds of arriving home each evening. Miss Ava Van Gilder glared.

'Make each one of the candidates your friend,' Biddy had instructed Elsie that morning over breakfast. 'Chat to them. Find out everything you can. Always good for us to have a head start and know who we're getting as assistant matron and what we will have to deal with.'

Biddy had given Elsie her pep talk before the

interviews had begun. Her advice had worked, until Miss Van Gilder arrived. She'd hoped the shared moment of lightness, the no milk and black tea, would break the ice, take her and Miss Van Gilder down an avenue of productive discussion. After all, she was there to be interviewed for the second most important job in the hospital. Elsie had liked all of the applicants until now. With a cup of tea balanced in one hand and a second lemon puff in the other, some of them had near told her their entire life story.

Gossip was the prime currency of St Angelus and every juicy titbit she could glean would further boost Elsie's status among the other domestics. You were only as relevant as the gossip you knew. Later that day, when Elsie and Biddy, along with Branna McGinty, the domestic on ward two, and Madge from the switchboard, met for their tea in the school of nursing – black for Elsie, swimming in milk for the others, chocolate butter-cream sandwich cake for all – Elsie could give them chapter and verse on the pros and cons of each candidate. That was the plan, although this candidate was proving a difficult nut to crack.

Employing an assistant matron was a big step in the life of St Angelus. There had been ripples of chatter throughout the greasy-spoon café at breakfast every morning that week. People coming up to ask Elsie when she thought the post would start. Elsie felt terribly important and grand. The keeper of the most important secrets in Matron's office. The truth was that people were more concerned than interested. St Angelus not only cared for the sick but via an efficient black market kept local families afloat. A system had developed over years and was based on a relationship of trust between Dessie as the head porter and Matron. No one wanted the system to end. Food, coal and a wage were all any war-widowed family wanted and Dessie could provide all three. A new assistant matron who would upset the rhythm of life at St Angelus could ruin all that.

As Elsie poured Miss Van Gilder's tea, in the kitchenette at the rear of the boardroom that also served Matron's apartment, she decided she had already made up her mind about the woman. Elsie could sense trouble a mile away. She hoped that her interview would be a disaster, a catastrophe even, and wondered if Branna had anything from ward two she could slip into the tea that would be quick acting and have a calamitous effect. She raced into Matron's office, which was also just off the administration corridor, and, picking up the telephone to the switchboard, dialled Madge to enquire about the whereabouts of Branna.

With a stroke of luck, Branna happened to be sitting next to Madge on the switchboard, having popped in for a quick cuppa. This was something Branna had done with increasing frequency since ward two had lost Sister Antrobus to casualty. Sister Antrobus was the most feared sister in the hospital. The manner in which she had used

Matron and played on her feelings had brought to the surface a latent loyalty in every decent person who worked at St Angelus, and that was almost everyone. Branna was no different. 'No one will ever treat me like a slave again,' she announced on the day Sister Antrobus was transferred out of gynae and into casualty. 'I'm taking no nonsense from the acting staff nurse. I'm starting as I mean to go on.' And that meant regular visits to the switch, which was situated close to ward two, and chats with Madge, who worked on the switchboard six days a week. Branna loved to slip into her small room and watch the board light up. She was fascinated by the way Madge could plug and unplug wires, start and end telephone conversations and, of course, listen in. If Madge ever nipped to the ladies, Branna would pick up the headphones and listen in to a conversation, quickly dropping them when she heard Madge reappearing.

'It's for you, Branna,' said Madge as she handed the headphones to Branna.

'For me? Holy Mother of God, who knows I'm here?'

Her cup rattled in the saucer as, leaping up from the stool, she almost stumbled in her haste to take her call.

'Branna, it's me, Elsie. Have you got any syrup of Senna in your bag, queen? I think we need something quick up here. Lord have mercy, there is a right one about to be interviewed.'

'Jesus, no, I haven't. I have nothing for the purging. Do you need something to act quick?'

'Well, if this one gets the job, I'm telling you now, we are all doomed. I'm putting milk in her tea, even though she said not to, because this woman needs to be shown a good time, but as God is my judge, it won't so much as reach the back of her throat before it turns sour. We have to do something to stop her getting through. This is an emergency, Branna.'

Elsie's voice began to rise. They had all heard the stories about the assistant matron over in Narrowgreen hospital. How she counted out the food rations, had the staff's bags checked before they left the kitchens at the end of each day, monitored the coal stores. Every week, a new story delivered a shiver to run down the spine.

'Elsie, are ye mad? You cannot poison a woman being interviewed because you don't like the look of her!' said Branna.

'It's not the look of her, Branna. You don't understand me. It's a feeling I have. It's in her eyes, Branna. Something unholy, it is. She makes the goosebumps stand up on me arms.'

Branna had nothing. Her locker was bare. 'I took some home from the medicine trolley on the ward only a week since. Night Sister gave it to me. Jesus, I only told Hattie Lloyd, but you'd think everyone in our street was bunged up. 'Twas gone by the following night. I swear to God it was sold.'

Elsie stopped for a moment while she digested

this piece of news. 'Is there nothing else that would make her temporarily uncomfortable, like, you know, unable to speak, or make her scream out in pain or something?' She felt the rosaries in her apron pocket burning into her thigh.

'Elsie, do you think my name is *Dr* Branna McGinty? I'm the ward orderly, not a flaming consultant. You'll be asking me to do your hysterectomy next. Jesus. You would have me locked up.'

'Oh, this is bad,' said Elsie. 'I've got a feeling in me waters and you know how they are always right. You can't fool my bladder. Been three times this afternoon. This woman, she will be no good for us. I swear she looks as though a smile has never cracked her face. I have to go now. I need the lavvy again. Me nerves are shot. I'll see yer for tea later.'

As Elsie trotted to the bathroom, she mulled over the fact that if the board decided that Ava Van Gilder was the chosen one, the new assistant matron, they would have nothing to give them a head start. She had not extracted a single fact from the woman. Back in the kitchen, she picked up the tea and with a heavy heart plopped in three spoons of sugar and poured in the milk. To hell with it, she thought. Live dangerously. It might put a smile on her craggy face.

She could hear the tinkle of young laughter emanating from the boardroom and smiled. That was Sister Haycock. Elsie remembered how Biddy had been worried that Sister Haycock didn't laugh enough. Well, she was laughing now. Elsie had liked the applicant who was now being interviewed. She was wearing yellow and Elsie had never seen anyone wearing yellow before.

'Now there's a lovely lady,' she whispered and thought to herself that she must telephone Biddy, with her being such a good Irish Catholic. It was a fact that the Irish had more prayers answered than anyone else, being as they went to Mass more often, and everyone knew that Ireland was the holiest country. She would ask her to pray for the lady in yellow.

Matron's dog, Blackie, shuffled in his basket in the corner. Elsie had to keep him hidden while they had visitors from the Liverpool District Hospitals Board. Blackie was now a grumpy twelve-year-old and had lived at the hospital in Matron's apartment since he was a puppy. But that was before the days of the NHS, and times were changing.

'Yes, Blackie, Biddy's smashing with the prayers. Always being answered, they are. Never lets her down at the bingo. I'll give her a call next.' With a sigh, she picked up the cup and saucer and left the warmth of the kitchenette to face the woman she had already nicknamed Ava Bone Grinder.

'Here's your tea then,' she said as she handed her the cup and saucer. 'I put the sugar in anyway.'

Miss Van Gilder made to protest.

'Go on, spoil yerself. I reckon they'll be calling

you in a few minutes or so. Now, where did you say you last worked?' She sat down on the chair next to her.

Miss Van Gilder stared at Elsie as if she were a maggot that had just crawled out of her apple. 'I did not say anything,' she replied. She looked Elsie up and down but failed to say thank you for the tea. Her meaning was as clear as day.

Elsie rose from the seat quicker than she had sat down. This was all going so badly. 'There's the toilet just along the corridor there if you need to spend a penny. I've just been meself. I wiped the seat and put a clean towel by the sink, so it's all nice and clean for you. The water's lovely and hot . . .'

There was a moment's silence before Miss Van Gilder replied. 'Thank you,' she said primly. Her pinched white face barely moved. She didn't smile. But then, taking Elsie completely by surprise, she spoke.

'Has each interview taken as long as this one?' she snapped.

'More or less,' said Elsie. 'It's Sister Haycock asking this lady a lot of questions. They seem to be taking it in turns. Very thorough, she is. But she can chatter, can our Sister Haycock. Her and Biddy, they never stop chattering some days.'

Miss Van Gilder's brow furrowed, her eyebrows met in the middle. 'Well, in my opinion, if an interview lasts for longer than an hour, someone is talking far too much, and I assume that must be your Sister Haycock.' She laid down her cup and saucer on the chair next to her, stood upright, smoothed down the front of her coat and without another word marched towards the ladies.

Without knowing it, Miss Van Gilder had just made her first big mistake. She had wrongly assumed that in the general scheme of things and, more specifically, in the hierarchal structure of St Angelus, Elsie was a nobody. That, as a mere tea lady, a domestic who fetched and carried, Elsie O'Brien could be treated as rudely as she wished and that whatever was said to her, a woman of so little consequence, would have no repercussions.

Miss Van Gilder had no idea that, when it came to the running of the hospital, the domestics at St Angelus held most of the power and they used it well. Between them all – Biddy, Branna, Elsie, Dessie the head porter and Madge on the switchboard – nothing went on in St Angelus that they didn't know about, make happen or mend. Elsie's gathering of information about who was to be the new assistant to Matron was a crucial element in this process of power and control.

What a nosey individual, thought Miss Van Gilder as she looked back over her shoulder and watched Elsie retreating down the corridor. She could hardly believe the woman was being so familiar and she gave an involuntary shudder as she walked. Having trained in the 1920s, she was used to hospital staff knowing their place. It was a place that was very lowly in the scheme of things. Their role was to be invisible; it was, if it couldn't be helped, to be seen but, like children, to never, ever be heard.

I hope one of the assistant matron's jobs will include the supervision and appointment of domestics, she thought to herself as she inspected the clean towel Elsie had laid out especially for her with a fresh shaving of soap sitting on top. This one will have to go, for a start.

As the lavatory door closed, Elsie doubled back. Miss Van Gilder had left her handbag under her chair. Elsie knew it was her only chance. It was now or never. If she didn't do this, she would know nothing, but if she did, it could provide her with information that the others would thank her for. Elsie could sense trouble. She needed the lavvy again. There was danger in the air. 'Do it,' she whispered to herself as she began to retrace her footsteps. 'Go on, do it.' She moved like a snake and then, realizing she was too slow, trotted back towards the seat.

Crossing herself as she stooped forwards, Elsie slipped the bag out from under the chair and in a flash unclipped the clasp. The two halves of the bag parted to reveal very little and Elsie's heart sank. A purse, a comb and a sheaf of papers. She glanced nervously towards the lavatory door. She would hear the chain flush before Miss Bone Grinder came out. In the small pocket on the side of the bag, she spotted a train ticket and, lifting it out, noticed it was a one-way ticket from Bournemouth. She peered in the pocket for the return half, but there was nothing. She wanted to remove one of the sheets of paper, but it was too late. She heard the toilet flush and swiftly snapped the clasp shut and returned the bag to the place where Miss Van Gilder had left it, tucked away under the seat.

Ten minutes later, entirely unaware, Miss Van Gilder placed the now empty national-issue cup and saucer down on the wooden chair next to her. Even though she would never admit it, she'd thought the tea had tasted delicious. She glanced appreciatively at the toffee-brown sludge of melted sugar granules clinging to the sides and for a brief second she felt lifted. Maybe she should start to take sugar in her tea, now that hospital rationing was ending. But no sooner had the thought entered her mind than she dismissed it and mentally shook herself back into grumpiness. The sugar slid down the sides of the cup into a despondent puddle.

As if on cue, she heard the now familiar sound of Elsie's footsteps as she came round the corner to collect the cup. The laughter in the boardroom had faded and the voices had lowered to a murmur; the interview was coming to an end.

The sound of a different, scurrying, pair of foot-steps filled the vast corridor as a lone probationer nurse, red-faced and anxious, made her way towards the boardroom doors.

A look of alarm crossed Elsie's face as she stepped forward to stop her. 'Where are you off to?' she asked as she put her hand out to halt the nurse. Elsie recognized her. She'd been in the most recent group at the preliminary training school, or PTS, as it was commonly known.

'Where are you off to, Nurse Moran?' Elsie repeated. She prided herself on knowing the name of every nurse in the hospital. It wasn't difficult. Once the probationers had passed their PTS, the names came to Matron's office to be allocated to the wards. Matron had had Dessie fix a huge blackboard on her office wall, on which she wrote the nurses' names as she moved them around the hospital, like pieces on a chessboard. Elsie thought Matron secretly imagined herself as a Wren in the War Office as she moved her troops around St Angelus.

'Sister told me to take this to the path lab,' Nurse Moran said, taking a glass sample-jar from underneath its brown-paper sheath.

Elsie gasped in disgust. 'Put it away, we don't want that up here,' she hissed. The jar was filled with what was obviously urine.

'But I can't find the path lab anywhere. Dr Davenport told me it was up the stairs and in through the big wooden doors.'

'Did he now?' said Elsie, thinking to herself that she would kill that man. She had told him herself earlier that morning that the interviews were taking place. She could picture him at that very moment, walking down the main corridor to the theatre where she knew he was operating this afternoon, giggling to himself. 'You take no notice of that wicked man,' she said. 'Jesus, the path lab isn't even in the main building. It's outside. Go through the courtyard, past the porter's lodge and then past the oxygen store. It's the wooden hut next to the mortuary.'

Nurse Moran looked as though she was about to burst into tears.

'Go on, hurry,' said Elsie impatiently as she turned her around and pointed her in the direction of the stairs. 'Sister Haycock will be out here in two seconds.'

The probationer's eyes widened and Elsie thought she might be about to cry.

'Go on, shoo now and you'll be fine. She will never know.'

In a pink flash, the probationer was gone.

Miss Van Gilder made to speak, but she never got her chance as the large wooden doors to the boardroom were suddenly flung open.

Out walked Emily Haycock, smiling warmly, chattering in whispers to the candidate she was accompanying into the corridor. Her small kitten heels clipped a tattoo on the wooden floor. The woman she was escorting was smart and young-looking. Her head was bent towards Sister Haycock's and she was listening intently to what she had to say. Both were smiling.

Well, she looks far too young, thought Miss Van Gilder. And no self-respecting ward sister wanting to become an assistant matron would wear bright yellow. Women wear that colour for one reason only: to be noticed. It's a husband she's after, and she's not the first. She coughed pointedly to attract Sister Haycock's attention. It's time this Sister Haycock noticed me and stopped chatting to that rain-beaten daffodil, she thought.

Emily raised her head and smiled in acknowledgement. The sound of a giggle filled the air and Miss Van Gilder felt her temper rising. She took a deep breath, swallowed and then fixed her face, ready.

'Miss Ava Van Gilder, hello. How are you? I'm so sorry to have kept you waiting,' Emily said as she walked over on her clippety kitten heels and held out her hand.

Miss Van Gilder stood up. Her back was ramrod straight, her handbag was clasped to her front and her hat did not so much as tremble a greeting. 'It is not Ava as in Gardner but Ava as in Arva,' she said as she proffered her hand.

She may have been short, with a small, wiry frame, but once met, no one ever underestimated Miss Van Gilder. The sharp, no-nonsense glint in her steel-grey eyes, the strength of her handshake and the timbre of her voice immediately disabused anyone of the notion that here was a caring and kindly woman.

Emily almost took a step back as Miss Van Gilder thrust out her hand and left it there, rigid and waiting. Goosebumps covered Emily's arms in response. Up until this moment she'd thought she'd got clean away with having selected candidates for interview on the basis of how nice their name sounded. It had worked astonishingly well. All five interviewed so far had been women with a modern approach and she could imagine any one of them taking the post. Now, though, it looked as if it was all about to go horribly wrong. She instinctively knew that this one was going to be trouble.

She blinked rapidly as the owner of the cold-as-a-wet-fish but firm-as-a-vice hand pumped her own arm up and down like the handle on a village-green pump.

'But I much prefer Miss Van Gilder at all times, if you don't mind,' the woman said. And then, as an afterthought, as though she'd remembered she was being interviewed, she added an awkward, 'Thank you very much.'

Emily felt herself recoil. If there was any way she could have prevented this woman from entering the boardroom, she would have done so. She momentarily considered fainting, as her mind frantically scrabbled for a way out of what she knew was about to become a treacherous situation. In a flash, she saw the small but significant achievements she had made since she had been in place slipping away.

Emily had tried her very best to drag St Angelus out of its entrenched, pre-war, 1930s' modes of behaviour, and that included everyone becoming a little less formal with each other. It was her dream to remove the ban on married nurses being able to continue working and she wanted the right assistant matron to be appointed, someone who would be on her side and would work on Matron to help achieve that objective. Matron was stuck in her ways and totally opposed. Emily needed an ally. A pincer movement was what was required. To convince Matron, or, if she resisted, simply to outvote her.

She desperately wanted an assistant matron who was forward-looking and modern. Someone who shared her goals. She had to ensure that the assistant matron's vote was one she could count on, as she would become a key member of the hospital management board. Not for a second did Miss Van Gilder look as though she fitted that bill and Emily heard her heart land on the parquet floor.

'Yes, quite, of course,' said Emily. 'We never use Christian names in the confines of the hospital, as you know. It's just that amongst senior staff, we occasionally do . . .'

Her words tailed off as she took in the almost raven-black hair, the fierce-looking glasses, the pinched lips, slightly hooked nose and pale eyes. The darkness of Miss Van Gilder's hair was in stark contrast to the paleness of her skin; she looked like a woman who had never met the sun.

A hard, expressionless gaze met her words and Emily felt as though she was shrinking before Miss Van Gilder's eyes. This woman is supposed to be forty-five, she thought, but she looks sixty if she's a day.

The previous applicant had been forty. She was smart and modern in her manner. Emily had taken to her right away and had even thought that this was a woman she could be friends with. She had admired her very fashionable dress-coat and had felt rather self-conscious in her own chocolate-brown twinset. If there were two things Emily needed more than anything, they were a single friend of her own age and some new clothes. Women who were dedicated to nursing became lonely spinsters in later life. Emily had seen it happen so many times and it was a future she dreaded. She knew she had to fight against it happening to her, but time was not on her side.

'Well, I don't think there is any doubt at all who the most appropriate candidate is,' said Matron at the end of the day, once Miss Van Gilder had left and Elsie had brought in the tea urn and sandwiches for the board members.

God, no, thought Emily. Not Miss Van Gilder. Please God, no.

'Do you have any questions for Miss Van Gilder?' Dr Gaskell had asked during the interview. His expression had been inscrutable and he had refused to catch Emily's eye beyond the one glance that so clearly said, Emily, what have you done?

'Yes, please, Dr Gaskell,' said Matron, whose face had lit up when Miss Van Gilder had entered the room.

Emily was almost in despair. They had taken it

in turns to lead the questioning of the candidates. Her own free run had been with the previous applicant; she'd been so desperate for the board to like the woman in yellow that she had asked too many questions and taken too long.

'What would be your approach to redressing the shortfall of nursing-staff applications we have experienced of late?' said Matron, leaning forward across her foolscap pad and holding her pencil as though ready to record every word Miss Van Gilder uttered. 'As you may know, the number of patients St Angelus treats is growing every day. The Liverpool District Hospitals Board has plans to build a new theatre suite and several new wards. Casualty now treats over thirty people a day. We are one of the busiest hospitals in the north-west.'

Miss Van Gilder didn't waste a second. 'There is no nursing cadet force at St Angelus, which is unusual, if you don't mind my saying. In Manchester, the hospitals have a full contingent. I believe St Angelus has relied too heavily on its reputation as a centre of learning for the treatment of TB.'

Dr Gaskell rose to his full height in his chair and shuffled the papers in front of him impatiently. As the regional clinical lead in TB, he was far from impressed. His manner said quite clearly that he wanted this interview to be over as soon as possible. In contrast, the representatives from the LDHB appeared to be lapping up her every word.

'We must search far and wide to recruit young girls into a cadet force as soon as they are ready to leave school,' continued Miss Van Gilder. 'When they reach seventeen, they can then begin full nurse training without the barriers new nurses often experience when commencing work in a hospital and meeting patients for the first time. They will be fully prepared for nursing and ill prepared for anything else. This is the only way we can ward off the modern-day notion that a man can do a woman's job. I am not a fan of male nurses. Never have been.'

Dr Gaskell raised an eyebrow. A normally wise and gentle man, he found Miss Van Gilder more irritating than almost anyone else he could remember having encountered. It was he who'd instigated the employment at St Angelus of former members of the forces' medical corps, encouraging them to take up roles in the hospital as part of their rehabilitation, and he hoped to employ many more, even though he'd met with strong disapproval from both Matron and Sister Antrobus. St Angelus had been the first to appoint male nurses from the post-war influx of 1952, and they were now becoming commonplace in every hospital across the country. However, he did not say this, just stared down at his papers.

Miss Van Gilder continued apace. 'I'm sure such men had their place during the war, out in the field hospitals, but not in a modern post-war British hospital. No, indeed, no place here.'

Matron beamed. The two charge nurses on the male surgical ward were the bane of her life. They were informal, disorganized, disobedient and far too loud. As far as she was concerned, taking them on had been the biggest mistake the board had ever made. But she had no choice. Every day she felt less and less in control of her own hospital as the new NHS flexed its muscles. She could not have agreed more with Miss Van Gilder. She liked this woman.

'I just have one more question, if you don't mind, Dr Gaskell?' Matron looked at Dr Gaskell and smiled.

He shifted in his chair and looked uncomfortable. 'Of course, but we must wind up soon, it is almost five o'clock,' he said with uncustomary impatience.

Matron knew Dr Gaskell was hurrying her, but she would not be rushed. 'There is a great deal of flippant and in my opinion silly talk about removing the ban on married nurses being able to continue working. How do you feel about this particular issue?'

Emily wasn't sure if Matron was even aware of it, but the manner in which she had phrased the question left no one in any doubt about what her own feelings were.

Once again, Miss Van Gilder dived in without hesitation. 'I could not imagine anything worse than a married woman nursing a poorly patient. Women who are married have homes and husbands to look after. They become pregnant. They would be tired before they even began a day of work. Nursing is a physical job. It requires every ounce of a girl's strength. After a day on the wards, she has none to spare and, frankly, I do believe there is something very distasteful and inappropriate in the idea that a woman in full possession of carnal knowledge should be tending to male patients. Not something the patients would be comfortable with, I am sure.'

Matron nodded approvingly.

Emily knew exactly what Miss Arva-not-Ava Van Gilder meant. Married women had sex. That was what Miss Van Gilder did not want to come into contact with. Women who had sex, who reminded her that she didn't.

Emily's only hope was that Miss Van Gilder was more than a world apart from the legendary Sister April, both in appearance and manner, and that this would be enough to put Matron off. Even though she'd left St Angelus way back in 1941, four years before Emily had arrived, Assistant Matron Sister April continued to be a familiar name at the hospital. She had a reputation for having been both kindly and modern, and everyone knew that Matron had had a soft spot for her. The whispers were that Sister April's departure had broken Matron's heart. Emily feared they were right. She sometimes wondered if the reason Sister April had left St Angelus was because she wanted to save her good friend Matron from any further heartache. But whatever the truth of it, Emily thought, Matron surely wouldn't want Miss Van Gilder in Sister April's place.

Elsie dusted the side table that held the sandwiches and tea urn. She couldn't possibly leave the room until she knew who the successful candidate was. She stole a glance over her shoulder. They were deliberating for far longer than she'd thought they would. She would need to find a way to prolong her cleaning-up process.

Pray to God it's not that Miss Bone Grinder bossy boots, she thought as she saw Emily nervously remove and replace the kirby grips in her hair. That would be a disaster. What in God's name was Sister Haycock thinking, putting a dragon like that forward to be interviewed? Was she mad?

Dr Gaskell smiled at Elsie, as though he could read her thoughts, which almost made her jump. She smiled back nervously as she rubbed an imaginary stain off the surface of the trolley and stacked the dirty water glasses before placing them on top.

Elsie had lingered during the process of every appointment made at St Angelus since 1931 and prided herself on always knowing who was to be the new member of staff before anyone else did. This time there was going to be a battle, judging by the tone of Matron's voice and the enthusiasm in Emily's, both of them championing entirely different candidates.

Now, as the clock struck five, she accidentally on purpose dropped a plate of crumbs on to the floor. 'Oh, sorry,' she said to no one in particular as she got down on her knees. 'I'll have to go and fetch the Ewbank for that now. What a mess.'

But no one was paying her any attention. So she got down on to the floor on her hands and knees to pick up the crumbs and shuffled herself out of sight and under the table. They would forget about her under there and she could hear every word. She was inches from the legs and shoes of Mrs Jolly from the LDHB. She couldn't help noticing the neatly tied laces on the brown brogues. She's got a nasty bunion, thought Elsie as she spotted the bulging lump on the side of her foot. No wonder she looks like she's chewing a lemon. Must be killing her.

Elsie wrinkled her nose. Mrs Jolly's feet had a strange odour of leather and sweat. She put her hand over her nose. She was dangerously close to sneezing.

Emily sat at the table and almost held her breath. She was dreading the outcome of this day more with every second that passed. She would not have minded any of the other applicants and was now almost wishing scary Sister Antrobus had applied.

Dr Gaskell was always Emily's ally on the board, but she knew he had to travel to Manchester that evening for the annual regional TB committee dinner. He'd even said to her at the beginning of the day, 'We need to be prompt here today, Emily.' He had taken to calling her Emily over the past few months. She thought it might be his little way of letting her know that he agreed with her that St Angelus was out of step with the way Liverpool was moving and they were all far too formal with

108

each other. She felt as though he was being almost paternal towards her. She hoped he would be able to stay until the end of the meeting.

It was now down to the representatives from the Liverpool District Hospitals Board to make their decision. Since the creation of the NHS, there had always been at least one LDHB member at any important meeting of the hospital board, but this was the first time that LDHB members had outnumbered St Angelus staff. Emily wondered if that was deliberate. 'Interesting,' had been Dr Gaskell's rather dry observation as they'd filed into the boardroom that morning. They weren't an inspiring-looking lot. Hatted and gloved, bespectacled and tweeded, the handbag-carrying four had marched into the room and, in an early indication of their self-importance, Mrs Jolly had sat herself down at the head of the board table without having been invited. 'Worrying,' whispered Dr Gaskell to Emily. That was usually his place.

There was something very deliberate and knowing about this little group of want-to-be hospital matrons. 'Is this a not so subtle way of the LDHB letting us know that we are no longer in charge of who works here?' Emily had whispered back to Dr Gaskell.

He raised his cup and saucer and drank from the tea Elsie had just given him. 'Terrifying,' he replied. 'St Angelus is a family. However, I'm not sure the Liverpool District Hospitals Board is aware of that.'

Mrs Jolly, the war widow of an army general, along with her three attendant officer-class war widows, had seemed less than impressed with the younger, more modern applicants they had interviewed. Coughs and sniffs and a general harrumphing had accompanied some of the questions Emily had asked the candidates. They are trying to put me off, Emily had thought. She had shot a look at Mrs Jolly, who had met Emily's gaze without so much as a flinch. Emily had begun to feel uncomfortable.

During the lunch break, she and Dr Gaskell conferred over their sandwich plate in the corner while Matron and Mrs Jolly appeared to be getting along famously. 'Where have these old boots come from?' said Emily as she sniffed a salmon-paste sandwich she'd taken from Elsie's trolley. 'Why have the LDHB sent these women?'

'I have no idea,' Dr Gaskell replied. 'But I have heard that the LDHB is kindly disposed towards those who make generous donations to hospital causes and positions. Healthcare in Liverpool is a bottomless pit and so I imagine all funds are gratefully received.'

'Just because you give money, doesn't mean you can do a job, though. Or that you have any idea what qualities are needed in a new assistant matron.'

'Ah, well, that is part of the problem. Not enough men left after the war to cope with the running of the NHS. It's only been in operation for five years, remember, and there just aren't enough women trained or wanting to work. The LDHB are turning for help to the widows of the men who probably would have taken positions of responsibility. To those who want to help, obviously. Which is how we have ended up with the likes of Mrs Jolly. They've been appointed to the board on the basis of status, class, generosity and who they were once married to. But many of them did help with the war effort. They probably have ability, just not the ability to choose the right assistant matron for us.'

This irritated Emily. The future of St Angelus was more important than a shortage of men and patronage. 'Why couldn't they have sent women who have experience in hospitals and nursing?'

'Well, as married nurses are not allowed to work, it's hardly surprising. Mrs Jolly, though, she was a code breaker during the war. They aren't idiots. It's just that they were all married to senior officers. They have a certain outlook and every one of them will be looking for an assistant matron who is just like them. That was why I asked you to filter the candidates. To ensure that they only had people like you to select from.'

Emily felt like she wanted to faint. If they were going to appoint a candidate who was just like they were, it would be Miss Van Gilder. 'Oh God, what have I done?' she said.

'Made a mistake?' he replied gently. 'Don't worry, Emily. If there is one thing I know about this hospital after my many years here, it is that it has a life of its own. Nothing happens that was not meant to. Everything works out for the best and, remember, this is your first meeting with Miss Van Gilder. Nothing is ever as bad as it seems, my dear.'

Now, as the afternoon was drawing to a close, the four ladies of the LDHB had stopped whispering and conferring among themselves. Emily was practically shaking with nerves. Surely they would not all agree on the same candidate, she thought. Surely they would not appoint someone that Matron, Dr Gaskell and she herself did not approve of. Or, perhaps more accurately in this case, just she and Dr Gaskell, as Matron and Miss Van Gilder had appeared to get along a little too well. That just could not happen. The decision would have to be unanimous, surely?

Mrs Jolly cleared her throat several times. 'There is no doubt in my mind who is the right candidate,' she announced.

You could be mistaken for Miss Van Gilder's sister, thought Emily as Mrs Jolly began to speak. You're so alike. And then it dawned on her that if Sarah Anne Jolly had applied for the position of assistant matron, on the basis of her name, all other attributes and achievements being equal, she would have been selected for interview too. Emily wanted to bury her face in her hands, but instead she smiled sweetly. She would give nothing away.

'The LDHB representatives are united in our decision. Miss Ava Van Gilder appears to be the ideal candidate. We are in desperate need of someone who is strong and resourceful to assist Matron in moving St Angelus forward to deal with the many challenges being presented in Liverpool today. The LDHB will be undertaking many new appraisals of the hospital. We shall assess whether or not the hospital is efficient in the manner in which it operates. It is no longer a voluntary hospital. We are answerable to Mr Churchill, the new department of health and the taxpayer. There is no room for error. The steps we are taking with the National Health Service have not been walked before and in Miss Van Gilder we have someone who will enable us to continue without losing our way.'

Emily wanted to cry. She had been taken in by the name, Ava Van Gilder, because it had sounded like the name of a musician or an artist. But what had arrived was a potential tyrant. Oh, what have I done, Emily thought to herself for the hundredth time. I should have applied for the job myself.

'Matron, please write and offer Miss Van Gilder the post of assistant matron forthwith. She is to assume her position as soon as possible. This hospital is all but buckling under the pressure of patient demand and we cannot afford to waste a minute.'

Mrs Jolly slowly rose from her chair. Once she was standing, the others respectfully followed suit. She folded her spectacles, placed them into their tortoiseshell case and snapped it shut. As far as she was concerned, they were done.

Without another word, the four members of the LDHB made their way to the door. Mrs Twigg, the nicest of the bunch, hobbled along at the rear. As she passed Emily, she reached out, gave her hand a small squeeze of sympathy and silently mouthed the words, 'I'm sorry.' Emily smiled meekly back, her eyes downcast. Mrs Twigg had been very sweet. Sweet but weak. It dawned on Emily that a name like Veronica Twigg would never have passed her selection criteria.

They didn't even ask us which candidate we liked best, she thought resentfully as she watched them go. Dr Gaskell met her eye. 'They aren't even applying for references,' she whispered to him.

'This is the new world, Emily,' he replied. 'I am sure someone somewhere will undertake that process. Yet another responsibility removed from our shoulders. It has begun: the transfer of power from the people who have run the hospital for so long, who know the patients, to the faceless bureaucrats in the NHS. I'm glad I'm an old doctor and not a young one like my son. I fear a monster is being created in the NHS. It will become a vehicle for people like Mrs Jolly, who have no clinical or nursing experience, to dictate to those of us who do. Even doctors. Don't be surprised if one day the likes of Mrs Jolly tell us how our patients should be looked after. And now, if you will excuse me, I have to catch my train.'

Emily was left alone in the room with Matron.

'Well, I thought they would have at least

consulted me,' Matron said to Emily as she gathered up the papers and pencils. 'However, no matter. As it is, they chose the candidate I would have voted for.'

'But, Matron, is it enough that we have her work record? No one asked why she left her previous hospital. Should we not at least apply for our own reference?'

'As it happens, I do know the matron at St Dunstan's. We trained together at the London, years ago. I shall drop her a line. I wouldn't take someone on, Sister Haycock, unless I knew their background, I can assure you. Regardless of Mrs Jolly and her posse.'

This did not cheer Emily, but she supposed it was a crumb of hope.

'However, I have to say, Sister Haycock, there are many roles I will be delighted to hand over. The running of the domestics, ward orderlies, porters and porter's lads, to begin with.'

There was a slight thud, which came from under the long table. It was the sound of Elsie's head hitting wood. But neither Emily nor Matron heard it as, still chatting, they moved into Matron's sitting room. As they walked, Matron cast a glance at Emily from the corner of her eye. She could tell she was downhearted and she sympathized. She knew how she felt. Disappointment was an emotion she had dealt with all of her life, on a daily basis. Her first thought as she woke every morning was that she was different and that she was about to face another lonely day. She lived with a secret and no one knew. Or so she thought.

'Come on,' she said. 'Cheer up, Sister Haycock. You will see. She looks to me like a very efficient woman. Just what we need. It is all about getting the job done. We have appointed an assistant matron, not a friend. Now, there is a bottle of sherry in my sideboard and a fire in my sitting room. Let's toast the appointment of our new assistant matron.'

As they closed the boardroom door, Elsie shuffled out backwards, on her hands and knees, from underneath the board table, the dustpan and brush still gripped in her fingers. She had remained deathly still throughout the final minutes of the meeting, determined to draw no attention to herself, and it had worked. They had all forgotten about her, as they knew she would.

'Well, they don't see me when I'm stood in the middle of the room with a teapot in my hand. All they see is the tea. I was as safe as houses under the table,' she said later to Biddy when she recounted the details of the afternoon. 'Sometimes it's just the thing, to be invisible.'

As she heard the latch on Matron's sitting-room door drop, she sprang to her feet, rubbed her head just where she had banged it on the table and pushed the service trolley out of the room, into the small kitchen at the back. She heard the sideboard door open and close in Matron's sitting room, followed by the clinking of sherry glasses.

'Well now, they won't be wanting any more tea.

116

And you can bloomin' wait,' she said to the pile of dirty crockery. She untied her wraparound apron and flung it on top of the plates. She was safe in the kitchenette. It was her domain. Matron never entered during daylight hours. She would not see the dirty dishes and Elsie would have it all cleared away by nightfall.

She opened the rear door so Blackie could make his way back to his basket in Matron's sitting room, then flew down the back stairs and out across the porter's yard in the direction of the greasy-spoon café where she had arranged to meet Dessie, Biddy, Branna and Madge. Oh, that woman is going to be terrible trouble for us all, and dangerous, too, she thought as she walked as fast as the rules would allow, past the school of nursing, trying not to break into a run.

Even Elsie, with her years of experience at St Angelus and her uncanny knack for predicting the future, could not have had any idea just how right she was.

CHAPTER 6

Lockie Keenan called in at the harbour-master's office to check if any of the ships waiting out at the bar would be sailing in to dock.

'Not a cat in hell's chance,' said the harbour-master. 'Everything that was in before Wednesday has been unloaded and the smog is so thick, it'll be hours before any of them can get in. There's even soot on the bleedin' smog. It's in my nose and everywhere. Never known it so bad.'

Lockie had expected as much. He'd left his horse in the stable and the rags over his cart. The smog was so thick, it was only because he made the walk to the docks every day and knew each step that he'd been able to find his way to the dock gate without getting lost. First the snow and now the smog, he thought to himself. It hadn't been the easiest of weeks. And there was more snow on the way, or so it said in the *Echo*.

Lockie traded between the docks and the processing plants. Lads like him bought jute off the ships as it was unloaded, then sold it on to processing works in the city ready to be spun into rope within the hour. Once the jute was done, they went back for the metal, to be smelted and coiled into brass wire. Much of what arrived at the docks was transferred up the hill with a horse and dray. Lockie used his horse to draw the cart all day long, but he knew the horse could do with the rest today.

'What's that package bulging out of your pocket? Brought me a present, have you? You're doing so well, Lockie, mine'll be a bottle of whiskey, please, and thank you very much.'

Lockie laughed. 'It's all saved, so it is. Every penny I can. Want to work for myself one day, not every other bugger. It's a Christmas present for Lily, down at McConaghy's. It's a while off yet, but I wanted to be sure to get her something. I've known her family a long time, and I know well enough, none of them will get her a present. She's like my little sister, that kid, and she needs a break. It's just a proper hairbrush, with a handle and things, nothing much.'

'You're a kind lad, Lockie. You'll make a lucky girl a good husband one day.'

Lockie chuckled again. 'I can't see that happening any time soon. Lily says I'm too fussy. I suppose I am. It's not me who's fussy, it's me mam. I daren't take anyone home to our house – you know what me mam's like.'

'Aye, I do. Since she's moved out of Clare

Cottages, she's got worse. Stop being so good at your job, Lockie, it's gone to her head, all the dosh you're taking home.'

Lockie grinned. The harbourmaster was right. His mother was nothing short of a social climber. Lockie had been able to afford the rent on a house – not just any house, a biggish house – and she had not stopped crowing since. He knew the kind of girl he was looking for was one like Lily, but they didn't make many like that. He'd known Lily since she was a baby. She was the closest he had to a little sister and he was the closest she had to a big brother. Lockie was the only reason Lily's stepfather refrained from using his fists as often as he used to, even when drunk, because he knew he would have Lockie down on him like a ton of bricks. And given that Lockie was six foot four and almost the same across his shoulders, no one wanted that.

While Lockie was chatting to the harbourmaster, Lily herself was walking down the landing of Clare Cottages on her way to work. Unbeknown to her, behind almost every window she passed on her way to the stairs, someone was making a comment about her.

'Look at her with her head high, who does that one think she is?'

'Feel sorry for that Lily, a lot to put up with, she has.'

On fine days, Mrs McGuffy and the other

women would gather on the landings and watch as the kids walked across the road to the school at St Chad's. Mrs McGuffy was always gruff but kindly towards Lily, more so than some of the others. She had the loudest voice and Lily often heard herself being discussed as she walked along the road. 'Would you look at the cut of that poor girl. Holding that family together, she is. Be in care, those kids would, if it wasn't for her. Someone would be ringing the welfare if she wasn't such a hard worker.'

Everyone in Clare Cottages had an opinion about Lily. She was too clever. Too proud. Too smart. Too put upon. Lily did not fit in.

Every Friday night, when Lily handed over her pay packet, she was given back the five shillings she needed for the bus. Her mother wasn't daft. No bus fare, no work, no money. If there was a way she could have kept it, she would.

Lily's mother hated Mrs McConaghy, Lily's boss. It was a hatred that had taken root only weeks after Lily had begun working at the plant, on the day the letter about her clothes had arrived. The letter had been delivered by Sister Therese and she'd wanted to die with the shame of it.

'I'm sorry, Mrs Lancashire,' Sister Therese had said, 'I'll have to read the letter to you. I promised that to Mrs McConaghy. She handed me the letter personally and I gave her my assurance. Lily is working in a proper job now and I have a sense of responsibility here. After all, 'tis I that recommended Lily for the job.'

She pinned Lily's mother to the wall using nothing but her eyes and began to read from the letter she had extracted from somewhere within her long black habit.

'I demand that Lily be dressed in clothes appropriate for her workplace. She is expected to be in the view of people who will bring good business to McConaghy's and, as a result, pay Lily's wages. I don't want anyone thinking I pay such bad wages that the girl who works in my office cannot afford decent clothes, shoes or a coat.'

Lily felt that there could be nothing worse in the world than having to stand and listen to Sister Therese as she read out that letter. Her cheeks burnt red with embarrassment. But not as red as her furious mother's.

'Who does that woman think she is?' Lily's mother had roared as Sister Therese finished. She flounced to the door and, hanging up her apron, pulled a headscarf over her curlers and said, 'Come on, you.' She grabbed Lily by the arm. 'If that woman wants her dressed all high and mighty for a job you got for her, Sister, then Father Brennan can provide the clothes.'

Father Brennan came from the next-door neighbourhood to Lily's mother's in Ireland. He knew her father and grandfather, to whom her decision to marry an Englishman had come as a great disappointment. Mrs Lancashire, née O'Hallaghan, had

122

arrived in Liverpool on the boat when she was fourteen. She sent letters home telling her parents she had married a good Irish boy from Dublin, so it was a blow when Father Brennan arrived and took up residence in the priest's house not yards away from the entrance to Clare Cottages. Her good Irishman had left by the time Lily was four. Her pretence was up, and not a letter had been returned since the day her parents discovered she had since married an English Protestant. There was worse – she'd been pregnant at the time.

'McConaghy wants you rigged out, does she?' Lily's mother muttered all the way along the landing.

Mrs McGuffy threw a bucket of boiling water and disinfectant down the steps before them and the smell of scorched urine filled Lily's nostrils. Not many children made it all the way to the toilet on the half landing or could endure the long queue before they had to relieve themselves.

'Watch me bleedin' legs,' Mrs Lancashire snarled at Mrs McGuffy as they walked past her.

There was no reply, just the sound of coarse bristles on concrete as Mrs McGuffy brushed the water down to the drain. As Lily came alongside her, she tried to smile, but her mother was holding tight to the arm of her cardigan and pinching her skin. It hurt. Mrs McGuffy gave her a kind look and smiled, squinting through the smoke from the dangling cigarette that appeared to be stuck to her bottom lip.

'And no mention of a penny extra in the pay?' Lily's mother continued. 'How am I supposed to feed the kids if I rig you out, eh?'

Lily let the irony wash over her. It was she who fed the kids, not her mother. She trotted alongside her mother, racking her brains to think of a way she could stop her knocking on the door to the priest's house. Her mother didn't even go to Mass; Father Brennan would surely have no time for her.

But her mother's anger was unabated. 'No, the fat cow doesn't think of that, does she?'

Lily stared at her feet as heads turned in the street to see what all the shouting was about. They turned back just as quickly. No one liked to make eye contact with Lily's mother, as that was a quick way to a mouthful of abuse.

'The state of her.'

'The poor girl.'

'A drunken slattern, her mother is.'

The usual comments floated on the air as they passed by.

Her mother marched her up to the door of the priest's house and banged loudly until it was opened by the housekeeper.

'Keep her in the hallway,' said Father Brennan from the comfort of the chair in his study. 'Make her wait for half an hour, that'll see the back of her temper. I know the family. All hot-heads.'

The housekeeper did as she was instructed and Lily's mother seethed until dusk began to fall.

After ten minutes, her need for a drink had increased as fast as her anger had faded. The door to Father Brennan's office opened and her mother, transformed, flashed a rare smile and begged for clothes for Lily.

Later that evening, Sister Therese turned up unannounced with a winter coat in her arms and a collection of boots and shoes. All previously worn, but each pair had some life in them yet. Lily's eyes had filled with tears. 'Here, some of them are just grand,' Sister Therese said. 'Would you look, a pair of stilettos, even. Won't you look the fancy one in those.' What Sister Therese didn't say was that she had spent the last few hours knocking on the doors of some of the finer homes in Liverpool, blatantly selling places in heaven in order to acquire the clothes Lily needed.

Lily was tearful with gratitude. She had almost died with worry and shame on her first few days at work because of the way she was dressed. Mrs McConaghy had noticed and wasted no time complaining.

'Here, don't cry so.' Sister Therese presented her always-at-the-ready handkerchief to Lily. ''Tis my fault, I gave your mother too much credit. I just thought they would be so pleased and proud that you had a grand job and would want to help. God love you, I will do my best by you, Lily, always. I am proud of you. The best pupil I ever had, you are.'

As she turned over in her hands and examined

a pair of sturdy brown leather shoes, Lily knew that she would never in her life, no matter what befell her, fail in the eyes of Sister Therese. And nor would she let her down. A new anxiety washed through her. She would need to prevent her mother from selling the shoes at the pawn shop, the next time she was desperate for a drink. Owning something worth having would bring with it a whole new set of unfamiliar problems.

CHAPTER 7

Maisie Tanner stood in her kitchen looking out through the window at the black night. She wiped a circle in the steamed-up window with a handkerchief she extracted from her cardigan sleeve. Snow had begun to fall yet again and she marvelled at the size of the flakes and how they melted the second they landed on the pane of glass. The range was pumping out the heat to cook the Yorkshire puddings, the last thing to go in. Balancing the heat on the range and allowing it to soar up to full temperature at the end of the roast was an art in itself, one she'd learnt from her mother and prided herself on having perfected.

'This weather is never going to end,' she said to her husband, Stan. 'All that rubbish you give me about Liverpool being in the Gulf Stream and how it should always be warm. It's bloody grim. Days of awful smog one minute, snow the next. I'm sure it can't be like this in the rest of the country.'

Stan opened the back door to flick his cigarette stub over the wall and into the entry running along the back of the house. Despite the heat from the range, an icy blast blew through the kitchen. Maisie popped her head out and pulled back the neck of her blouse to let the cold breeze waft across her breasts.

'You feeling the heat, love?' asked Stan. 'Not like you, that.'

Maisie took a long breath and sighed at the touch of the snowflakes melting against her burning cheeks. She looked across the back-yard wall and her eyes rested on the chimneystacks atop the row of houses opposite, pumping smoke into the night sky. On some nights, snow or not, some of those chimneys stood cold and forlorn. Always the same houses, always the same families. War-widow homes, or those with ageing men not able to complete a full day down on the docks. But Sundays were special. There was always a roast and a fire in every home, and if there wasn't, someone would help. Maisie had lost count of the times she'd seen a bleak chimney on a winter's Sunday and sent Stan round to the same house with a bucket of coal. But tonight the dark kitchen windows on every house opposite were, just like Maisie's, opaque from the steam lifting from three veg boiling on the range. Some houses would have meat to go with it, some wouldn't.

'You all right, love?' Stan placed his arms around Maisie's waist and hugged her to him. She hadn't been herself of late. Quicker than usual to snap, unable to sleep.

'I think it's the change of life, Stan. It's got me

a bit early. I'm definitely going to lose me looks now, but at least we won't have any more kids, eh?'

Stan grinned. 'Well, you know what they say, don't you – every cloud has a silver lining.'

'What, so you do think I'm losing my looks?' Maisie sounded agitated. She was the most glamorous woman on Arthur Street and always had been.

'No, I didn't say that. *You* did. You will always be the most beautiful woman in the world to me, even when you're sixty.' It was time to change the subject. 'Our Pammy looks well, doesn't she, love? It's nice to have her round on a Sunday, with her friends and all that. She's doing all right for herself up at the hospital, now she's put all that trouble behind her. Who would have thought that? With our Pammy being as gobby as she is.'

'God, Stan, let's not count our chickens, eh? She came that close to being thrown out, telling Matron where to ger off and kicking up a fuss about that aborted baby.'

Stan chuckled. 'Yes, she did. That's our Pammy all right! But she was doing the right thing. And look who saved her, eh? Look who stuck up for her. Emily Haycock.'

'Stan, d'you think it's time I told our Pammy about Emily Haycock? About her being there when our Lorraine was born?' She stood stock still for a moment, remembering that god-awful night in the air-raid shelter. 'I still think that's the reason Sister Haycock fought so hard to get our Pammy

129

taken on as a nurse. Sure of it. Who would have thought that, me calling little Emily Haycock from George Street Sister?'

'We've been through this a hundred times, love! There must be a reason Emily hasn't told Pammy she knew her when she was a kid, or that her own family copped it in the George Street bomb. I reckon she wants our Pammy to think she got on to that course at St Angelus all on her own and not because there was once a connection between her and us. If Pammy knew who Emily was, she might begin to wonder whether that had anything to do with it, like. It might make her doubt herself, and none of us want that now, do we?'

'I expect you're right, Stan.' She sniffed. 'Must be the change. Keeps making me feel a bit sad. I wish me mam was still here, I don't half miss her.' She took her handkerchief out of her apron pocket and dabbed at her eyes, which had filled with tears.

'Eh, eh, come here, love,' Stan said and wrapped his arms around her. 'Don't cry. I know you miss your mam. God, we all miss her. She was a big part of this family. I would have fretted every single day of the war if I hadn't known your mam was with you. I felt as safe as houses knowing she was looking after you all.'

Stan felt uncomfortable. This was not a situation he was used to. He was out of his depth and it upset him to see his Maisie, who coped with everything life threw at her, so upset.

Maisie rested her head on Stan's shoulder as she spoke. 'That was just it, though. The houses weren't safe. Mam was never the same after '41.'

'Do you need any help, Mam?' Pammy shouted in through the kitchen door.

Maisie sniffed again and, extricating herself from Stan's arms, tucked her handkerchief up the sleeve of her cardigan. 'No thanks, love. I'll be two minutes. You lot start helping yourself to the roasties. Lorraine, come and carry the gravy in. And Stan, put a shovel on the fire to keep us going, will you.'

She patted Stan on the arm and he breathed a sigh of relief. This was more like it. His Maisie shouted out her orders all day long.

'Lads, little Stan, have you all washed your hands?'

The instructions fired out of the kitchen in rapid succession and hardly anyone answered with anything other than a 'Yes, Mam'. Maisie was now smiling, her sadness wiped clean away by the fact that there was nothing she loved more than having the St Angelus nurses who Pammy worked and lived with over for a Sunday roast. It had become a tradition that whenever Pammy had a Sunday off, she almost always brought home whichever of her nurse friends also had a day off. It also gave Mrs Duffy the Lovely Lane housekeeper a break. Today, the girls were all together: Victoria Baker, Irish Dana Brogan and Beth Harper. It was the first weekend Beth had had off in almost an entire year, since she had first started on the wards as a probationer. But Beth never complained. Studious, diligent, committed, she dealt with whatever came her way, even if it meant missing Sunday lunch at the Tanners' house.

Stan had thrown the coal on the fire and popped back into the kitchen to rinse his hands under the tap. 'The lads have done theirs under the outside tap on their way back from the outhouse,' he said. 'I watched them meself.'

Routine, discipline and order were the key principles of life on Arthur Street. Big families needed hard-and-fast rules and hand-washing before meals was one of them.

Maisie bent down to take the Yorkshire pudding out of the oven. 'I'm worried about this fresh snow, Stan. These girls better eat up quick and get back to Lovely Lane in case it sticks. The last lot has only just melted. I've never known it so bad.'

'Well, you've got a short memory, it's nowhere near as bad as '47. Anyway, it won't stick, honest. It never sticks here, queen. We're too close to the Mersey and the Gulf Stream. Liverpool is warmer than you think.'

'Oh, for God's sake, Stan, shut up about the Gulf Stream. Just because you went to a desert during the war. Here, make yourself useful now and carry these in.' Stan took the salt cellar and a dish of apple sauce from Maisie. 'Anyway, stranger things have happened than a settling of snow. Who would have said we'd have the daughter of a lord sat around our table! No one else in these streets would dream of having a Victoria Baker round for a Sunday roast, would they?'

Stan looked into the front room and saw the girls laughing. 'Victoria is teasing the boys.' He smiled at Maisie as he spoke.

'Well, to be fair, Victoria only has to look little Stan's way and he's a mess. He can't speak and blushes as red as a beetroot.'

'I think he's in love,' whispered Stan. 'Ah, well, no teasing him. It's a powerful thing, is a young boy's first crush. I remember it well.' He winked at Maisie, who had turned to the tap to rinse her hands. He came up behind her, circled his arms around her waist and nuzzled his face into the side of her neck. He felt like he wanted to protect her after her tears. It was the only way he knew how to make her feel better. He would make love to her later, he thought to himself. That always cheered her up.

'Ger off, Stan!' squealed Maisie as she wriggled out of his grasp. She only half meant it. She would have happily stayed in his arms all day; there was no better place.

Stan had been away for the duration of the war. He was one of the first to sign up and they had both been shocked at the speed of his departure from Lime Street station, less than a week later. He had just one forty-eight-hour leave, which had resulted in the arrival of Pammy's younger sister,

133

Lorraine, nine months later. Not a day had passed in all the years he was away when Maisie hadn't felt sick with worry. Telegrams came and went. Hearts stopped when the whistle on the telegraph boy's bike rang down the street, but it was never for Maisie. Although her heart broke for whoever it was who was about to receive the telegram they all dreaded, often about a boy she'd known from school or the streets, she thanked God every night it wasn't her Stan.

She turned and briefly kissed Stan on the lips. 'Later,' she whispered. 'Later. We have our lot, Pammy's friends and one Victoria Baker of Baker Hall to feed.'

Stan patted Maisie on the bottom and winked. 'Later' was enough to make him the happiest man in Arthur Street. There wasn't a night when he closed his eyes and a memory of his worst days didn't flash before him. Back home now, the last thing he did every night before he fell asleep was reach out and touch the warm body of his wife and give thanks to God that he'd survived. His house and family had survived the Blitz. He was in their bed, her heart beat next to his, and they were alive.

'Maisie, Lady Victoria is one of our Pammy's friends. She's a nurse like the rest of them, you don't have to single her out for a special mention.'

'I know that. I just can't help meself bragging, though, every time she's been here. You've got to admit, she's lovely and, Stan, she says that when she's qualified, she's going to invite us to her wedding. Imagine that!'

Stan couldn't keep the grin from his face. When his Maisie became excited, she looked like the young girl he had married on the best day of his life.

'I'll make sure we buy you the nicest frock in Liverpool for that, queen. I still can't understand a word she says, mind. When is she going to learn to speak like the rest of us?'

'Don't be ignorant, Stan, she just talks nice. I'm hoping our Lorraine picks it up from her. I don't want to hear Victoria talking like us. I want our Lorraine to do well for herself, to get out of here and talk like a lady. I don't want her growing up in Arthur Street. Look at the state of the place – bloody river rats and bomb rubble everywhere.'

'Our Lorraine? Do us a favour, Maisie. She'd get beaten up if she went to school talking like Victoria. You don't want our Lorraine talking posh.' Stan lowered his voice to a whisper so that Victoria couldn't hear. 'We used to beat up the lads from Waterloo Grammar when I was a kid, for talking posh, like. They were sitting ducks for us, when they were waiting for the bus. Mind you, can't beat them up for talking posh now. They all live in big houses over the water and work in banks and go out for fancy lunches and drive cars and things.' He began to chuckle.

Maisie sighed. 'And that, Stan Tanner, is my point. That is exactly why I want our Lorraine to do better, so she doesn't grow up into a senseless blockhead like you.'

Before Stan could answer back, Maisie stooped down to retrieve the Yorkshire pudding, perfectly risen in its large enamel dish.

Both Maisie and Stan walked into the front room and the sight that greeted them made Maisie's heart melt. The table was set, cutlery laid, earthenware dishes piled in the middle. The small fire was roaring up the chimney and on the burnt and tattered fireside rug lay the youngest Tanner boys. Tired of waiting, they had settled back down, their faces buried in comics. Victoria was on the chair nearest the fire, with Lorraine perched on her knee as she painted Lorraine's nails. Dana and Pammy had been on the settle and jumped up as Maisie and Stan walked in.

'Look at me nails, Mam,' said Lorraine as she flashed her fingers in Maisie's face. 'Don't they look lovely?'

Maisie laid her dish on the table and moved Lorraine's hand further away so that she could examine it properly while at the same time instructing Dana and Pammy to lift the trestle over to sit on.

'Well, they do look nice. I get it all over me fingers when I try.'

A collective gasp went up from the girls and there was a rush to the table by the boys. A smile of pride crossed Pammy's face as they all took their seats, ready to eat.

'Oh, Mrs Tanner, you are simply the tops!' said Victoria.

Maisie shot Stan a warning look. He grinned and raised his eyebrows.

Dana couldn't take her eyes off the pork and almost licked her lips. This was the nearest she got to the roast dinners her own mammy served at home in Ireland. It was all here, in Maisie Tanner's house. A Sunday at the Tanners' was one of the few days Dana stopped feeling homesick and guilty. Having promised her mammy she would visit home lots, she had managed it only once and the guilt sat heavily with her every single day.

'Now, you have to eat up, all of you,' said Maisie. 'But you can't stay and listen to the radio tonight. You won't believe this, it's snowing again, and despite what clever-clogs Stan says, it looks like it might stick. Are you all in early tomorrow?'

'I'm on the children's ward,' said Dana as she gratefully lifted up her plate to accept a huge slice of pork and a large helping of Yorkshire pudding. Yorkshire pudding was cheap to make and came with every roast, regardless of the meat. The more Maisie could cram on the table, the happier she was. Sunday was the day she pushed the boat out.

'Take as much as you want, love,' said Maisie. But Dana held back, even though she could quite happily have eaten the lot.

'Victoria and I are on male medical together,' said Beth. 'I called into the office to look at the

137

off-duty for next week. There are four of us on tomorrow, and Staff Nurse told me there's a new probationer from Mayo. Dana, you might know her, she's called Bridget Moran.'

Dana had her mouth full and was unable to answer.

'But the big news is, Mam,' said Pammy, 'that there's a new assistant matron starting and the third years say she's going to stir everything up. I'm not looking forward to that.'

'How do they know that if she hasn't started yet?' Maisie asked.

Pammy had loaded a roast potato into her mouth, so Victoria answered for her. 'Well, because Matron is so busy, she leaves most of us trainee nurses to Sister Haycock and Sister Ryan, and they are just dotes. But the rumour flying round is that the new assistant matron looks like a hawk and has the charm of a dragon. She is by all accounts absolutely beastly and I'm not sure who has even met her yet.'

'We'll just have to make sure we do everything by the book. No calamities.' The other girls fell quiet for a moment as Pammy had the good grace to look sheepish. Pammy was the architect and executor of all the calamities that occurred in Lovely Lane.

'What do you think, Stan?' said Maisie.

Stan hadn't understood a word Victoria said and so instead he replied, 'It's lovely this, Maisie,' nodding his head at his heavily loaded plate.

'The thing is, Mam, it's like a big family at St

Angelus. Everyone gets on with everyone else. There are no dragons and we don't want one now.'

Everyone fell to polishing off their dinners and soon the only sound in the room was that of munching. Even the boys were quiet as they ate.

During the clearing up, Stan picked up the Saturday *Echo* from the night before and read out the headline. 'Eh, Maisie, I see they got that fella who left that young girl for dead in the entry. Caught him in Durham, they say. A vacuum-cleaner salesman, he was. It says here he tried it again with another young girl in Durham and they think he's done it before as well. I don't know what the country is coming to. What did we fight for, eh? Not for animals like him to make the streets unsafe for our girls. I didn't put my life on the line for the likes of him, that's for sure.'

'She worked at St Angelus, that girl, Da,' said Pammy as she stacked the dirty plates. 'She was an administrator in casualty. I'm not sure if she will be back after that. Not sure I could.'

'I had to take her down to theatre,' said Victoria. 'She was admitted to ward two. She was a right mess, the poor thing. I saw Matron actually cry.'

'Cry?' the girls all said at once.

'Matron's allowed feelings,' said Beth. 'Just because she gets the job done, doesn't mean she's not human.'

'Oh, I know, Beth, but you wouldn't think she'd cry. She's hardly soft, like, is she?' Pammy was surprised. She'd had her own run-ins with Matron in the past and Matron had far from cried then. It was Matron who'd made Pammy cry.

'Doreen, her name was,' said Victoria. 'Used to see her coming in through the back gates sometimes. She's one of Dessie's protégées. He's always looking out for someone, is Dessie.'

'That's right, love,' said Stan. 'Says here her name was Doreen. Gives her address and everything, says she worked at the hospital. What a shocker. She'll be tainted for life now, poor girl. Used goods and all that.'

Maisie gave a sympathetic tut and shook her head, but she didn't say anything.

'I wonder if your Matron will give her her job back. A lot of employers wouldn't, not after something like that, you know.' Stan closed the paper. 'You girls take care going home now, do you hear me? Mind you, it would be a foolish man who tried to take advantage of you lot. You'd terrify the living daylights out of anyone up to no good. You lot scare the life out of me.'

The kitchen filled with noise. Pammy complaining that the boys never had to wash up. Dishes clattering as Victoria and Beth washed and dried. Maisie taking a crumble out of the range. Stan fiddling with the radio while outside in the dark night, the snow silently fell.

CHAPTER 8

Dana had awoken early and was immediately aware that something was not quite right. Her window looked out on to the street and as she lay in her bed, puzzled, trying to work out what was unusual about the morning, it suddenly dawned on her. Lovely Lane was completely silent. There was no traffic. No buses. No footsteps or voices. No park-keepers shouting or dogs barking. Nothing. Just an eerie silence on account of the snow.

She snuggled back under her eiderdown but found it impossible to sleep. Being a farm girl and used to rising just after dawn for farm duties and milking, she still found it difficult to sleep past 5 a.m. The air in her room was cold and she suspected the fires hadn't been lit yet. The only sources of heat in the nurses' home were the large fire in the hallway, the small but fierce fire in the sitting room and the large stove in the kitchen, which also heated the morning room, two steps up from the kitchen, where the nurses ate. Three times a day, the lads who worked for Dessie at the hospital would come by and stock up the fire baskets and scuttles. The maids raked out the ashes first thing and, thanks to a strict timetable of duties, the fires burnt all day long through the long winter months. But today, with the snow, it seemed likely there wouldn't be any buses, in which case neither the maids nor the Lovely Lane housekeeper, Mrs Duffy, would be able to make it in.

Dana quickly washed and dressed and made her way downstairs. Breathing a sigh of relief as she entered the main hallway, she discovered that the coal scuttle and log basket had been filled by the porter's lad the previous evening. He must have come round after she and the girls had returned from the Tanners' house, before the snow had got too heavy. She sparked the fire into life by blowing on the old embers, which were buried under a blanket of ash, then screwed up Saturday's *Echo*, which Mrs Duffy always left in the basket. She heaped on the kindling from the bucket, then added the coal and the logs.

More than a little satisfied with her efforts, she stood and watched as the flames licked up the chimney. I reckon I'm going to be everyone's favourite this morning, she thought as she tiptoed over to the window to the side of the front door. She was filled with excitement at the sight that greeted her. Unable to help herself, she tripped up the stairs to wake her friends, starting with Pammy, whose room was halfway up.

'Oh my giddy aunt,' squealed Pammy as she

142

flew to the window. 'Are we the only ones in the house? Mrs Duffy will never make it in, we'd better get cracking.'

'I've already lit the fire,' said Dana. 'I'm going to wake Beth. Bet you anything you like, she will be downstairs and organizing the kitchen before you can say sausages.'

Dana was right. The smell of toast cooking and the sound of a kettle whistling soon filled the home as Beth laid the table with cups and hummed as she worked. There was nothing Beth loved more than a challenge and being in charge.

As housekeeper at the nurses' home, Mrs Duffy's first duty of the day was to ensure her nurses were well fed before they began a long shift at the hospital. Seeing as the Crossville buses stood abandoned at the pier-head depot, looming like a row of green, snow-capped ghosts against the River Mersey, she had no choice but to walk the two and a half miles from her home to Lovely Lane.

The streets were soft and quiet, the snow as yet sullied only by the most conscientious members of the city's workforce, who slipped and stumbled their way to work in their inadequate footwear. Mrs Duffy made as much haste as she was able. Where and when she could, she grabbed hold of shop windowsills and dustbins to steady herself. The back of a bench took her safely on to a bus stop and then she found a low stone wall. She dropped her handbag twice as she slid and slipped and almost fell. It was treacherous underfoot, but Mrs Duffy had responsibilities, and despite the weather and her age, she was resolute that she would arrive at the nurses' home in time to meet the provisions van from the St Angelus kitchen. It supplied her with everything she needed to feed her nurses their breakfast and evening meal.

What will they do if I'm late, she thought as the cold bit through her gloves and into her fingers. They will freeze this morning. No fire. No breakfast. Poor lambs. As she slid her way through the streets, she couldn't stop worrying. What if the van doesn't arrive? I have nothing in the kitchen. Goodness me, they have poorly patients to care for and they can't do that on empty stomachs. I have to get there. They'll starve without me.

Finally, she turned the corner into Lovely Lane and was mighty relieved to see the familiar black van of the under-porter, Jake Berry, partly covered in snow, parked on the street outside the front door of the nurses' home. At least she thought it was the street – the snow was so deep, it was impossible to tell where the road ended and the pavement began.

Jake had left the noisy engine running and as Mrs Duffy approached, a huge lump of snow slithered off the heated bonnet and on to the road with a soft thud.

'Morning, Jake!' she shouted. 'You're a sight for sore eyes, I can tell you. I was worried I wouldn't make it in time to catch you. I wasn't even sure you would get here yourself. You've done a grand job driving that van, God bless you. I'm right out of bread and bacon, heaven only knows what I would have given them for breakfast.'

'I'm a sight for sore eyes? What about you! How did you manage? I thought I'd be handing the bacon over to the nurses to cook themselves.'

'And that, Jake, is exactly what I was dreading. God alone knows what state I would have found the kitchen in. There's no one to wake them. They will all still be sleeping in their beds. What a mess this flaming snow is.'

'I've left my Martha in bed,' said Jake. 'I told her: let the fire warm the house a bit before you get up. Stacked it up, I did, and left the door to the stairs open so the heat would get up to the bedroom. I took her a cuppa and some toast with her knitting bag and that is where my princess and our baby will stay until the fire is roaring.'

Jake had been promoted by Dessie from porter's lad to under-porter just around the time that he'd married Martha, who, until that point, had worked as the maid in the St Angelus doctors' sitting room. A job secured by her mother, Elsie, Matron's housekeeper. At St Angelus, the staff looked after their own.

Jake opened the doors to the back of his van and pulled out a wooden tray loaded with everything Mrs Duffy had asked for on the list that she'd sent back with the van the previous morning. 'Bread, bacon rashers and butter coming up first, is that right?'

Mrs Duffy bit down on the woollen fingers of her snow-encrusted gloves and pulled each one off with her teeth. Having freed one hand, she scrabbled around for the gaoler-sized bunch of keys in her holdall. 'How's the baby coming along then?' she asked, stalling for time as she fumbled. She'd almost run out of breath from the effort of trudging through the snow and her words staggered out on the end of long gasps.

'It's coming along nicely, thank you. All good so far.' Balancing the large wooden tray, Jake spun round and kicked the doors of the van shut with his heel. 'We haven't told too many people. Martha says it's too early yet, so I just do as I'm told. As long as she does the same and stays in that nice warm bed, everything should be well in the world. Wouldn't you say, Mrs Duffy?'

He could barely see ahead of him as he held the tray out in front of his chest and picked his way to the short flight of stone steps leading up to the front door. The snow was so deep, it was difficult to tell where one step ended and another began. Mrs Duffy smiled to herself as she located the keys. She extracted them from her bag with a flourish and a smile, like a magician producing a paper bouquet.

There was not a single person on any of the dockside streets, down on the docks, or working in St Angelus who did not know that Martha Berry was expecting a child. But only a very small number of people knew it was most definitely not her first child, and in a community where gossip spread faster than chickenpox, that was nothing short of a miracle.

Mrs Duffy followed Jake and held on to the stone balustrade as she took the snow-covered steps one at a time with great concentration. 'I don't know how you got the van here. God in heaven, I don't. There's not another thing on the road.'

'I can take no credit for that,' shouted Jake over his shoulder. 'It was Dessie. Would you look at the van – he's wrapped chains round each of the wheels like a hairnet. Worked like a dream, it did. I could hardly believe it. Have you ever heard the like? Says he learnt it in the army. He's been at the hospital all night, working on all the trucks and carts. He's going to run out of chain soon.'

'The poor man, he'll have no fingers left.' Mrs Duffy tutted as she shook her head. 'There's a reason why that man returned a war hero, and that's the truth,' she said. She admired Dessie as much as everyone else who knew him. 'I doubt there is much that could put our Dessie's nose out of joint. A bit of snow wouldn't stop him in his tracks, despite the cold. Not with what he must have been through. It must seem like nothing to him.'

'Do you think, Mrs Duffy, that if Dessie wore all his medals at once, he would be able to walk?'

Mrs Duffy was laughing so much at the image of Dessie staggering under his medals that she didn't see Jake take a tumble. What she did see was the tray flying up in the air, and the packs of bacon and the bread spiralling and turning. Then came Jake, landing with a thud on to his back at the bottom of the steps.

He blinked and as soon as he'd recovered from the shock, began to laugh. Mrs Duffy, reassured that he was not seriously hurt, began to laugh again too.

'I knew that would happen,' he yelled. He was laughing so hard, he couldn't stand up.

Mrs Duffy tried to pick her way through the deep snow and back down the steps to help him, but she was laughing so much, she could barely move. And anyway, she was frightened to death that she would end up the same way.

'No, no, you stop where you are,' Jake shouted to her. 'I'll get meself up.' His legs scissored uselessly on the slippery snow. Just at that moment, the large wooden door to the nurses' home was flung open and Jake's shame was deepened by the sight of a group of St Angelus nurses staring at the two of them. They gasped in shock at Mrs Duffy, almost bent in half as she clung to the stone balustrade of the steps, and Jake, lying on the floor making snow angels as he flapped his arms and legs.

Beth Harper picked her way down the steps and was the first to reach Mrs Duffy. She grabbed her by the elbow as Pammy Tanner staggered down to grab the other side.

'How in God's name did you get all the way

here?' Pammy exclaimed. 'Mrs Duffy, you want locking up! Do you not think we could survive on a piece of toast?'

'What time did you leave home?' This from Dana, who was by now rescuing the loaves of bread and shaking off the snow. Food was always the first consideration for Dana.

Just as Dana spoke, Victoria Baker appeared. 'Jake, will you pick up that bacon! Quick!' she shouted. 'There's a dog behind you.'

Jake clambered on to his knees and outstared a curious stray dog that was perched in mid stalk at the bottom of the steps. It had smelt the bacon, left wherever it had been sheltering and was now fixing an unwavering stare on the four-pound pack of rashers wrapped in greaseproof paper and lying on the ground.

'Don't you even think about it, big fella,' whispered Jake as he edged slowly on all fours towards the packet. 'Go on now, away with you! Don't touch it.' As Jake reached out and took the bacon, the dog sat down and wagged its tail, then leapt forward to lick Jake's face.

'Oh, would you look at him, he's frozen!' squealed Pammy. Mrs Duffy was now safely on the top step and Pammy picked her way towards the dog. She felt its neck for a collar.

'Mrs Duffy, can we bring him in for a warm by the fire and a rasher? Please! Can we?'

Dana, who had lived all her life alongside farm dogs, could not believe what Pammy was asking.

'Saints above, my mammy would have a fit if I had ever brought one of the farm dogs into the kitchen. They lived on scraps, bones and pig feed, slept in the barn and grew well on it. Leave him, Pammy, he's fine. I've seen him coming in and out of the park and at the bus stop, being given titbits by passengers as they get on and off the bus.'

'That's as maybe, but there are no buses or passengers today. And look at him, Dana, there's not a scrap on him. That's probably all he has to eat, the odd biscuit from people going in and out of the park.'

The entrance to the St Angelus nurses' home was situated directly opposite the entrance to Lovely Lane Park. Lovely Lane ran all the way up to the Dock Road. At one end of the lane were buildings that had once been the homes of sea merchants, and at the opposite end were the homes of the dockers. Between them sat the park. The two ends of Lovely Lane were worlds apart.

Pammy knew she had a point and she played it well. There would be no one visiting the park today. The dog would surely go hungry if she didn't intervene.

Jake returned to the van and unloaded the next tray. 'He looks half frozen, the poor scraggy thing,' he said as he passed Pammy on the way up the steps. She was also half frozen, shivering on the steps in her short-sleeved pink cotton nurse's uniform.

Mrs Duffy was in the hallway and the girls heard her exclaim, 'God in heaven, who lit the fire in the hall for me? I've been here twenty-five years and that has never happened before.'

The nurses on day duty had also been taken by surprise when they'd walked into the kitchen to see Beth buttering a mountain of toast. 'Only one and a half slices each, I'm afraid,' she said. 'Load up at break time when you get to the greasy spoon.' They would have to walk the mile and a half to the hospital and work for a further three hours before it was time for the traditional milky coffee and hot buttered toast at break time and the mood in the house was not a happy one.

'Please, Mrs Duffy,' pleaded Pammy. 'Matron has Blackie in a basket in her office, she won't mind. Matron loves dogs, she does.'

Mrs Duffy loved dogs too. Her job at the nurses' home precluded her from ever owning one. She spent most of the day away from her own home, often returning only to sleep at night. The dog looked up at her and tipped his head winningly to the side. 'Would you look at him!' she exclaimed, already sounding like a woman on the verge of wavering. 'He's a big scruffy dirty grey thing. I've never seen a dog with such a coat. It looks like it's made of steel wool and it's all different lengths.'

Pammy looked as though she would never step indoors again unless Mrs Duffy said yes. Her teeth began to chatter.

'Ah, go on then, bring him in. But just for a

warm, mind, and a rasher. After that, he's back outdoors. Do you hear me? And no arguments.'

Pammy grinned. 'Come on in, big fella,' she said to the dog. It needed no encouragement and bounded up the steps after her. 'What shall we call him?' she said to the others as she reached the top.

A Scouser through and through, born and raised on the dockside streets, Pammy would have snuck the dog into her room if she'd needed to. Either that, or she would have taken him to her mam and dad's. The Tanner brood would have loved him. There was no dog at home now, but over the years she'd brought back too many strays to mention. Liverpool was full of stray dogs wandering the streets and every dog they'd ever owned was one she had brought home on the end of a length of dirty string, having found it down by the docks.

'Well, just looking at the state of him, maybe we should call him Scruff,' said Dana.

The dog stopped in its tracks. It had been following the pack of bacon, which had disappeared into the kitchen. It looked up at Dana with wounded eyes.

'Wash your mouth out,' said Pammy, offended. 'Don't you be listening to her, big fella.' This comment was addressed to the dog.

'Scamp is a good one,' chirped Victoria, who had spent her life around dogs.

Pammy looked pleased. 'Yes, I like that. Scamp then, everyone, what do you say?'

'I say it's a waste of time naming a dog who is

going to be here for no more than an hour,' said Beth as she walked past with the second tray from the van, loaded with flour and Mrs Duffy's remaining food order. 'I'm going to help Mrs Duffy grill this bacon. We only have forty-five minutes, nurses, before we have to leave, and so do you, matey.' This to the dog, who was quickly working out who its friends were.

'Can you give me a lift in the kitchen, please, Victoria?' Beth was an organizer, through and through. She had got herself off to a rocky start at Lovely Lane when she had appeared to prefer the company of Celia Forsyth, the least pleasant of all the student nurses, and the members of the knitting circle, who were firmly controlled by Celia and very much under her thumb.

As Victoria and Beth walked into the kitchen, Pammy grabbed Jake by the sleeve and whispered, 'How is Martha?' She had nursed Martha on ward two when she'd lost her first baby and almost died in the process, thanks to a back-street abortionist. The whole affair had almost got Pammy sacked. She had got to know Martha very well.

'She's great, Nurse Tanner. Asks me every day have I seen you, like. She won't be going back to work at St Angelus. She's my wife now and I'm going to look after her and our baby good and proper.'

'You can tell her I heard the consultant telling Sister Antrobus that he's looking forward to delivering your baby himself. We all have to look after each other at St Angelus, don't we, Jake?'

Jake failed to answer, but the sober nod he gave Pammy made it clear that he would never talk about Martha's days on ward two. Jake and Martha had a future to look forward to. Their baby was on its way. The past was in the past. He would never speak of it again and neither would Martha.

Jake slid the final wooden tray back on to the runners and, lighting up a cigarette, jumped into the driver's seat, slipped the van into gear and, with no sign of another vehicle on the roads, turned a perfect circle and headed back towards St Angelus. He spotted the dog in his rear-view mirror, running down the Lovely Lane steps and heading towards the park with the packet of bacon he had just delivered hanging from its mouth and Beth in hot pursuit. Jake began to laugh. Blowing out his smoke, he said out loud, 'You look like trouble, you scraggy dog,' and, dropping a gear, he made his way up the steep road to the rear gate of the hospital.

CHAPTER 9

The overnight snow soon melted. Stan had been half right. The Gulf Stream had warmed Liverpool back into life before Mrs McGuffy, who had sat up half the night darning gloves in order that her children could spend more than five minutes outdoors at any one time, had finished. But the cold and the damp had taken their toll. And the smog, which had preceded the snow and lasted for three whole days and nights, had been filled with flecks of soot and wrought its own particular havoc. The wards in St Angelus had quickly filled with the weak and elderly.

'Here's my sputum pot, Nurse Harper. Will you take it for me?' Mr Trimble called to Beth as she and the other nurses assembled by the long, polished, central ward table to await Sister's arrival and find out who would be sent for the first coffee break.

Backs and beds trolleys had been dismantled. The tubs of zinc and castor-oil cream, and the wads of gauze and surgical spirit, used for the treatment of bed sores, were neatly lined up, and the leftover sheets and draw sheets had been returned to the linen cupboard ready for the next round of bed-making. Dressings trolleys had been wiped down and sterilized with Dettol. Rubbish and dirty-laundry baskets had been left by the ward doors for the porter's lads to collect, and from the dirty sluice room came the clatter and clang of the enamel bedpans as they were cleaned and placed on the hot pipes to dry.

Beth had stopped for the first time that morning and was examining her own feet. Her black lisle stockings had got soaked all the way up to the middle of her calves as she'd walked through the wet slush from Lovely Lane to the hospital. Having finished the morning duties, she now saw that the dark black stain had faded and she could almost feel her toes again. She was ready for her coffee. It was always the same: following the morning bed round, she and the others felt slightly weak and sick. They needed sustenance after having lifted and shifted big dockers with muscles the size of a crane up and down and in and out of bed. Male medical was hard work and saw the end of many a nursing career with the near breaking of a slender seven-stone back.

'Of, course, Mr Trimble.' Beth walked swiftly across the ward to his bed with a bright smile.

'Ah, you're a good'un, Nurse Harper. The sight of it sitting on me locker makes the wife sick. She told me if it's still there this afternoon when she visits, she's not coming any more until I'm discharged. Got a bit of a sensitive stomach, she has. It makes her feel a bit queasy.'

Mr Trimble's expression was forlorn and anxious. Beth smiled as she attempted to reassure him. 'Well, not everyone has stomachs of steel like we nurses do. We are immune to queasiness. We wouldn't be able to do this job if we weren't.'

The new young Irish probationer, Bridget Moran, hurried to Beth's side. 'Nurse Harper, the man in bed sixteen wants to use the bedpan, but we've only just cleared them away and Sister said the next round would be at twelve now, before lunches.'

Beth looked down the ward towards bed sixteen. The patient weighed at least fifteen stone. Nurse Moran looked as though she would struggle to come in at six and a half. 'Well, if he's desperate, he has to have one. And believe me, you'd rather he did than deal with the consequences.'

Nurse Moran looked terrified. Beth smiled. Sister Crawford was in charge of ward seven. She had worked at St Angelus for all of her life. She was strict but fair and kind, and she was a sister most nurses looked forward to working with. Ward seven was one of the toughest wards in the hospital and Sister Crawford knew it. She also knew that happy nurses made a happy ward and that on a happy ward the bells rang less often and the patients recovered sooner. She was known as one of the nicer sisters and the only sister that Matron regarded as an equal. Yet the young probationer was terrified of her. God help her when she gets to meet Sister Antrobus on casualty, thought Beth.

Bridget was the youngest of six sisters and the first to be accepted on to the State Registered Nurse training course at St Angelus. Her five older sisters were all State Enrolled and lived and worked in different parts of the country. Coming from Mayo in the west of Ireland, she was a beneficiary of Emily Haycock's determination that no nurse would be discriminated against as a result of where she came from. If a young woman could pass the entrance exam and the interview process, if she could demonstrate both compassion and competence in equal measure, then as far as Sister Haycock was concerned, it was of no relevance where the potential nurse had been born and to whom. The memory of the way Mr Scriven had tried to block the appointment of Nurse Tanner just because she came from Arthur Street still stung. Emily was keen to avoid this ever happening again and wanted to introduce a policy of removing applicants' addresses from the forms before they got as far as the board.

Standing in front of Beth on her first day on the wards, Bridget was frozen with fear. She had worked so hard during the bedpan round that her scalp prickled. Her shoulder-length dark hair was tied back into a ponytail and her bright and watery pale blue eyes were filled with apprehension as she waited for Beth to reply.

'Wheel a commode to him,' said Beth. 'He's on

bed rest, but he can manage the commode. He only came in last night and they have yet to decide what his problem is. Can you manage that on your own, do you think? It will be easy, just make sure you put one hand under his arm and guide him so that he doesn't fall. He might be a bit giddy once he's upright, if he hasn't been on his feet for a while.'

Bridget blinked. 'A commode?' she repeated.

'Yes, you know what that is, don't you, Nurse Moran?'

This probationer reminded Beth of Dana, only with Dana there was someone driving when you looked into her eyes. This poor girl looked vacant and terrified. Beth had already heard that she was the cleverest girl in PTS on paper but that she had only just scraped through her practicals and that was thanks to all the help she'd got from Sister Ryan. Everyone knew that Sister Haycock was especially keen on the bright ones. She was always saying how the practical skills could be taught but that a probationer either came ready with intelligence or they didn't. Looking at Nurse Moran now, Beth wasn't so sure Sister Haycock had got that right.

'Err, yes, I do know what a commode is, Nurse Harper. 'Tis that big heavy chair on wheels, is that right?'

Beth almost laughed out loud. 'Yes, it is. And if you lift up the wooden lid, there is a bedpan concealed underneath.' She spoke slowly and carefully. It seemed as though Nurse Moran might have trouble understanding what she was saying.

'Sure, and I sit him on the seat with the lid up?'

'Obviously,' said Beth, becoming exasperated. 'Because if you don't, there will be one almighty mess to clear up and Sister Crawford will have you for her morning break.'

Bridget looked as though she was about to burst into tears and scuttled away with a worried frown. Beth went from feeling irritated to feeling sorry for her. Though she was only in her second year, Beth's PTS days already felt like light years ago. Those first three months had been the worst. On a first placement a probationer barely saw the outside of the sluice room and spent almost the entire time with bedpans – giving them out, clearing them away and scrubbing them up. All to be ready to start again two hours later.

Beth watched Bridget as she headed back towards the sluice room, her head down, scurrying along, studying her shoes as she went. She probably feels very hard done by, thought Beth. I know I did.

She turned her attention back to Mr Trimble. She had noticed his wife during visiting hours on a previous occasion and had watched as Mr Trimble had slipped his pot off the locker and placed it under his pale green counterpane. He was a recovering TB patient. After eighteen long months in isolation, he'd been transferred to the main medical ward following a series of consecutive TB-free sputum samples. As was the routine, he would have a sample a week taken until he was strong enough to return home. Although there was no longer any blood in his sputum, former TB patients were left with a persistent cough.

'I will take this pot to the dirty sluice room for you and bring you back a clean one. Then just before visiting, I can do the same and you can keep the clean pot under your covers, just in case you need it, until visiting is over. How is that for a plan?'

Mr Trimble looked weak with relief. 'Oh, thank you, Nurse Harper. I don't like to make the wife feel ill when she comes. Before I came into the hospital, if I felt a bout of the coughing coming on, I would nip to the outhouse where she couldn't hear me coughing up. I spent more time in the outhouse than I did indoors. She can't help it. Makes her sick, it does.'

'No wonder you've ended up with a nasty chest infection then, Mr Trimble. What with the smog and the damp and you living right on the river.'

'I know, Nurse, I know. But what can I do?'

'Nurse Harper.' Sister Crawford was now out of her office and walking up the ward towards her. Beth could tell she was in the mood for giving orders. 'Nurses!' she said, louder than was usual, and clapped her hands together. 'Right, we are fairly quiet on here today following our discharges yesterday, but tomorrow we have five admissions and four on the operating list, so let's have a few hours' scrubbing with our good friend Dettol.

Diluted to ten parts of warm water, of course, will we now?'

She surveyed her nurses with enthusiasm.

'The domestics will see to the flowers and vases that have been left by the patients who've been discharged. They will clean the windowsills and wash down the lower paintwork on the walls, up to bed ten today. I will have two nurses on bed frames and lockers, two on the ward furniture and two making sure we have enough dressings sterilized in the drums ready for the post-ops tomorrow. Ah, Nurse Harper, I almost forgot.' Sister Crawford extracted a small tube from her pocket and held it out to Beth. 'Doctor has asked for a sample from Mr Trimble's sputum to be taken down to the pathology lab for culture and analysis. Can you see to that for me? Label this tube and take it down yourself before you clean the pot out.'

Beth took the glass tube from Sister. It was sealed with a rubber bung and had a blank label on the side. 'Yes, Sister. Of course, Sister,' she said.

'Right, set to, nurses. It is 10 a.m.; we should be finished with the cleaning for twelve, in time for backs and beds. The probationers have been told to clean down the walls in the dirty sluice room when they've finished scrubbing the pans.'

As Sister walked away, there was the faintest of groans as the assembled nurses divided themselves into groups.

'I'll do anything,' said Beth. 'I don't mind lockers

162

or beds, but I just need to sort out this lovely sample here first.'

Victoria Baker was on the same ward and working the same shift. In a loud voice so that the others could hear, she said, 'We can clean beds and lockers together, Nurse Harper. I will fetch the trolley while you sort out that specimen.'

In the dirty utility room, Beth examined the small-necked tube Sister had handed to her. Big clumsy pot. Small-necked glass tube. This was not going to be easy, she thought. However, not for nothing was she known as the most studious of the Lovely Lane nurses. No one doubted that she would one day be a matron, or a ward sister at the very least.

She was still pondering how to transfer her specimen when Victoria opened the door. 'Come on, you. You're taking ages, what's up?'

Beth explained.

'Just tip it in,' said Victoria.

Beth held up both the sputum pot and the test-tube for Victoria to examine. 'The neck's too small, and I don't want to contaminate the specimen any further.'

'Amazing, isn't it . . .' said Victoria as she pressed the foot brake on the trolley and left it outside the door. Squeezing inside, she leant over the long sink and they both stared at the pot and the test-tube. 'Everyone in the whole world thinks nursing is a glamorous and lovely job. No one really knows what we have to do, do they? If my Aunt Minnie knew that I spend half my day wiping the bottoms of grown men, or if she'd seem the manual evacuation of rectum I had to perform yesterday on Mr Whiteside, she'd be dragging me out of this ward as fast as you could say sputum sample.'

'Don't tell her then,' said Beth. 'Let her think you just keep an eye on drips, take temperatures and wipe the brows of the good-looking doctors, if that makes her happy.'

'Happy? The only thing that will make Aunt Minnie happy is if I tell her I'm not going to see Roland again. What she wants is for me to accompany her to all those functions in London that she thinks will yield someone more suitable.'

Roland was Victoria's boyfriend and he had already asked her to marry him. She'd had no hesitation in saying yes and they were due to be married just as soon as she completed her finals. He was the brother of Dr Teddy Davenport, who worked with them at St Angelus and was the object of Dana's adoration.

'If I leave St Angelus, that will be my life gone. Controlled by Aunt Minnie. Since Father died, she's been pretending to love Roland, but really she is desperate to get me hitched to one of her friend's sons. She doesn't care which one, just as long as he has a frightfully posh name and a flat in Mayfair so that I have no excuse to not spend half of my life with her, in London. Give me ten impacted Mr Whitesides any day.'

Beth winced at the thought. 'Lordy, it must be bad.'

'Fighting to keep Roland in my life and refusing to live in London are my sole preoccupations.'

'You aren't going to let your aunt have her way and leave your Roland, are you?' asked Beth. 'I think he's lovely, the bee's knees. He's such a perfect gentleman, and he's so kind too. You don't often notice that in a man. You make such a perfect couple.'

'No, of course not. But he does keep pushing for us to be married sooner. He doesn't want to wait for more than another two years and if I marry, I'll have to give up nursing and I don't want to do that. I love my job. I'm as hardy as a pair of old boots now. I can manage anything! Remember how I used to heave and retch like a baby when I first started.'

'Sister Haycock is really working on that marriage thing, you know,' said Beth. She had taken the rubber stopper off the test-tube and laid it down on the wooden surface. 'But I've heard that all the ward sisters are up in arms against it. They don't want married nurses on the wards. Sister Antrobus said she would hang up her cap and leave St Angelus if they changed the rules.'

'Maybe it's because they don't like to be faced with women who might have had a better time between the sheets the previous evening than any of them have had for the past twenty years, or their entire life even. It's the reason why some of them don't like gynae or maternity. A baby is a product of, you know, doing "it". A swollen belly is a reminder of what they've missed and some them have become more like nuns than nurses. Especially Sister Antrobus.'

'Spinster sisters – they are their own best argument for allowing nurses to work when they're married,' said Beth, who was the only one of their close-knit group who didn't have a boyfriend. Small, bespectacled and slightly intense, married to her vocation, she was the one most likely to end up living in the accommodation block above the main entrance of St Angelus and becoming one of the spinster sisters they were discussing.

'Have you met the new probationer yet? Nurse Moran?' she asked.

'Only briefly. I've just seen her pushing a commode down the ward. It looked as though it weighed more than she did. She was huffing and puffing and so I walked up to her and asked if she'd taken the brake off. And she said, "The brake? No, what brake?" Honestly!'

Both Beth and Victoria began to giggle.

'So I kicked off the brake and she pushed so hard, if Staff Nurse hadn't been heading in the other direction and put her hands out to stop it, she would have gone flying.'

'Were we that green and gullible when we started?' asked Beth.

'It seems like so long ago, I can't remember. Not you, Beth, you were always Nurse Clever Clogs.'

Beth turned back to the sample. 'Right, you will

not defeat me.' She was talking to the pot. She wrinkled her nose to push her glasses further up her nose. It was a technique she had developed to prevent her from having to touch her face during sterile procedures.

'Go on, just slip it in,' said Victoria. 'Have a go.'

Beth looked up at Victoria. She was secretly impressed with her. She was someone Beth had had down as being almost too posh to nurse. A refined young lady of breeding. That was obvious as soon as she opened her mouth. But she'd taken to nursing like a duck to water.

'Do you know, Victoria,' she said, 'if anyone at the beginning had asked me, I would have said that you wouldn't have lasted six months as a nurse. I think it's wonderful that you are the one complaining about having to give up nursing if you marry because you want to carry on and sit your finals.'

Victoria was still studying the pot. 'Could you have imagined me doing this, Nurse Harper? I mean, even emptying a bedpan threw me when we first got here. I couldn't do it and never, not for weeks, could I get the top sheet to measure exactly without using the eighteen-inch rule. I used to throw up when patients were sick. Do you remember when I grabbed the kidney dish from the patient who was heaving so badly, she made me ill. I was sick in it before she had a chance, and then she threw up, all over my apron. God, that was a bad day. Sister Antrobus almost roasted me and complained about me to Matron. I thought I was done for. But nothing fazes me now. I'm even looking forward to my spell in the operating theatre.'

'Ah, eureka!' said Beth as she took down a clean pot from the shelf above their heads. 'I've just got it. I know how to do this.' Juggling her pots around, she obtained the specimen she needed, picked up the test-tube and, grinning, held it in front of Victoria's face.

Victoria emitted a retching noise.

'Are you all right?' she asked.

'Yes, of course I am,' snapped Victoria. 'Just got a bit of wind, that's all.'

'Hmm,' said Beth as she began to write Mr Trimble's name on the test-tube label. 'I am going to have this signed off on my assessment sheet this week with Sister Ryan at the school. I'll ask Sister Crawford if I can do a few more. Shall we see if we can take them together? You could do a few too? That would be it then, collection of specimens ticked off on our assessment sheets.'

Victoria didn't have time to answer as in one heave she discharged the entire contents of her breakfast into the sink.

Beth left the dirty utility room with her test-tube held proudly out in front of her, en route to the pathology department, leaving Victoria holding on to the side of the cold stone sink. 'Tough as old boots indeed!' She chuckled as she walked away.

Just before she left the ward, she turned back and saw the second coffee group assembling. Behind them, she saw that the curtains around bed sixteen were still drawn and were billowing outwards. There was no sign of Nurse Moran, who was due on second coffee.

What on earth is going on in there, thought Beth. Slipping the test-tube into her top pocket, she walked back down the ward.

When she drew back the curtain, she could barely believe her eyes. For several seconds she was unable to speak.

The young probationer was standing on top of the patient's bed, precariously swaying from side to side and clinging with one hand on to the curtain, stomping her feet up and down as she tried to regain her balance. Beth's mouth opened, and then closed again.

The pale green counterpane and the pristine white sheet were covered in dirty footprints from the crêpe soles of Nurse Moran's regulation black shoes.

The patient was kneeling on the pillow in hospital pyjamas; the bottoms were halfway down, around his knees, and he was clinging to them. He looked terrified. Possibly no one had ever been as delighted to see Beth as he was just at that moment.

Nurse Moran let go of the curtain for just a second and grabbed the large wooden commode chair by the handle. It was also precariously balanced on top of the bed, swaying unsteadily in front of her. She gripped the chair with one hand as she let out a little squeal and held the other out to the patient. As she leant towards him, both she and the commode listed to the side and she had to grab on to the bedside curtain once more to steady herself.

She was breathing hard and furiously. Letting out short gasps from the exertion, she held the curtain tight and yanked both herself and the chair back into an upright position. 'Come here, take me hand,' she gasped to the patient. 'I'll hold the commode while ye sit on the seat, ye won't fall off.' She looked over at Beth. 'He won't do what I'm asking him, Nurse Harper. Can ye help? He won't listen to a word I'm saying. He's being mighty uncooperative.' And then, in a smaller, fainter, almost pleading voice, 'I'm scared we might fall off,' she said as her eyes filled with tears.

Beth was also about to get tearful, but hers would have been tears of laughter. However, her first consideration was the patient and she held herself together, even if her mouth kept opening and closing like a goldfish's.

'Please, Nurse,' the patient said pleadingly, 'she wants me to sit on that thing on top of the bed and she can't even hold it straight herself. I'm scared to death I'll end up on the floor and I'm desperate to go.'

Beth placed her hand on his arm to calm him. 'You stay there. Don't move an inch. You cannot possibly sit on a commode perched on top of a bed for a bowel movement.'

The patient looked as though he could have kissed her. 'I could never have managed it,' he said. 'I need a bit of peace and quiet and a copy of the *Echo* before I can go, Nurse. I'd be terrified of landing on the floor. That little thing can't hold the weight of that big chair and me, on top of a wobbly mattress.'

Nurse Moran, her legs apart to better balance herself, was now holding on to the commode handle with two hands, and the wild swaying had subsided into a gentle rocking. 'Come on now, up, would you?' she said irritably to the patient.

'What are you doing?' hissed Beth.

Nurse Moran looked startled. 'What am I doing?' she said, confused. 'You told me that the patient was on bed rest and to give him the commode, you did. That was what you said, wasn't it? You did, I heard you. "He's on bed rest, but he can have a commode."'

'Yes, but . . .'

'God, it was an awful job dragging it on top of the bed. Have ye felt the weight of it? I near killed meself. 'Tis awful unstable now I have it up here.'

Beth didn't know what to say. Surely the probationer couldn't be that stupid?

'Please don't look at me like that,' said Nurse Moran, 'as if you're mad with me.'

Beth was certain she was about to burst into tears at the very least. Or hang herself from the bedside curtain, she looked so desperate.

'You said I was to put me arm under his shoulder

171

to help him, but sure, if I do that, the commode will fall on the floor and it would go with a hell of a clatter and I might even break it and hurt someone. 'Tis awful dangerous up here.'

Beth put her hand to her mouth. She was finding it hard to control her laughter. But she knew she had to resolve the situation fast, before Staff Nurse became aware that she was two short on the second coffee. Or, worse, if Sister came looking for them.

'Look, we need to get you and the commode down from the bed without you falling on top of the patient,' she said.

The patient was now clinging on to the metal headrest and looked as though he was about to climb the walls. His face was full of fear and his rear end was exposed. 'Don't let her near me, Nurse,' he whispered to Beth. 'She's mad, she is. Mad.'

Beth lowered her voice to speak to Nurse Moran, who was once again wobbling from side to side. The black footprints across the newly made bed were getting worse by the second. 'Please God, let Sister Crawford be on the end of a very long phone call,' she said. 'Nurse Moran, when I said to fetch the commode because he was on bed rest, I didn't mean to put the commode on to the bed.' She was exasperated now. 'I meant to put it by the side of the bed, so that he could just swing his legs over and slip across to it by holding on to the arm rest. You were to put your hand under

172

his shoulder to help him. He would only have needed to put one foot on the floor for a second.'

Beth watched as realization swept over the face of Nurse Moran. The tears quickly followed. 'Oh God, I'm such an eejit.'

'Here, I'll take the wheels.' Beth reached over and grabbed the two front wheels. The commode steadied and ceased swaying. Pulling the wheels to the edge of the bed, she held on. 'You climb down now. I have it and we can both lift it off together.'

'I can't,' said Nurse Moran. 'I can't move. I'm scared.'

Beth could see it was difficult and, having realized her mistake, Nurse Moran was now as scared as the patient.

'OK, slip down on to the bed, slowly. Sit on the bed and then swing your legs over the side.' She turned to the anxious-looking patient, who was probably now desperate for a bedpan. 'I'm so sorry,' she said.

'That's all right, Nurse. You see to the young nurse there. She looks as scared as I feel. I think she must have mistaken me for King Tut.' He began to giggle.

Beth, picturing him on top of a commode on top of a wobbly mattress being held upright by a slip of a probationer nurse holding on to the handles, also began to giggle. The patient reached out and grabbed her arm and they were both on the verge of being helpless with laughter. Only

Nurse Moran, who was by now kneeling on the bed with a tear-stained face, looked serious.

Beth was disintegrating. The tears were pouring from her eyes. 'Get down, please,' she gasped between seizures. Tears were also pouring down the patient's cheeks as he grabbed the sheet to cover his dignity and held on to his belly while he laughed. His eyes met Beth's and they were both lost. Totally helpless with laughter.

The probationer slipped on to the floor and grabbed hold of the back wheels, but Beth could not move for laughing. 'Oh God, help me, please!' she gasped as her knees collapsed into the side of the bed frame, supporting her weight and that of the commode. The patient, who was in as bad a state as she was, held out his arm to steady her. She leant forward, her abdomen and her cheeks hurting from laughing, and was about to lift the wheels of the commode when the curtains flew open to reveal Sister Crawford standing there, furious.

'What is all this commotion about?'

As Sister took in the chaos in front of her, the ward fell silent. All chatter ceased as everyone listened with bated breath.

Sister found her voice following a moment's hesitation and, almost for the first time in many years, shouted on her own ward. 'Nurse Harper, what on earth is going on here?'

The curtains were open and every pair of eyes in the ward, patients' and nurses' alike, were fixed on bed sixteen. Beth heard the sharp intake of breath. The commode wobbled, the probationer screamed, the patient roared with laughter and the commode tilted dangerously backwards. Beth turned her back on Sister Crawford and almost threw herself across the bed to catch it. As she did so, she heard the test-tube in her pocket snap.

CHAPTER 10

At Christmas, the plant closed for a week. Not that this was the choice of the McConaghys. They would have opened on Christmas Day, given half the chance. But Christmas was as special for the Irish diaspora on Liverpool's dockside as it was anywhere else in the country. Few ships came into the docks and there were even fewer men sober enough to unload them. So, in spite of themselves, the McConaghys allowed their furnaces to cool, the spinning machines to stop and the coils of hot metal to settle as they locked the plant floor for the first time since Michaelmas.

This year, Mrs McConaghy decided to close the office after lunch on Christmas Eve. She had her sister and brother-in-law and her niece, Amy, coming over for Christmas lunch and she wanted to get off early herself. Regardless of how much she trusted Lily, she would never leave anyone alone in full charge of the office, the cast-iron safe and the large bankers' drafts it contained.

'Amy is turning into a very beautiful young woman,' she said to Lily. 'Someone will snap her up in a flash.'

Lily had heard a great deal about Amy. After all, she was Mrs McConaghy's only niece, and with them having no children of their own, it was only natural they should take a special interest in her. But there was something in Mrs McConaghy's tone, a catch of concern in her voice. Lily wasn't sure she ever wanted to meet her in the flesh. Her reputation had run ahead of her faster than the boyfriend had raced down the path when her parents had caught them on the new bouclé sofa.

'Here, take this as your Christmas box,' Mrs McConaghy said as she slipped an envelope into Lily's hand. 'And I got the cook at home to make two Christmas cakes, so that I could bring one in for you. Don't you fret, it didn't cost me a thing apart from the ingredients, so don't be worrying about that.'

Lily was too spellbound to be fretting about anything. It was the very first present she had received in her entire life and she blinked as the tears burnt at her eyes. Mrs McConaghy took the lid off the cake tin and all Lily could do was blink. It was iced and in the middle there was a hand-made figurine of two skaters on a frozen blue lake. Around the edge were miniature trees covered in little red bows. Lily briefly pictured the expressions on Joe's and Katie's faces when she took it home. But she was quite sure this could not be happening and that in a moment Mrs McConaghy would say that there had been some mistake.

'Are you sure this one is for me?' she asked as she looked up from the tin.

Mrs McConaghy's hands flew to the gold crucifix around her neck and she rubbed it between her finger and thumb as she replied. 'Yes, and that's not all, either. You have been a hard worker this year, Lily and, well, Sister tells me you work like a demon at home too. So I thought you deserved a bit of a treat.'

Lily looked at the envelope with suspicion until Mrs McConaghy said, 'Go on, take it, it's for you.'

She wondered what Sister Therese had told them. She hated pity more than anything. Sometimes a neighbour would stop her on the landing at Clare Cottages and in a sympathetic voice would ask if there was something she needed. There were things Lily needed, but no one could give her a set of parents who could remain sober for longer than four hours. Or who thought more about their kids than they did about their next pint of Guinness. No, Lily was on her own. She never called upon the help of neighbours. She would manage.

Lily blinked at Mrs McConaghy like a lamped fox. She had no idea what to say. She hadn't been worried about the cost. She had yet to absorb the fact that Mrs McConaghy was being so kind and had given her a present.

'It's got candied peel in it that I dried and made myself,' said Mrs McConaghy. 'I smelt of lemons for days. Did you not notice?'

Lily hadn't noticed a thing. She was amazed that

178

Mrs McConaghy made something called candied peel. It sounded delicious, even though she was not entirely sure what it was. They had never had a Christmas cake at home, although she'd seen them standing to cool on the kitchen windowsills of her neighbours' homes. 'I'll do that one day,' she had whispered to herself one morning in October as she'd walked past Mrs McGuffy's and inhaled the smell of molasses and fruit and warm Christmas spices.

She stammered out a thank you, then placed her basket on the desk and quickly peeled back her birdcage cover. She had to stop herself from snatching the cake. She wanted to place it inside her basket as quickly as possible and then she would know for sure it was hers. Mrs McConaghy lifted it out of the tin. She had wrapped it in greaseproof paper tied up with string. Lily's heart beat like a trapped bird in a cage as she feared that Mrs McConaghy might change her mind and ask for it back. In a flash, she slipped the cake into her basket and fastened the cover back over it. Relieved that it was now really hers, she looked up and smiled.

'Well, we don't see that smile very often. And to think, all it took was a fruit cake. Sure, I would have brought one in before, had I known.'

'The kids will love it, Mrs McConaghy.' Lily's voice sounded strange even to her. She wanted to get out of the office and away. She could not relax in the knowledge that the kids at home could really have this until she was on the bus. 'Thank you. Thank you very much,' she stammered.

'It was them I made it for, Lily. Oh, I know you'll have a slice, but I wanted the little ones to have a treat and I also knew that it would mean a lot to you. I like to help where I can.'

Lily made O-shapes with her mouth. She had never known Mrs McConaghy to help anyone before now. She had seen grown men walk down the steps of the plant in tears, in the early days before Lily had assumed charge of calculating the weekly wage packets. If a man was paid short and challenged Mrs McConaghy, he always lost.

Unbeknown to Lily, Sister Therese had told Mrs McConaghy all about the children and Lily's situation at home. She no longer needed to be asked twice. The less she saw of Sister Therese, the better.

'Here, don't you go forgetting the envelope. Put that in there too, to keep it safe.' No one had asked her to give that to Lily. That had been entirely her own idea. She had looked into her own heart for that little treat and the joy she'd got from putting the ten pounds into an envelope and giving it to Lily had been like no other pleasure she had ever known. She felt alive for the first time in a long while.

At first, Lily thought it was a Christmas card. The office wall was covered in cards from customers and traders. Some of them had been addressed just to Lily herself, with lovely messages of appreciation, and she had so wanted to take them home, to show to Joe and Katie, to decorate their barren house at Clare Cottages. But Mrs McConaghy had pinned them up on the wall with all the others. As Lily picked up the envelope, it occurred to her that it felt flimsy, not firm enough to be a card. 'What's this?' she asked.

Mrs McConaghy beamed from ear to ear and looked towards the door. The furnaces were still firing and it would be another hour before her husband and brother-in-law appeared.

'Look, open it now, would ye. There are some shady characters around at this time of the year and I don't want ye opening it on the street or the bus.'

Lily opened the envelope and almost fainted as she extracted the twenty brown ten-shilling notes. 'Mrs McConaghy, is this for us?' she gasped.

'No,' replied Mrs McConaghy. 'It isn't for "us". It's for you. For a new pair of shoes and for some clothes of your own. They have some lovely little red boots with a furry lining in that shop in St John's market for two pounds and two shillings. If you ask, they might knock the two shillings off.'

Never in a million years would Lily spend two pounds on herself. Not when there was Joe and Katie to see to first. Joe had no shoes. He would be first. 'I don't know what to say,' she said again.

'You are very special to us, Lily.'

Lily noticed Mrs McConaghy's cheeks were burning red and her eyes were bright and sparkling. She had partaken of a few sherries during the day. A bottle had stood open on her desk and she'd drunk to a prosperous new year with every trader who had called into the plant. Her eyes were misty.

'I don't know how we would manage without you, Lily. 'Tis just a sign of my appreciation. Sometimes I think you are better than family to me. My own niece, Amy, won't come near the place.'

Mrs McConaghy had gone from a reluctant acceptance to being terrified of losing Lily, but it had taken three long years to get to this point. This was the first time she had properly acknowledged Lily's importance, and now she was suddenly better than family. Lily knew how valuable she was to the business. If she left tomorrow, they would struggle and be thrown into a tizzy of incomprehension. Both Mr and Mrs McConaghy's health had deteriorated over the past three years and they had aged rapidly as a result.

'And this, Lily, is for you, but you cannot open it until Christmas morning.'

Mrs McConaghy held out a flat package wrapped in coloured tissue and Lily was truly speechless. Wide-eyed, she lifted the basket cover again and slipped the parcel inside.

'Thank you.' Her words were little more than a whisper.

'No, Lily, it's me who should be saying thank you. Now, off you go.'

Lily was determined to make the ten pounds spread as far as twenty and keep every penny a secret from her parents. She'd have to. Once they knew she had it, the lot would disappear within hours. She fought the urge to want to make them proud of her with pragmatism. She knew exactly how they would spend it. The horses at two thirty in the bookies. The pub at three. Pie van at five. Back to the pub and home at midnight. Shouting and fighting. Sick of the sight of each other. Every penny gone. And the following morning, neither would remember a thing. Lily knew this. It had happened before.

She had asked her stepfather for some of her wages back for food, after he had ripped the packet from her one Friday night and disappeared straight out of the door.

'I don't know where your money is,' he'd said. 'Don't call me a liar or you'll get the back of me hand.'

She didn't call him a liar, but she got the back of his hand anyway.

'You little bitch, just because I'm not your own father, you think you can speak to me any way you want. Look down your nose at me. Keep your money from me, me who puts a roof over your head. You ungrateful little madam.'

And then she felt the force of his hand. Felt the wall against the back of her head and a fistful of hair being ripped from her scalp. Then it was over.

Despite her headache, she had still arrived at McConaghy's on time. That was the day Lockie took one look at her and then flew to the pub and pinned her stepfather to the wall. 'One more time.

Once more, old man, and I will kill you with my bare fists, do you understand that, you snivelling, stinking coward?'

Lily's stepfather had shaken and cried like a baby, but it had worked; he hadn't hit her since. A man whose brain was almost pickled in alcohol and who forgot most things did not forget Lockie's warning.

Lily fastened her coat. She was reluctant to let go of the handle of the basket, in case it, along with the cake, her money, her present and her birdcage cover, should disappear. She had so little of her own, the birdcage cover was important to her.

'Thank you again, Mrs McConaghy.'

Without knowing why, and for the first time ever, she reached up and kissed her boss on her Coty-smelling powdered cheek. For a fraction of a second, she wallowed in the sensation of being hugged by a motherly figure. She inhaled the warm, perfumed smell, felt the pleasure of another's arms around her shoulders, noticed the prickly down against the side of her face. For a moment, she wanted to cry. A strand of hair began to tickle her cheek and she felt Mrs McConaghy giving her the faintest squeeze.

'Do what you have to do to have a good time, for all of you,' said Mrs McConaghy. 'I don't mind how you spend it. Whatever way makes you happy. Merry Christmas, Lily.'

★   ★   ★

'Where has all that coal come from in the shed?' her mother exclaimed later that night when she opened the door to scratch around for a few lumps at the back and was met by a black mountain.

Lily had called into the coal merchant's immediately she'd alighted from the bus. The coalman was busy, told her everyone came in for extra fuel once the Christmas money started to arrive.

'I never heard him shouting. Did he deliver to everyone? Who's paid for that?' Her mother stood staring down at the heaped shovel in her hand, as though she couldn't quite believe it. 'Jeez, the coalman has turned into fecking Father Christmas.'

Lily didn't respond. If she told her mother she had money for coal, she would want to know what else she had money for. And it didn't stop at the coal. The cupboards were filled with food, and for half a crown Lily had bought a turkey late on Christmas Eve in St John's market.

'And where did the money come from for that?' her mother asked on her way out to the pub. 'What the hell is going on around here?'

Lily knew that as it was Christmas Eve, her parents would be out until later than usual. They would stagger into St Chad's at midnight and then straight back into the pub after Mass until the early hours.

'Mr and Mrs McConaghy gave it to me,' she replied with a clear conscience. It was not a lie; they had, in a way. Lily was aware that her mother would assume that Sister Therese had been involved and that any chance of selling the turkey in the pub would be thwarted as a result.

Lily had taken the children with her to the market. Joe was pushed along in his old pram, to carry the turkey back, and Katie held on to the side. They had been amazed by the noise and the sawdust. By the messenger boys whizzing past them on bikes with huge wicker baskets on the front, and by the bright overhead lights and the calls of the traders attempting to offload the last of the turkeys and sprouts before dark.

Mrs McConaghy's ten-pound present made the difference between a cold, miserable Christmas and a warm, comfortable one. Lily even managed to buy a small present for each of the children without them knowing.

With Joe and Katie finally asleep and tucked up in bed, Lily slipped out to midnight Mass. She knew Sister Therese would expect to see her there and would miss her if she wasn't. She heard her parents arrive in the back of the church as the pub spilled in through the door. 'What am I doing here? I'm not even a Catholic,' she heard someone shout in a drunken slur. It sounded like her stepfather. She died inside and, looking up at the cross, asked one question. Why?

'Lily!' Sister Therese called above the crowd outside as Lily hurried through it to make her way home. 'I have presents back at the convent. I will pop them in in the morning after Mass. Where are your parents?'

They both looked over at the heaving throng visible through the windows of the public house, already shouting out their orders for drinks.

'Are you all right, Lily? Are you managing?' Sister Therese's heart nearly broke. If she could have one prayer answered tonight it would be for someone or something to make Lily smile. To share her burden and lift the weight from her shoulders.

'I am, Sister. I am managing well.'

For the first time, Sister Therese believed her.

Lily woke earlier than was usual on Christmas morning. She had been roused in the early hours by her parents' noisy return home. She wondered how they had found their way or even remembered where they lived. She heard her stepfather try to use the bucket and miss as the sound of his steady stream of urine hitting the wooden floor filled the air. She had done her best to clean the kitchen before she left for Mass. She would have another mess to clean when she rose. Now she wanted to make sure the kids woke to a clean, urine-free kitchen, a roaring fire and a delicious breakfast. She had bought bacon and eggs in the market and she would fry bread in the fat that was left in the pan.

The sulphur glow from the street lamps slipped into the room and the air was cold. She looked down at Joe. His breathing was even. The side of his sleeping face had taken on a marmalade glow. There was still the faint wheeze but no rattle. His thumb was placed firmly in his mouth and the arm of a well-worn teddy, all that was left of Lily's once beloved bear, was clutched in his hand.

Lily stroked his wispy blonde hair back from his face and, bending down, kissed his cheek. The lone arm of the teddy smelt pretty bad and she wondered if she might persuade him to throw it on to the fire to say thank you to Father Christmas for his toy train. She wished she had some paper to wrap the train in, to enhance the excitement, delay the surprise.

Joe began to stir.

'Stay asleep, little fella,' she whispered into his hair. 'I'm going to light the fire. Sleep for a bit longer.'

Happy to have heard Lily's voice, with his free hand he grabbed on to her finger and, like he had as a newborn, he grasped it tight. Within seconds he was once again relaxed as he flipped from wakefulness into a deep sleep.

Lily had bought hair ribbons and colouring pencils for Katie, as well as a hand mirror and a bar of sweet-smelling soap. A toy train and books for Joe. She had also purchased a Cadbury's bar of chocolate each, a Satsuma and some nuts. Conscious that she had nothing to wrap it all in, she decided that just before she woke them, she would place two little piles at the foot of the bed.

It had been hard enough buying the presents in the first place. With her heart pounding, she'd left Katie with Joe in the pram while she ran around the perimeter wall of the market, where the non-food stalls sold their wares. It took her no more than ten minutes and when she'd passed a fruit-and-veg stall, she bought the fruit and nuts and asked the vendor to place them in the paper bag with the toys.

'How many kids you got, love?' the fruit-and-veg man had asked.

'Two,' she replied. Not realizing that he thought they were hers.

'You must have started early, queen.' He laughed. 'Here, I'll throw in a few extras. Closing in half an hour, I am.'

She couldn't get her change back from him quick enough, keen to return to her siblings and the pram.

'Didn't mean to cause any offence, love,' he shouted after her. 'Merry Christmas.'

Now, on Christmas morning, with the bedroom door open, the light from the fire in the kitchen lit up the room and warmed it through within minutes. Lily knew it was a dreadful waste of money, but she couldn't help it. She wanted to make it a nice morning for Joe and Katie.

She placed the presents at the bottom of the bed and then listened for the snores of her mam and stepdad. They were sound asleep and she just hoped that as the pubs were closed today, they would behave and not take their bad heads out on them all.

'Wakey, wakey!' She laughed as she tickled Katie.

'Come on, monkey, wakey, wakey!' And then to Joe, 'I think Father Christmas has been and left you something at the bottom of the bed.'

There was no further need to try and wake them. It was as though they had both received a shock. They sat upright together and then the room was filled with screams as, wiping the sleep from their eyes, they scrambled to the end of the bed, hardly able to believe what they were seeing. It was the first Christmas morning they'd woken up to presents.

'Lily, Lily, would you look,' said Katie as she gasped and held up her mirror. 'God, isn't it just beautiful.'

Joe was silent as he held his toy train in his hands and turned it over and over.

Lily's eyes filled with tears as she watched Katie cradle the mirror in her hands, scared to drop or break it as she looked at her own wide-eyed and speechless expression.

'Would you look at you! You'd think that Father Christmas had brought you the crown jewels,' she said as, excited beyond belief, they began to chatter all at once as they examined the colouring books and pencils.

'Come by the fire now,' she said, 'we won't be going outside.'

But she couldn't stop them moving to the window. The noise of the neighbours' children, even on Christmas morning, began to filter through the walls. They dived to the window, clutching their presents and, behind them, Lily's heart sank.

The children from the happy families, those whose fathers worked every hour they could get down on the docks and whose mothers cleaned at St Angelus at night when their children were all tucked up in bed, pushed bikes and toy prams out on to the half landing and into the courtyard.

'Oh, Lily, would you look at that toy pram. It's white and red, isn't it beautiful?' said Katie, her colouring books forgotten and her face pressed up against the glass. 'It's Sheila. Can I go out, Lily? She will let me play with her, won't she?'

The air was pierced by a shrill scream. It was Joe. He'd seen the little boy from next door pedalling up and down the courtyard on a tricycle.

'Why didn't Father Christmas leave us any of those, Lily?' asked Katie. 'I would have loved a doll.' This wish was whispered almost into the glass and Lily had to strain to hear her.

'It doesn't matter, Katie,' said Joe, 'we have got all these. We have the best presents.'

'Yes, you have. You can do colouring all day in the warm. You can go out and play any old day,' said Lily.

But under her breath she cursed the children of Clare Cottages. How could she compete with the parents who put money in the 'club' down at the shop every week and another two bob in a jar every week of the year to save for Christmas. She had watched in envy over the past week as the women of Clare Cottages had struggled up and down the stairs with string bags bulging with jars and tins and hams banging against their shins. Rationing was still in force, but the black market down on the docks enabled those who were canny enough to push their own boat out at Christmas time. It was as if the good women of Clare Cottages had gone mad, desperate to buy every new food commodity available in the shops or that had arrived into port and fallen off the back of a ship.

'Now, who is going to help me make mince pies?' said Lily cheerfully. 'There was a recipe in Mrs McConaghy's magazine and she gave it to me and I have all the things we need. We can use a milk bottle for a rolling pin, can't we, Katie?'

She clasped Katie's hand as the little girl shivered with excitement at the thought of baking. It was so novel, it was as exciting a prospect as a new bike.

'Come on then, clothes on. Let's go! We have bacon and fried bread for breakfast. Now, isn't this the best?'

How her parents didn't wake up with the whoops of excitement, she had no idea. She hoped in her heart that they would sleep all day.

Everything is going great, Lily thought to herself as they made the pastry, just the way Sister Therese had taught her at school. The children giggled as the flour covered them all and Lily became enveloped in a white cloud.

'Merry Christmas, everyone!' They heard her voice before she was even through the door and Joe ran forward to meet Sister Therese.

'Come here and help me, would you, Joe,' she

said. 'Here you are, Katie, these are for you.' Sister Therese did have wrapping paper and the present she handed to Katie was enormous and looked twice as inviting as Lily's had earlier that morning.

Lily felt her heart sink for the briefest moment. She wished she could have had more time to prepare, but until yesterday she'd been dreading Christmas. It was still less than twenty-four hours since Mrs McConaghy had handed Lily her envelope and even Lily was wide-eyed at the transformation one gift had made to their fortunes.

'What is it?' asked Katie, almost breathless. 'Is it for me?' She held it at arm's length and looked as though Sister Therese had just placed an unexploded bomb in her arms.

'Well, now, why would I be giving it to you if it was for someone else? Do you think I've struggled all the way here and up those steps on my own with my arms full to bursting, only to find out I've come to the wrong house? I had to make the journey twice.' Sister Therese winked at Lily. 'I haven't forgotten you,' she said. 'Does that teapot have anything in it? I'm near parched from the holy smoke.'

Lily felt frozen in shame. She'd been so busy running around the market buying for Katie and Joe, she'd forgotten to buy anything for Sister Therese. Her face burnt with embarrassment. She wasn't even sure that nuns could accept presents, but still, she would have liked to have at least had something to show how grateful they were for all her help.

'Sit on the floor to open them,' Sister Therese said.

'Can I?' asked Katie, who despite Sister Therese's instruction looked dubious and sought confirmation from Lily before daring to move with such a big parcel in her arms.

Although she wanted to fetch Sister Therese her tea, Lily couldn't move from the spot. She could not take her eyes off Katie's face as, crouching, she slowly placed her box on the floor and, casting nervous glances towards Joe and Lily, surveyed the first real present she had ever been given.

'Come on then, Katie,' said Lily. 'Open it up. I'm not leaving until I see what you have.'

Katie, unsure what to do, picked at the edge of her present. 'I want to see what Joe has,' she said.

'Do you know, someone once told me that a big box wrapped up in paper is the best thing in the world that you can give a child. Doesn't matter what's in it. It's just the wrapped-up box they love.' Sister Therese kept her eyes on Katie and inclined her head towards Lily as she spoke. 'Who would credit it now. You wouldn't think so, looking at this one now, would you?'

Katie smiled up at her and finally, feeling reassured, proceeded to rip the paper from the present with gusto.

A perfect and exquisitely dressed doll was lifted out of the box. She was wearing a pale blue silk dress and, for a brief moment, it occurred to Lily that the doll was dressed better than Katie would ever be. It was a doll more beautiful than either Lily or Katie had ever seen.

There was a moment of silence as Katie held out the doll before her. 'Is it really for me?' she asked again. Unsure. Scared. Reluctant to let her heart soar with the surge of love she felt for the loveliest thing she had ever seen until she was absolutely certain it was safe to do so.

'Well, it's not for Sheila McGuffy. Of course it's for you,' said Sister Therese.

Katie slowly hugged her doll to her, and burst into tears.

Lily dropped to her knees. She instinctively knew what was wrong. Katie did not believe that this doll was something she could keep once Sister Therese had left the house. She was torn between her sudden rush of intense love for the doll and the disappointment she knew would follow when her parents saw it. They would sell it for sure. Or pawn it. Their sole mission in life was to secure money for drink.

Sister Therese dropped to her knees next to Lily. 'This is yours for ever, Katie,' she said. 'Now, you need to stop crying and think what name you're going to give to your baby and where she is going to sleep tonight. Have ye room in the bed for her?'

Katie nodded her head vigorously and wiped her eyes with the back of her hand.

'Well now, isn't that just grand. I always think Alfreda is a nice name. I knew a Sister Alfreda once.'

Katie wrinkled her nose. Suzy had been the name that had flown to the front of her mind. Lily smiled at Katie. She knew that, as grateful as Katie was, the beautiful doll would never be christened Alfreda.

'Now, listen here, you. While I have a cuppa, I want you to choose a name for your dolly, and don't be influenced by me. But you have to make me a promise.'

Katie looked solemnly towards Sister Therese.

'You have to bring her with you to Mass. Is that a deal?'

By now it was Lily's eyes that were filled with tears as she watched Katie undo the string ties in the box that were holding her doll upright. And then she held her doll across her front like a baby and silently rocked her.

Lily noticed that Joe had been standing next to her, still and silent, holding her hand. She moved closer to him and ruffled his soft, morning hair. She was subconsciously letting Sister Therese know there was another little one and her heart constricted in pain at the thought she might have forgotten him.

'Oh, Joe, there you are. Come here with me while I show you. I would never forgot you,' said Sister Therese. She opened wide the door on to the landing and before them all stood a gleaming red tricycle with a wicker basket fastened to the rear with a white leather strap.

Lily grasped Joe's hand tight and Joe let out a gasp.

As Joe sat on his bike, almost speechless with delight, one thought ran through Lily's mind. Within days, her mother would try to pawn or sell these wonderful gifts and she would now have to come up fast with a way to prevent that happening.

Let them have their day, she thought, as she went to make tea for Sister Therese. She would not let her parents spoil this, their best Christmas Day ever. But her spirits sank at the thought of their broken hearts when the inevitable moment came and her siblings arrived home from school to find the presents gone.

'And here, Lily, this is for you.' Sister Therese reached down into her bag and brought out the smallest present. 'Go on, open it.'

It was a gold crucifix on a fine gold chain and Lily let it slip through her fingers.

'Go on, put it on. I want to see you wearing it before I go.'

Lily did as she was told and then said, 'I had a present from Mrs McConaghy too.'

'Well, isn't that the thing. Let us see it then.'

Within seconds, Lily had extracted the thin present from under her bed and laid it on the table. She untied the string as though it were spun from a spider's web and eventually lifted out a beautiful green paisley scarf.

Sister Therese could not hide her delight. 'Well, imagine that. If you don't look like the most beautiful girl in all of Liverpool wearing that, I don't know who would.'

Lily had no words as she tied the headscarf and, picking up Katie's now forgotten mirror, examined her reflection. For the first time, she saw herself as the woman she would one day become.

As Sister Therese made her way across the road to St Chad's, she met Father Brennan on his way over from the house.

'Did you do your deed?' he asked.

Father Brennan had long argued that the children needed to be taken into the home at St Chad's and then the welfare contacted, to give them a better chance of being raised as Catholics.

'I have, and I know you disapprove, Father, but if you had seen their faces . . .' The Lancashires were her biggest challenge. She had always felt her best option was to support Lily and the children at home. It was her policy with all the families in Clare Cottages.

'Sure, St Chad's would be full to the gunnels if every child who needed care was brought into the home. How would we manage?'

Father Brennan waved his finger at Sister Therese. They had many a disagreement about the children who lived in Clare Cottages. 'You do a fine job, Sister, but mark my word, the day will come when we have no choice. You are arguing with the Lord over this one, so be careful. He always wins.'

Sister Therese had a heavy heart. She was just as worried about Lily. The children were her world. If they were taken into care, where would Lily go? What would become of her? No, she would leave things as they were. And Father was wrong, she was not arguing with the Lord, not yet anyway. She knew that soon something would happen that would show them the way. She felt that something good was about to pass. Something that would change Lily's life. That was what the Lord was telling her.

'The only person I do battle with around here, Father, is you,' she said with a wry smile as they both blessed themselves and walked under the arch into St Chad's.

Father Brennan shook his head. Sister Therese always got what she wanted. From everyone she met, and always from him. And now it looked as though she might also have God himself wrapped around her little finger too.

CHAPTER 11

The second she walked through the door of the processing plant office, Lily knew something was not quite right. The bell above the door jangled and announced her arrival to the empty room. She looked up at the huge clock, positioned above the door to the back stairs that led down to the processing plant floor. She had made it. The large black minute hand told her it was two minutes to eight. She shivered. The office was unwelcoming, the fire unlit. It was cold and empty and then she saw that her desk had been moved to face the wall, where there was no window and very little light. Lily frowned. She had sat in the same place, near the fireplace and facing the window, since the day she'd arrived.

In her place and even closer to the fire, directly opposite Mrs McConaghy's own desk, someone had placed a smart new leather-topped desk and a leather swivel chair.

Lily looked around her. 'Hello,' she shouted. 'Mrs McConaghy?' There was no response. The bell above the door jangled in a slightly disappointed tone as she slowly closed the door, her

200

eyes never leaving the new desk. She surveyed it as she would an intruder. 'How did you get in here?' she whispered. 'Who carried you up the steps?' Mr and Mrs McConaghy were getting far too old to do any heavy lifting themselves and in Mrs McConaghy's case, she was rather too fond of the newly arrived French fancies in Sayers, so she no longer moved as well as she used to.

The office was freezing. The furnaces that warmed the upstairs rooms had been run low over the Christmas break and down in the yard she could hear the coal being shovelled into the wooden skips on runners and wheeled across the concrete floor ready for to start them up again. Soon, with the help of the huge gas pokers, the plant would fire back into life, and in an hour or two the office would be as warm as toast again.

Lily didn't want to remove her coat until she'd begun to feel the heat from the furnaces and had lit the fire in the office. She peeled off her gloves and, pushing them into her coat pocket, began her usual morning routine. It had taken her over an hour to walk to work. The roads had been almost deserted due to the thickness of the smog, and her bus had failed to turn up. It was as if time had frozen as the people of Liverpool hibernated indoors. She filled the Burco urn using a large copper jug and, placing her ear against the side, reassured herself that it was working as she heard the faint hum of the first simmer. She lit the fire and used the old bellows to coax it into life, then walked around the office taking down the Christmas cards that were pinned on to the wall. Her breath hung before her in opaque, milky clouds and her frozen fingers struggled to remove the brass-topped drawing pins with her soft and splintered nails.

All the while, her eyes kept wandering to the imposing new desk and chair. Just like Katie, when she'd been presented with her new doll, she kept thinking to herself, that can't be for me. Surely not? Can it?

She couldn't think who else it could be for. It must be for her. A ridiculous thrill began to run through her veins at the thought that it might be a second Christmas present, given in acknowledgement of how hard she worked. Did the McConaghys really appreciate her so much that they thought she was worthy of a brand-new desk and chair?

The bell above the door announced the fact that she was no longer alone. It was accompanied by an icy blast of air around her ankles. Turning from the wall, she saw Lockie, stamping his boots.

'Shut the door, Lockie,' she almost shouted. 'It's cold enough in here with no furnace lit, and the fire hasn't got going yet.'

Lockie turned to face back outdoors and looked towards the river. 'Have you seen out on the docks? There's no ships coming in. The ones that are have already been unloaded and there's nothing waiting out at the bar. Harbourmaster says the fog out at sea is as thick as pease pottage. It'll be worse onshore by tonight.'

Lily smiled at Lockie. She liked to think that they were friends, but really, it was more than that; he was an ally. Someone she could chat to when Mrs McConaghy went out for her morning walk to the cake shop. Lily had no romantic notions or feelings towards Lockie, but she enjoyed his company and although she would only admit it to herself, apart from Sister Therese, he was her only friend.

'I nearly fell over twice on my way to work,' she replied. 'Have you got the horse out?'

'No way. He's still tucked up in the stable. There's no point. I've nothing to put on the cart if there's no ships in.'

'Why aren't you tucked up in bed then? You can have a day off, you lucky thing.'

'No point in being in me bed, Lily, if there's no one to keep me warm, is there?'

Lily blushed to the roots of her hair. 'Get lost, Lockie,' she said. 'Even if there was, you would have to get up to feed the horse.'

Lockie stamped his feet up and down on the coconut mat and closed the door behind him. 'Where is everyone?' he asked, and then he let out a long, low whistle. 'Wow, you've gone up in the world, haven't you! Would you look at the cut of that desk.' He walked over to the new desk and ran his fingers across the embossed green leather top. His finger traced around the gold filigree inlay.

'I don't know. I don't know what to think. It can't be for me, surely?'

Lily handed Lockie a mug of tea. It was her first job of the morning, to make everyone tea. In a second, she would carry a tray down on to the plant floor with two pint-sized mugs. One for Mr McConaghy and one for his brother-in-law.

She hated doing it and was filled with embarrassment and regret when she walked back up the wooden steps with the empty tray at her side. She would see the eyes of the other men as they glanced at the empty wooden tray and, occasionally, at Mr McConaghy as he drank his tea. Some would arrive for work with glass bottles full of cold tea. Some with nothing at all.

She would have happily made a cuppa for everyone. After all, there were only a dozen men on the plant floor. She had suggested as much once to Mrs McConaghy and had been roundly scolded for even daring to consider the workers.

'Would you like me to make a tea for everyone?' she'd asked during her first week. Her own had left a bad taste as she thought of the men working in front of the huge furnace, parched.

'Tea? For everyone? No, I would not. 'Tis not a charity we run here. This is a workplace, not a kitchen. There is a water pump in the yard. They won't die of thirst.'

Mrs McConaghy's tone had been so scathing, Lily had never mentioned it again.

'Give them tea and they'll be after a cake and a sit-down next.'

Like yourself, then? Lily had thought the words,

not daring to say them out loud. She had to keep her opinions to herself. She needed her job.

It was many weeks before she joined Mrs McConaghy in a cup of tea in the morning again. Her cup and saucer sat on her desk unused, her own small, silent protest in solidarity with the men downstairs.

Lockie placed his cup on the new desk.

'Pick it up,' said Lily. 'You idiot, it will burn the leather.'

'Oh, well, get you. All protective now. Worried I'll mark the grand desk. Stop kidding me, Lily, you know this new desk is for you. All I can say is, you are really making your mark here. They must think very highly of you because the McConaghys wouldn't spend a penny they didn't need to. Unless of course . . .'

'Unless of course what? There's no reason it would be for me, is there? I can't believe it's for me. Do you really think it can be?' She bent her head in to whisper this, even though there was no one in the office to hear her.

'I do think so, yes. Who else is going to sit at it? Mrs McConaghy would never give up her own desk.' Lockie took a package out of his pocket, wrapped in brown paper and tied with string. 'Here, Lily, I have something for you.'

'For me?' asked Lily, eyes wide and inquisitive. 'Are you sure?'

'Of course I'm sure. It's a bit late, as I didn't see you before the break, but Happy Christmas, Lily.'

Lily's eyes filled with tears and she hurriedly wiped them away with the back of her hand. She carefully undid the paper and her smile widened in wonderment. It was a hairbrush. Made of polished wood and bristle. She had never seen anything so handsome. She'd always longed to have such a thing to brush her long chestnut hair.

'Oh, Lockie . . .' she whispered, but she could barely speak.

'Come here, you daft lump!' Lockie scooped her into his arms and for a second he rocked her.

She felt the coarse wool fibres of his donkey jacket scratch against her face and for a moment she let her cheek rest and take in the smell of the jute that Lockie hauled up and down, on and off the cart all day long. She was like a sister to him. Someone he had known for all of his life. He protected her, cared for her, but she knew he most certainly did not think of her as any more than that, and nor did she of him. He was a special person in her life and she loved him for it.

Lockie pulled back and held her away from him by her shoulders. 'Did you get through Christmas all right, Lily? He didn't hit you, did he? If he did, tell me. I swear to God, I will kill him if he did.'

Lily sniffed. Lockie handed her his handkerchief. It was pristine white and crisp. Lily knew that Lockie's mam was the proudest woman in Liverpool and she would never let her son set foot outside the house without a clean handkerchief in his pocket. She was also a woman of strong opinion, and that opinion was particularly strong with regard to the Lancashires.

'No, they were in the pub or asleep for most of it. Sister Therese bought us presents. Lockie, it was the best Christmas we ever had.'

'Well, it looks to me like it's getting better. You never know, that desk could be your Christmas present from Mrs McConaghy.'

Lily laughed. 'Don't be daft. She bought me a beautiful scarf. I've hidden it under the bed and the kids' presents are in Mrs McGuffy's.'

'Have you thought of telling the McConaghys how tough it is at home?'

Lily shook her head.

Lockie didn't have to ask why. He knew why. Lily was proud. She would rather die than tell the McConaghys that both her parents were alcoholics and that she was the only thing that stood between little Joe and Katie and the care home.

The new desk was a mystery. They both looked over towards where Mrs McConaghy usually sat. Her chair was placed right next to the safe door. Lockie was right, she would never move. She guarded the door to the safe with more diligence than St Peter at the gates of heaven.

'She gave me a big cake for Christmas and some extra money,' Lily whispered. 'She's not all bad. Just a bit mean sometimes.'

'A bit mean?' said Lockie. 'Are you kidding me? Well, there you go then. If she remembered you at Christmas, it's obvious, isn't it? They are pushing you up in the world, Lily. Making sure people give you the respect you deserve. That's why they've put the new desk in. Look, they are both going to either retire or kick the bucket very soon. Who else can run this place if that happens? You have well and truly taken over. Was that not always the plan, Lily?'

Lily blinked. It was as though Lockie was speaking in a foreign language. She had no idea what he was talking about. 'I only know how to do the banking, the ordering and the wages, Lockie,' she whispered, scared that someone might come through the door and hear her. She was loyal to the McConaghys, despite their frequent displays of selfishness, and Lockie's words made her feel uncomfortable. 'I don't know anything about the processing, down on the floor.'

'Don't come the innocent with me, Lily.' Lockie smiled. 'You also look after the office, barter a price with the traders, make all the decisions. What is there left, other than for the likes of me with horses and carts to turn up from the docks? The men who work on the plant floor have done the same job all their lives. They know how it works. Processing jute into rope and metal into wire isn't women's work. You've got it made here, girl. Play your cards right and all this might be yours one day. And when it is, Lockie here can help you out. I've had me eye on this place for a while. Neither of them has a clue, Lily. This place, it could be ours.'

Lily's expression was frozen somewhere between terror, disbelief and hope. For a fraction of a second, she dared to hope.

'And now, sit at your new desk and let's try it for size.'

The moment was gone. The warm smell from his jacket, the compassion in his eyes, gone.

'I can't, Lockie,' said Lily. 'I daren't. I just have a feeling about it. I'll have to take the tray downstairs for Mr McConaghy and his brother-in-law soon.'

'You can do that in a minute, but first, let's have ourselves a little swing in this chair.'

Lockie flopped into the green leather chair and placed both of his hands on the polished wooden arms. Then, planting his feet on the floor, he pushed off until the chair swivelled round and round.

Lily put her hand over her mouth and began to giggle.

'Have you ever seen anything like that!' Lockie exclaimed as the chair slowed down and he jumped off.

'I thought you were going to spin right off, I did!'

'Hang on, let me see how it works.' He removed his cap and, holding it in his hands, bent down and looked underneath the seat. 'Well, blimey, that's a nice bit of engineering, that is. It'll need a regular drop of oil, I would say, but those springs will last a lifetime. Well forged, they were. Come on, you, try it for size.'

He took Lily's cup and saucer out of her hand and, placing it on the desk, pushed her backwards into the chair, grabbed the arm, and spun her round and round and round.

'Lockie, stop. Lockie, don't,' was the only protest Lily could make as, caught off guard, she found herself flung back in the chair while Lockie propelled it round. She clung on to the arms for dear life.

She saw his face, she saw the door, she saw his face, she saw the door, she heard the bell. She saw Mrs McConaghy.

Her head was spinning so fast, her thoughts could not keep up, but she heard the laughter in Lockie's voice fade, sensed the atmosphere in the room changing as quickly as the temperature was dropping, felt the fresh blast of icy air from the open door.

Lockie grabbed the arm of the chair and Lily was flung forward. She tried to stand, but her legs failed to work and she slumped to the floor. She felt nauseous and dizzy, like a child who'd been spun round in a playground game of blind man's buff. Her legs were like jelly as she tried to grab the edge of the desk and heave herself up from the floor. She wanted to die with the shame of it.

Lockie stretched out his hand and with one pull she was on her feet. She swayed backwards slightly. Lockie pushed her forward. She was aware of something else hitting her senses. A smell. Of flowers, of scent. A lingering memory from the inside of the chemist's shop.

Her eyes focused as for the first time she realized that there was a young woman standing next to Mrs McConaghy. She had dark hair cut short below her ears in a sharp bob. Her lips were red, her hat made of fur, her coat woollen, and it was she who smelt of loveliness.

'I will ask once more. What on earth is going on here?' said Mrs McConaghy, who looked dismayed.

'Yes, do tell. We would love to know, wouldn't we, Auntie?'

The young woman purred as she placed her handbag on the new desk. Lily looked down and saw that her red leather booties had grey fur poking out around the ankle, matching the fur of her hat. For the first time in her life, Lily felt envious. She looked down at her own brown leather shoes, now years old. They had been worn every day since Sister Therese had acquired them on her behalf and were now stained almost black by the wet and the snow. Her feet were so frozen with the cold and the damp that her chilblains throbbed. She would have loved to own a pair of booties just like those.

'Is this my desk, Auntie?' asked the young woman.

'Yes, it is, Amy. I was hoping to have a word with you, Lily,' Mrs McConaghy added, with a hint of guilt in her voice. 'This is my niece, Amy Curran. She will be working here from today.'

Lily heard the faintest intake of breath from Lockie.

So this was the famous Amy. She of the escapee boyfriend.

Amy now sat on the edge of the desk and crossed her legs one over the other. Placing her hands on the green leather surface, she leant to the side. 'And who does this belong to?' she asked as she picked up Lily's cup and saucer.

Lily held out her hand to take the cup. She wanted to speak, but the realization that, just as she'd suspected, the desk was not for her, had made her tongue thick and immobile. She was angry with Lockie for having raised her hopes when, really, she should have known better. She saw her new hairbrush lying on the desk and held her breath, but it was too late, Amy had also seen it.

'Oh, is this for me? Is it a welcome present? Why, thank you.'

Amy picked up the hairbrush and walked to the mirror. She brushed her hair and Lily's heart stopped. It was the only new thing she had ever owned, apart from the headscarf, and she had been too afraid when she opened it to touch the brush to her hair. She had wanted to savour the moment. To let her hair down and brush her long locks slowly. Words failed her as Amy took the brush and, in one swift movement, opened the drawer of the desk and dropped the brush in.

Lily felt the tears prickle. It was all too much. Some days, life was too much. How could it be Amy's desk? She didn't work at the plant. That was where her desk lived.

She almost visibly shook herself. She would let

the crushing disappointment wash over her. Of course the desk wasn't for her. Why would it have been? Finally, she found her voice.

'I'm sorry, the cup is mine. I will move it now.'

Mrs McConaghy failed to make eye contact with Lily. That was the first time that had ever happened. From somewhere inside, a sense of injustice rose like bile in Lily's throat. She could never defend herself at home, and now, even at work, people were walking all over her.

'Please could I have my hairbrush back?' Her voice was a whisper.

'What did you say?' asked Amy. A menacing smile playing at the corner of her lips. She was making Lily squirm, she knew it and she was enjoying herself.

'Can I have my hairbrush back, please. You have put it in the desk drawer.'

'Oh, this.' Amy pulled open the drawer and held up the hairbrush. 'Well, all I can say is that Auntie must be paying you too much.'

She slapped the hairbrush down in the hand Lily held out. The palm of Lily's hand stung.

'Well, I'm off,' Lockie announced.

Lily realized he had moved from her side and was already standing by the door. He looked sheepish and shifty. He was obviously embarrassed.

'There's no ships in, Mrs McConaghy. Reckon I won't be back now until the morning.'

Lily wanted to run to the door and grab Lockie's arm and pull him back into the office. Don't leave me, she thought. Don't go. I don't want to be alone with this Amy. But it was too late. The bell above the door jangled again and without a backward glance, Lockie was gone.

Mrs McConaghy didn't waste any time. 'Amy is here to learn the ropes, Lily, and it's down to you to teach her. She will be working here from now on, won't you, Amy?'

Amy made no reply. She smiled at Lily. Not a friendly smile, but one that said, not if I can help it.

Amy was so perfect, she made Lily feel ugly and inadequate. Her clothes, her make-up, the way she spoke, her confidence and audacity, the way she swung her legs to and fro under the desk and smiled her half-mocking smile at Lily. It all made Lily feel thoroughly foolish.

She was also stunned by the new side she was seeing to Mrs McConaghy, who was at the sink, pouring the tea. She had never made a cup of tea in all the time Lily had worked there. She assumed it must be for Amy, and she was right. Mrs McConaghy waddled over, carrying the best cup and saucer. The one they kept for when Mr O'Hara from the bank called by.

'Here you go, warm yourself up. Don't spill any, though, on that beautiful coat.'

Lily's mouth fell open in disbelief. It was instantly apparent that Amy was making the most of being the only niece of the childless Mr and Mrs McConaghy. She clearly had them wrapped around her little finger and was benefiting greatly from the prosperity of the business. The way Mrs McConaghy had run her hand along the sleeve of Amy's coat told Lily one thing: she had bought it.

Lily wondered if being made to work in the office was Amy's punishment for having been caught with a boyfriend. That question was answered when Mrs McConaghy spoke.

'You see, Amy, all this will be yours one day soon, so you have to learn how it all works. And the only way to do that, love, is by working here, in the office, and learning from your aunt and Lily here. But of course you will be the boss. You understand that, don't you, Lily? Amy is family.'

Lily's heart sank. Working for the fashion-conscious, apparently cheeky, spoilt and lazy Amy was not an attractive prospect. She remembered all the whispers she had heard about her down on the plant floor. She liked Amy's father, but he was a soft man who was pushed around by the McConaghys. She knew he'd been hurt by the stories about his daughter.

'You're going to teach me the ropes, are you, Lily?' said Amy, her eyebrows arched as she removed her coat and handed it to Lily.

Lily's arm almost hit the floor. The coat was as heavy as little Joe. It was soft in her hand, and warm. A sweet aroma wafted up from the lining and Lily resisted the urge to press the coat to her cheek. To feel the quality, inhale the femininity she knew she did not possess, and absorb the warmth.

'I will teach you what I know, Miss Curran,' said Lily softly.

Mrs McConaghy smiled and looked more relaxed. 'That's a good girl, Lily,' she said as she made her way to the stairs leading down to the plant. No doubt to tell Mr McConaghy that Lily had been 'not a bit of trouble', thought Lily.

Amy's face softened. 'I'm Amy, Lily. That's all you have to call me.'

'Well, you know I'm Lily. I have to start the order book this morning and the time sheets for Christmas Eve have to be entered into the pay book.'

'Oh God,' groaned Amy. 'I don't want to be doing any of that stuff.' She looked towards the door.

Lily noticed that she seemed distracted, as though something else entirely was occupying her thoughts.

'Who was that bloke in here when we came in?'

'Who? Lockie?' asked Lily, surprised.

'Well, there was no other bloke in here, was there, when I arrived? Unless overnight I've become as stupid as you look?' snapped Amy.

'It was Lockie,' said Lily. Her cheeks burnt with shame from the insult as she hung up Amy's coat on the stand. For a fleeting second, she let it brush against her face while she took a deep breath.

'What was he doing here then?' said Amy as she strode around the office, picking up ledgers, examining what was written on the side and then dropping them again in disgust. Before Lily could answer, she snapped, 'I can't believe I'm being punished like this. In this dirty place. Hardly glamorous, is it, Lily? So, go on, what does he do?'

'He's one of the traders. He brings goods up from the docks, usually jute, quite often metal, and sells it to your uncle.'

'Does he make good money doing that?' Amy had walked over to the window and her gaze took in the full length of the Dock Road, the cobbles, and the dark grey river that blended into the dark grey sky all the way to the horizon.

'He does. They say he will have his own processing plant soon. Lockie is always the first down the docks every morning. It's the horse I feel sorry for.'

Amy turned around and folded her arms. 'Don't waste your sympathy on the horse. It's me you should be feeling sorry for, because I can tell you, this is the last place I want to be. You see out there . . .' Amy checked that she had Lily's attention. 'Out there is the Atlantic and it doesn't stop until it reaches New York. That's where I should be, New York. Not in this hellhole.'

Lily made no comment. She sat down at her desk and opened a ledger. The hellhole, as Amy referred to it, had kept her in employment and her siblings fed for three years.

'Is he married?' Amy barked the question. She stood with her back to Lily, still facing the river.

'Lockie? God, no. Who would marry Lockie?' Lily almost laughed. 'He lives at home with his mam and dad.'

'Does he have a girlfriend?'

Lily was taken aback. 'No, not as far as I know.'

'Is he sweet on you, Lily?'

Lily spluttered her response. 'No, never! Of course not.'

Amy turned round and stared at Lily long and hard. Satisfied that Lily had answered her truthfully, she replied, 'Good. Right, he will have to do then.'

And much to Lily's relief, that was the last word Amy addressed to her all day.

CHAPTER 12

On Sunday, Lily had taken the children to Mass and prayed that Mr and Mrs McConaghy would have very long lives and see no need to rctire in the near future. Spending a week with Amy had been a trial. Her selfishness knew no bounds.

'Oh God, Lily,' she'd said every time Mrs McConaghy left the room, 'is this not a living hell? I was not cut out for this. I've only been here a few days and it's killing me.'

Lily didn't see any point in telling Amy that she'd been there for three years and considered her job a lifeline. Even if she had told her, Amy wouldn't have cared. Amy was interested only in conversations that revolved around her.

'Tell them you don't want to work here,' said Lily.

'I wish I could! Never once when they were paying for my schooling did they say that it was because I was to be locked up like a prisoner in a dirty office all day long, in front of books and columns of boring figures. Lily, am I not better than that? Look at me. Do I look like someone who should be sitting at this dull, dull desk?'

As she spoke, she kicked the new desk with her foot and sent the chair spinning backwards into Lily's desk.

Despite herself, and despite Amy's condemning attitude, Lily began to laugh along with her.

'Oh God, we are both delirious with the tedium. Lily, does this powder match my complexion?' Amy had a habit of completely changing the subject without a second's warning, leaving Lily struggling to keep up. 'I don't want to be like Auntie, with a big orange line under my chin and around the side of my face.'

She clicked open her compact and studied her reflection in the mirror. She did this a dozen times a day.

Lily stepped over to her desk and gently removed the accounts Amy was supposed to be working on for her auntie. Mrs McConaghy had gone into town to meet a friend who was visiting from Ireland and would be back shortly. Lily had already learnt how to disguise her handwriting in order that Mrs McConaghy wouldn't guess she was doing Amy's work.

Lily, who had never owned a compact and only occasionally saw one of the women in the cottages wearing powder, had no idea what to say. She looked at Amy, who was pouting her lips in the mirror, licking the tips of her fingers and smoothing her eyebrows.

'It does suit you, Amy. You look lovely,' she said. It was the truth. Amy did look lovely. Of course she was dissatisfied, sitting in the McConaghys' office. Someone as beautiful as Amy was surely cut out for an entirely different life, thought Lily.

Outside the back door of the office, at the top of the stairs down to the processing plant floor, was a small wooden balcony, and at the bottom of the stairs was a tall, padlocked iron gate, to which only Mr and Mrs McConaghy and their brother-in-law held the keys. This ensured that traffic went only one way, from the office down. It prevented anyone on the plant floor from having access to the office, or, more critically, the safe. The only time the traffic changed course was on payday. The front door of the office opened on to a steep flight of concrete steps that led to the street. When traders had made their delivery to the plant at the rear, they received a note confirming the weight of their goods, then moved their wagons or drays round to the front and called into the office for payment.

As a way of amusing herself, Amy stood on the wooden balcony and waved to her father down on the plant floor.

'A real family girl, is Amy. Dotes on her, her father does – well, he did until . . .' Mrs McConaghy said several times to Lily, but she never went further than that.

Lily, who often used one word where others might have used five, never replied. She simply could not imagine being close to her own stepfather. But not for one minute did she think that Amy stood on the balcony to wave to her da. Amy was waving to the world, or at least to anyone who would look up at her and pass her a compliment.

'That's a nice frock, Amy,' someone would shout up when her da was out of earshot.

'Who did your hair today, Amy?' shouted another.

'Have you got yourself a fella? Good-looking girl like you?'

'Is there a pocket in your knickers, Amy, to keep the money your uncle is making?'

Lily wondered why Mrs McConaghy hadn't noticed that Amy only stood on the balcony to wave to her da just as he was leaving the plant floor, never when he was in the middle of working or had just arrived.

Lockie had provided Amy with her biggest distraction. She watched him through the window as he went up and down with his cob and cart, from the old dock to the door of the processing plant and back again, three, sometimes four times a day. He bought his jute as it was unloaded on the docks, transported it in cartloads up to the plant, and sold it to the McConaghys for a higher price. Lily would then take his delivery sheet, enter the figures into the ledger and then pass the banker's draft to Mrs McConaghy to sign. After which she would count out the cash or hand him a banker's note as payment.

Lockie had begun to pay Lily compliments of

late and she found she was enjoying them. She now looked forward to Lockie's deliveries whenever a ship came into the old dock. He had built up her confidence and made her feel less of an ugly duckling as a result of having to spend her days sitting in close proximity to the beautifully turned-out and fashionable Amy.

'Are you sure there is nothing going on between you and Lockie?' Amy had asked her a dozen or more times.

Each time, Lily had responded with the same comment. 'Amy, he is more like a brother to me. We were born neighbours and I've known him all me life.' But Lily was confused. Lockie was changing and she didn't know why.

When no one was looking, Lockie had begun whisper to Lily, 'Go on, Lily, come out with me tonight for a drink. You can trust me, we've known each other for years. I will treat you right, you can trust Lockie. Haven't you always been able to? Let me take you out for a bite and a walk about town.'

Lily's answer was always the same. 'I can't, Lockie. I have to look after the kids when I get home. You know I have responsibilities.'

'Let me come home and help you then, Lily,' he would plead. 'I'm one of nine, I'm used to kids, it doesn't bother me. Bloody hell, I know your mam and stepfather – isn't the reason he keeps his fists to himself because he knows he will have me to deal with if he doesn't?'

'He's from such a decent, hard-working family, is Lockie,' Mrs McConaghy would say. 'I knew his mother's family in Ireland. They have great religion and the old folk never touched a drop, any of them.' Mrs McConaghy always smiled fondly when she spoke of Lockie.

Lockie's interest, Mrs McConaghy's opinion and even Sister Therese's praise of Lockie set Lily's thoughts on a new path. Maybe she should say yes to one of his many invitations. He knew what her life was like.

'Go on, will you, Lily?' had been the last thing he'd said to her when she pushed him away. Maybe she shouldn't push any more because when she had, she'd seen a different look in his eyes. One of hurt and rejection.

'Even a worm can turn,' Mrs McConaghy said as she watched him from the window as he ran down the steps, shoulders hunched. 'You need to be careful there, Lily.'

'What are you whispering about then?' Amy had returned from the cloakroom and joined Lily and her auntie at the window. They all watched as Lockie jumped up on to his cart.

'We aren't whispering,' Lily snapped back, expecting Mrs McConaghy to give her away. She was embarrassed at having being caught out and terrified that Amy would discover the real reason.

'Seems that way if you ask me.' Amy twirled her bobbed hair in her fingers. 'Auntie?'

Mrs McConaghy ignored her question and said,

'Right, I'm off down to Sayers. 'What's your fancy today, girls?'

Amy looked Lily up and down with her perfect Max Factor kohl eyes, Goya lips and ill-concealed contempt. She took in Lily's worn clothes and shoes and Lily watched as a smile began at the corner of her mouth and then quickly disappeared. 'You would be lucky to land a good-looking bloke like Lockie. I've been making some enquiries. Every girl around here has her eye on him. He's first division, is Lockie, Lily. Looks, money and prospects. Way out of your league, love.'

Lily's breath left her body so quickly, she felt as though she had been dealt a blow to the stomach. Of course, Amy was right. But even if she couldn't have Lockie for herself in that way, he was her friend. Her only friend. He spoke to her like she was already his and she was his social equal. She felt her face redden under Amy's immaculate gaze. Looking down in shame, she stared at her shoes. Second-hand, scuffed, dirty. Every morning she sneaked into the toilets as soon as she arrived at work, slipped out the sodden piece of cardboard and replaced it with a fresh one. Without turning her head, she looked at Amy's shoes. Polished, leather, a kitten heel and a neat T-bar with a pearl-button fastening on the side. Why on earth did Lily think anyone would consider her someone worth talking to? Least of all Lockie. He could have any girl he wanted.

Lockie was good-looking. He was well built from

his hard physical work. His eyes were blue and twinkled with mischief and his dark hair was slicked back under his cap, giving his jawline a sharp edge. He worked hard, his business was growing and he had wonderful prospects in a city that was recovering from the war. Lily loved the freckles that dappled his nose and cheeks. But, there was no use in her daydreaming. No man would take on another man's children and she would never leave home without Katie and Joe.

Amy was right, Lockie was way out of her league. She felt crestfallen, committed to a life that would be shared with a pair of alcoholics until Joe was old enough to work, and by then it would be too late. She would be old and unattractive and past the marrying age.

'Oh God, you didn't really think you had a chance there, did you, Lily?' Amy roared with laughter.

'No, no, I didn't, not like that. I've known Lockie since I was a girl, he's always looked out for me,' she stammered. Her words were coming out all wrong and she knew that Amy would never believe her anyway.

It was Lockie who had shown the interest. Lily had done a good job of holding him at bay and making sure that there was no ambiguity. Her pride was intact. Lockie had not been misled. She had simply behaved like a lonely girl enjoying the company of the childhood friend who made her laugh.

At home time, Lily needed to change the cardboard in her shoe and as she did so, she overheard Amy talking to Mrs McConaghy.

'Auntie, do we have to have someone from Clare Cottages working here? Her hair smells some days and she wears the same things all the time. And have you seen the state of her shoes? They don't have soles and they're full of holes with cardboard stuffed in. She's not up to your standard, Auntie.'

'Her clothes are a darned sight better than they were on her first day,' replied Mrs McConaghy tartly. 'If you want to know what rags look like, you should have seen her then. Are you offering to do her work, Amy? Because unless you are, it might be best to keep your opinion to yourself. I know for a fact that Lily visits the public baths and the Clare Street wash house every week. I don't know how she manages it. Hardest-working person I know.'

'Look, queen . . .' Mr McConaghy had come into the office. Sensing a row brewing, he wanted to add his tuppence worth. Lily had never taken to him. He was a mean man and often treated the men who worked for him unkindly. 'Look, Amy, one day this will all be yours and you'll have to learn that in order to get on in business, you have to get along with everyone and employ people from all walks of life. We can't just employ girls like you, Amy. It's necessary to take on riff-raff because they have to do the grind so that we can get on with making the money.'

Lily waited for a moment and then, when her

breathing was calm enough so as not to make her appear flustered, she walked back into the office with her head held as high as she could manage.

'Goodnight, Mrs McConaghy,' she said as she passed the older woman. She had meant for her voice to sound firm and proud. It let her down and came out as nothing more than a squeak.

'Goodnight, Lily. See you in the morning.'

Lily said no more, but as she went out of the front door, she let it bang shut behind her.

The following day, Lockie tried his luck one last time.

'I can't,' said Lily. 'I've told you a thousand times, Lockie, I have responsibilities. Why don't you ask Amy?'

'Amy? No, she's not for me. Too expensive and high and mighty. Money burns a hole in the purse of women like Amy. Lily, are you mad? You can't live your life looking after your brother and sister. You know that now, don't you?'

'I do, yes, but it's difficult.'

'What do you mean, difficult?' he asked. 'What does difficult mean, Lily? That tells me nothing.'

'It is just very difficult. They need me . . . .' Her voice trailed off. She wasn't even convincing herself. She had toyed with the idea of taking up Lockie's offer, but Amy had killed off the happiness she'd felt at his attentions.

This time Lockie didn't wait for any further explanation. He snatched his draft out of her hand

228

and turned away. Lily's heart belonged to little Joe, but she hoped Lockie would remain her friend.

'What were you talking to Lily about, Lockie?' Amy had sidled up to Lockie at the door just as he pulled it open with some force, ready to leave. Their silhouettes were dark and framed in the morning sunlight and neither of them saw the frown cross Lily's face when, turning from locking the safe, she caught sight of them.

'Nothing, Amy, just chatting,' Lockie replied.

But Lily saw it the moment it happened, as Lockie turned around and took a second look at Amy. She saw the temptation of possibility cross his face. How could it not? Amy was smiling up at him and fluttering her Rimmel-coated eyelashes. Her lips had been freshly painted ruby red and she always smelt of powder, petals and sweetness. Lily, who owned nothing in the way of make-up or cosmetics, could only wonder at how she did it.

The previous evening, she had wandered into Woolworths as she waited for the bus home and looked at the palettes of eye-shadow colours and lipsticks. She was in awe of the nail varnishes and the ten different fragrances of talcum powder. As she smelt one of the bottles of perfume, she recognized it as belonging to Amy. It was the smell that filled the office in the mornings. Gardenia. She knew it was a smell she would never want to own herself.

As Amy looked up at Lockie, she was almost

licking her lips. She was pretty and she knew it, and now so did Lockie. 'Do you want to take me out, Lockie?' she said. Lily blinked, hard. She could barely believe the audacity of Amy asking Lockie out, just like that. 'Go on, you know you want to. I am so bored in this office all day. Why don't you take me to the pub after work? I'd let you. Go on, Lockie, I dare you to ask me.'

Lockie gabbled a reply that went something like, 'I can't really, Amy, I'm meeting up with the lads in the Grapes, already promised. Err, have to go now,' and before he left, he threw Lily a look that told her it was her fault.

He would never ask her out again. She had turned him down once too often and, set against the eager Amy, she had been found wanting. Lily felt relieved. She wished him well. She wished him better than Amy.

But as the door closed behind Lockie, it felt to Lily as though the brightness of the day had left with him. The office suddenly seemed dull and the sense of loss and loneliness that hit her took her by surprise. Her heart crunched as she wondered if he would ever speak to her again.

Mrs McConaghy, who had stepped out of the office momentarily, returned. 'Come along, girls, neither of you earn us a good day's profit by chatting to traders.'

'I'm sorry, Mrs McConaghy,' said Lily straight away.

Amy didn't say a word. She flounced back

down into her chair with the grace of a sack of potatoes and, picking up her pen, pulled a face at Mrs McConaghy behind her back.

From that day on, Lockie spent less time dawdling in the office than he had before. There was less chat and banter and, one day, he didn't speak to Lily at all, just addressed Mrs McConaghy directly as she handed him his banker's draft. Lily watched him through the window as he ran down the steps two at a time. Her heart felt heavy at the sight of him. He was the only person who had ever enquired about her life or paid her any attention. She couldn't have him for a boyfriend and it appeared he didn't want her for anything else. In her naïveté, she had supposed that their banter and chatter would carry on as before, but it had almost stopped dead. She had spurned a suitor and lost a friend. Her eyes filled with tears.

'Well, if you ask me, you were a fool letting that boat sail, and that's a fact,' said Mrs McConaghy as she locked the safe.

Lily looked back at her in shock. She had no idea Mrs McConaghy had been aware of her conversations with Lockie.

'It's a pity, especially as he's doing so well. Works hard, that young man does. Brings us twice as much as he did when he first started. Mr McConaghy said we need to box clever or Lockie will be opening his own processing works and we will lose his business. Seems to me he is casting his net in another direction altogether, in more ways than one. It doesn't do to set your eyes above your station in life, Lily, if that is what you've done. You won't do any better than Lockie, and sure, I can't see any other reason why you would spurn a nice fella like him. He would have been a very nice catch for you. God only knows what you thought you were doing. Never mind, his loss is our gain. You'll be working for us for a little longer now then. No marriage taking you away.'

Lily turned back to the office window. Lockie had jumped on to his cart and was lifting the reins to wake his nodding cob. She willed him to look up at the window, but she knew he wouldn't. She had been honest and that was all she could do. She couldn't change her life and she couldn't just head off and leave little Joe and Katie to be taken into the home on Menlove Avenue. Besides, she had enough on her plate.

Joe had been ill that morning and Lily had begged her mother to stay at home with him. 'Please don't go to the alehouse until I get back, Mam. Please don't leave him,' she'd pleaded as she left the house. 'His breathing, it's really bad today. Can you take him to the doctor's?'

'I will if I have to, now it's free,' her mother said with a scowl. 'But the last time I did that, they made me take him to St Angelus and we just sat there all day and then they told me to take him home again. They said it's all in his head, remember? And I believe them. They all told me that, up at the hospital. So what's the point of me taking him? I'm not going through all those shenanigans again.'

Lily knelt down beside Joe, who was lying on what passed for a rag rug in front of the fire. At least her mother had been concerned enough to light the fire; that was some blessing. Joe was flushed and pink, his wheeze louder than usual. He was struggling. The air in the house was blue with her mother's cigarette smoke. Joe coughed and choked.

'I'll be home as quick as I can, love,' Lily whispered to him. 'You just stay there and don't move. Are you all right?'

Joe opened his eyes. They were filled with fear. The only person he felt safe with was Lily.

'Don't fret. You know I'll be straight home, don't you? If you feel a bit rough or sad, just think to yourself, "Lily's back soon." You got that?'

'I'll be good, Lily,' Joe wheezed. 'Can I play with your hair?' he begged.

Lily smiled. Joe liked to wrap his fingers in her long chestnut hair. Sometimes, when she was sleeping, he would carefully undo the knots of the rags she tied in her hair at night and take them out one by one, in order that he could better run her hair through his fingers.

Lily planted a kiss on his brow, then placed her hand on his forehead. 'I won't be long. Katie will be home from school before I'm back from work. She'll look after you.'

Joe had tried to smile, but he was distracted by his own discomfort and looked unconvinced.

When six o'clock came, Lily laid down her pen, shot out of the seat and took her coat off the hook.

'Well, you are keen to leave, aren't you,' said Mrs McConaghy. 'You are a good worker, I'll give you that, and you have a lovely hand, but you're always quick to be out of the door.' She sniffed in disapproval, but Lily didn't care. She had struggled to put Joe to the back of her mind all day long while she'd been working and she was now desperate to get the bus home and reassure herself that he was all right.

'Amy has already left.' Lily's voice was little more than a whisper, but Mrs McConaghy had heard her.

'Yes, well, she was running an errand for Mr McConaghy.'

Lily knew this was not true, but she had little interest in Amy; it was Joe she was concerned about. Without another word, she ran out of the door.

Sitting on the steamy bus, Lily wiped a circle in the misted-up window and looked out into the dark night. The street glowed amber from the sulphur street lamps. Shop lights were being extinguished and black-out shutters, relics from the war that were still used in places, were slammed shut and locked as workers made their way home. The only buildings to bustle and brighten as the night wore on were the public houses.

As the bus pulled into the stop outside the Grapes, the pub door flew open and noise and light from its welcoming coal fire spilled out on to the pavement as workers piled inside. There was no mistaking what Lily saw. Amy in her fur-trimmed coat and high heels was standing outside the pub door and she was holding Lockie's hand. With a jolt, Lily sat back in the seat. She willed the bus driver to move on quick lest either Amy or Lockie should jump on board. It was the last thing she had expected to see. The shock sent a wave of prickles running across her skin.

'You stupid girl,' she whispered to herself as she took one of Sister Therese's handkerchiefs out of her pocket. She had no idea why she felt so lonely. It was the glimpse of the pub, of people having fun, of office- and shop-girls like her rushing to meet each other and have a drink in front of the open fires in the amber-lit pub. She noticed their clothes, their shoes, their handbags and their Outdoor Girl make-up, the uniform of the shop-girl, and pulled her wicker basket further up her knee and closer to her, almost hugging it protectively. Inside was a scone and two barley sugars Mrs McConaghy had dropped on her desk as she'd passed her the luncheon-meat sandwiches she'd provided for lunch. Lily had been so hungry and light-headed, she'd eaten all of the sandwich and now she felt sick with guilt and anticipation. What would she find when she arrived home?

The bell on the bus rang and as they pulled away she let out a sigh of relief. She would know soon enough. As she sat back on the hard green leather seats, she thought to herself, you are someone, Lily, who must never expect nice things to happen to you. But even as she thought this, her heart was contracting with pain at having seen Amy with Lockie. She knew Amy well enough by now; if she wanted Lockie, she would have him.

Lily blinked away the tears and took rapid shallow breaths to steady the burning in her chest. Most of the time she looked on the bright side. When Joe cuddled up to her in bed and twiddled her hair, she knew the love of a mother for her child was no greater than what she felt for her little brother. But today had been a bad day, spent worrying about Joe, being stung by Mrs McConaghy's comments and ignored by Amy. And now, seeing the man she had known her entire life holding hands with another, she could not help feeling sorry for herself and the miserable life she led. His interest had made her feel validated. Now that it was well and truly gone, she felt wretched and worthless.

Her eyes were red by the time she climbed the concrete steps to the half landing and walked along the walkway to their front door. The light was on and the fire was lit, but the house was unusually quiet. As she entered, she saw that Katie was at the chipped Formica-topped table eating a hot supper and Sister Therese was sitting on one of the four hard wooden chairs with Joe on her lap. 'Your mam and da are out, Lily,' Sister Therese said. 'Katie here came and got me. She thought that Joe was getting worse.'

Lily glanced at Katie, who was looking a little sheepish. 'It's OK, love,' she said as she went over and kissed the top of her sister's head.

Sister Therese continued. 'Joe here, he's had a bad day, but we are over the worst of it now, aren't we, little lad?' She jiggled Joe up on her knee to make him more comfortable and gave him the biggest smile. 'His breathing began to ease at around four o'clock and I would say that he is much better now.'

Lily looked down at Joe. She had spent many days like that with him on her lap and she knew the signs; he was very much over the worst. His inhalations were almost the same length as his exhalations. The wheeze had become a whistle. Lily knelt down on the floor and threw a shovel of coal on the fire. The bucket was full. Sister Therese had been busy.

'I got the coalman to drop a hundredweight of coal into the coal house, and he doesn't want paying, before you waste your breath objecting,' she said.

Lily wanted to kiss her. She knew the cold often made Joe's chest worse. But this did not prevent her parents from drinking away the coal money, no matter how often the facts were presented to them. They would sit in the warmth of the alehouse without a second thought for their children, as long as they had a tankard in their hands.

'What am I going to do, Sister Therese? How much longer can we go on like this? I feel at the end of my tether.'

Lily began to cry and Sister Therese stroked her hair. She wished she had an answer. She had a dozen families like this, who depended on her to hold things together. Families whose fathers had returned from the war more useless than they'd been before they left. Lost, damaged or just plain lazy, they took solace in the public house, and as there was a pub on almost every corner, they were spoilt for choice.

'Shall I visit the welfare officer tomorrow, Lily?' Sister Therese asked the question she knew Lily was dreading having to answer. 'I think these two will have to come into our care in the home at St Chad's, but the welfare might have different ideas. What do you think? I won't do it without you, but your mam, she lied to me. I popped out for the Angelus Mass and she told me she would stay with them both, but when I returned, she was gone. We can keep them until they are fourteen. You would have to remain here, or you could find lodgings. I will help you to do that. You have no life here, child. If we don't do something, this will be it for you, for ever. I can see no way out.'

Lily buried her head in Sister Therese's lap. In just one day it felt like she had lost everything.

CHAPTER 13

Biddy was delighted to see that the bingo hall was only half full when she arrived.

'I'm going to try and get there a bit early,' she'd said to Elsie that morning at the hospital, when they'd stopped for a tea break. 'I hate those new red shiny seats. My backside keeps slipping off. I can't get meself up on to the flamin' things.'

She purchased her bingo books and, stuffing them into her coat pocket, trotted over to the seat she hoped would still be vacant. It was Welsh Hattie's seat, which made her want it even more. A grin of sheer pleasure slipped on to her face as she secured the coveted stool, even though it took three attempts to haul herself up on to it, putting one hand on the new high tables and her foot on the dazzlingly shiny chrome rest.

'God in heaven, I deserve to win for this effort alone,' she muttered as she undid the buttons on her coat, cursing herself. 'Jesus, I should have took it off before I started the climb up.' Out of breath, she turned round to see if Elsie had come in yet and almost fell off the stool as it swivelled round with her. She grabbed the table and swore. She decided to leave her coat on until Elsie arrived and could help her.

There was more than the bingo at stake tonight. Biddy had sent a nervous Elsie on a spying mission and she needed to know whether or not Elsie had been successful. 'Keep your eye out for any letters or notes from Miss Van Gilder to Matron, or from Matron to her. You get to polish the desk every day, it shouldn't be hard.'

Elsie had frowned. 'But what if I get caught?' And Biddy had felt her patience slipping away faster than her pay packet.

'You won't get caught, soft girl. Wait until Matron has gone on her rounds, or takes that vicious little dog of hers down to the park.'

Matron was nothing if not a creature of habit and every day at 1 p.m. exactly, whatever the weather, she took Blackie on his daily walk around the Lovely Lane Park. Blackie had a temper as dark as the colour of his coat. Nonetheless, Matron loved him like a child. He spent most of his time in a basket behind her desk and the only time he didn't accompany her was on her morning and evening ward rounds.

Biddy knew Elsie would deliver. If she could have spent the time in Matron's rooms herself, she would have, but that would have raised suspicions. Elsie being caught at Matron's desk would need no explanation. Elsie had been Matron's housekeeper for many years. She had polished the large oak desk every single day and was a valuable source of important information, but Biddy had never asked her to write anything down before. This deviation from the norm had spooked Elsie somewhat.

Biddy cast her eyes across to the ladies' toilets. She would need to go soon. 'Thank the Holy Mother for small mercies,' she said as she slipped her hands below her rear and across the seat to make it look as though she was smoothing her coat beneath her. She was dry. She had Sister Haycock to thank for that and for forcing her to seek help. Sister Haycock had transformed her life. Before, she would never have made it at a trot from home to the bingo hall without having some kind of accident. She blessed herself. It was a miracle. Almost as much of a miracle as the fact that she was perched on one of the few shiny red plastic-covered stools not ripped across the middle and ready to snag at her stockings.

'You'll be in trouble on that stool,' said a gentle voice from behind her. It was Doreen O'Prey, the clerk from casualty. This was her first week back at work since the attack, and tonight was her first time out. Her mam was with her.

'I don't give a monkey's, Doreen. Hattie Lloyd can whistle. First here as far as I'm concerned. Where are you sitting, love?' she asked in a kinder voice. 'Amongst friends, I hope. Mind you, everyone here is your friend, Doreen, you don't need to fret. Are you holding up, love?'

Doreen gave Biddy a look loaded with gratitude.

'I am, thanks, Biddy. I'm expecting there will be some who won't be able to help themselves. Best get it over and done with, eh? I've been long enough in ward two and indoors.'

'Oi, you, what you doing on my seat? Give it back!' Welsh Hattie squealed in her Swansea accent as she dashed through the door.

'Get lost! Does it have your name written on the bottom?' said Biddy in a tone few dared to challenge.

Elsie was just behind Hattie, handing over her shilling to the doorman and waving her hand in the air to signal to Biddy she was there. 'Keep me a seat,' she mouthed to Biddy as Hattie made for the stool next to Biddy.

Biddy placed her bag down on top of the vacant stool with a definitive thud and folded her arms, glaring at Hattie. Few women argued with Biddy. Hattie took the message with little grace and, pulling a face at Biddy, flounced off.

'Please yerself,' she threw over her shoulder as she made for the nearest empty seat. 'You're the hard-faced one, aren't you,' she said to Doreen as she stormed past. 'I wouldn't be showing me face around here for a while. And you, Biddy, you wonder why the Irish have a bad name in Liverpool. Very churlish behaviour, that is.'

Biddy snorted. 'Well, if ye want to know why they call the Welsh dirty, take a look at yer kitchen floor when you get home, and wonder no more.'

Some of the women sitting around giggled and

some told Biddy to hush. Others gestured to Doreen to come over and join them. The lights were dimming and the bingo caller stepped on to the stage to take his place. Bingo was a serious business. No distractions were tolerated, not even from Biddy.

The sound of handbags being clicked open and shut filled the hall. Woodbines, roll-ups, Swan Vesta matches, pens, spectacles, handkerchiefs and boiled sweets were being extracted and laid in the middle of the long tables, ready to begin.

The room smelt of damp wool and cigarette smoke as the wide old radiators pumped out the heat. The sound of the rain danced on the tin roof of the hall and against the windows and Biddy blessed herself and gave thanks for having made it in before the heavens opened. Elsie had not been quite so lucky.

'Jesus, I thought I would never get here,' said Elsie as she took off her headscarf and, shaking it, sprayed rainwater all over Biddy. 'Was that Hattie having a go at poor Doreen?'

'It was. How did you guess?'

'Oh, give me a break. When did that woman ever not seize the chance to be mean to someone? No, I knew it, the minute I saw Doreen. Hattie's mouth must be dripping blood from the sharpness of her tongue.'

Elsie unclipped her handbag and began to mine her essential possessions for her regular Monday night of entertainment. All the women who worked at the hospital spent two evenings a week at the bingo, Mondays and Thursdays. The addicted, and there were many, travelled on the bus to Everton on a Friday and, away from the priest's prying eyes, to the Dingle on a Sunday night too.

Biddy looked over to see where Doreen had settled. 'Ah, that's a stroke of luck,' she said. 'She's sitting with Maisie Tanner and the crowd from Arthur Street. They'll take good care of her.'

Elsie looked up and waved to Maisie. 'Her Pammy's going to be on casualty soon, she'll be working with Doreen now she's back. She's a brave girl, after what she's been through.' A hint of sadness had slipped into Elsie's voice and Biddy detected it immediately. Elsie had had her own problems with her Martha before she'd married Jake and the worry had taken its toll.

'Don't be fretting, Elsie,' Biddy said in a no-nonsense tone. 'Your Martha is the happiest girl around here now and maybe Doreen will be one day too. It's all in the past. Doreen is a brave girl, she's moving on and isn't that tough to do with the likes of Hattie Lloyd sniping at your back? But she's no braver than your Martha. She's had her trials too and it all worked out for her.'

Elsie sighed and, nodding her agreement but making no further comment, continued to extract her bingo paraphernalia from her bag.

Biddy watched as Elsie's belongings began to fill the table. Along with the usual accoutrements of the game, Elsie took out her lucky leprechaun from Galway, her lucky pencil, which had been blessed by the priest back home, a brown paper bag of broken biscuits – 'in case we get a bit peckish; never like to be without food' – a penknife in a leather sheaf in case her pencil lead snapped, and her Bible.

'Elsie, we are at the bingo, not on retreat,' said Biddy, exasperated, as she eyed the Bible.

'You know I can't win a penny if I don't have everything with me,' whispered Elsie. 'I have me lucky bloomers on too – you know, the ones with no elastic at the bottom of the legs. Helps me to get on and off the stool easier. They don't cut the blood off at the top of me legs if they slide up. I felt faint once.'

'Would ye help me off with me coat?' Biddy put her arm out straight and gripped the table. 'I thought you were getting here a bit earlier. Did you do what I asked?'

Elsie grabbed at the cuff of Biddy's coat and began to tug. 'I would have been here ages ago, but Miss Bone Grinder wasn't happy with her room and I had to make up the guest room for her. The one the visiting consultants use. I thought Matron would kick up a fuss, but, no, not a bit of it. She let her pick whatever room she wanted. Imagine that! I always keep that room for when Dr Gaskell has one of the big nobs from the TB committee staying, but now it's Assistant Matron's.'

'When is her first proper day?' asked Biddy as she changed hands and held out the other arm.

'Eyes down, ladies!' shouted Al, the caller. 'Does everyone have a full set of books? Beryl is coming round now, so if you are feeling that little bit extra lucky tonight, buy another couple of books. I've kissed each one as a bonus, you lucky ladies.'

Beryl, showing off her beehive hairdo and enormous bosom, minced past the end of the tables with the bingo books held aloft in her hand, looking more like a magician's assistant than the woman who worked as a cleaner by day and a bingo-hall attendant by night.

'That's a Playtex bra she's wearing,' said Elsie disapprovingly as she finally removed Biddy's coat. 'Makes the nipples stick up and out.'

'What in the name of God are you talking about, Elsie?' asked Biddy as she folded her coat and slipped it under the desk.

'Beryl, the caller's assistant. Look at her.' Elsie nodded without any subtlety whatsoever towards Beryl's breasts as she passed them.

'Extra books, ladies,' Beryl purred in an affected voice. 'Sixpence for one, a shilling for three.'

'I saw her in T.J. Hughes yesterday, buying two. They have them in from America. A bit too in-your-face if you ask me. If anyone is feeling an extra bit lucky, it must be Al, because I can't see any man around here with the money to throw away on Playtex bras – and not one but two! It's him what's bought them. She never got the money for them from her Sidney. They're definitely carrying on, those two. Fancy taking money from a man to buy a bra.'

'It's not the bra he's giving her money for, Elsie. And besides, you're only jealous,' said Biddy. She couldn't tear her eyes away from Beryl's breasts. They looked as though someone had blown them up. They stuck out at the ends in two firm points. She looked down at her own. They rested on one of her extra belly folds. 'No matter how much money I had,' she said to Elsie, 'it would take more than a Playtex bra to do anything with my pair. I doubt a crane would work.'

'And eyes down, it's number four, the number of teeth on a whore.'

'Talking about your missus, again, Al?' a woman shouted from somewhere in the direction of where Hattie was sitting.

Al grinned and, rolling his eyes, continued. 'And it's all the sixes, clickety-click.'

Both ladies looked down at their books; only Biddy placed a cross in a box.

'Anyway, Bone Grinder, she's ready for action,' Elsie whispered. 'She'll be out and about in the hospital very soon, if you ask me.'

Al had called four numbers and Elsie hadn't got a single one. She motioned for Beryl to bring her an extra book for the next game and extracted her purse.

'Did you copy anything from the note she sent to Matron?' asked Biddy, who'd just got legs eleven.

'Dirty Gertie, number thirty,' Al called.

'That your mother-in-law then?' shouted Hattie,

who loved to flirt with the caller, the only woman in the hall not to have realized that Beryl had beaten her to it.

'Ooh, don't spoil my evening, Hattie,' shouted Al. 'I'd rather have to put up with a vicious dog than my mother-in-law. At least a dog lets go.'

The women in the hall roared with laughter at the joke they had heard Al tell so many times before. It wasn't just about playing the bingo, although that was exciting enough. The women met in the hall for a laugh, for the craic. Something to keep them going through the days of never-ending, repetitive, hard, physical work.

'Line!' A shout rang out and the hall filled with the sound of groans from thwarted would-be winners.

'One more number and I would have had that,' said Biddy. 'I was nearly there. I feel lucky tonight, I do.'

'Would you do the honours, Beryl, please, and check that line. I need a drink,' shouted Al as he picked up his pint of Guinness and let it pour down his neck, closing his eyes in ecstasy.

Elsie took advantage of the gap in the calling. 'I copied as much as I could. Here, I couldn't really understand all the writing, but I did me best.' She took a sheet of paper out of her bag with her purse and thrust it at Biddy before locating her sixpence.

'It's a line, Al!' shouted Beryl as she handed over the half-a-crown prize money. 'And don't spend it all at once,' she said to the lucky lady as she minced away towards Elsie with her extra book.

'Who was that?' asked Elsie.

'I couldn't see,' Biddy replied. 'One of the women down at the front.'

'The kitchen girls are down there tonight,' said Elsie. 'Like they need any luck. Not one of them leaves St Angelus with an empty bag. It's no coincidence their kids are the fattest on the street. Saw one of them taking home a whole tray of jam sponge only last week.'

'I don't begrudge them that,' said Biddy. 'After all, they work for a pittance. You forget how well paid you and I are, Elsie.'

Elsie harrumphed, but she couldn't argue. She and Biddy had worked their way up to the top of the pile. Making sure no one toppled them was a constant pressure, yet the army of St Angelus domestics below them had little idea how much they owed to the united forces of Dessie, Elsie and Biddy.

'Settle down, ladies,' shouted Al. 'We are off again. Two fat ladies!' he called, and Biddy and Elsie marked their books.

'What those kitchen women don't know,' Elsie said, 'is that it's us being one step ahead of everything what keeps their jobs safe.'

Biddy was reading the note Elsie had copied from Matron's office. 'Keep your eye on my numbers, Elsie,' she snapped as she read. When she'd finished, she folded the sheet in half and, opening her handbag, slipped it in.

'Is everything all right, Biddy?' asked Elsie.

'Well, it's nothing that can't be sorted, but 'tis

a fact, the biggest threat to our jobs is putting herself to bed right now, I'm guessing, in the accommodation corridor.'

The shout 'House!' pierced the air and they looked across and saw Hattie waving her book around.

'Bring your book to the front, please, Hattie,' shouted Al. 'I need to see a full house for meself.'

'Oh, for God's sake. Did she buy her books from the Holy Mother herself or from Sandra at the door?' said Elsie. 'She wins almost every week.' Each woman played to win, but no one liked it when someone they knew was repeatedly lucky. Harmony on the streets was achieved by virtue of the fact that they were all equal. Everyone struggled to the same degree.

'I'm calling in to Dessie's on the way home to show him this letter,' said Biddy. 'Are you coming with me?'

'I can't, Biddy. I would, but Jake has had to go and help one of his aunties in Bootle and Martha is on her own. Said I would call in on me way back. She's really feeling the pregnancy now. Getting bigger every day.'

Biddy felt a pang of jealousy. With none of her children living at home, all of them having flitted and none of them having been in contact for years, she never saw her grandchildren. Biddy was as alone in the world as Emily Haycock, she just hid it better because, unlike Emily, Biddy's job as housekeeper at the school was of little importance in the hierarchy of St Angelus.

'What auntie? I never knew he had an auntie in Bootle,' said Biddy, who was always suspicious of behaviour that was out of the ordinary.

'He said she was at the wedding. You would have seen her. There were loads of them. That's the problem with weddings today, full of widows and men with false legs or arms or wearing eye patches.'

'We can't help the effect of the war, Elsie. Nothing we can do about that.'

The room began to settle down once again as Hattie made her way back to her seat, but not before she'd caught sight of Biddy and Elsie and thrown them both a raspberry. 'Shame you aren't sat with me, ladies. Missed out on a drink, you did there. Always generous with me winnings, I am.'

Elsie and Biddy grimaced back.

'That's not all you're generous with, is it, Hattie,' said Biddy.

But Hattie didn't hear as she slipped back into her seat with her neighbours and workmates from the hospital kitchens.

As they turned the pages of their book to begin the next game, Biddy pondered on the contents of the note Elsie had copied. She had done well. It was a letter written by Miss Van Gilder to Matron about hospital staffing. Next to the words *domestic staff* she had written the words *agency, efficiency, cost-effective, electric floor-cleaners*. Biddy had no idea what an agency was, but she didn't like the sound of it at all.

'I can feel it in me water, we are going to have trouble on our hands with this new assistant matron,' she said to Elsie.

They were a formidable team when it came to dealing with trouble, but Biddy knew, as useless as she thought most men were – and personal experience had played a huge role in influencing her opinion, her husband and sons included – she could achieve only half as much without the cooperation of Dessie.

She didn't really enjoy the rest of the game. The word *agency* ate away at her and she wanted to discuss it with Dessie as soon as she could.

Elsie didn't enjoy the game much either. While she had been watching Biddy's card, number thirty-two had come up, but Elsie had failed to mark it. She had been busy lighting a ciggie and putting her bag back down and trying to see what was on her own card when she heard one of the other women shout out, and the moment was gone.

'Was that house?' Biddy asked. 'That was bloody quick. Must have got nearly all of them.'

'I don't know, can't see.'

And then they heard Maisie Tanner. 'Isn't that great, everyone, it's Doreen!' And the tin roof almost blew off as everyone began to cheer and clap and whistle, even fickle Hattie Lloyd.

'Oh God, she would have killed me if she'd known,' Elsie said to her daughter, Martha, as she sat down in her kitchen an hour later. 'The house was hers. I was supposed to be watching the numbers, but Doreen got it instead.'

'Ah well, that's nice, Mam. Doreen deserves it. You did Doreen a good turn there. She hasn't worked for weeks, she could do with the money. Don't tell Biddy, then,' Martha said as she poured them both some tea. 'How much was the prize?'

'It was only two pounds, but she would have found it useful. God, I feel awful. I panicked. I could have told her and she could have claimed it because her number was called first. She would have bitten me head off though, and that's a fact. Maisie Tanner sent round a hat and we all put a shilling in and Maisie gave that to Doreen at the end of the night. She was a mess, Doreen. In floods of tears. You should have seen the state of her, but I think she was happy too.'

'It's no wonder she still gets a bit tearful. Thank goodness Matron kept her job open for her, though. Poor Doreen, imagine if she'd had to go and look for another one after all that. Sometimes Matron is her own worst enemy, don't you think, Mam? Everyone thinks she's as tough as old boots, but she is a good woman for all that.'

Elsie nodded. She knew Matron better than most. 'How long will Jake be then?' she asked.

'He will be on the bus now, I guess. His aunt's moved into one of the new tin houses and she wanted him to put up a curtain rod.'

'When that baby arrives, you make sure he's not

253

at everyone's beck and call,' said Elsie. 'He can stop doing favours for people when he's a dad. Which reminds me, could you ask him to pop into mine after work tomorrow? There's water on the floor under the kitchen sink and I cannot for the life of me work out where it's coming from,' Elsie added without a hint of irony in her voice.

'Mam, I'm going to ask Auntie Biddy to be a godmother to the baby. Her and Uncle Dessie. What do you think?'

Elsie put her cup down and thought for a moment. 'I think that would make her day, Martha. Biddy always needs to be fussing about someone. I feel sorry for her, but I can never tell her that. Not one of her kids contacts her. You do that, Martha. Your baby can have two nanas in one street for the price of one.'

CHAPTER 14

Miss Van Gilder fastened the silver buckle on her assistant matron's belt and then drew back the heavy curtains on the tall, mullioned windows which overlooked the frost-covered car park of St Angelus. She could tell by the painted pictures of Squirrel Nutkin that the children's wards ran adjacent to the accommodation block. As she looked across, every now and then she would catch a glimpse of a nurse with a baby or a child in her arms, pointing out of the window to passers-by in an attempt to soothe the fretting child.

'Mummy will be here soon,' she could imagine the nurse was probably saying.

No, Mummy would not.

Miss Van Gilder had read only that week that there were moves to allow parents to visit their children when they were in-patients; that there was a school of thought suggesting that separating children from their mothers could do psychological harm. 'What a lot of old rot,' she had exclaimed out loud. She would never allow that to happen. She had been at St Angelus for just a few days and could already tell that rules needed to be tightened there, not relaxed.

The westerly wind that blew across from the Mersey had frozen her to the bone, and the frost had been in permanent attendance from the day she'd arrived. She thought of St Dunstan's and how she had moved from pillar to post ever since, under a cloud. When Sister Haycock had contacted her requesting a name and address so that St Angelus could ask for a testimonial, she'd been thrown slightly. It had to be St Dunstan's. She would be safe. Matron at St Dunstan's was too arrogant and proud. She would do anything to avoid any criticism being levelled at the running of her hospital. There were moves to force her to retire, but she was resisting. No, the matron at St Dunstan's would not say a word. No one else would catch up with her. Not here, she thought to herself. I am too far north for anyone to know me. Not here.

Matron had been away since she'd arrived, visiting her elderly mother, and today was to be their first formal meeting. Miss Van Gilder had not wasted her time, however, and had made it her business to visit every ward and department in the hospital and to announce, in her own special way, that she had arrived. She had only clashed with one sister, Sister Antrobus, who had quite recently been put in charge of casualty. The air had bristled with resentment the moment the two women met.

'I would like to go through with you your reporting of admissions and how you allocate patients to beds, please,' Miss Van Gilder had said.

'And why would that be?' Sister Antrobus had enquired. 'It is done the same way it has been done in this hospital since 1932.' She had pulled herself up to her full height. The fine, downy hair on the back of her neck prickled with mistrust.

'And that, Sister Antrobus, is exactly why I would like to take a look. I am amazed that Matron has not felt the need to bring the reporting procedure into line with NHS protocols.'

'And what would they be?' asked Sister Antrobus. 'We allocate patients to the wards with empty beds. It isn't brain surgery. In the winter, we are often tight and we can have children on the geriatric wards, but we do what we have to do. Unless of course, in your role as assistant matron, you can magic up some beds.'

'Why were you moved from ward two?' Miss Van Gilder didn't mince her words. Not a muscle moved in her face; her jaw was set, her eyes fixed on her prey.

Sister Antrobus was speechless. Caught unawares. She had been diminished by her past indiscretion, then forgiven by Matron, but only just. Her lip wobbled, her gaze faltered. She folded her arms firmly across her chest, to protect herself and ward off any further attacks, but it was useless, she was beyond help.

'Well?' Miss Van Gilder smelt blood. Her first

blow had wounded her opponent. 'Gynae is a coveted ward. Never in my life have I known a sister walk away from gynae. Not unless she was going mad or sickening for something, or, of course, if she had misbehaved. There used to be a consultant on that ward, I saw his name entered in the book of death certificates. He's gone too, by all accounts. A consultant and a ward sister, both at the same time. I never heard the like, but you have.'

'I have no idea what you're talking about. It was a coincidence.'

'Too much of a coincidence, if you ask me. I will get to the bottom of it. Nothing escapes me. Now, bed reporting.'

Sister Antrobus swallowed hard. She thought she'd been given a lucky break. That on casualty she would have the chance to heal her wounds. But the arrival of Miss Van Gilder had put paid to that and Sister Antrobus dreaded what would be the outcome if she found out.

If Miss Van Gilder was unimpressed by Sister Antrobus, she was practically at war with the domestics.

'The hospital is run like we're one big family,' the cook in the main kitchen had told her as she opened and closed the store cupboards.

'Everyone gets on with everyone else around here,' the head porter, Dessie, had said.

'We have all worked together for years,' said Betty Hutch, one of the night-time cleaners.

She knew what they were doing. They were warning her. Don't upset the apple cart. Little did they know, that was exactly what she intended to do.

She had begun by telling Elsie O'Brien that the room she had made up ready for her was not suitable. The impertinence of the woman, she thought, when she recalled how Elsie had told her that she kept the other room for when Dr Gaskell had visiting guests. Who did she think she was, a mere domestic, taking a decision like that?

'I am afraid that simply won't do,' she had said to Elsie, who had personally escorted her to the room.

'Well, that's the only room, other than the visitors' rooms. There's nothing I can do now. Matron won't be back for a few days, her mother's taken bad.'

'Has she not left a telephone number? Surely there must be a way she can be reached?'

Elsie had fingered the note folded in her apron pocket. It was the number of the nursing home in Lytham St Annes where Matron's mother had lived for the past ten years. Reluctantly, she confessed that she had the number, and Miss Van Gilder wasted no time in making the call herself.

After a brief conversation with Miss Van Gilder, Matron had asked that the telephone be passed to Elsie. 'I am quite sure that Dr Gaskell will have no objection if you offer Miss Van Gilder the visiting consultants' rooms,' she said.

Elsie wanted to object, but she knew that was not her place. There was something about Miss Van Gilder that made her flesh crawl. With a sigh, she quickly excused herself from the company of Miss Van Gilder and went off to air the bed and give the visiting consultants' rooms a once-over. Within minutes, the story of the unhappy new assistant matron had spread across St Angelus like wildfire.

'You will now be in the rooms next door to Sister Haycock,' said Elsie as she struggled to carry Miss Van Gilder's case into her new accommodation. Miss Van Gilder stood and watched without offering any help. Opening the door with one hand, Elsie set the case down with a thud on the polished wooden floor. She made a mental note to reward herself that night at bingo with a cold Guinness, for having kept the room as clean as she did, even though it was only ever used four times a year.

'She is as quiet as a church mouse, is Sister Haycock,' she said. 'You will have no cause for complaint being next door to her.'

Miss Van Gilder made no comment. She failed to smile and simply nodded her head in approval as she took in the room. She ran her fingers along the mantelpiece over the fire and fingered the curtains at the window as she glanced out. A pair of seagulls almost collided as they passed mid flight on the other side of the glass, catching her off guard and making her step back in alarm.

'Don't be worried about the seagulls now, they are never away from the place,' said Elsie. 'Forever hitching lifts back and forth on the ferry, they are. It must be bad out at sea as there's lots of them about today.'

'Indeed,' replied Miss Van Gilder.

Elsie, having gathered her strength, lifted up the suitcase once more and lugged it with little finesse into the bedroom. 'Do you want me to do your unpacking as well, or can you manage?'

'No, I do not. I can see to my own unpacking.'

'All right, well, please yourself. There are clean towels on the end of the bed. I've scrubbed the bath, but Sister Haycock keeps it immaculate anyway. The greasy spoon is open until after the night staff break at midnight.'

Elsie waited for a thank you. None was forthcoming. The silence told her she was dismissed.

When Matron returned from her leave, she summoned Miss Van Gilder to her office.

'Come and sit by the fire,' she said. 'The cold is just dreadful. Sister Antrobus tells me the bed count is full on the medical wards due to bronchitis and influenza. Are your rooms warm enough?'

'They are, thank you, Matron. And besides, a bit of cold never killed anyone.'

'Oh, I think Sister Antrobus might disagree with you there,' said Matron as she closed the door behind her. The number of patients who'd died that day from pneumonia was already much higher than usual. A situation Matron was sure was not helped by the cold houses some of their patients had to endure.

'Warm or not, I'm not altogether sure how much longer any of us will be able to remain living on the hospital premises,' she said. 'The Liverpool District Hospitals Board has approved plans to convert the entire accommodation corridor into a ward for emergency admissions. I have no doubt that soon they will be giving us orders to find our own accommodation outside of the hospital grounds.'

'Well,' Miss Van Gilder replied, 'in that case, we shall have to move into the Lovely Lane nurses' home, which would be a far better solution, in my opinion. Much more homely and comfortable. I am surprised, Matron, I have to admit, that we don't have rooms in the Lovely Lane home, what with it being such a beautiful building.'

'Well, it was your predecessor, Sister April, who put a stop to that,' said Matron as she led Miss Van Gilder to the comfortable chair by her roaring fire. 'When the war started. Sister April felt that the nurses needed a break from the more senior staff and that it would be much better to separate the qualified staff from the junior nurses. And I have to say, it has worked very well. As Sister April used to say, we can't act as if our young nurses need supervising when they're off duty and at the same time expect them to have the responsibility of saving lives on our wards.'

Matron bent down to stroke Blackie, who was stretched out in front of the fire. He made a continual low growling noise in his throat. If there was one thing Miss Van Gilder hated more than children, it was dogs, and Blackie clearly knew it.

'Well, Matron,' replied Miss Van Gilder, sucking in her cheeks disapprovingly, 'I have never been a fan of living above the shop, as it were, but if we are to hold on to the ban on employing married nurses, moving out of hospital accommodation will make life a little more difficult. Very few nurses could afford to pay for their board out of their salary. Not that I am complaining. At least we're paid enough to keep us in comfortable lodgings in our old age.'

Matron nodded and stoked the fire.

'But, frankly, I would have thought that there were other matters the LDHB would want to concentrate on before it considered emptying out the sisters' rooms. There are areas of hospital operation which I believe require more immediate attention.'

Matron bristled. Blackie growled.

'Other areas? What areas exactly, Miss Van Gilder?'

Matron was disappointed. She had looked forward to the arrival of Miss Van Gilder. She had judged her to be someone who was firm but also compassionate and flexible in her approach. She was sure the board members had seen those qualities too. Qualities they all realized were required in a hospital that was struggling to cope with the post-war demands of a rapidly healing and developing city. The number of babies being born was a challenge in itself, but there were also more and more young men ending up in casualty, now that there were so many more scooters and motorcars in the streets. Liverpool, so recently devoid of the young men who had been away fighting for King and country, was once again alive and vibrating with energy, and St Angelus needed to keep pace.

Miss Van Gilder spotted the shadow of concern that had crossed Matron's face and feared she had overstepped the mark. It would not be the first time. Proffering her opinion where it was not wanted or required had always been her problem. If she had not been quite so forceful with her opinion, she might have been in Bournemouth still.

She smiled a bright and disarming smile and tried to rekindle their earlier friendliness. 'As you'll have understood, Matron, from the letter I sent you outlining cost-efficiencies I have encountered in other hospitals, this is an area in which I have some expertise. Perhaps I could spend some time getting to know St Angelus a little better and in the process produce a report for you. A new pair of eyes to take a fresh look at the way we do things. And then, Matron, you could use it as your own, to help with the expansion plans for the hospital. After all, easing the burden of the matron should be the primary consideration of any assistant matron worth her salt.'

Matron softened. The smile returned. Blackie settled back down on to his tartan rug. The danger had passed.

'Why, Miss Van Gilder, that is an excellent idea. I must tell you, I have managed to hold them off evacuating the sisters' rooms and demolishing the old ward block. But the proposed building programme in itself makes my eyes water. I have no idea how we could deliver a normal service to patients with the amount of disruption we would be expected to endure. A report on how we might make improvements to the hospital without the degree of bulldozer destruction proposed by the board would be very welcome indeed.'

Elsie arrived with the tea tray and laid it down on the small coffee table between them.

'I think that, as well as the building, we could make some changes to how the hospital is staffed. We do seem to employ an army of people. Many hospitals are looking at money-saving measures, and in particular they're reviewing the ways in which they clean the hospital and provide meals to patients.'

Elsie didn't move a muscle.

'I have some very exciting ideas with regard to how we can reduce our spend and staffing levels. We employ far too many domestics, it appears to me.'

Elsie spilt the spoon of sugar she was about to drop into Miss Van Gilder's tea.

'I would also like to develop my ideas regarding a nurse cadet force.'

'Ah, I see,' said Matron. 'The person you need to speak to there is Sister Haycock.'

'Well, I would like to, but she has been very elusive. She appears to be out almost every evening. Returns at nine o'clock, does a little washing, and is out again by eight in the morning. I have never known anyone to wash so often.'

'Yes, I have noticed that myself. However, we are all entitled to our private lives, Miss Van Gilder. As long as Sister Haycock isn't breaking any of the hospital rules or behaving in a manner which is inappropriate or would bring shame upon the hospital, she is entitled to behave in private as she pleases. I have known her since she was a young nurse. It is a fact, she was not my choice for the position of sister tutor. I was overruled on that one by our TB specialist, Dr Gaskell. However, she has more than proved herself as being both able and, dare I say it, excellent in the execution of her duties. She has a way with the student nurses which brings out the best in them. And as a result, she now has my unconditional support.'

Miss Van Gilder wasn't sure she shared that sentiment. She found complaint with almost everyone and everything and she was quite sure that Sister Haycock would present no challenge in that regard. As a woman who had no private life herself, she was deeply interested in everyone else's and had already decided that she would make it her business to find out exactly why Sister Haycock did so much washing in the laundry room and ran so much hot water late at night. After all, how did one know whether rules were being broken if the perpetrator had yet to be caught?

'Now, Miss Van Gilder, I think we need to establish a time when you and I can meet and discuss the week. May I suggest that every Monday morning we meet here in my rooms at eleven o'clock for coffee and you, being my eyes and ears, can tell me what concerns or indeed pleases you. I am being called to so many committee meetings across the city and even have to catch the train to London later this week for a matrons' conference. Would you believe it, there are some people in this new NHS who consider that matrons lack the correct management skills to run hospitals. I had no intention of travelling all the way to London at first, but when I saw that particular item on the agenda, I made it my business to secure myself a place. Just who do these people think they are?'

Miss Van Gilder began to relax. She tut-tutted and shook her head in conspiratorial disbelief. This was more like it.

'Why, thank you, Matron, yes, a weekly meeting would be an excellent idea. I am sure I shall have a great deal to report back to you for consideration. There will not be a part of this hospital or a single person I won't know all about, I can assure you.'

'Excellent. Right, well, this all sounds very positive. I'm delighted that you could join us. Let me call Elsie back with some of her delicious biscuits to celebrate and we can start today as we mean to go on. I keep forgetting that we can have biscuits whenever we want them now, do you?'

Miss Van Gilder, not being fluent in small talk, stammered a response. 'Er, well . . .'

'Have you met Blackie?' asked Matron as Blackie growled.

Miss Van Gilder flinched. Matron almost frowned.

As Elsie placed the biscuits on the plate in the kitchen, she answered the kitchen phone. It was Biddy.

'The note you copied from Matron's desk, it's come up trumps, Elsie. It had a hospital name on it, St Dunstan's, and I have the address for your woman in St Dunstan's, the one I was telling you about yesterday. She's from Ballina and her sister is Cathy, in the kitchens, lives on Waterloo Street. Cathy asked her in her letter did she know your one, the Bone Grinder, and sure she did. I said I would send a letter off to her tonight with what we want to know and my address. Is she there now?'

'Oh God, she is, Biddy, and she has a right funny way about her. There's something fishy about that woman, make no mistake, and she's going to be big trouble for us all.'

Biddy almost sighed. Elsie was a worrier and Miss Van Gilder sent Elsie into a spin. 'Stop your fretting, Elsie. Get round to mine tonight and we'll send the letter off. If she's hiding something, as God is true, we will find out what it is.'

As Miss Van Gilder drank her tea and ate the delicious caramel biscuits with Matron, her hostility to the chilly north-west began to fade. St Dunstan's felt like a million miles away. It had been a close thing at St Dunstan's. Too close for comfort. But this was a fresh start. She would not make the same mistakes. From now on, she would take much more care.

'I suggest you let me deal with all the post as well, Matron. I can open the mail and settle the more trivial issues. Anything of concern, I can place on your desk for you to deal with. After all, what is the point of having a dog and barking yourself?' Miss Van Gilder couldn't help herself as she set her chin at Blackie.

At the mention of the word dog, Blackie's head shot up.

Matron did not feel comfortable with this suggestion but had no idea how to object. Miss Van Gilder was quite correct. Her job was to assist her in her matronly duties. Hadn't she just said herself how busy she was? Was it not the case that this week alone she was away from the hospital for three full days? 'Well, that will be very kind of you,' she said, reluctantly.

'Excellent, I shall have the porter deliver all the

post to my desk each morning and we shall work out who deals with what from then on. I shall handle all the tedious and less important correspondence.'

Miss Van Gilder looked into the leaping flames and thought to herself, yes, at St Angelus I shall cover myself in glory. No one will wag any fingers at me here.

CHAPTER 15

Lockie had drunk too much. He knew it, but Amy had been in the mood to drink and he couldn't stop her.

'Wait for me outside the plant at six,' she'd said to him as he collected his banker's draft that morning, and he had. They'd been sitting in the Grapes pub ever since, on the small pew next to the fire.

Amy wasn't really Lockie's type. He was a quiet, hard-working man who wanted a simple life. He watched the footie with his dad on Saturdays and called in to the pub after the match on the way home. He lay in bed on Sundays to catch up on his sleep and gave Misty an extra-long groom. He went to the pub with his dad for a lunch-time pint, ate the roast dinner his mam cooked and then visited his nan.

That was Lockie's life. Orderly. Nothing unusual happened to knock him off his beat and he liked it that way. He had never met a woman who wore make-up, until he met Amy. He had never met a woman who flirted with men, until Amy. When Amy spoke to Lockie, he wanted to run a mile,

271

but instead, he was captivated by her red lips and the wafting aroma of something that had no place in a kitchen.

'I have to work in the morning, Amy,' he said. 'I need to be up at five. I want to meet the *Cotapaxi*. She's out at the bar, due to be first in. When she docks, I want to be down there for the jute offloads.'

Lockie was always the first in the queue. The broken bales and the ripped sacks were all his, for a lower price, and he took those too. That was how he managed to save over ten pounds a week. It would be more, but he always slipped a green note to his nan on Sundays.

'Use this for the Guinness and the bingo, Nan,' he would say as he placed it on her dresser. She would light her pipe and pretend she hadn't heard him. Pride always came before grateful acceptance of a pound note.

He also helped out his mam, paid the rent and supplemented his dad's wages as a docker. All was good in Lockie's world and this was a result of his own endeavour and enterprise. But nothing gave him as much pleasure as the ever-growing pile he had on deposit in the bank. He checked the amount each month and surprised even himself. Not long now.

'I'll have enough soon, Da, to rent my own yard and buildings and employ my own men with no need of money from the bank. There will even be enough to buy this house one day. I can get extra carts and with a bit of luck start some of my own processing. I'm doing well, Da.' He knew it was true. He worked for it and nothing was going to stand in his way. When he had saved up enough money, he would cut out the middleman. These thoughts filled his mind day after day. They propelled him out of bed at four thirty on the coldest, dampest mornings and they sustained him through the longest working day.

Amy smiled. 'What are you thinking about, Lockie?' she asked.

He picked up his tankard and finished the last of his beer. 'Sorry, Amy, I was wondering what price the captain of the *Cotapaxi* will put on the spoilt sacks in the morning. He's new to this port. Never seen his name on a manifest before. The new ones are always a bit tricky.'

Lockie's mind was always on the business. He knew how to work hard and save money, but not how to say no to Amy. As she talked on and on, he couldn't help comparing her to Lily, and Amy came off worse, by far.

'Well, you should be thinking about me, not the captain of the *Cotapaxi*,' said Amy sullenly.

The parrot on the bar chattered away to the customers and they had to speak louder than was usual to rise over the sound of chinking glasses and laughter. Above the line of the semi-opaque window opposite, Amy could see that it was dark. Night had truly set in. She had no watch on and there was no clock on the wall in the snug, but she guessed that it must now be about nine. She would have to get a move on. Her parents were away, making a second attempt at a holiday, and she was supposed to be staying with the McConaghys. They had all watched her like a hawk since that awful night. A night that haunted her every day.

'You have brought my rheumatism on something awful,' her mother complained. 'My nerves are so bad.'

And then her father had snapped. He had dealt with the entire fallout since he'd found Doreen, and he continued to be filled with shame. Both Amy and her mother knew he was at his wits' end. So when he said, 'I need a holiday,' her mother did not object. She daredn't.

Doreen had not spoken to Amy since that night, but Amy was haunted by everything that had happened. It had been seven weeks and three days and she was counting every minute.

'I'm going home tonight for clothes, Auntie,' she had said to Mrs McConaghy. 'I haven't enough. And I'm off to the hairdresser's later on, it's the only time she can fit me in. So I'll stay at Mammy and Daddy's.'

Mrs McConaghy had no chance to object and, frankly, she liked her niece more when she wasn't living with her. 'The truth is, I can't think of her in the same way since the incident,' she said to her husband. 'She has had everything in the world given to her on a plate, that one, and yet she has no friends. Lost the one she did have, such an awful thing to have happened. Thank God our name wasn't in the *Echo*. It could have been bad for business to be associated with that whole awful affair. The girl could have died. I still don't think we know the truth about what happened and she has brought shame on us all. She should have been sent away.'

'Your sister has always been more interested in herself than she ever was in Amy,' Mr McConaghy replied. He took a long pull on his pipe.

'Yes, but look at Lily. From what Sister Therese says, she has nothing but the dress she stands up in, and would she behave in that way? Not in a million years.'

Mr McConaghy snapped open the pages of the *Echo* and, looking at his wife over the top, replied, 'You don't buy loyalty or good behaviour, 'tis earned. Lily must have good parents to be as good and hard-working a girl as she is.'

Mrs McConaghy twisted her handkerchief around in her fingers. That was not what she'd heard from the likes of Sister Therese and Lockie, but she had to step carefully. She was also worried about Amy. She had woken that morning to the sound of Amy vomiting in the bathroom and as far as she was concerned, there was only one reason that happened to a woman. It would be her sister's problem to deal with, but if she was right, Amy could not stay in Liverpool. The scandal would be bad for business and she would not tolerate it. If her sister and brother-in-law put up a fight, they could wave goodbye to their five per cent as far as she was concerned. She nursed her cup and saucer and stared into the fire as her husband flicked over the pages of his newspaper. No, I can't be right. I'm letting the worry and responsibility for that girl run away with me, she thought to herself. It's a bug. I'm wrong. She drained her cup and promptly forgot her concerns about Amy.

Amy and Lockie had been in the Grapes since work had finished. Amy had made sure he was waiting for her at the bottom of the steps, under the watchful gaze of Mrs McConaghy as she stood at the side of the office window. She watched as Amy ran down the steps, as Amy knew she would. She had told her auntie that she was going to have a quick drink with Lockie before she took the bus to the hairdresser's. It was just one more lie heaped on to the others she seemed to have to tell daily. As she approached Lockie, she took him by surprise and reached up and kissed him full on the lips, with passion. She wanted Mrs McConaghy to believe another lie she was preparing, that she had been dating Lockie for weeks, in secret. She wanted her to report this back to her parents. To make them believe she had been too nervous to confess that Lockie was her secret beau.

As Lockie spoke, Amy plotted. She needed to get him out of the pub and soon. She also had to make sure that, for whatever reason, the barman remembered them. What had to be done could not be done there. Time was running out. It had been weeks now. Ben had not come back to find her since her father had chased him out of the house. But it was too late, the damage had been done.

Lockie began to slur and Amy looked at his face. His red hair had caught the glow of the fire and looked as though it was alight. His eyes were soft and blue, his birthmark had deepened to almost black, and she thought to herself, he will do. All things considered, he will have to do.

'Let's go back to my house, Lockie.' She sidled across the wooden pew and, slipping her hand down to the base of his back, whispered in his ear as she kissed the side of his face.

'Amy!' Lockie exclaimed and shot away as though her touch had given him an electric shock. 'That is not a proper way for a lady to behave. Wasn't it enough, kissing me in broad daylight like that in the street?' He looked around the pub frantically to see if anyone had noticed.

Amy wanted to be noticed. She sighed. This was going to be so much harder than she had first thought. Why couldn't Lockie just be like other men? Why couldn't he be the one trying to get her to go home with him?

Jesus, am I not just irresistible, she thought. She felt affronted. In any other circumstances, she would have told Lockie where to sling his jute and stormed off. However, tonight, that was a luxury she did not have. 'I'll fetch you a chaser,' she said, 'and then we'll leave.'

'No you won't,' said Lockie. 'Are you mad, Amy? No woman goes to the bar.'

A minute later, he was back by her side. A dry amontillado and a refilled pint jug sat between them.

'Lockie, if you don't want me to kiss you here, come to my house then.'

Lockie stared at Amy. She looked at his eyes and saw them darken. His facial muscles tightened and a nerve in his jaw twitched.

'Your da?' he croaked.

'He's away. Look, how about I make you a fried-egg butty and then you can leave after a quick kiss and a cuddle. Go on, you're safe with me, Lockie. And besides, you've had nothing to eat yet tonight.'

As they left the pub and stepped out into the chilly night air, Amy slipped back into the bar. She handed the landlord a five-pound note and as she did so, she blew him a kiss. 'Here you go, mate,' she said. 'Get the parrot a budgie for a friend.'

The landlord looked at the note in his hand and his mouth dropped open. But before he could speak, Amy had gone.

Half an hour later, Amy reached up with her key to open the front door. She found herself quite looking forward to what lay ahead. Her problem solved, her goal achieved, and another conquest. That always made her feel good.

Lockie moved ahead of her into the hallway. Closing the door, Amy went to switch on the light, but she was already having second thoughts and knew she would have to move fast. Jesus, he could pass out with the drink soon, she thought. Turning to Lockie, she dropped her handbag to the floor, placed her arms around his neck and kissed him.

His hands slowly came up and unfastened hers from around his neck. 'Amy,' he whispered, 'we can't.' His voice was thick and slightly pleading. It was a tone she had not heard before. A thrill shot through her. She was nearly there. Just a little more effort.

'Oh, Lockie, don't disappoint me,' she whined. 'I have been looking forward to this,' she whispered and she kissed him again. He groaned as he opened his mouth slightly. He was yielding. She was winning.

She gently pushed him against the wall, wriggled her slim body in between his legs and pressed herself against him. She felt him harden as she undid his belt and slipped her hand down the front of his trousers. He slid down the wall. Come on, she thought to herself, want me. He didn't. He allowed her to push him, but he didn't want her. There was a reluctance, a hesitation, and then the thought struck her: God, he's a virgin. He's scared.

Her hands worked instinctively, coaxing and encouraging until he was beyond staging any pretence of serious resistance.

'Come along, Lockie,' she said as she took him by the hand, 'I have something to show you.'

An hour later, lying in her empty bed, which smelt of beer and sex, Amy smiled. 'Thank bloody goodness,' she said as she slipped her hands down on to her belly. There was the faintest mound. It might mean nothing more than she had eaten too many of her auntie's cakes. But Amy was taking no chances. The sickness in the morning could just be that she wasn't used to all the sugar her auntie couldn't get enough of. But she had to make plans, just in case. Sugar didn't stop a monthly and she had not had any sign of one. She was sick of running into the toilet every time she thought it might be coming, only to be disappointed. It was not uncommon for babies to be born a couple of months early. If she had to, she could say that. Plenty of others had and did.

But she had a better plan. Her number-one plan. She would find Ben and tell him, because if he knew she was pregnant, he would surely want to do the right thing. To care for them both. She would find him and she would tell him she needed just five minutes to talk to him. She missed him. She missed the fun. The nights out, the laughs. She resolved that tomorrow she would call round to his house and see if he was there. To the address she had memorized. But Amy was no fool. If the worst came to the worst and she couldn't find him, Lockie would do. And if she needed to prove that Lockie was the man who had made her pregnant, there were plenty of witnesses. The barman wouldn't forget the red-lipped, well-dressed girl who'd given him a five-pound note for a budgie.

CHAPTER 16

'Stand in line, lads,' shouted Dessie to the group of apprentices known as the porter's lads. The lads were in the hospital yard awaiting inspection.

'Come on, lads, stop larking around. Tom, give Harry his cap back, please, now.'

That was all it took, a dip in Dessie's tone, and the sound of boots on cobbles filled the air as sparks flew from the steel heel-tips and toe-caps. The lads shot into their places as fast as bullets fired from a gun. Not one of the lads would willingly upset Dessie. He commanded their respect, just as he'd commanded the respect of many of their fathers when they'd served in his regiment.

Dessie took all of his apprentices from the poorest houses along the Dock Road. Those where a father had fallen during the war. Few of his boys came from a home where both parents were still alive.

Each morning was the same. Across the road from the hospital stood St Angelus church. By the time the last bell had rung out at 8 a.m., the porter's lads were in two rows, standing to attention. Dessie had replaced his army parade ground with the porter's yard at St Angelus. If his lads were to be ferrying laundry baskets and vegetables, repairing tiles or buildings, stoking up the furnaces or running between kitchens, wards and doctors' and nurses' homes, they had to begin the day spick and span. Dessie insisted on each one of them visiting the public baths on their day off for a full wash down, and they had to come from a home where there was soap available every day.

Dessie's inspection began at the beginning of each shift and there were two shifts per day. Twenty-four lads on the day shift, which began at eight in the morning, and ten on the night shift, which began at eight in the evening. Dessie undertook both inspections himself. Towards the end of the day, after the patients' suppers and prior to visiting time, Dessie would allow those boys who had worked hard and done well to leave for home, with no deduction from their pay. Every lad worked his hardest and spent his life in fear of disappointing Dessie.

'Don't you let Dessie down. He's a good man, giving you that job. He knew your da, you know.' Those were the words that chased at the back of each porter's lad as he ran down the road to St Angelus each morning.

'Get out of that bed and away to your job! There was never a porter's lad injured or died at the hospital, not like down on the docks or in a muddy field like your da,' mothers would shout to lads who were turning over in their beds for 'just another five minutes'.

'How's our lad getting on, Dessie? Is he doing well?' Dessie would be asked often down at the local shop. A son with a job at the hospital was a source of pride among those who thought they had little to be proud of, even if their menfolk having made the greatest sacrifice of all in the war should have made them prouder than anyone. But when paying the rent and the coalman was your weekly struggle and you lay awake wondering how you would make the money stretch until the next pay packet arrived on Friday night, it was hard to feel anything but anxious.

The hospital provided the lads with a uniform of brown overalls, but Dessie insisted on freshly washed hands and faces and highly polished boots at the start of each shift. He demanded that the glint on the lads' boots match the shine that would have graced their own fathers' boots when he was sergeant of their regiment. He felt a paternal duty by proxy towards the boys. Having no children of his own, he was well aware that his army of porter's lads filled that gap.

This morning, Dessie was being harsher than was usual. The prospect of a visit from the new assistant matron, Miss Van Gilder, or Miss Bone Grinder, as she had already become known, hung over him like the worst of a morning smog. It had depressed his spirits.

'Look at the state of your boots, Bryan,' he

shouted to one of the newer recruits. 'Your toe-caps look as though they have just arrived back from Dunkirk, and I was there, so I know what I'm talking about.'

'Sorry, Dessie, sir.' The porter's lad looked sheepish.

'Right, you can spend the entire day on the bins then, Bryan, as a punishment. I'm not having those shoes on any corridor or ward inside the hospital. Miss Van Gilder would be down my throat in a flash if she saw you. If you have run out of the Cherry Blossom at home, there's a tin and brushes in the lodge, as you well know. Call in tonight before you leave for home and give them a good going over. I'll be there. I'll show you how your dad used to have to do his, every single day.'

Bryan nodded. The war had ended only eight years ago, but to the fatherless boys, the memory of the dads they'd hardly known was already fading. There was no blacking at Bryan's home. There was only his money and his mother's cleaning money coming in. It was spent on food and the rent and what was left over went on coal for the fire. His mother was running a house on a boy's wage. Dessie made a mental note to send Bryan home with blacking and an extra shilling. He didn't want to embarrass the lad, but he had to understand, Dessie was a man of standards. St Angelus was run like clockwork and, never mind the assistant matron, Matron herself could spot a pair of dirty boots a mile away from her office window on the first floor.

'Make sure you put the newspaper underneath first and give a good spit on the leather.'

As he spoke, Dessie looked down at the leather on Bryan's boots. They appeared as though a good polish might see them off. He sighed as he pushed his cap back on his head and wiped his brow. He bought the boys steel heel-tips out of his own money and they lived in a large jam jar on a shelf in the porter's lodge for the lads to help themselves. They helped save the boot leather. He was well aware that the nineteen shillings a week the lads earned was not enough to keep siblings properly fed and buy a new pair of boots.

Bryan was in trouble, but he knew how to take his punishment. 'Yes, sir,' he answered again. 'Sorry, Dessie.'

Dessie placed his hand lightly and with sympathetic understanding on the boy's shoulder. 'Right, the lot of you, Jake has the rota, so listen up and set to. No slackers now. Plenty of lads after your jobs, you know.'

There was never a truer word spoken. One mother had stopped Dessie on his way up the lane only that morning.

'Honest to God, Dessie, I don't know what we would have done without you. They've stopped taking them on at fourteen down at the docks and that's because the bastards know the war pension stops just as soon as the lad hits fourteen. The harbour board is trying to starve us out of our homes. The work's slowing down, not as many ships coming in, and there's a rumour that they want to sell our houses to the corpy and build new ones.'

'I wouldn't worry about that,' said Dessie. 'They were talking about that before the war. Said every house should have a bathroom, too – that'll be the day.'

'Everyone is fighting to get on a gang down there to keep a roof over their head. I don't know where it's going to end. We would be lost without our Tom's money from the hospital, and he's got prospects, hasn't he, Dessie?'

Dessie never wanted to lie. There were prospects, but they were few and he was finding it a continuing struggle to justify having twenty-four day lads. Miss Bone Grinder had demanded he present the worksheets to her and there was no doubt in Dessie's mind that she was going to be a difficult customer to satisfy. She had sent shock-waves through St Angelus and she had only been there for a matter of days.

'Right, you lot. Jake, read out the rota.' Dessie turned to Jake and almost dropped his clipboard. Attached to Jake's wrist by a length of bailing twine was a scruffy grey dog. 'What the hell is that?'

The porter's lads were still standing to attention, but their two regimentally straight rows began to titter.

'Don't blame me, Dessie. Mrs Duffy told me I had to take him away from the nurses' home this morning and it wasn't even me what took him there.'

'Why has she given him to you then?' asked Dessie as he removed his cap and scratched his head.

'She said she hasn't been getting along with the dog. Keeps nicking the food. She said I was to ask you if he could live in the porter's lodge. Said he's driving her mad down at Lovely Lane. Keeps leaving his hair all over the place and she doesn't want him there no more.'

'God in heaven, the lodge is not an animal sanctuary, Jake, 'tis a hospital we are running here. And besides, he will scare the cats away, and if that happens, we will be overrun with the river rats.'

As Dessie scratched his head, Victoria and Dana were crossing the porter's yard on the way to their wards.

'Scamp!' shouted Victoria.

Scamp recognized her voice and pulled and pulled at Jake until he dragged him over towards her.

Dana shrieked. 'Don't let him jump up on the aprons or we'll be shot.'

Jake pulled Scamp down. 'Sit, boy, sit. Do you think you could take him back with you tonight, Nurse Brogan?' he said. 'Dessie is not happy. You know how he looks after the cats and they do a useful job around here, they keep the river rats away and the mice too, and there's plenty of them around the bins. Mrs Duffy said I had to take him. I think she found him on your bed and was none too happy, Nurse Baker.'

'Did she now?' said Victoria. 'Oops.'

Dessie had given the lads their jobs and, having dismissed them, walked over to join Jake.

'Look, Dessie, we all know, do we not, that with Mrs Duffy there's a way to work her,' said Victoria.

'Aye, and if anyone can, it's Victoria here,' said Dana as she grinned at Victoria.

'Right, well then, nurses, if you can collect him and walk him back down tonight, that will be just great. Would you do that now?'

'Of course we will, Dessie. You keep him safe in the lodge and we will collect him and have another word with Mrs Duffy. I have all day to think of a plan and a very good excuse.' Victoria was stroking a spot just between Scamp's eyes that made the scruffy grey dog slowly collapse on to his side on the ground. They all began to laugh.

'Sure, I thought she had quite taken to him,' said Dana, whom Scamp had won over from the moment he arrived, despite her protestations.

In the distance, marching across the yard towards the red-brick arch, Dessie saw Miss Van Gilder. She was steaming towards them in a manner he would have praised in one of his soldiers. 'Disperse, quick, all of you – Jake, nurses, and the dog!' he said as he walked towards the archway to head her off.

Dessie had yet to see the assistant matron smile. This cold morning, she was about to disappoint him as she scrutinized each entry on the worksheets.

'There is talk of piped oxygen being brought to each individual hospital bed. It was a standard requirement in my last hospital.' She turned to Dessie, pushed her spectacles up her nose with her index finger and waited for him to respond with a suitably awed expression. There was none and so she continued. 'I am proposing in my report for Matron and the board that it should be done here too. Once a contractor has been appointed to lay the piping, we can dispense with at least half of your scruffy little lads running around the wards delivering oxygen bottles.'

Dessie's heart sank. The lads from the Dock Road weren't the brightest. The clever boys passed the eleven-plus and went on up to Waterloo Grammar, where they gained the best education in the land and left with certificates, cauliflower ears and fluency in Latin.

'I shall look forward to that, Assistant Matron,' he lied and, out of habit, raised his cap and saluted, as, her own inspection over, she marched away.

'What's up, Dessie, has Miss Bone Grinder been 'aving a go again?' Jake bounded into the hut and found Dessie poring over the worksheets.

'Yes, she has indeed, Jake. Is it that obvious?'

Dessie was genuinely surprised. For ten years, he had taken orders from regimental sergeant-majors. He had faced down Jerry snipers that were so close, he could see the whites of their eyes. He was immune to the sound of gunfire and exploding shells and had lost count of the number of men who had died in his arms. Nothing had ever scared Dessie and when death hovered close by, he had let his fingers run over the gold crucifix he wore under his shirt along with his identity tag and sent death on its way. He had tried the same tactic with the new assistant matron. It had failed.

'She tells me she wants to bring piped oxygen to the beds in the wards and that the lads will have to go.'

'Jesus wept, really?' The cheery smile fell from Jake's face. He lit the gas ring in the lodge and filled the kettle. Jake's most important role of the day was the making of the mid-morning drinks. He proceeded to line up the twenty-four pint-sized, enamel mugs, freshly scrubbed by the night-porter lads. Chipped and brown, the mugs were washed only once a day, a two-in-the-morning job.

'Is there anything we can do about that?' Jake banged the kettle down on the gas ring and flopped on to the wooden chair on the opposite side of Dessie's wooden desk. He removed his tobacco tin from the inside of his jacket. It felt as though he'd already done a day's work. 'Shall I roll you one?' he asked. 'You look like you need it.'

Dessie nodded as, with an expression of great solemnity, he set his spectacles back on his nose and studied the ward repair chart.

The porter's lodge was nothing more than a glorified pre-fab hut. It contained a desk, half a dozen or so rickety wooden chairs, cast-offs from various waiting rooms, a coal burner with a steel chimney piped straight out through the roof, which pumped out heat all day long, and a sink with a scrubbed wooden draining board next to a large gas ring. At the back of the hut stood an outside privy, which housed two toilets with polished wooden-plank seats across them. Porter's lads could often be heard shouting, 'Coming for a crap and a smoke,' to each other as they ran back from their various jobs to the yard for the morning break. The lads came from homes with large numbers of children where toileting was a communal affair.

The walls of the hut were stippled with old nails from which were tied loops of string and clip-boards. Above each nail Dessie had written the relevant task on the wall. *Worksheets*, *Oxygen Deliveries*, *Laundry Out* and *Laundry In*. There were sections for outer building repairs, call logs from the wards, plumbing repairs, leaks and squeaks, furnaces to be stoked and fired, patients to be moved, theatre light bulbs to be changed, and dressing drums to be collected and delivered to the furnace for sterilizing. The running of St Angelus hospital was coordinated like a World War Two field operation and it was all master-minded from Dessie's field hut.

Some of the boys had to take their breaks

292

outdoors as there was not enough room for everyone to fit into the hut at the same time. When the weather was especially bad, some would take their pint-pot mugs down to the stoke hole, to warm their bones and dry out. The warmth induced increased merriment and high jinks and always resulted in either Jake or Dessie having to chase the lads down and chivvy them back to work, out into the freezing cold.

As the kettle in the lodge began to whistle, Jake took down a large pub ashtray from the shelf running above his head. 'Reckon if we are all having a cuppa, this fella can have one as well?' He looked down at Scamp, who had made himself a home under Dessie's desk.

Scamp's head came out from under the desk and his ears pricked up as he looked towards Jake. He instinctively knew when he was being talked about.

'I'm going to phone the station in a minute,' said Dessie, 'to see if anyone has called in to report him missing.'

'Are you serious?' said Jake. 'The streets are overrun with stray dogs.'

'Well, you never know, he may be someone's pet. I would hate to think that some old man or lady, or a nipper, even, is pining after their lost dog. Not all families are as poor as those down on the Dock Road, you know, Jake. Many live a different life altogether.'

'Oh, I know that, Dessie.'

Jake was now filling the large metal teapot with scalding water. He gave the tea leaves a big stir with a metal screwdriver, then poured in a bottle of sterilized milk. Satisfied it had all mixed in, he tipped what he assumed to be the correct amount of sugar from the canister into the pot. Then he covered the huge teapot with a ribbed knitted cosy his mother had made, set the gas light on low and placed the pot back on to simmer. 'That teapot is bigger than your head, Jake,' his mother had complained as she darned the sides together with wool.

'What are we going to do about Miss Bone Grinder then, Dessie?' asked Jake. 'We can't have her putting the lads out of work, can we? She's all over the bloody place, pushing her nose into everything. Every time I turn around she's there, asking questions.'Dessie removed his cap, rubbed his scalp, frowned, and replaced it. 'Well, it seems to me we are stuffed, Jake. Things are changing. You can tell that yourself, can't you?' He sounded uncharacteristically bad-tempered.

'Yes, but not here, Dessie. These are our jobs, nothing can change how it is here at St Angelus.'

'I wish that were the case, Jake, but you can't stop progress. Look at your lovely house and how you're doing it up. All the new-fangled gadgets you've bought for your Martha. You know, soon there won't be any work for women to do at home, with all these gadgets. The next thing you know, they will be wanting our jobs.'

Jake laughed out loud. 'Never, Dessie. Women are smarter than we think. Why would they want to come here and be dictated to by the likes of Miss Bone Grinder when they can let their men go out to work while they stay at home and put their feet up?'

Dessie smiled. 'I wouldn't let a young mother hear you say that, Jake. If you spent a week at home with a gang of kids, you might change your tune. Anyway, what we have to do is find a way to keep the lads on and I know two women with better brains than you or I who might be able to help with that. Time for me to have a meeting with Biddy and your mother-outlaw, Elsie.'

Jake felt a sense of relief at Dessie's suggestion. He was only too aware exactly how formidable Elsie and Biddy were. He began pouring the already milked and sugared tea from the huge metal pot into the mugs – the lads complained if it boiled when the milk was already in – and finished with the clean, oversized, Bakelite ashtray.

'Here you go, Scamp lad,' he said as he placed the ashtray full of tea on the floor.

Scamp's tail wagged as he drank. Dessie watched him and for the first time that morning, his expression softened.

'Ah, I can see that look in your eye. You're going soft on the dog, aren't you, Dessie?'

'No I am not,' said Dessie indignantly. 'I have more important things to think about today.' Jake transferred the twenty-four mugs on to a wooden tray and carried them over to Dessie's table. He could already hear running feet pounding across the yard. Jobs done, the lads were always ready for their tea. 'They must smell it brewing,' Jake said. He looked towards the open door and was surprised to see young Tom, one of the lads, standing there with a large metal tray covered with a cloth. 'Quick, get the hell in,' he rasped as he grabbed Tom by the shoulder and dragged him inside. Stepping back towards the door, he scanned the yard to check for Miss Van Gilder.

'Is that from cook, Tom?'

'Yes, sir,' said Tom. 'She gave it to me when I delivered the veg trolley from the vans. That's my rota today, you told me.' Tom's eyes widened, worried that he might be in trouble.

'Yes, Tom, I know. Don't worry. What has cook sent and did she give you a message, Tom?'

'She did, Dessie. She said . . .' Tom took a deep breath. He appeared to concentrate for a long time and then he said in a very clear voice, articulating the words carefully, 'The manhole is open.'

Jake had lifted the cloth from the tray to take a look. 'Oh, this is the gear,' he said to Dessie as he licked his lips. 'Fried eggs on toast.'

Dessie was up from behind the desk and took the tray from Tom as he spoke to him. 'When you've had your tea and your slice of egg and toast, Tom, go back to the kitchens to collect the baskets and say this to cook, "Jake will deliver." Have you got that, Tom?'

Tom repeated the words slowly, but it was hard for him to concentrate as his mouth was watering at the smell from the tray.

Dessie looked at him and was filled with pity. 'Go on, lad, take the biggest slice before the others get here.'

Tom's face lit up and he beamed as he lifted a slice of the toast and fried egg, treating it as though it were a newborn baby, terrified of dropping a crumb.

'There you go, Tom, you are the first today, mate,' said Jake. 'Take a chair and here's your tea. Now, what was that message Dessie gave you for cook?'

Dessie and Jake watched in amazement as Tom began to drink his tea. He blew and blew at the scalding liquid and then began to drink. Dessie and Jake were lost to him; he had only one thing on his mind. Once he began to drink, it was almost as if he could not stop. He gulped and blew and gulped and blew and gulped until he was breathless and the pint pot was empty. With a gasp, he set the pot down with a thump on the ledge. His eyes looked almost as if were in a trance as he regained his composure.

'Tom, when did you last have a hot drink, lad?' asked Dessie, trying to keep the concern from his voice.

'It was here, yesterday, Dessie, sir,' answered Tom.

Dessie and Jake exchanged a glance. This was

not a rare occurrence, but they had a solution. Dessie would call on the boy's mam and tell her that Tom needed to be fed properly or he would lose his job and there would be no money at all. Dessie needed to make such a call about once a month. Money was often diverted by parents from his lads' stomachs to the pub counter.

'What's the message for cook, Tom?' repeated Jake.

Tom had eaten the first chunk of bread and answered in a perkier voice. 'That Jake will deliver.'

'That's it, lad.' Jake patted him on the back.

'Amazing the difference a milky tea with sugar in makes to the lad and his memory,' he said.

Dessie nodded in agreement. 'Aye, it is. Here's the key for the coal yard.' He took a long key tied with a piece of string down from one of the hooks. 'Fill a sack up for cook and drop it into her cellar later. That's a fair exchange, if you ask me. A breakfast for all the lads for a bag of coal.'

All the houses along the Dock Road had a manhole cover next to the front door that opened on to a coal cellar, reached by a wooden door inside and a flight of steps down. Even if they were old, pregnant or sick, women spent their days going up and down the steps with a bucket, or just a shovel, once a bucket became too heavy to carry.

'You sort out the lads' break, Jake. I'm popping over to the school of nursing to speak to Biddy and arrange a pow-wow. Assistant Matron doesn't know it yet, but when our lads' jobs are threatened, we mobilize the St Angelus underground. Miss Bone Grinder has met her match.'

'What about your egg on toast?' asked Jake. 'Are you not going to eat it before ye go?'

Dessie turned back from the door and looked down at Scamp. Scamp sat upright. He looked at Dessie and licked his lips. 'Give mine to the dog,' he said, as he put on his cap and strode across the yard.

CHAPTER 17

'We are totally mad, you do know that, don't you?' said Dana to Victoria as they walked towards the wards. 'Anyone else would think we'd lost our marbles, trying to keep a scraggy old dog at the nurses' home.'

They both stopped in their tracks to let Tom cross in front of them as he carried the hot tray.

'Gosh, he's in a hurry,' Victoria said. 'I know they would, but I had a dog my whole life and he slept on my bed until he died when he was fourteen. I think about him all the time. I would love Mrs Duffy to let us keep Scamp. It's what's missing at Lovely Lane, don't you think? A nice obedient dog, waiting for us all to come home after a hard day in the wards. What could be better?'

Dana shook her head in disbelief. 'Obedient? Which dog did you have in mind, Victoria? Not that mangy thing over there, the dog Mrs Duffy had to chase off the dining table, the dog who ran off with the joint of ham in his mouth yesterday, would that be him?' She gave Victoria a wry smile. 'No wonder he's been sent up here. Now, though, we must have a hand wash before we step onto the wards or anywhere near a patient.'

'Cooee!' Pammy's voice rang out and both girls turned their heads and watched as she waved frantically towards them then disappeared in to the cloakroom just outside casualty.

'It's her first day on casualty today and guess who's working on there with her?' said Victoria as they waved back.

'Who?' asked Dana, intrigued by Victoria's tone.

'Your Dr Teddy, who do you think?'

Dana blushed. She had been dating Dr Davenport for a year. What with his gruelling junior doctor's on-call rota and her studying to pass her PTS, it was difficult to get an evening off together. He frequently worked five days and nights on the trot. During the day, he performed his usual houseman duties on the wards and in the clinics. At night, when the more senior consultants and doctors were at home or tucked up in bed, the patients were his responsibility. Teddy Davenport was the first to admit, he could often grab a full five hours on the army camp bed in the doctors' night room. 'It's surprisingly comfortable, in fact,' he had told Dana when she'd asked how he managed to sleep night after night on a sheet of canvas strung across a wooden frame. His nights off were few and far between and it was more by luck than management that they managed to see each other at all.

'Oh, I knew that he was starting on casualty.'

Dana laughed. 'Not for long, though. He's planning the summer holidays already, so he is. He's becoming really insistent that we stay in a hotel, by the seaside, but I need to go home to visit my mammy and daddy, to the farm, in Ireland. How do I tell him that's the last thing I want but I have to do it? Honest to God, wouldn't I just love to go to the seaside or to London or anywhere I've never been before. He has not a clue, it could rain every day when I'm in Ireland. What kind of holiday would that be for Teddy? A waste of time it would be for him, that's what, and besides, if I ask him, he might think I'm being too presumptuous, you know, inviting him home. I'm in such a pickle.'

'Well, get you,' said Victoria, 'stuck for choice.' Victoria's boyfriend, Roland, was Teddy's brother and both nurses had discussed on more than one occasion the possibility that they might one day be related by marriage.

'Teddy's own parents are both dead, as you know,' said Victoria, 'so I can see that he might find it difficult to understand your obligation to travel home. But he and Roland both miss having parents at home, as I'm sure he's told you. Their mother died when they were both very young. I think there was a third child involved, but Roland has never said and I don't like to ask. I knew their father, but I was only a little girl at the time. The Davenports were – still are – a very old family firm of solicitors and they took care of all our

302

family's legal affairs. Have done for generations. Everyone expected Teddy to follow his father and Roland into the business, but he was adamant that Roland could take it over and that he would break the mould and become a doctor.'

It had been Roland's idea that Victoria should go to St Angelus to do the nursing training she was so insistent on undertaking, because that was where Teddy had recently qualified as a doctor. She and Roland were already engaged, but she was determined to complete her training before they got married. 'When I marry you,' she told her fiancé, 'I will do so as Staff Nurse Baker. My Aunt Minnie will despair and my mother will beam with pride from her grave.'

Roland had known Victoria's mother. He knew that there was a link for Victoria between her mother and nursing. Her mother had taken care of all the walking injured who'd been discharged from military service during the war and had returned to Bolton and its environs. While she was tending to the sick, no one had had any idea that she was very unwell herself, her weak heart a legacy of her childhood rheumatic fever. She had passed away very suddenly.

'Really, I didn't know all that,' said Dana. 'What was Teddy's father like?' She was intrigued to know the inside information on his family. He very rarely spoke about home and had mentioned his parents only once, when she'd asked him a specific question. She got the distinct impression that it was not a subject he wanted to talk about and so she had never broached it again.

'Well, he was injured during the war and my mother and I used to cycle out from Baker Hall, me on my little bike, carrying the dressings in my basket. A lot of the men had terrible leg ulcers. Mother used to give me the dressings because I couldn't break them if I came off my bike. I just remember their father as a wounded man. A quiet man. He'd been my family's solicitor for years, my grandfather's as well, I think, and the Davenports were advising the Bakers even before then, as far as I know.'

'How old was Teddy at the time?'

'Well, he was older than me, younger than Roland. But, you know, I can't really remember Teddy. He was the cheeky one of the two. Roland was very much the responsible older brother and that was apparent even to me as a ten-year-old. Teddy was always up to something and I think he was the closest to his mother, but, do you know, they never mention her. He was usually up a tree, if I remember rightly.'

Dana smiled at the thought of her precious Teddy as a little boy. 'I don't mind telling you, Victoria, I'm slightly jealous that you have that history with Teddy that I just don't.'

'Ah, well, you know how to rectify that, don't you, my lovely. You just have to make sure you have a future.'

'Yes, but look at you with the ring on your finger

and your secret nights in hotels. The two of you have a fine time. Teddy and I only get to see each other once a week.'

Victoria put her arm around her friend's shoulder. 'You know what, I'm going to suggest to Roland that instead of you dragging Teddy back to the farm, where you will end up working, he invites you both to Bolton. Or even that you both sneak away somewhere. How about the bright lights of London? You can buy a fake wedding ring. No one will know.'

Dana looked mortified. 'Victoria, I'm Irish. I can't do that. My mammy would skin me alive. God, no. I envy you, but I could no more sleep in the same bed as Teddy before we were married than fly to the moon. God knows, I want to, though, but I sure don't want to go straight to hell either. It's all right for you, Lady Baker, you aren't even a Catholic.'

'Gosh, you Catholics and your guilt. It's just as big a sin for an Anglican, you know. You just have to use your brain – would God really be that cross if you had a bit of fun?'

Dana gasped. 'Victoria, yes, he would. It might be different for you, you and Roland are engaged to be married, but honest to God, if I gave in to Teddy, why would he want to marry me? There would be nothing to marry me for. I don't have money or a big house or anything. All I have is me. A farm girl from the west of Ireland. For the life of me, I don't even know why he likes me. He could have any nurse he wanted.'

'Well, that is just nonsense. How about because you are one of the nicest and, with your red hair and your blue eyes, the prettiest nurse in the hospital. It's Teddy who is the lucky one, not you. And when it comes to the big house, neither do I have one any longer, but I do know what you mean. I am probably a bit more relaxed about these things because my parents are no longer around. I have no one to let down. And you know what, if I did become pregnant, I would take some pleasure from the expression on Aunt Minnie's face when I told her. She would leave the country probably, unable to face the scandal.'

'Hush, Victoria. That would be awful. Be careful, you don't want that to happen.'

'Well, I'm not sure how I'm going to be able to prevent it for much longer, sweetie. The one thing I've learnt is that what's quite enough for us is nowhere near enough for a man. Not for Roland, anyway. He's never had enough.'

Dana blushed furiously. Her experience of sex before Teddy had been a near rape by Patrick, her neighbour from back home who'd followed her to Liverpool and been arrested as a peeping Tom. There were many reasons apart from the weather why a visit home was an unattractive prospect, but she would have to face it.

Teddy could not have been more different to Patrick if he tried and with his gentle manner and soothing charm he'd laid to rest her fears about intimate contact. He was sweet and patient, but lately he'd taken to mentioning in the most subtle way that Roland was enjoying an entirely different kind of relationship with her close friend Victoria. With every date, Dana could feel the pressure building. His latest salvo had been the suggestion of a holiday.

'We can go somewhere where no one knows us,' he'd said. 'To the Lake District or the coast. We could book in to a nice little hotel.' They had been kissing goodnight at the time, in the front seats of Teddy's car, parked a hundred yards away from the front door to the nurses' home. Teddy didn't mention whether it would be one room or two and Dana didn't ask. She could guess what the answer would be.

'I'll have to write home first and see if I'm needed on the farm,' said Dana as a way to stall things. She could almost feel Teddy's exasperation.

'If they've managed without you all this time, why would they suddenly need you when you have two weeks off?' he pleaded and kissed the side of her neck. As he did so, his hands began venturing towards places they never had before.

Dana placed her hand firmly over Teddy's and guided them back to her waist. 'Give me a week to find out,' she said. 'Just a week.'

That had been over a week ago and their next date was looming. She would telephone home tonight. She was almost certain what the outcome of the conversation would be, but at least she wouldn't be lying to Teddy.

'Anyway, one thing about Pammy being on casualty with Teddy,' said Dana, 'she can tell me what he gets up to. It's not as if he isn't known for his high jinks. I must ask him one day how many nurses it was he dumped into dirty-linen trolleys. She can keep an eye on him for me. Or, knowing her, he can tell me about her antics.'

Both nurses laughed. Dana went off to her ward, but Victoria had a few minutes to spare and decided to wait for Pammy to come out of the cloakroom so she could wish her luck on her first shift in casualty.

Pammy Tanner was a true cheeky Scouser. A nurse who got herself into numerous scrapes but was loved by every patient who came into contact with her. She had always liked Teddy. He was the first doctor she had set her eye on. She had been stunned to discover that he already knew Dana, but she hid her disappointment well and soon transferred her adoration to the new gynae consultant, Mr Oliver Gaskell. Pammy was not alone; every nurse at the hospital had been disappointed when the rumour spread that Dana had landed the very attractive Dr Davenport.

Pammy was now one of Dana's best friends. Just the other weekend, they had all been out dancing together. Teddy with Dana, Pammy searching for Oliver Gaskell. Ever since the night of the last doctors' dance and a particularly smoochy number, she had been convinced that Oliver Gaskell was in love with her. 'He's just shy, that's all,' she said when Teddy had very gently asked if she was sure that he carried a flame. 'I know he likes me, Teddy. He probably thinks that because he's a consultant and I'm still training, he might get me into trouble with Matron or something, but he won't. Mrs Duffy is a dote and we can wrap her around our little fingers, can't we, Dana?'

Teddy was not convinced. He liked Oliver Gaskell well enough as an acquaintance. He respected him as a skilled obstetrician and gynaecologist, and he was in awe of his war record. He often had a last pint with him down at the pub, but when it came to women, well, if Dr Teddy Davenport had had a sister of an eligible age, he would have kept her well away from Oliver Gaskell.

As she came out into the corridor, Pammy saw Teddy take the steps to casualty two at a time. She pushed back the errant wisps of dark hair under her cap and refastened a kirby grip. She was about to shout to him but stopped as a probationer nurse hurried alongside him. She watched as Teddy opened the door for the trainee. She was willowy and pretty, one of the September intake girls. Her name was Sarah and she was living at Lovely Lane. Pammy felt a shiver run down her spine. There was something about the way she laid her hand on Teddy's arm that made Pammy's hackles rise. She instinctively knew she would have to keep an eye on Nurse Sarah Makebee and Dana's Teddy.

'Here, let me,' said Teddy, as he held open the door.

Even from a distance, Pammy could tell he was dazzled by the girl's beauty. She tutted, then turned and caught sight of Victoria.

'Would you look at her,' whispered Victoria, nodding at Sarah Makebee. 'It's as if her uniform was designed with the sole purpose of enhancing her beauty. She just looks great in it, doesn't she?'

'She looks more than great,' said Pammy. 'Does she actually eat? Has anyone actually ever seen her swallow anything? Look at the size of her waist. It's tiny.'

Both nurses had stopped still in their tracks and they stood in awe of the perfectly coiffed hair swept over and under her perfectly starched and upright cap. Pammy's hand slowly raised to feel her own. Yes, as she'd thought, the ends were already flopping.

'Beth doesn't like her,' announced Victoria. 'Says she has a boyfriend who's a doctor in London. Beth thinks that, for a probationer, she's a bit of a know-it-all.'

'Oh, for God's sake, if that's what Beth thinks, that means she's clever as well as pretty. That's not fair.'

'Well, fair or not, she's just turned Teddy into a bowl of jelly, so keep an eye out there, Pammy.'

'You can depend on it, Vic. As if I haven't got enough to do, working with Sister Antrobus yet

310

again. I'm convinced Matron has put me on casualty deliberately.'

Pammy set her chin as she marched towards casualty. Teddy and Nurse Sarah Makebee disappeared into the gloom ahead of her and the door swung back and almost smacked her in the face.

CHAPTER 18

Pammy felt like trembling as she walked in through the casualty doors. She looked to see which way Nurse Makebee and Teddy had turned, but there was no sign. She spotted Sister Antrobus in her navy-blue uniform, belt and tall starched white cap. She was talking to the new assistant matron and they appeared to be deep in conversation. Pammy almost groaned out loud. The nurses' home had been swirling with rumours and stories about the new Miss Van Gilder.

'They say she made Sister Antrobus swear the other day,' Beth had said over breakfast at Lovely Lane one morning. 'Apparently, Miss Van Gilder asked Sister to demonstrate her procedure for ordering clean dressings and to show her exactly how she calculated her weekly requirements.'

The rumour had spread around the hospital like wildfire and Beth didn't skimp on the drama. 'Can you imagine!' she continued. 'So Sister Antrobus told Miss Van Gilder that she'd been a ward sister since St Angelus had its own sterilizing ovens in the kitchen and that she could do the ordering in her sleep. "I don't need to keep records of what I order and why," she said. And then . . .'

Beth's face was animated and the girls were transfixed as they tucked into their breakfast toast.

'And then, Miss Van Gilder said, "Well then, you will have no difficulty explaining your process to me, will you? Things are different now. You will need to keep a record and I will check it every week.""'

The girls giggled, imagining the steam coming out of Sister Antrobus's ears, her eyes burning red, her cap flaring into flames . . .

'Anyway,' continued Beth, 'after Miss Van Gilder left, Sister Antrobus stormed into the office, slammed the door and said, "Bloody Germans!" And Miss Van Gilder isn't even German, she's Dutch.'

'No!' they all exclaimed.

'Fancy being so rude about the Germans. We are at peace now,' said Victoria.

The only person who didn't bat an eyelid was Pammy. 'What are youse all so shocked about? You think there's anyone in Liverpool has a nice word to say about a German? We were bombed to smithereens, you know. Anyway, aren't I the lucky one, Assistant Matron won't be bothering me – it'll be too busy in casualty for anyone to have time for an old bossy boots like her, and Sister Antrobus will have us all run ragged, for sure.'

Casualty was very different from the wards.

There was no continuity of care or consistency of patients. Everything happened by the minute and on demand. No two hours, let alone two days, were the same.

As Pammy approached the desk, Sister Antrobus looked up from the ledger she'd been studying. It seemed as if Miss Van Gilder was towering over her, even though she was shorter. This illusion surprised Pammy.

'Nurse Tanner!' Sister Antrobus exclaimed, looking both flustered and relieved to see Pammy, which also came as a surprise. Sister Antrobus and Pammy had had an unhappy time together on ward two and Pammy thought that she must be the last person Sister Antrobus wanted to see walking on to casualty.

But there was no time for pleasantries as the voice of Doreen, the casualty clerk, rang out from behind her counter. She was holding the telephone in her hand. 'There's a blue-light job due in in ten minutes, Sister. Woman hit by a tram down on the pier head.'

Sister Antrobus shook her head. 'We get one a week at the moment. Why can't people watch where they're walking?' She didn't expect an answer to her question as she looked about the unit to take in what was happening and where to make space.

'And there's a young boy in the waiting area. He has breathing difficulties . . .'

Sister Antrobus was very obviously about to bark

an order when Pammy caught her eye. 'Why is your cap askew?' she snapped.

Immediately, Assistant Matron butted in too. 'Are you wearing make-up?'

Pammy ignored Miss Van Gilder and chose to answer Sister Antrobus. 'Oh, I'm sorry, Sister Antrobus, it must have been the wind. I was a bit late getting out this morning – blame Scamp, not me.' She grinned and, lifting her hand to her cap, readjusted her errant kirby grip as she tried to make the flopping sides stand upright.

Miss Van Gilder looked as though she was about to bite her head off for not replying as, to either side of them, nurses moved chairs and screens around to prepare for the emergency. Pammy was eager to join them.

'What on earth are you talking about?' retorted Sister Antrobus. 'Blame Scamp? Who on earth is Scamp? I didn't ask you for an extravagant excuse steeped in a lie, I asked for an explanation.'

Pammy wondered whether she should fight her corner or let Sister Antrobus win. It was, after all, her first day on casualty and she was desperate to make a good impression. She had only just recovered from the commotion she'd caused when she'd insisted that a baby aborted at twenty-eight weeks that had lived for a few short moments be afforded a visit from a priest and a proper burial. It had led to her being suspended from ward two.

She bit her tongue hard. She could hear the voice of her mam, Maisie, ringing in her head.

'Don't get into any more scrapes, Pammy. Be a good girl now.' Pammy had thought this extremely unjust. At the very least, she had uncovered the behaviour of a very dishonourable doctor.

'Sorry, Sister Antrobus,' Pammy said in a timid voice that she very rarely used.

Sister Antrobus sighed. 'Nurse Tanner, the little boy on the chairs, could you transfer him into a cubicle quickly, please. His breathing is really rather laboured.'

Miss Van Gilder looked over towards the child. 'A psychosomatic case if ever there was one,' she said in a very loud voice. 'All neglected children have breathing difficulties. It's their mother they need. You can tell a neglected child a mile off by the sound of the wheeze.'

Sister Antrobus didn't look the slightest bit surprised by Miss Van Gilder's comments. 'Yes, well, anyway, please look after him, Nurse Tanner. The houseman has arrived and our senior casualty doctor, Dr Mackintosh, is on his way down. I think he wants to bring in someone from the infant health service, but there is no one available yet.'

'Yes, Sister Antrobus, right away,' said Pammy as she took her cue to remove herself from the presence of Miss Van Gilder.

Pammy threw her cape into the staff room as she passed by. She missed the hook and heard it slide down on top of all the other capes which had also missed the hook and sat in a pile on the staff-room floor. She took a quick glance at herself in the mirror. It was impossible for Pammy to walk past a mirror without sneaking a peep. She loved the new black eyeliner her mam had bought her and she'd hoped that, unlike on the wards, she'd get away with wearing it on casualty. So far, so good. She'd sidestepped Miss Van Gilder's scrutiny and she wondered if Sister Antrobus had deliberately rescued her.

As she walked towards the waiting area, she looked around to see what the other nurses were doing. She already had the sense that it was going to be a case of learn as you go on casualty. Everyone looked much too busy to have the time to show her what to do or where to start and the tension in the atmosphere was palpable. Nurses were rushing about with trolleys and drip stands, the clip-clop of their shoes reverberating off the polished wooden floor. Against the perimeter wall were cubicles containing beds, some of them screened off with plain, sage-green curtains. A male nurse disappeared into one, carrying what appeared to be a bucket filled with plaster of Paris. Pammy could hear a faint whimpering from within. Another set of curtains were pulled back and a staff nurse waved at Pammy, handed a set of case notes to a doctor, made a brief comment and tripped across to Pammy.

'Are you OK?' she asked. 'Is it your first time on casualty?'

Pammy only had time to nod before the nurse rattled on.

'Thank God you're here, it's been mad. I've worked here for fifteen years and it's no quieter now than it was during the war. We all thought once the bombing was over it would be back to normal, but the past couple of years have been mad. Mad, I say.' She shook her head as if she couldn't quite believe what she was saying herself.

'Right, I have to be quick. There's a blackboard and chalk in the office to mark up your patient's name and details and we keep those on the board until point of transfer to a ward. That way everyone can see at a glance what is happening and where. When you wipe the details off, you fill in this daily record, in triplicate using the carbon paper. You give them to Doreen in the office and she keeps one and at the end of each day sends the other copies to Matron's office and to Assistant Matron, so don't miss anything off. Matron likes to know everything that happens on here during the day.'

Pammy instinctively took a deep breath and stood a little taller. She was going to be under close observation on casualty, one way or another.

'You also have to record each case into this book.' The staff nurse indicated a very large thick black book that was lying open on the desk. 'We all use the patient notes here on the unit, doctors and nurses alike, and the notes leave here with the patients during transfer to the ward.' She flashed a harried smile at Pammy. 'We don't normally have trainee nurses on here. Some of the sights could put you off nursing for life, but in truth, we couldn't run the place without you all, so we're very relieved you're here, I can tell you. We even have a probationer – a Nurse Makebee; do you know her? – that's a first for casualty too, but honestly, we are so busy. They had an RTA in here last night.'

Pammy looked puzzled.

'A road traffic accident. Sadly, the driver and his passenger died. And we had a pair of twins delivered in cubicle three – decided to pop out before the porter could transfer the mother to maternity. She had no idea she was pregnant. Tiny, she was. Came in with abdominal pain and bingo, half an hour later she's a mother of twins. Anyway, do you understand how we record what happens? It's most important.'

Pammy blinked. 'Er, I think so. Where do I get the patient's notes from?'

'There, on the ledge.' The staff nurse pointed at a pile of buff-brown, pre-lined notes. 'Doreen keeps them topped up. Come and meet her now.'

Pammy felt mildly embarrassed. Everyone who worked at the hospital knew of Doreen's story. Pammy had noticed how pale she looked and the sadness in her eyes told their own tale. She spent her working day sitting behind a counter manning a telephone and hammering away at a typewriter, issuing forms in triplicate and dealing with difficult patients and exhausted ambulance drivers.

Doreen didn't hear them approach as she tapped

away on a sheet of paper that was to be inserted inside a set of patient notes.

'Doreen, here's our new student nurse.'

As Doreen turned, Pammy recognized her face from the front page of the *Echo*. She looked to Pammy as though she needed a good meal and a laugh. One of my mam's Sunday dinners is what she needs, she thought.

Doreen raised a hand. 'Hiya,' she said. 'Let me know if you need anything. I'm right here.'

'Thanks. I think I have it all,' said Pammy with a huge, encouraging smile that said, I know all about you and I'm here too. 'I'm Nurse Tanner, by the way,' she said to the staff nurse as they turned away.

'Lovely. I'm Staff Nurse Imping and I've just taken a call for your patient from the infant health service registrar. Dr Davenport – he's the on-duty houseman – is going to be in charge of the little lad with the help of Dr Mackintosh until the paediatrician arrives. He's up on the children's ward at the moment with the twins from last night. I think that little lad has been in here before. When you have his name, ask Doreen to look out his notes for you. She'll be able to find them in a flash. All the ambulance drivers report to her and she clerks the patients in; the walking wounded do it themselves. Got all that?'

Pammy blinked again. 'Yes, of course I have,' she said and grinned.

'Great. I know it's a lot to take in, but there's

only one way to learn on casualty and that's to be thrown in at the deep end. I'll come back and see you when I've finished with this chap.' She nodded towards a cubicle. 'He sat on the gear stick in his new car and somehow the end came off and got lodged in his rectum.' A loud roar echoed through casualty. 'Oops, maybe not any more, eh!' she added. 'Looks like that one's been sorted out now.' And she disappeared behind the curtain.

Pammy grabbed a sheaf of notes from Doreen and walked over to the wooden chair in the waiting arca where a young woman was sitting with an obviously poorly little boy on her lap.

'Hello, love,' Pammy said. 'What's up with you then, little mite?' As she spoke, she sat down on the chair next to the young woman, extracted her pen from the long, thin pocket in her uniform dress and opened out his notes on her knee. She reached out and took the little boy's hand in her own and smiled at him. He was obviously in distress.

Pammy and her cohort had spent a week studying lung disease with Sister Haycock. They had learnt enough so far to know that in Liverpool lung disease was a daily killer. Children and the elderly were particularly susceptible to chest infections, pneumonia and TB. They were victims of the thick, suffocating, soot-tinged smog produced by the cool, damp atmosphere around the River Mersey and the high number of coal fires in the city. Pammy had grown up on the dock streets and a bronchial baby was something she'd seen many times before.

The pretty young woman accompanying the little boy looked anxious and fretful.

'Don't worry, love,' said Pammy as she placed her hand over the top of the young woman's hand. 'We can get him sorted out, I'm sure.' But she could tell by the fearful look in the girl's eyes that her reassurance wasn't working and that the girl's distress was deep rooted. She placed the back of her hand on the little boy's forehead. 'Well, I'll just get a thermometer, but he doesn't appear to have a temperature and that's a good thing. What's the little fella's name? Can you say your name, love?'

The little boy looked up at the young woman, his eyes pleading.

The girl looked at him lovingly and obliged. 'His name is Joe Lancashire and he's nearly four. I'm his sister, Lily.'

'Smashing,' said Pammy. 'Can you both go into the cubicle here and I'll take down some details while we wait for the doctor to arrive.'

Five minutes later, Joe was lying down on a casualty bed with the cot sides up and a thermometer protruding from his bottom. Lily's wasn't sure Joe would have agreed to let her take him to the hospital if he'd known that was going to happen, but he was so distressed and finding it so hard to breathe, he appeared to neither notice nor care as he lay on his side with Pammy gently cupping his knees to his chest.

She removed the thermometer swiftly. 'There, you see,' she said as she wiped the thermometer, shook the mercury back down to the bottom and laid the thermometer down in an enamel kidney dish of diluted, opaque white Dettol. 'His temperature is fine and that's a relief. Now, just a few bits and pieces to ask you while we wait for Dr Davenport. What's your address, love?'

As soon as Lily mentioned that they were from Clare Cottages, Pammy fought to prevent her eyebrows from rising. Clare Cottages were notorious across Liverpool and everyone knew the place was nothing like its name implied. It had been drilled into Pammy since she was a child that she was never to wander up towards the cottages.

Little Joe began to cry. Not loudly or with any obvious fear or anguish, just the gentlest of sobs, which came through trembling lips as his tears began to flow.

'Oh, love.' Lily bent over him as he lay on the bed. She'd had no time to tie up her hair that morning and it fanned out across the bed and buried her brother under a blanket of glistening chestnut.

'He's just a bit frightened, Miss Lancashire,' said Pammy gently as she placed her hand lightly on Lily's back. 'It's the unfamiliar surroundings, the strong smell. It used to scare me too, and I work here.'

Lily lifted her head. She was bent over Joe in

an awkward position, but she slipped her arm under his shoulders and looked up at Pammy. 'I think he's probably too hungry to be worried about the smell. I didn't have time to give him his breakfast before we left the house. He was just too poorly.'

Lily failed to mention that there was no breakfast to be had in the house and that Katie had gone to school with an empty stomach.

Today was payday down at the processing plant. It was Lily's job to tot up the worksheets and prepare the pay packets with the amounts carefully worked out and written on the front of the envelopes in large, clearly distinguishable writing. In three years, she had never missed a payday at work. As she sat in the hospital waiting for the doctor to come and see little Joe, she felt panic rising inside her like bile. She was terrified that Mrs McConaghy would use her absence to not pay the men. Mrs Mc Conaghy would be struggling. It was so long since she had calculated the pay, Lily was sure she would have forgotten even how to add up the worksheets. Amy wouldn't have a clue and besides, over the past weeks, Amy had been coming into work later and later each morning.

In her head, Lily ran through the stages of the payday routine. She always had to complete the calculations by 2 p.m., at which point she placed the empty pay packets on Mrs McConaghy's desk. Then the ritual began. The unlocking of the safe, while Mr McConaghy stood guard at the front door. The meticulous counting out of the cash into each envelope. The locking of the front door with the large set of jangling keys as Mr McConaghy came over to the desk and re-counted. The locking of the safe, and the 'All clear, my dear,' from Mrs McConaghy as the doors were once again unlocked.

And yet, to Lily's amazement, despite the meticulous routine, they still managed to make mistakes.

When the bell rang at 6 p.m., the gate at the bottom of the wooden steps would be opened and the men would line up on the stairs and the balcony, waiting patiently outside the door for Mrs McConaghy to hand each of them their weekly pay, just enough to support a family until the following week. The distribution of pay was done in a man's own time, not the McConaghys'. Mrs McConaghy liked to do it slowly, to ensure that each employee knew how lucky he was. She would often blow on her diamond ring and give it a polish on the sleeve of her cardigan before she began the handing-over process. It was as if this subconscious affirmation of her wealth imbued her with a feeling of security and superiority, though Lily was never sure if she knew she was doing it.

'I'm two shillings short,' was a common complaint and it would be met with groans from the men. A complaint always delayed the process by about ten minutes, which was especially unwelcome when the men were itching to get to the pub across the road.

'Might be just as well if I took the pay straight to the Red Admiral and didn't bother giving them the envelope,' Mrs McConaghy would say to Lily as the last man filed down the steps and straight through the pub door directly opposite.

Lily was meticulous in her calculations and the mistakes were never any fault of hers, as the men well knew. It was always down to Mrs McConaghy, who somehow had trouble counting out the exact amount into each packet. Two shillings would put a meal on the table and no man could afford to be short-changed.

If Lily missed an entire payday, she knew there would be a commotion in the office and she was terrified that this might result in Mrs McConaghy seeking to have her replaced by someone from a more stable home environment. Someone without a poorly little brother. Her sister Katie had sensed her panic earlier that morning.

'Shall I go to the hospital, Lily?' she'd asked her when they discovered that both their parents were too drunk to rouse.

'No, love, you go to school. You must never miss a day of school.' Lily didn't want to tell her that if her seven-year-old half-sister walked into the hospital with a three-year-old boy, the welfare office would be telephoned and neither of them would return home. They would be straight into one of the many children's homes dotted around the city.

Pammy had already taken in the poor state of

Lily's and Joe's clothing and yet it was obvious that someone had been making an attempt to keep the boy clean. His face was almost as white as his neck was black and a tidemark skimmed his chin and divided the clean from the dirty. He smelt strongly of camphor oil.

She had recently read an article in the *Liverpool Echo* about how, when the new housing was eventually built out at Huyton and Speke, the families from Clare Cottages would be the first to be relocated and the cottages would then be demolished. It had been confirmed as the worst housing in Liverpool. Infant- and child-mortality rates were higher in the cottages than in any other part of Liverpool.

'How long has he been like this?' she asked.

'He was like it when I got home from work last night. I put some camphor oil on his chest, but this morning he was no better. He was panicking and he seemed really frightened. I'd never seen him like that before, so I thought I had better bring him here. He usually gets better after a few hours, but he's been like this since last night.'

While Lily spoke, Pammy counted Joe's respirations and took his pulse. 'Where's your mam?' she asked and looked up sharply when there was no answer. She guessed that Lily was no more than seventeen, which surely meant she couldn't be wholly responsible for such a young and poorly child.

'She's had to go to work,' Lily lied. Lily knew

the hospital was a dangerous place for her and the children. It represented authority, had links to the welfare board. She needed to keep her mouth shut. Her only friend was Sister Therese and she was at Mass. When she'd realized that, Lily had decided that Joe couldn't wait. Even though her instincts told her to hang around at the convent until Mass was over and she could ask Sister Therese what to do, a stronger impulse drove her to rush to the hospital.

Dr Davenport pulled back the curtain with a flourish and joined Pammy and Lily. He picked up the notes and said, 'Hello, er, Mrs Lancashire?' It was a question more than a statement as he looked down at Lily's ring finger.

'No, Doctor, I am Joe's sister. Our mam is at work. She left before he woke up, so she didn't know how bad he was and I thought I had better bring him down.'

Lily was talking faster than normal. She knew it and so did Dr Davenport.

Teddy smiled at Pammy, took his stethoscope out of his pocket and said to Joe, 'Can I listen to your chest, young man?'

Joe nodded his head, his blonde hair bouncing and his blue eyes wide with apprehension.

Teddy blew on the end of his stethoscope to warm it and, placing it on Joe's chest, listened hard as an expression of great concentration fixed his facial features into a deep frown. 'Ah ha,' he said loudly. 'I thought as much. That watch I lost last week,

Nurse Tanner . . .' He was now looking at Pammy. 'It's in there.' He tapped Joe on the rib cage, lightly.

Little Joe grinned from ear to ear, before he began to cough violently.

Turning his attention to Lily, Teddy added in a low voice, 'The senior casualty registrar will be down from the children's ward in a moment; he's the doctor who actually knows what he's doing. I thought I would just pop along and see if I could help in any way before he gets here. How is your breathing now, Joe? Is it worse than, say, last night?'

Joe nodded his head frantically.

'Has the camphor oil I can smell filling the entire casualty department helped any?'

Little Joe opened his lips, about to speak, but Teddy put his hand on Joe's.

'On second thoughts, don't you speak, little man. Best you conserve what breath you have for the vital questioning from the doctor who looks after the nearly-four-year-old little boys with trouble breathing. Not three or five, mind, we have other doctors for them, he's just the nearly-fours man. He's been waiting for weeks for you to arrive. Lives in a cupboard, he does, until one pops in. The last nearly-four-year-old we had in stayed with us for a little while, being looked after by these gorgeous nurses in pink dresses, and when it came time for him to leave, he didn't want to go home. Can you imagine that?'

Lily smiled as he spoke and thought that she for one could imagine just that.

Joe's eyes widened. 'He's been living here, waiting for me?' he wheezed.

'Oh that's right, little man, and shall I tell you something else? He's the only doctor in this hospital to carry a bar of chocolate around in his pocket. The doctors who look after the threes and fours, they can't get near the key for the chocolate cupboard.'

Despite his obvious discomfort, Joe's eyes had lit up and he was beaming from ear to ear. His face was a picture of wonderment.

'You will see for yourself exactly what I mean,' said Teddy to Lily, whose eyes had filled with tears of gratitude for nothing more than that he'd made Joe smile. She wanted to say to both Pammy and the doctor that they weren't used to such kindness or attention. That never in his life had anyone other than Lily spoken so many kind words to little Joe or been as concerned as this doctor so obviously was.

No sooner had the words left Teddy's mouth than he heard Dr Mackintosh talking to Doreen. 'Excuse me a moment, please,' he said to Lily and disappeared beyond the curtains.

Dr Mackintosh was scanning the entries in the big black book. He appeared dishevelled, with a stethoscope flung around his neck. He was unshaven, his shirt was crumpled and his copper hair was tousled.

'I'm so sorry,' he said to Teddy. 'I've been here since the day before yesterday. We have so many poorly bronchial babies on the ward. The air in Liverpool, it's tough.' His accent was Scottish and his voice was gentle and full of authority.

'So I hear,' Teddy replied. 'I bet you'll be glad when all this talk of a Clean Air Act for Liverpool comes to something.'

'I wouldn't put money on it happening any day soon,' Dr Mackintosh replied. 'It's in the hands of the politicians. If London hadn't had that dreadful smog, a Clean Air Act wouldn't even be on the cards. They say four thousand people died in London as a result of that smog, but do you see any politicians asking how many people died in Liverpool? And even if it does become law, apparently it will be down to each city corporation to decide whether or not they accept it. If the children of local politicians had died as a result of the smog, it would have been passed by now.'

Hearing that made Teddy furious. He'd heard quite a lot about the issue from Oliver Gaskell, whose father, Dr Gaskell, had spent the last year travelling up and down to London to give his expert opinion on it. He knew that Dr Gaskell was frustrated with the progress.

'There's a chap, an MP called Nabarro,' said Dr Mackintosh. 'He's trying to push the government along by bringing in some sort of private bill. But right now we need to attend to this very important young man you have behind the curtain.'

Both doctors walked back into the cubicle.

Teddy smiled at little Joe and winked. Little Joe tried to wink back, but his breathing was so laboured it was all he could do to inhale.

Dr Mackintosh examined little Joe thoroughly and spent what was actually minutes but felt like hours to Lily listening to his chest.

Folding his stethoscope in half, he pushed it into his pocket and looked at Joe. 'Right, young man, we have a little problem here. I'm going to need you to be admitted to St Angelus for a wee while.'

Without waiting for a reply from Joe, he turned to Pammy and Dr Davenport. 'I'm going to give him some aminophylline. Nurse, could you set up for an intravenous injection, please.'

He then turned to address Lily. 'Mother, would you like to step outside and we can have a little word.'

Lily looked from Pammy to the doctor, a pleading expression in her eyes.

Reading the signs, Pammy spoke for her. 'This is his sister, Dr Mackintosh. Joe's mother had left for work before Miss Lancashire here noticed Joe's breathing was worse than usual.'

'Really? With a wheeze as bad as that? How could your mother have slept a wink? He must have kept the whole street awake. How could she have not noticed?'

Dr Mackintosh had been working in the casualty department at St Angelus since the end of the war. He had trained in Edinburgh and worked in

Glasgow before travelling south to Liverpool during the war years. He had witnessed enough cases of neglect to have given him a sixth sense.

'Our mam, she works hard, she's a heavy sleeper,' said Lily anxiously. She cast a glance at little Joe and hoped he wouldn't say anything. She had used this line once before at the doctor's and little Joe had piped up, 'No that's wrong, Lily. Our mam doesn't go to work, she's in bed.'

Dr Mackintosh walked over to the seats and beckoned for Lily to sit down. 'How long has he been like this?' he asked, his voice brimming with gentle concern.

Lily fumbled for an answer. Just as she was about to reply, Teddy's voice rang out from a gap in the curtains. 'Er, Dr Mackintosh, do you think you might have forgotten something?'

Dr Mackintosh looked at Teddy with a puzzled expression on his face. Teddy stared at the pocket in his doctor's coat and nodded his head furiously. He had parted the curtains and was holding them from the inside. Lily thought he looked ridiculously funny, like a talking head hanging on to the outside of the curtains. Lily also thought Dr Mackintosh and Teddy were the kindest people she had ever met.

'Forgotten something . . .?' Dr Mackintosh furrowed his brow and then Lily watched as a twinkle lit up his eyes. 'Ah, well now, excuse me,' he said to her as he stood. 'Have I got this right, is Joe a nearly-four-year-old? Yes, he is, I see now,' he said, looking down at the sheet of paper he'd written on as he walked back behind the curtains.

Joe nodded his head furiously.

'Well now, you see, I wouldn't have known that. You are a big man for four. I thought you were at least five. Dr Davenport will tell you, I've been waiting a very long time for a nearly-four-year-old to come into casualty because, you see, here in my pocket I've been carrying around with me a very special piece of chocolate for the next nearly-four-year-old who comes in. And it looks like that is you. Are you sure this young man is only nearly four years old, Dr Davenport, and you aren't having me on? He looks like he's clever and big enough for school to me.'

Teddy put on a very grave face and picked up the notes Pammy had left on the side of the bed. 'Well, Nurse Tanner has put down that he is nearly four, but you know what she's like. You have to watch her,' he said to little Joe. 'Turn your back and her hand is down Dr Mackintosh's pocket and nicking the chocolate as fast as you like. She's been after that special chocolate for nearly-four-year-olds. Watch out, here she comes.'

Dr Mackintosh pulled a Cadbury's chocolate bar out of his pocket and snapped off a large chunk. 'I have to keep some back,' he said to little Joe. 'Nearly-four-year-olds are like buses, you never know when the next one will come along.'

Joe took the chocolate and turned it over and over in his hands, looking at it in wonder. Then, holding his arm out to Lily, he gasped between breaths, 'Take it home for our Katie, Lily.'

Again, tears filled Lily's eyes. 'I will not. You can keep it in your pocket for when you're feeling better.'

'Trolley is ready, Doctor,' said Pammy as she bustled in behind the curtains.

'Just one minute whilst I explain to Miss Lancashire here what it is I am about to do.'

Anthony Mackintosh took Lily by the arm and led her back towards the hard wooden chairs. Over his shoulder he said, 'Could you get this young lady a cup of tea, please. She will be here a wee while yet.'

'Of course,' said Pammy. 'Right away.'

'And a biscuit or two wouldn't go amiss, Nurse, thank you. Now, what your brother has, we see often here in young children. He has no temperature, he isn't sickening as such. There is an irregularity in the pattern of his breathing. He is struggling to exhale, to breathe out, and you may have noticed that his chest bone protrudes slightly, even at his young age, which we call a pigeon chest. The learned doctors in this land think that what your brother has is a breathing condition that is psychosomatic, that is, it is all in his head. According to them, the wheeze you hear on the top of his breathing is actually the child crying out for his mother.'

Anthony took in the expression that shot across Lily's face. Nothing in these situations escaped his attention.

335

'Now, it may interest you to know that I don't hold with any of this, but in a funny way I have to, because I can't prove it is anything else. My own suspicion is that there is something inflammatory, and certainly not infectious, going on, but I just can't prove that.'

Lily looked confused. Anthony leant forward on the seat. He felt sorry for this young woman. She obviously loved her little brother very much.

'I'm sorry. I hope I'm not making this sound too confusing and complicated. Look, the wee lad needs an injection right now to help with his breathing. We have to give it to him very, very slowly, but when we have, I'd expect that he'll be well enough to go home in a few days and he won't be giving that chocolate to anyone, least of all his sister. But if he isn't any better, I cannot let him go back home until I know the attack has stopped.'

Lily smiled and as she did, Anthony Mackintosh's heart leapt. Her hair was unbraided and hung in a voluminous, unkempt mass around her shoulders, framing her face and making her features look small and vulnerable and her eyes wide and apprehensive. He knew that there was a secret behind those eyes and for a split second he had an urge to know what it was. To know the real reason Joe had come in with his sister and not a parent.

Pammy pushed a trolley towards them. On it was placed all the equipment she needed and a cup and saucer. 'Here you go,' she said to Lily. 'I've put two sugars in the tea and two custard creams on the saucer too.'

Just at that moment, Miss Van Gilder strode up. 'Has casualty become a café now, may I ask?' Her tone was so sharp that Lily wanted to drop the cup and saucer. Everyone felt the chill breeze that blew across the casualty unit with the arrival of the new assistant matron.

Pammy suddenly remembered something the nurses had been talking about the week earlier. Beth Harper had said that Sister Emily Haycock from the nursing school had threatened to jump out of the window when she heard whom Matron had selected.

Joe began to whimper. Assistant Matron's tone had frightened him, even though she had not said a word to him directly and had spoken over his head, but as Lily came back around the curtains, her tea and biscuits abandoned under the condemning eyes of Miss Van Gilder, he held out both of his arms towards her.

'This boy,' Miss Van Gilder barked at Dr Mackintosh, 'we all know this condition is a psychiatric problem, so why is he here? By that wheeze, I suspect that his mother is absent for much of the time. It is an established fact, Doctor, that the wheezing child uses the wheeze to gain attention. It is a cry for help and an indication that the mother is failing in her mothering duties.'

Teddy thrust his hands deep into his pockets.

Pammy instinctively moved towards the top of the bed, stroked little Joe's hair back from his face and whispered, 'There, there, now.' As she did so, she looked at Lily with an expression that said, 'Don't worry, we are here.'

Dr Mackintosh spoke. 'Assistant Matron, I am well aware of the clinical opinion based on these symptoms. As the senior registrar at St Angelus, I don't require your clinical analysis, thank you very much, and if you don't mind, I would like to alleviate this little boy's symptoms without delay. My opinion is that he has been breathing in this manner for far too long and if he continues, there may be consequences.'

Assistant Matron puffed out her chest and pushed her glasses up her nose. Her dark navy dress, worn at the longer length, which had been common during the war, made her look even more severe. Her overly frilled cap on top of powder-black hair and steel-rimmed glasses failed to project any degree of femininity or compassion.

'As you wish, Dr Mackintosh. You are indeed the senior registrar. However, if I believe that money and beds are being wasted on the feckless in this casualty unit, I shall have to report it to the board.'

Anthony Mackintosh rose to his full height, which was a daunting six foot two inches. 'That is entirely your prerogative, Assistant Matron. However, at this moment, mine is the treatment of some rather distressing symptoms being experienced by a nearly-four-year-old little boy. Although you could be forgiven for thinking he was five.' Dr Mackintosh smiled at little Joe in an attempt to wipe away the look of fear which had flooded his face.

'Dr Davenport, could you hand me the amino-phylline, please. Nurse Tanner, let us find a vein now, shall we? It will take me about half an hour to administer this drug. It must be done very slowly. If given too quickly, it can lower the blood pressure to a dangerous level, which is why I would like his blood pressure taken every four minutes, please, Dr Davenport.'

Miss Van Gilder had stomped off in a huff and Lily, entirely forgotten about as the doctors and Pammy focused all their care and attention on Joe, slumped down on to the wooden chair. She picked up the cup of tea; it was now cold, but she didn't care. It had sugar in, which was a rare thing. Lily's mother sold their sugar coupons to get money for alcohol. There was talk of the coupons ending soon and Lily couldn't wait. One less income stream to be spent in the pub. The cold milky tea was the first thing to pass her lips since teatime the night before. She gulped it down and it tasted delicious. Taking the two custard creams from the saucer, she slipped them into her coat pocket to take home to Katie, as a treat.

Dr Mackintosh took almost forty minutes to administer the aminophylline and when Lily was called back into the cubicle she noticed it had had an effect. Joe was breathing much more easily and his expression was free from panic.

Dr Mackintosh washed his hands at the sink and as he dried them, he walked over to Lily. 'As you can see, he has improved, but not as much as I would have hoped. I would still like to have him on the ward.'

Lily didn't know what to say. She was so grateful to this kind man who had made Joe laugh and the words that were tapping on her brain, demanding to be spoken, were simply not enough.

Dr Mackintosh looked at Lily for what even he knew was too long.

He was thirty and single and hadn't had a girl-friend since his student days. His life since the war had ended had been entirely taken up by the study and practice of emergency medicine. Any number of the nurses he had encountered over the years could have been his wife by now, but he was someone who liked a challenge and felt that something worth having had to be worked for. He had been offered his uncle's GP practice in Aberdeen six years ago but had opted to stay in emergency medicine instead. Its rapid pace of change excited him and he enjoyed trying to keep up with the daily uncovering of new diseases and drugs. Liverpool was one of the most demanding cities in the country to work in, with high levels of industry and poverty and a booming birth rate, and he loved it.

He had met a hundred young boys like Joe, but the young woman who had accompanied her brother had stirred something in him. She was so earnest. So sincere. And her pride, well, that was plain to see and made her all the more intriguing.

Half an hour later, Lily was heading down towards the docks and the processing plant. If she was quick enough, she would have time to make up the pay packets and that would include her own. She would be able to get home with enough food for Katie's tea and then back down to the hospital to visit Joe on the ward. She had been told she would be allowed to visit tonight and then the sister on the children's ward would tell her when she could next visit. Nurse Tanner had said that might not be for another week, if little Joe was to be admitted for a long stay. Lily knew her mother wouldn't be in the least bit bothered about how long Joe had to remain as an in-patient.

Dr Mackintosh had been quite clear about his expectations and the long road ahead for Joe.

'I'm going to keep him in here for at least a couple of weeks,' he'd told her, 'and, to be honest, with a chest as pronounced as his, maybe longer. I have a friend who is a specialist in London who is visiting soon and I may ask him to take a look at Joe. He's working on the theory that this could be an inflammatory condition, not psychosomatic, and I want to do anything I can to support him. And besides, I think Joe has an enhanced chance of getting better in here, where it's warm and there's good, hot food. Would you agree with me? I expect you have a tough time worrying about this young man, don't you?'

Lily had looked up at the gentle giant. She wanted to say so many things to him. That she didn't know people like him existed. That if someone had told her that St Angelus could make Joe so much better, she would have brought him in long ago. But all she could manage was a faint 'Thank you.'

'You are very welcome. It's my job, to make nearly-four-year-olds better.'

A smile spread across Lily's face. It was met by a smile appearing on Dr Mackintosh's.

Lily noticed that he had dark circles under his eyes, which were bloodshot. He looked exhausted, and yet he'd had so much time for Joe and been so patient with him. More than anyone else other than Lily had ever been.

'I hope to see you visiting maybe, on the ward?'

For a moment, Lily was taken aback. She hadn't been aware that Dr Mackintosh was speaking to her. She nodded, feeling awkward and embarrassed. She thought of her mother coming to the hospital, demanding to see Joe, as she surely would as soon as she sobered up. She would turn his illness into a reason for people to take pity on her, for the neighbours to flock to her offering comfort and a spare shilling and a bottle to help. The thought that she would storm in here and sully this caring, calm atmosphere with her brashness was something Lily could not bear to contemplate.

Her voice was filled with sadness as she replied, 'I have to go to work now, but I'll be back soon. Thank you, Doctor.'

And in a flash she was gone, out of the door and down the steps, leaving Dr Mackintosh wondering what on earth was wrong with him.

Teddy was at his side. 'I saw you,' he whispered.

'You saw what?' asked Dr Mackintosh.

'I saw the way she made you smile, put a twinkle in your eye.'

'You did no such thing. Do you know, since you've been dating Nurse Brogan, you've gone soft in the head.'

They could both hear Miss Van Gilder's voice at the sisters' station and they both winced. Without wasting a second, Dr Mackintosh called out to Pammy, 'Nurse Tanner, could you please arrange for this young chap to be transferred up to ward three.' He walked over to the desk and dropped his hand towel into the linen basket as he passed.

As he had guessed she might, Assistant Matron had an opinion. 'Is that entirely necessary, Doctor?' she asked. 'You have said yourself that his breathing is much better.'

'Miss Van Gilder, when you have spent seven years dealing with chest conditions, as I have, I will happily invite your opinion on my cases. But until such a time and for as long as we are under the auspices of the NHS, clinical decisions regarding children are my responsibility. I shall exercise my judgement as I see fit. That's if you don't mind?'

Miss Van Gilder bristled and turned away. 'I shall return later, Sister Antrobus. It is very clear to me that we need additional supervision on casualty. I will ensure that some semblance of normality returns to this department.'

As she finished speaking, she bustled towards the main entrance, where she bumped straight into Nurse Makebee and almost knocked her out of her way. Nurse Makebee dropped the half-full bucket of plaster of Paris she was carrying all over the floor.

'Oh, that poor nurse,' said Teddy, who was about to start completing Joe's notes. 'I'm going to go and help her before that woman eats her alive.'

Pammy was speechless. Unusually for her, she could think of nothing to say. She watched helplessly as Nurse Makebee responded to the outburst of vitriol she received from Miss Van Gilder. She was contrite but retained her dignity, seemingly unfazed as Miss Van Gilder tore her off a strip then flounced out through the main doors.

Teddy had rushed to help Nurse Makebee a little too quickly. He knelt down on the floor, scraped the plaster of Paris into the bucket and called for the orderly, and within seconds he was standing upright again with the now tearful Nurse Makebee in his arms as he tried to comfort her.

Only Pammy saw her smile as he led her towards the sink to clean the wet plaster from her apron. Nothing escaped her and she caught every last trace of meaning that beamed from Nurse Makebee's eyes in Teddy's direction. You fool, Teddy, she thought. You fool. I'm really going to have to watch you, miss.

CHAPTER 19

Sister Antrobus stormed out of Emily Haycock's office as Biddy walked in.

'What's got her goat?' asked Biddy. 'She's flying down those stairs and as God is my judge, I have never seen her walk as fast as that before.'

'She's not happy about Miss Van Gilder.' In despair, Emily dropped her head on to her forearm on the desk. Then, lifting it again, she said, 'Apparently, Miss Van Gilder is not happy with the way ward sisters take the nursing assessments and then tick off the tasks in the workbooks. She thinks it's a job for herself. That trainee nurses should be answerable to her, even on casualty, with all that goes on there.'

'And has she spoken to you?'

'No, she hasn't mentioned a thing to me. I've heard her moving around in her room next to mine on the accommodation corridor and that's about the sum of it. We haven't spoken a word since the day of her interview.'

'Well, it seems to me you need to change that pretty fast because that woman is trouble. Tell me, what is an industrial and domestic cleaning agency? I've never heard of such a thing, but it doesn't sound good to me and we know it's something she is talking to Matron about and Matron doesn't seem to be putting up much resistance.'

Emily groaned. 'Do you think the board knew what they were doing when they said she was the one they wanted? She was the one I liked the least. I reckon they don't like me. They think I am too young for the responsibility I hold. They appointed her to spite me.'

'Well, if they did or didn't, there's nothing you can do to change anything, so there's no point in complaining. I'm going to go and get us some tea and a slice of brack from the kitchen. You and me, we need to make a plan.'

While Biddy made her way to the kitchen, Emily walked over to the window, pulled up the sash and placed half a slice of seed cake she had popped into her pocket on the sill for the gull. She looked sideways to where it had taken to resting, in the guttering behind a large pipe, and watched as it craned its neck upwards at the sound of the sash rising.

She had told her stepfather, Alf, about the seagull and had been amazed at the lucidity of his response. 'He's a young one, queen. They often fall out of the nest and can't get back and so he will have made his own way to the guttering. Keep feeding him and once he has his strength up he will fly down to the docks with the rest of them. Have you told your mam? Show the boys, they'll

love that. Our Richard, he'll look after it for you.'
It had all been going so well until that point. In
Alf's mind, his wife and sons were all still alive.
The bomb had never fallen and all was good in
the world.

Emily heard a loud clattering noise outside. It
was the delivery of coal to the furnace and she
watched as the bags were lifted one by one from
the cart and dumped on to the blackened cobbles.
Miss Van Gilder was down below and she watched
as the porter's lads visibly shrank in fear as she
strode past.

She let her head rest against the cool window-
pane and, placing her hands on the ledge, she
sighed. There was something about Miss Van
Gilder that disturbed her. The woman didn't feel
right. It was as if she was an act, playing out the
role of the formidable assistant matron. Only in
her case she was trying to tone down her fierce-
ness, not ratchet it up.

Emily thought she would like to move out of
the accommodation block if she could. She needed
a life outside of the hospital. It was too consuming.
She thought and spoke about nothing else and she
knew that wasn't right. But housing in Liverpool
was so scarce, it would be almost impossible. Her
stepfather Alf would spend the rest of his life in
the nursing home for war veterans. She had visited
him there almost every evening since he'd been
admitted and tonight would be no exception. In
fact, she was looking forward to seeing him. She

would tell him all about the new assistant matron, she would let off steam and complain and moan and rant. And when it was all over, he would forget every word within seconds. His senility was about as bad as it could possibly be, except for one fact: he sometimes knew who she was.

She watched as Dessie came into view. He straightened the cap of one of the porter's lads as he passed and they both looked down at the lad's gleaming boots. He gave the boy a fatherly pat on the back and, extracting something from his own pocket, pressed it into the boy's hand. With that, the lad ran off to join the others.

What a lovely man you are, Dessie, thought Emily. She guessed he had passed forty. He had the air of a man who had seen and known life. She had never heard him mention the war, but had heard others speak of his medals and bravery. 'No one gets a medal for making the tea,' she whispered and as she did so, the window steamed up with her breath. Watching Dessie with his kindly way softened her heart. He reminded her of Alf.

She had a sudden pang of loneliness and regret at her solitary circumstances. Oliver Gaskell had tried to win her back after she'd seen him with Pammy Tanner at the doctors' social, but she'd rebuffed all his calls and notes. She might be alone, but she had her pride. She would keep searching for a man who matched up to her Alf. Her mother would have expected no less.

Just as she turned to move away from the window, Dessie looked up, as if he had sensed her watching him. He smiled and slowly raised his hand, and she waved in response. Without knowing why, a grin spread across her face as Dessie doffed his cap and mock-bowed to her up at the window.

Blushing, she moved away and back towards the desk at the sound of Biddy's returning footsteps.

Biddy placed the tray down on the desk. 'Have you ever seen a slice as big as that?' she asked.

'Isn't everything in this life made better by a slice of cake.' Emily smiled. 'Biddy, can we have a chat?'

'A chat? God in heaven, we chat all the time.'

'This is personal, Biddy. There is something I want to help you with, with regard to Miss Van Gilder and the St Angelus mafia. Oh, I know you all exist. You and Dessie and Elsie, and Madge from the switchboard, and some of the others, you're as thick as thieves and you're always one step ahead of everyone else. Come and sit down with me. Not at the desk, over here by the fire. I'll take my tea.'

The two women carried over their cups and plates.

'You know I can't get out of these chairs once I've sat down,' Biddy complained. But secretly she enjoyed the fireside chats that Emily occasionally invited her to share.

As she put her cup of tea down on the side table, Emily heard a gentle patter outside the window.

Without turning her head, from the corner of her eye she saw the seagull move halfway across the red sandstone ledge. It stopped and looked into the room to check it was safe and, sensing it was, scuttled towards the seed cake, picked it up and scuttled back to its safe place with the cake in its beak. Emily smiled, pleased with the gull's bravery. Yesterday it had taken over an hour for it to venture out towards the food she'd left.

'Biddy, I have made a huge mistake and I don't know what to do about it. Miss Van Gilder is spying on me. I've never seen her, but I know she's doing it. I hear her footsteps on the other side of the wall when I'm washing Alf's clothes and pyjamas in the laundry in the accommodation block. Every night when I switch off my light, I hear hers go off just after me, as though she's been waiting. The woman is giving me the creeps. I also think she is bad for the hospital. We have to do something. If she carries on, I think Sister Antrobus is going to have a stroke.'

'And that's a bad thing?' enquired Biddy with a look of surprise on her face. 'No, I'm only joking, having a bit of craic! Don't look so horrified. I have no notion what was in the head of those do-gooders when they appointed her.'

There was a moment's silence. Both were aware that Biddy had chosen not to mention that it was Emily who'd been in charge of sifting the applications.

'Biddy, I think we need your team of ladies –

and before you object, I know you have one, you can't hide it from me – to keep an eye out. There is something about Miss Van Gilder which does concern me.'

'Right you are,' said Biddy. 'But it may not surprise you to know, we are already way ahead of you.'

Emily's mouth dropped open.

'Now I have a bit of news of me own. We have tracked down someone who works in St Dunstan's, her previous hospital. She's a ward orderly, a sister of Cathy's in the kitchens here. We've written to her – Dessie helped us – and we're waiting for a letter back, but it sounds to me as though she may have some interesting information. If there is anything to know, we will find it out.'

Emily bit on the last slice of brack and finished her tea. 'That was blooming good cake, Biddy. OK, here's what I propose. Can I come in on your little mafia meetings? We need a plan. I will find out about the agencies and report back to you, if you let me know what your friend Cathy finds out from her sister.'

Biddy smiled. 'Well, it's nothing fancy. We meet in my house every so often. It's generally on a Sunday night with a pie and a bottle of Guinness. Fancy that, do you?'

Emily grimaced. 'Well, I can eat the pie.'

'OK, my house it is then. I'll let you know when we've had a reply to our letter.'

Over in the administration offices, which were situated at the end of the accommodation corridor, Miss Van Gilder began to open her own post. She was delighted with the first letter, which was from the Acme cleaning agency.

Dear Miss Van Gilder,

Thank you for your letter requesting further details of our services. We would be delighted to provide you with a quotation for the cleaning of St Angelus Hospital.

ACME see the establishment of the NHS as an opportunity for cleaning agencies such as ours who wish to specialize in the cleansing of NHS facilities. Procurement of our services would both save St Angelus a great deal of money and improve the cleanliness of the hospital.

I would be happy to meet at your earliest convenience in order that we may evaluate the best way forward and ensure that my estimate fully meets your requirements.
Yours sincerely,

Capt. T. J. H. Oldsworth

'Excellent,' she said out loud. That is a meeting I am looking forward to, she thought. But I must take every care to ensure that everything is in order. No one must be able to point a finger.

Everything as it should be. No mistakes. She made a new file clearly marked: *Cleaning Agency Proposals*.

The second letter was not so pleasing. It made her heart race and her skin tighten in apprehension. She swallowed hard as she instantly recognized the scrawly handwriting on the envelope. It was there in her hands. The envelope was addressed to Matron, but she was safe. She had it.

Breathing in, she steeled herself. She turned over the envelope with a flourish and cut through the paper with a single sharp slice. She let out the long breath she was unaware she had been holding.

Dear Matron,

Thank you for your letter requesting a testimonial in writing for Miss Van Gilder.
I sadly have to inform you that Miss Van Gilder's time at St Dunstan's was not a happy one.

Miss Van Gilder continued to read.

Without taking her eyes from the letter, she walked across to the fireplace and, placing one hand on the mantelpiece, read it again.

'Well, well, I got the better of you, you old witch.'

Resisting the temptation to tear the letter into tiny pieces, she let it float down on to the fire, where it instantly caught alight. She watched as the flames engulfed the accusing words.

'The problem with you, Matron, was that you

thought you were cleverer than me, didn't you? It was only by chance that you thwarted me, and you have been the only one.' She rested both of her hands on the mantelpiece and watched as the paper crackled and burnt until, before her eyes, the words became nothing more than a gossamer film of grey ash.

'You with your girly kiss-curls on an old woman and your fancy notions.' She spat the last word into the fireplace and a streak of spittle landed on her chin. She wiped it away with the back of her hand as she swallowed hard. Her face glowed red, burning with the heat from the fire, and her eyes stung.

She walked back to her desk. As she picked up the next letter, her hand was shaking violently; she placed it back down on her lap and rubbed her thighs until the shaking stopped. She couldn't concentrate. The fear of almost having been caught haunted her thoughts. It refused to go. If that had happened, she could not have lived with the shame. There would have been only one way out and, even now, she was not sure that she would have been brave enough. One more time, she thought. We just need one more time and then it's done.

CHAPTER 20

Dana had been tucked up in her bed in the Lovely Lane nurses' home since 9 a.m. on the dot and now, in the middle of the day, she lay there wondering what it was that had woken her. She could hear the whispered voices of the maids, who she knew were being quiet so as not to disturb her. She had been temporarily transferred on to nights on the children's ward because almost all of the night staff had gone down with flu.

She'd been terrified when she was told to report to Sister Haycock's office. But she was soon put out of her misery and informed that she would be the most senior member of staff on children's.

'But I'm only partway through my training,' she'd said to Sister Haycock.

'Needs must, I'm afraid. There is a staff nurse on ward four, she will be keeping an eye on you. You can always call Night Sister if you need her, and I'm in the accommodation block. There is a lot of help on hand and besides, it's great training. The best nurses are those who've been thrown in at the deep end.'

Dana felt proud at having so much trust placed in her.

'There is so much new thinking with regard to paediatrics,' Sister Haycock had said. 'It's an interesting area and you may find it's something you want to specialize in. I will look out the article I read in the *Nursing Times* this week and lend it to you. It's all about the proposed new NHS policy for allowing daily parental visits to children on the wards. The thinking being that it does more harm than good, keeping parents away.'

Dana could imagine how Miss Van Gilder would feel about daily visiting for parents. She had already garnered a reputation for being rude to visitors.

'The new policy is one I wholeheartedly agree with,' continued Sister Haycock.

Dana couldn't agree more. Her heart tightened at the sound of children crying out for their parents.

'Some of the doctors are pressing for a children's intensive-care unit and that could be just up your street, Nurse Brogan. Work hard on children's, use this opportunity to learn well, and if you're inclined to apply when you qualify, you would have my support.'

Dana had thought that when she qualified she would want to be placed on casualty. Having been born to the twice-daily routine of milking cows, she loved the unexpected and the anticipation of what could come though the door next. There was a much more light-hearted atmosphere on casualty. A camaraderie among the staff, doctors and nurses alike that sustained them through the worst events.

But all she said was, 'Thank you, Sister Haycock. I shall do my best.'

'I can't believe I've been given such responsibility,' she'd told the girls and Mrs Duffy that evening.

'Well now, that is one exhausting ward,' Mrs Duffy said. 'I know that from every nurse who has worked on nights on children's. You will have to listen to me, Nurse Brogan. You have to look after yourself on nights or you can quickly become run down. And once that happens, 'tis the Devil's own job to get you right again.'

Dana gave Mrs Duffy a hug. 'Mrs Duffy, seeing as you and my mammy write to each other every week, it would be more than my life's worth not to listen to you.'

She hadn't really been surprised to discover that her mammy had written to Mrs Duffy to ask if she was attending Mass every Sunday. From this one letter a regular correspondence had been struck up, in which every aspect of Dana's well-being was discussed.

When Dana arrived back from her night shift, not an hour after the girls had left for the day shifts, Mrs Duffy was waiting with her breakfast ready and a hot-water bottle already warming her bed.

'I know you nurses get cold feet after a night shift and it is terrifically hard to warm them up.

Takes hours, it does,' Mrs Duffy said. 'No nurse finishing a night shift can sleep without a hot-water bottle, even in summer. Oh, some try, but they always give in.'

Dana smiled to herself. How right Mrs Duffy was. She was right about everything. One day Mrs Duffy had struggled to get to work in the smog, had arrived late and had forgotten Dana's hot-water bottle and Dana had lain awake with cold feet for hours, unable to sleep.

There were two children's wards at St Angelus, situated at the top of a long flight of wooden stairs. Wards three and four. Three was children's medical. Four was children's surgical. There was one nurse on each ward at night, with a torch-carrying orderly floating in between. The night shift was seven nights on and seven nights off.

Sister Haycock had been right to place Dana on children's. She adored the work, even though it was hard. However, just lately, the equilibrium of the wards had been upset with visits from Miss Van Gilder, which were becoming more and more frequent and, to Dana, intensely irritating.

This morning a thought plagued her and was keeping her awake. It was the man she had passed at the back gates as she'd left the hospital.

She had seen him before, three times in total, standing just inside the hospital gates, looking up towards the accommodation block. It was the little boy, Joe, who had pointed him out to her when she took him a hot chocolate after lights out.

'Who is that man, Nurse?' he had asked her.

It was late, her ward round had finished, most of her patients were asleep and she was more interested in the book she had brought with her to read to Joe. She was thrilled at how willing he was to learn.

'I don't know, Joe,' she said as she glanced out of the window. 'Looks to me like he's waiting for someone. Maybe he has a relative in the hospital.' Dana looked at the man for a brief moment. In his mid thirties, smart. He was standing with both hands in his pockets, and when he saw Dana framed in the large window he walked away, towards the road.

'He is often there, Nurse,' said Joe. 'I waved to him yesterday and he waved back.'

'Well, there you go, Joe. He's harmless enough then.'

She decided not to tell anyone. They would think she was exaggerating because there was no pattern to his being there. It wasn't as if he came every night. She thought she'd seen him again yesterday; he didn't look at her, just walked up the steps of the main entrance to the WRVS stall. He stopped and she noticed that he bought a cup of tea and sat on one of the chairs. He kept looking at the main doors as though waiting for someone to appear. He's obviously a visitor, she decided. Poor man, I hope it isn't too awful for him, she thought. He has a sad face.

'Come here, little fella, give us a hug,' said Dana

and, despite the strict rules about not sitting on the bed, she flopped down next to Joe. 'Right then, what page did we get up to last night? If you do well, there's something in my bag for you in the cloakroom.' Her eyes twinkled.

'What?' asked Joe. 'Is it something nice? The doctor gave me another piece of chocolate today, but he said I wasn't to tell Sister.'

'God job I'm not Sister then,' said Dana as she ruffled his hair. 'No, it's not chocolate, although it is cake. Mrs Duffy made flapjacks in Lovely Lane today and she sent me in with a slice for you. I told her you were my favourite patient and every day she asks me all about you. She's going to be heartbroken when you go home.'

Joe grinned from ear to ear. 'Will you go and get it now?' he asked with a cheeky grin.

'No, I will not. Not until you've shown me how much you've improved with your reading today.'

The night-light cast a glow over Joe, and Dana thought he looked like an angel as she glanced at his face. The bed was in the middle of a small cubicle and on either side were two large, square-paned windows, one of which overlooked the car park, which was as black as the moonless night outside. The other looked out on to the corridor, lit by the red night-lights. As Dana turned a page, she was startled to see Miss Van Gilder standing against the far wall of the corridor, watching her through the glass. Her face glowed like that of a deathly ghost and Dana couldn't help herself as she let out a shriek. Leaving Joe, she went to answer the hundred questions Miss Van Gilder fired at her every single night. If anyone or anything makes me leave this job, it will be having to deal with this woman, thought Dana as, with her best professional smile, she strode out to meet her.

'It's as if she doesn't trust me to look after them,' said Dana to the staff nurse on ward four. 'She wanted to know every detail about every child. That was after she tore me off a strip for sitting on Joe's bed. Does she not realize, I can hardly sleep during the day for worrying about this lot.'

It wasn't long after Miss Van Gilder had left that a young nurse came flying in through the office door to Dana, who was folding away the patient records Miss Van Gilder had asked to see.

'Nurse, it's Benny, his respirator has slipped out. Staff has asked if you can help. The orderly will stay on here.'

Dana felt her heart pounding in her chest in a way she had never experienced before. Nursing children was a far greater responsibility than nursing adults. She had found it difficult to articulate to the others why that was so, but it was. Here, on the children's ward, she worried, brought each child home in her heart. She dreaded an emergency, and now there was one, with little Benny. He was in a coma and it was his respirator that kept him alive. Her feet felt as if they were stuck to the floor.

'Has he arrested?'

'No, it's still pumping, he's getting some of the oxygen. But quick, she needs you.'

Dana flew to the cubicle. Just as the nurse had said, the tube which allowed the air to pump into Benny's lungs and was keeping him alive had become detached and was lying on his little chest.

'His chest has stopped inflating,' said Staff Nurse. 'I've called for the doctor, but I'm going to try and get the tube back in myself, though it may be too late.'

Dana could tell she was trying to keep the panic out of her voice. 'What can I do?' she asked. The sight of Benny had spurred her into action.

'Here, place your hand behind his head and hold him steady. This machine is so temperamental.'

Dana put her hand behind Benny's neck and his mouth fell open.

'Yes! Thank God,' said the staff nurse. 'His endotracheal tube is still in place.'

The respirator at the side of his bed pumped and whirred away as its bellows moved up and down, up and down. It was still blowing oxygen at Benny's mouth and nose, but it needed to be reconnected to the tube in his airway to make it work at full capacity.

'Cut me some fresh tape,' said Staff Nurse over her shoulder, and without a second's thought she picked up the respirator tube and slowly slid it back down and through the rubber airway. Using the tape the orderly handed to her, she fixed the tube to the side of Benny's face and the rubber tubing to the cot.

'How did it happen?' asked Dana. 'God, he could have died without the oxygen.'

'I've no idea,' said Staff. 'Maybe he had an involuntary movement and his hand pulled the tube out, or maybe he came round for a moment and tried to pull it out himself. I'm going to call Night Sister and ask for help. We need someone to sit and special him. He is specialled all day, so why is it they think, given that he's in a coma, the night is any different from the day? Thank God this happened when the Bone Grinder wasn't here. She would have had me sacked for that, I'm sure.'

When all was calm again, Dana headed back to her own charges. She took in every cot and bed with a sweep of her night torch as her heart slowed back down to a normal rhythm. Joe was sleeping, the book open on his bed, a smile on his face. Dana moved to the head of his bed to switch off his reading lamp. Brushing the hair back from his brow, she whispered, 'God, you are a proper little angel, aren't you, Joe Lancashire.' Remembering her promise, she scurried back to the cloakroom, extracted the flapjacks Mrs Duffy had sent for Joe and slipped them into his locker.

CHAPTER 21

Knowing that Joe was being cared for at St Angelus and that he was getting three meals a day was a blessing for which Lily could never give enough thanks. In the days immediately after he was admitted, Sister Therese had visited him twice and brought back reports of his recovery. Visiting hour was once a week on a Sunday afternoon, two until three, but the sister on the children's ward had not dared argue with Sister Therese.

'The doctor came over to see me when I was there this afternoon,' Sister Therese said to Lily and Katie as they left Mass one evening. 'He was asking after you, Lily. I told him you were well and good and he said to be sure to tell you that Joe is in good hands and being well looked after.'

Lily had no idea why, but she blushed and looked down at her shoes. What Sister Therese had said was innocent enough, but it made her heart beat faster. A thrill of excitement shot through her belly to think that, with all the people Dr Mackintosh had to deal with every day, he had remembered her and asked after her.

'Now, you two, we have special tea at the convent tonight for our new postulant and you are both my special guests. You would not believe the gorgeous ham the butcher on the market gave me for not a penny in return.'

Lily smiled up at Sister Therese. She could believe it only too well. She'd probably promised him that there was a particularly special place in heaven for butchers who were generous.

'How's your mammy and daddy?' Sister Therese dropped her voice to a whisper.

Lily did not know how to answer. They hadn't seen her stepfather for a couple of months. Her mother came home at some point each night to sleep.

Sister Therese did not mention to Lily that she'd seen her mother standing on the pub steps at two o'clock, an hour before the pub was due to open, with the two other women who were the notorious drinkers of Clare Cottages. She also didn't say that at the time she was on her way back from visiting little Joe. There was a lot that was left unsaid.

At the convent, Lily and Katie were treated to the best meal they had ever sat down to. As they tucked into hot potatoes, ham and vegetables, followed by steamed jam pudding and custard, Sister Therese told Lily her plan. But not before Lily had noted how much pleasure the nuns sitting around the table took from the simple things in life. How much they all whooped for joy when the cook upturned the pudding bowls. The way their faces easily creased into smiles and laughter. It was a joy to watch them chatter and talk and eat. It dawned on Lily how little she smiled.

'You know that Katie has come along in leaps and bounds at school, don't you?' Sister Therese said to Lily. 'And we are aware that this is in no small part thanks to yourself, coaching her at night and all the rest. Just a year ago, I thought that Katie was a lost cause, but now I can see hope.' She flashed Lily a reassuring smile. 'Will you help us arrange for her to be sent to the boarding convent across the water? It's in the middle of the most lovely countryside and the girls who live there, well, they are the nicest lot. It's run by Sister Joseph and she is just a dote. Sure I have no idea how they learn anything, the girls run rings around her. Would you?'

Lily did not hesitate. She would miss Katie with all her heart, but now that Joe was in hospital she knew that the biggest worry in her life was making sure her siblings were fed and clean. Tears pricked at her eyes. 'We will make it happen,' she said.

Katie had overheard. 'Can I take my dolly with me, Sister?' she said as she slid from her chair and stood by the side of Sister Therese.

Katie's doll had lived in the convent since the day Sister Therese had persuaded the pawnbroker to give it back to her after their mother had pawned it in exchange for an afternoon in the pub.

'Of course you can, because I say so. Now, why

don't you go and see her. She's sitting on the shelf in the visitors' room and I think she misses you.'

Katie's face broke into a grin as she slipped Sister Therese's hand and skipped away. As both Lily and Sister Therese watched her disappear, to the joy of the nuns, who cooed over her as she passed, Lily said, 'This is the nicest tea we have ever had. Thank you. It's lovely that Katie got to enjoy it and thank you for seeing Joe. I can't wait to go and see him on Sunday.'

'I think you will be astounded at how well he looks.' Sister Therese smiled. 'Lily, I want to get Katie into the school after the summer. Can you cope with that? We may have to do something a little devious to persuade your mammy to sign the forms, but sometimes God gives me permission to do things like that. We have his blessing, if it's for the betterment of a life on earth.'

Lily wanted to throw her arms around Sister Therese's neck, but instead, she gracefully accepted the handkerchief she held out to wipe away her tears.

The strict visiting regime was unbearable. As Lily pushed her way to the front of the queue on the following Sunday, she peered through the ward windows, her first impulse to reassure herself that Joe was actually still there and alive.

She bumped into Dr Mackintosh while she was there. He happened to be on the ward during visiting hours.

'The nurses have Joe in the steam tent each day,' he said, 'and I don't know about you, but I think he's looking much better.'

'I've never seen him look so well,' Lily blurted out as a smile spread across her face.

Joe was indeed looking much better. He had put weight on, been regularly bathed, fed and fussed over, and was out of the cold and thriving.

'He's a bit of a favourite with the nurses, isn't that right, eh, Joe?'

It was Joe's turn to blush.

Never once did Dr Mackintosh ask where their mother was.

Dana Brogan, who was now back doing day shifts at the weekend, thought she should warn Lily about the ward sister's rules. 'It is highly unusual that Joe's mother does not visit,' she said. 'We only allow parental visiting. Sister would have my guts for garters if she knew you were his sister. She's on her Sunday off, but, honestly, when it comes to taking him home, Sister will want to see his mother here or she will be making enquiries.'

Lily's face burnt as Dana delivered her warning from the foot of the bed. Dana whispered in as low a voice as she could to save Lily embarrassment, but they were both aware of the sound of silence and ears straining to hear every word.

'She works, Nurse,' was all Lily could manage in response. 'Long hours. She asked me to come . . .'

Dana knew plenty of families in Ireland where the children survived on their wits as parents worked every hour of the day to make ends meet. 'Look, I'll be covering up for you as much as I can,' she said. 'He's the loveliest little lad I've ever looked after, aren't you, Joe? So clever, he is, being as he's only nearly four.' She winked at Joe, who, now that he was feeling much better, winked back.

'Where did you learn to do that?' Lily exclaimed as she pulled up the chair next to the head of his bed.

'Would you like a cup of tea? asked Dana. 'Let me fetch you one.' There was something about Lily that made Dana feel protective. She sensed that Lily was as vulnerable as Joe in her own way.

'Look what I have for you,' Lily said as she took a white paper bag out of her basket and handed Joe a packet of mint balls. She glanced at the lockers belonging to other children and saw that they were piled high with treats and toys in a variety of coloured wrappings. Joe's locker was bare and contained only his water jug. Next to him on the bed was a soft toy that Lily had never seen before. 'Who's this?' she asked as she picked up the bear and, holding it to her, smelt it. The bear was bathed more regularly that they were at home, she guessed.

'It's Mr Bear, Lily. Nurse Dana gave him to me. She said, while I am in hospital he is to be my special bear, to look after me and make me better. And look, Lily . . .' Joe leant over, opened his locker door and removed a book. 'Nurse Dana reads this to me when she has time and she's teaching me the words too.'

Lily picked up the book and turned over the front cover. Her eyes misted over. There is something behind why the nurses of St Angelus are called the angels, she thought. Nurse Dana had certainly taken a shine to Joe. Very few people had been as kind to her brother as she had.

'Nurse Dana always brings me hot chocolate and gives me extra biscuits, and last night, Lily, she brought me apple pie. She said the lady who looks after her in the home where she sleeps sent it in with her, especially for me.'

'Did she now? Well, aren't you the lucky one with all these ladies fussing over you.' Lily's heart folded as she spoke. Not only was Joe better looked after in St Angelus than he was at home, he was better loved than he was by his own mother too.

Despite her worst fears, their mother hadn't shown the slightest inclination to visit Joe in hospital. Now, as Lily passed away the hour listening to Joe, a new panic set in as she wondered how she was going to convince their mother to come to the hospital when the day came for Joe to be discharged. The dreadful truth was that Lily's mother truly didn't seem to care any more whether or not the kids were taken into care. She had barely noticed that Joe was in hospital and only yesterday, as she'd fallen over the threshold, had she asked where he was. The condemnation of the nuns had once stirred her into short periods of sobriety, but not any more.

There was only one woman who could help. Sister Therese.

'If I don't have help, I don't think they will allow him to come home, and he is looking so well,' Lily explained.

Sister Therese listened but looked concerned. 'Lily, Joe's condition is because of the way your mother treats him. Do you not think it might be an idea if we let the hospital staff decide what is best for him?'

'No!' Lily raised her voice to Sister Therese for the first time in her life. 'Katie and I are managing, you know that, and when she goes to the school, I will manage just as well. Joe isn't a baby and from September he will be with you in the boys' school.'

'Now, isn't that the truth,' said Sister Therese. 'Well, there is no ward sister ever threw a nun out of a hospital, so I shall call in this evening after Mass and visit. I will make sure they know that there is someone helping you, and you know, Lily, don't you, that I always will. Joe will have a good lunch down at the school every day, I will make sure of that.'

'I don't know how I am ever going to be able to thank you enough for all you do for us.' Lily's voice broke with emotion.

'Come on now, stop. We are too busy for that. 'Tis you who does all the work and deserves all the praise. I'm keeping Katie here after school to feed her. One of us will bring her across when I know it's time for you to arrive home from work. That's one less job for you to worry about. And next Sunday, we shall visit Joe together. Maybe they will let him back with us then.'

Lily breathed a sigh of relief. Saved from the ward sister and her probing enquiries. 'We couldn't manage without you, you know,' she said.

'Child, I have never known you to miss a Sunday at Mass, and do you know what that tells me? That you understand family. We are all one family, God's family, and every Sunday you come to his house, we all do, and we are as family to one another. I help you and will do so until the day the good Lord calls me, because that's what families do.'

Lily also found unexpected kindness elsewhere, in Mrs McConaghy.

'Use the phone to call the ward,' she pushed Lily one day. 'I want to know how the little lad is, never mind anyone else. Don't let Mr McConaghy see you, though,' she whispered. 'Ring when he's down the steps on the floor.'

This did not make Lily feel uncomfortable. Joe was her priority. 'Thank you, Mrs McConaghy, that's very kind of you.' It was heartening to know that Mrs McConaghy was on her side, worried for her.

'That's quite all right. I've only met the little lad once, but sure, he has the face of an angel.'

Lily remembered the day. It had been her week off, a few weeks before Joe was admitted. His chest had been bad, her mother was chain-smoking and Lily was sure this made his coughing worse. So she'd pushed him out in the old pram and taken him to see where she worked.

Mrs McConaghy had spotted her and came running down the steps. She clucked around Joe like a mother hen.

'How do you do it, Joe?' Lily said to him as they walked back home. 'Every woman is putty in your hands. God help the girls when you grow up.'

Joe was always quiet when his breathing was bad. Talking took far too much effort. He had turned his face to the River Mersey and the ships being unloaded. 'I want to be a docker, Lily,' he'd croaked.

Lily smiled. Not in my lifetime, she thought. There is better for you out there, Joe. But to his face, she replied, 'You will. Just like your da.' She could have bitten her tongue off. No one had seen his da for weeks and she knew in her heart that they were never going to again. It had only taken him fourteen years and a few hours of being sober, but the penny must have finally dropped: if he left home, he would get to keep his pay packet to himself and wouldn't have to share it with his drunken wife. The next payday, he was off.

'Go and find the bastard, your stepfather! He's on the docks somewhere,' her mother had screamed when she became aware that her husband was not just lost but gone.

But there were five thousand men working on

374

the docks and Lily guessed he could have gone as far as Seaforth. 'He's gone, Mam, and he isn't coming back,' she said. First her father had gone. Now Katie and Joe's father had left too. It seemed he'd never got over the threat from Lockie, telling him what would happen if he ever used his fists on Lily again. It was as if the wind had been taken out of his sails. 'He's gone, and we know how that works, don't we, Mam? He won't be coming back.' There was a determination in her voice that caught her mother's attention and from that moment on her stepfather's name was never mentioned again.

Not long after Joe was discharged – into the persuasive hands of Sister Therese, who had accompanied Lily as promised – spring arrived, without fanfare or warning. Liverpool simply woke up one morning and there it was. The swallows flew in, the sun shone and the trees burst into bud. Lily walked to the bus stop with a new bounce in her step. Her feet were dry and the westerly breeze lifting off the Mersey was milder, allowing the sun to warm her skin. And Joe was home. Her mind wandered, as it often did, to her final conversation with Dr Mackintosh at the hospital. 'I hope we don't see you in here again, young man,' he'd said to Joe. Lily had smiled and thanked him. She thought the doctor's eyes had seemed to hold an entirely different message, but she knew she was being fanciful.

The feeling of new life and wellness that spring

had brought evaporated for Lily as soon as she entered the office. She was finding the flirting between Amy and Lockie almost intolerable. Not because she held a shred of remorse or envy, but because Amy's behaviour made it hard for Lily to leave work on time and get back home to Joe. Amy was responsible for some of the work now that the plant was getting busier, and whenever Amy didn't finish her tasks, Lily had to do them for her.

'If you don't take me out somewhere special tonight, Lockie,' Amy trilled, 'you won't get another chance and that's for sure. It'll be our last date.' She swung around in her chair and pouted her red lips at Lockie.

Lily watched as Lockie grinned. Amy had done it, she had got what she wanted, and Lockie was completely smitten.

'You will be sorry later that you challenged me, Amy.' He laughed. 'I'll be back at six to pick you up.'

Amy looked delighted as she swivelled back round in the chair. It had all worked to plan. Of course, she hadn't slept with Lockie again since. If she'd been lucky and hadn't got caught out, she would have no need of him. Nonetheless, she had made sure that first night was witnessed and noted.

'God, I am so sick of this place, aren't you?' Amy whispered so that Mrs McConaghy couldn't hear her.

'I've been here for almost four years now, you've only been here for weeks, how can you be so bored?' Lily replied.

'Because of this, that's why.' Amy picked up the order ledger she had been working on and let it bang back down on the desk. Dust flew up and filled the air. 'I swear to God, I'm going to go crazy if I don't get out of here soon.'

'And how do you think you can make that happen?' asked Lily. 'This place will be yours when your aunt and uncle retire.' Her irritation at the way Amy and Lockie carried on in front of her had made her bolder than she had ever been before.

'Not on your nelly,' said Amy with grit in her tone. 'I'm not spending a day longer than I have to in this filthy place. I am worth more than spending my days in this hole, Lily.'

Lily leant back in her chair and sighed. 'It's time for me to make the tea,' she said.

Not once had Amy offered to make the tea. Lily didn't mind. Filling the urn, swilling out the leaves from the huge brown earthenware pot, washing the cups and saucers, it all gave her time to think. She concentrated hard when she was working on the accounts, so making the tea let her stretch her thoughts to other things. Like Joe's health, the disappearance of her stepfather, and her mother's new abode, which appeared to be the pub.

Mrs McConaghy always brought the milk back when she went out to buy the cakes. It was her daily indulgence and Lily knew that she ate one on the way back. The crumbs, which adhered to the corners of her mouth, were a dead giveaway.

Lily wondered if, by the size of her, it was only one she indulged in.

'Is it that time already?' Mrs McConaghy said as she looked up at the large clock over the doorway. 'I'd better be fetching the cakes or they will have all gone. Sayers is becoming a very popular little shop these days.'

Lily dried the cups and, leaning against the draining board, folded her arms and waited for the urn to boil. She was deep in thought, irritated with herself and the fact that the face of Dr Mackintosh continued to appear from nowhere when she was least expecting it. On the page of a ledger. In the frame of the window. At the front of her mind as she made the tea.

She was roused from her wandering thoughts by the sound of the urn bubbling.

'Come on, Lily,' said Amy. 'I'm gasping for my tea.' She came and stood beside Lily and shovelled three spoons of sugar into her cup. 'I don't know what's up with me,' she said. 'I can't stop eating sugar and I'm going mad for cake. I have to stop, though; this skirt wouldn't fasten this morning.'

Lily looked down as Amy showed her the undone button on the waistband of her skirt. 'You have a waist the size of a wasp, Amy,' she said. 'It's unnatural to have your skirts so tight. It's just your body objecting, that's all.'

A worried look crossed Amy's face. 'That had better be all it is,' she said.

Before Lily could answer, the door to the office

swung open and a bowler-hatted man in his forties strode in. He looked anxiously about the office.

Lily saw the blood drain from Amy's face. 'Ben! What are you doing here?' she gasped.

'I saw your aunt leave. I've been waiting outside. I have two minutes and I'm not going to waste a second, Amy. First, don't you ever go to my house and speak to my wife again, do you hear me?'

Lily stood stock still with the teapot in her hand. The atmosphere in the office was tense and she didn't dare move.

The noise of the men on the processing floor, the sound of the compressor and the banging on the benches could be heard loud and clear as Amy struggled to speak.

'I didn't,' she whispered.

'Yes, you did. There is only one person that I know of who fits the description of a tart.'

Lily took in his smart suit and his bowler hat. His tie was dark and crisp and his shirt was as white as the snow which had plagued them that past winter. In his hand he held a tan-coloured briefcase that concertinaed at the sides.

'I needed to speak to you.' Amy had found her voice.

'No, you did not, and you never will again. I never want to set eyes on you, you little whore. How dare you go with your whining lies to my wife! Set foot near my door again, Amy, and you will regret it. You and the rest of your common family. You don't want to cross me, Amy. Do you understand?'

379

Amy nodded.

The full pot in Lily's hand began to weigh her arm down. The musky smell of the tea leaves in the scalding water assailed her nostrils. For a fleeting second she wondered whether she should throw the pot at the man. Or call for Mr McConaghy to come up from the floor. But she was rooted to the spot.

As quickly as he had arrived, he was gone. The bell above the door jangled violently as he stormed out.

Amy, as white as a sheet, turned to check that the door to the processing plant was closed. Turning back to Lily with her eyes full of tears, she whispered, 'Lily, you won't tell anyone about that, will you? Not even Lockie. Definitely not Lockie.'

Lily put down the pot and walked over to Amy's side. 'Of course I won't. Here, don't cry. Why was he so angry? God, I've never met such an unpleasant man. Amy, I was scared for you. He's not a man to be crossed.'

Amy collapsed into her chair and wiped her eyes. 'Oh, don't I know it. The bastard. He didn't tell me he was married, Lily. I thought the woman who opened the door was a cleaner.'

Lily suppressed a smile. The wife thought the heiress to a processing plant was a whore and Amy thought the wife of the businessman was a cleaner. Takes one to know one, she thought, then mentally slapped her own wrist for thinking such things.

'He lives in Woolton, in a big house. I met him

380

in the bar of the Grand. Told me he was single. A man about town and of considerable substance, he said. He's in the shipping business. Import and export, whatever that means. I believed every word he said and we were having just the best time, Lily. He said he loved me and everything. Then, one night, something awful happened and he just never turned up again. So I thought I'd got it wrong and I went back to the bar to find him, and my parents were giving out at home, threatening to throw me out, and I went every night, Lily, but he never came back. I never heard a word. He didn't say a thing to me. Nothing.'

'You poor thing,' said Lily as she handed Amy her cup. 'Your auntie will be here in a minute with the fancies, so dry your eyes, quick. If she sees you crying, she will want to know why. It's a good job she never saw him coming up the steps.'

She looked out of the window at the street. It occurred to her that she felt more sympathy for Amy than she would have expected. She almost felt the shame of her humiliation. She wondered whether this was because Amy's sheltered and privileged upbringing had left her so unprepared that when an unpleasant surprise did befall her, she received special consideration simply because she was unused to things not going entirely her way.

She took her handkerchief out from her sleeve and held it out for Amy, who appeared to have none of her own.

'I just went to the house to see if he was there

and waited to catch a word with him, I swear. I thought something bad had happened to him.'

Amy burst into fresh tears and Lily had no idea what to say to comfort her. She was distraught. Just as Lily put her arms around her, the bell jangled again and Mrs McConaghy bustled into the room with her arms full.

'Heavens above, what on earth is going on here?' she demanded as, having deposited the cakes on the table, she rushed to Amy's side.

Lily responded without a second's hesitation. 'Amy isn't feeling very well, Mrs McConaghy. She has terribly painful monthlies.'

Mrs McConaghy began to fret. 'Oh, Amy, you poor girl. 'Tis the most awful thing, the curse we women have to bear.'

Lily thought of the time she herself had really had unbearable monthlies, so bad it had taken all her effort to sit upright, but Mrs McConaghy would never have known.

'Would you like to go back home to your bed?'

Amy nodded. 'Please, Auntie,' she said and, playing along, placed her hand on her abdomen. If only what Lily was saying was true, she thought. She would have taken all the pain in the world to see her monthly return and take away the anxiety she was now feeling every minute of the day. Standing quickly, too quickly for someone in pain, she made her way to the door.

'Your coat, Amy,' said Lily as she lifted it down from the hook and followed her to the door.

As they stood at the top of the steps, Lily wrapping Amy's scarf around her neck as though she were Katie, Amy whispered, 'You won't say anything, will you?'

'Never, Amy. Of course not. I can keep a secret.'

'That's my girl, Lily. We have to stick together, eh?'

Lily nodded. She was still none the wiser, but she knew there was something deadly serious Amy was keeping from her.

CHAPTER 22

Matron had asked Emily to attend a meeting in her office at 9 a.m. sharp. Emily was never late and arrived on the dot.

'Miss Haycock, come in, sit down.' Matron had opened the door herself. It felt to Emily as though she had been hovering on the other side, waiting for her.

Matron and Emily had not always seen eye to eye. Matron had regarded Emily, a nurse she herself had appointed to the hospital, as a traitor when she'd gone on to apply for the director of nursing job. She worried that it would be only a matter of time before Emily was after her job.

'Come along, into the office, quickly.' Matron appeared agitated. 'Miss Van Gilder won't be here for half an hour, but I suspect she will arrive early. She always seems to be one step ahead of me. Part of me thinks she will guess I have invited you early.'

'Goodness, what is the matter?' said Emily as she headed towards her usual chair, on the opposite side of Matron's desk. A thrill shot through her. It was clear that Matron was now finding Miss Van Gilder tiresome, just as everyone else in the hospital was. This was welcome news.

Blackie lifted his head in the basket as his tail wagged in recognition of Emily. Deciding she was worth getting up for, he stretched his aching body, yawned and padded over for a stroke.

'My, haven't we come a long way,' said Emily, who remembered the times she'd come to Matron's office with food in her pocket, just in case she needed to ward him off.

It was too much effort for Blackie to walk all the way back to his basket, so he flopped on to the carpet instead, his head resting on Emily's foot.

Emily removed the biscuit from her pocket that Biddy had given her for Blackie. She now carried them as a treat, not armour. It had taken the best part of a year, but it seemed to Emily that the moment she had won Matron over, Blackie had followed suit.

'Elsie is bringing in the tea,' said Matron, 'while we take a look at this.'

She handed Emily a document. It was six pages long and Emily scanned the individual headings. *Main corridor. Ward block. Theatre block. Maternity. Kitchens.* The list went on and on.

'What is this?' she asked.

'Miss Van Gilder thinks that the hospital spends too much money on ancillary staff. She wants a complete reorganization of how we do things and I'm afraid that she has blocked me into a corner.'

'You? How?' Emily was unable to hide her incredulity. She had never heard of Matron being backed into a corner by anyone. Matron was one of the most formidable women she knew. She might have been on the wrong side of sixty – no one was really sure of her age, and no one dared ask her – but Emily knew that some matrons kept going until they dropped. Not all had transferred on to the new NHS contracts; some were still employed under the old voluntary hospital and trust contracts. And Emily didn't see Matron leaving St Angelus for a long time to come. This feebleness in the face of Miss Van Gilder was alien to her.

'Well, I let her persuade me to allow her to review every aspect of how the hospital functions. She said she would produce a report for the board. I agreed, but, frankly, Sister Haycock, I had no intention of providing the board with a report full of suggestions as to how we turn the hospital upside down. The Liverpool District Hospitals Board can manage that quite well without any input from me or anyone else at St Angelus. Anyway, not only has she completed a draft of her review, she has made some very dramatic suggestions and has even gone outside the hospital and obtained proposals as to how her changes might be implemented. That document before you is a preliminary quote from a cleaning agency which appears to propose that we sack every one of our domestics.'

'What? No! We can't sack an entire community of women.' Emily looked down at the sheet in dismay. 'They all take a wage home and keep a family going. Have you seen the houses they live in? Have you seen Elsie's? The house next door to hers was bombed and it's still there. The wooden staircase still intact, open to the elements. If these women had the means, they wouldn't work here, they would be off. To better housing and a better life. They need their jobs at St Angelus.'

'Do you think I don't know that, Sister Haycock?' Matron's voice was quiet but firm. 'Do you think I have kept Elsie here all these years because of her intelligence or her wit?'

They both heard a clatter from the kitchenette as something hit the floor.

'I have done my best to support every war widow I can. I have no intention of anyone cleaning the wards other than the women who have done so since before the war, but I don't have the authority I used to. The NHS is running before it can walk. It seems to me they just want to turn everything upside down, and what for? Nothing I have seen happen yet has anything to do with the patients. It's all about money.'

'Can't we just tell her we have an obligation to our staff and we won't be implementing these changes? It is just a report. Her report. Her suggestions.'

'If I could, I would. But she has already, without even consulting me, included the presentation of the proposal on the agenda for the next board meeting. And, again without even asking me, she posted the copies to the members of the LDHB. They already have the agenda. If Dr Gaskell hadn't tipped me off, I would never have known, because I am the only person she has failed to send an agenda to. Now, why would that be? Am I being overly suspicious? Does that not sound very odd to you?'

Emily shook her head. She wanted to enjoy this rare moment with Matron, being united in one cause, not battling over the usual old chestnuts. But this was too urgent a situation for indulgent reflection. The livelihoods of dozens of women were under threat from Miss Van Gilder's proposals, and it felt as though the woman had only arrived five minutes ago.

'Good heavens, she hasn't wasted any time, has she?' said Emily as she turned over a page and read the list of porter's lads to be laid off as part of the new regimen. 'But I don't understand. How can they save money by sacking most of our work-force? They will only have to pay other women and boys to do the same jobs.'

'Yes, but look at this.' Matron pushed her glasses up her nose and stood behind Emily. She jabbed her finger at a column of figures. 'That is how they'll save their money. They will re-employ our domestics but pay them two pounds less per week.'

'They can't do that, that would cut their wages almost in half!' Emily jumped to her feet and walked towards the fireplace. 'Most of these women are widows with children over fourteen. They can't collect their war-widow's pension any longer. They need their jobs. How are they going to manage to survive with no money coming in and no men to go out and work? Matron, our workforce comes from the homes of fallen soldiers. Men who gave their lives so that St Angelus could remain safe.' Emily took a breath. Her own loss fired her emotions and she took a second to regain her composure.

Matron stepped in. 'Exactly. My sentiments entirely. Our job isn't just running a hospital. It isn't only about making the sick well. We are a family with a legacy and it is a legacy we must honour, together. Here, for goodness' sake, drink your tea and eat a garibaldi before she arrives. I've never known a woman to eat a plate of biscuits as fast as she can.'

Emily took a deep breath and sat back in the chair. She looked up at Matron fussing and in the midst of her concern she also felt happy. Here they were, she and Matron, working as a team, and it felt good. They had a mutual enemy in Miss Van Gilder and, united, they would thwart her plans. Emily had envisioned the Bone Grinder and Matron becoming the best of friends, but that hadn't happened. This brought Emily some relief.

Matron poured Emily some more tea and, placing her own cup in her saucer, sat back in her chair.

'Many of our domestics were young married

women when they started at St Angelus, earning pin money. I was young myself then. I'm not against all married women working, you know, Sister Haycock.' She gave Emily a wry smile. 'And now they are war widows, no longer working for pin money to supplement their husband's wage, looking after each other's children, a way of earning a few treats. That pin money now buys the food and pays the bills. That is how much the war changed things around here. I know some of them think I am as tough as old boots, but I do understand. What was once their pin money is now their only income. I do understand that.'

Emily smiled and nodded. 'I think they know that, Matron. You have a following amongst the domestics.' She failed to add that in equal measure she was feared by the student nurses.

'She will be here in a minute. Any suggestions?'

'I will have to have a think, Matron, but why don't we hear what she has to say anyway? Maybe when she says all this out loud, she will realize how awful it all sounds. At least we now know what we are up against.'

'Apart from all this, she's driving Sister Antrobus mad. It's like two stags locking horns. And I have to say, I admire Sister Antrobus; she isn't cowed by her. Miss Van Gilder has been asking her for the most ridiculous things and, frankly, Sister Antrobus is earning a lot of sympathy from the other sisters. We will have a revolution on our hands soon if she carries on like this.'

Emily finished her tea and, leaning forward, laid her cup and saucer on the coffee table. 'Poor Sister Antrobus,' she said as she raised one eyebrow.

'I know you don't mean that, Emily.' Matron gave another half smile. 'I know that until recently she was the most feared sister in the hospital. Who knows, maybe one day you will grow to like her.'

The irony was not lost on Emily, who had spent years battling Matron in order to get her own way.

'To think, it used to be my visits to the wards that everyone dreaded. But what the nurses didn't seem to realize was that I timed my visits for when the wards were at their quietest. After the drug rounds. Whereas Miss Van Gilder turns up unannounced at all hours. The nurses always start from the premise that I am out to get them. It just shows you, I earned myself a fearsome reputation without even trying that hard.'

Neither of them heard Elsie tiptoeing slowly back into the kitchenette. She had been hovering with her ear to the half-open door ever since she'd dropped the sugar bowl, and she'd heard every word.

Branna was waiting on the other side of the door and Elsie almost shrieked as she bumped into her.

'What did she say? What's the latest?' Branna hissed. She had nipped out from her cleaning duties on ward two, desperate to get the news.

'I have no idea,' said Elsie. 'Other than Matron has not employed me for me intelligence. It's just as well. What use would that be when I'm scrubbing her bath?'

Branna had no idea what Elsie was talking about. 'Is Miss Van Gilder there?'

'No, not yet. Miss Haycock is, though. And Matron. Mighty pally they are too.'

'Right, I'm off back before Sister or anyone misses me. I only came for a natter, but my time's run out now. I didn't want to disturb you when you were spying. I have news from Madge. She's coming on Sunday. Written down some interesting phone conversations to do with the Bone Grinder, she says. She's bringing all her notes with her.'

'Ooh, good. That sounds promising,' said Elsie. 'Did she say what she had?'

'No, you know Madge, she likes her news to make an entrance. She thinks she's Mata Hari, but we won't discourage her, will we? She did say someone's been looking for Miss Van Gilder, keeps ringing the hospital. Anyway, she will tell us all, for sure. See you at Biddy's on Sunday night.'

Elsie opened the door to Matron's office in an exaggerated manner and entered the room pushing a tea trolley and wearing a beaming smile. Before she had finished pouring the fresh pot of tea, the door opened again, without the customary knock this time, and in strode Miss Van Gilder.

'Ah, Matron, Miss Haycock,' she trilled. 'Here early, I see, Miss Haycock. And yet I made a point of being here ten minutes early myself.'

Emily felt both confused and surprised and had no idea how to respond.

'When you have finished pouring the tea, could

you leave the room promptly, please,' Miss Van Gilder snapped at Elsie.

Emily's and Matron's eyes met. Matron's brow arched.

It's her audacity, thought Emily. Everything she says and does is out of the ordinary, a surprise. She knocks Matron on to her back foot and Matron has no time to recover before she knocks her back again.

Elsie was concerned about Matron too. She retreated to the kitchenette but decided she would stick around and give the place a good clean. She might pick up some more useful information. She prepared everything Matron ate. Matron was not a cook, but she was no eater either. Elsie often discovered a meal she'd left her the night before hidden in the bin, covered in paper, in the hope that it be wouldn't noticed. 'When you live alone, Elsie,' Matron had explained once, 'food is not easy to swallow. Even the lovely dishes you cook and leave for me. Sometimes they're hard to eat, alone. They stick in your throat and taste of sadness.'

She felt sorry for Matron and it dismayed her to see that her efforts had ended up in the bin or the dog's bowl. Everyone in the hospital looked up to Matron, but she spent her evenings on her own, sitting at the large dining table in her apartment looking out over the empty car park.

Elsie had worked for her all the time she'd been at St Angelus. When the gossip spread across the hospital about Matron's feelings for Sister April,

Elsie had wanted to lash out at anyone who dared to say a word against her. Her heart bled for her boss. Matron would never know love. Never have children. Elsie couldn't think of anything worse. 'Being who she is must make it very lonely for her,' she said to Biddy on a regular basis. 'It's not like she can tell anyone or talk about it. It must be the worst thing in the world to be born like Matron. So lonely.'

An hour later, Emily strode back into the school of nursing. 'Biddy!' she shouted into the kitchen as she mounted the stairs to her office.

Branna hid behind the kitchen door, holding a cup of tea in one hand and a cigarette in the other.

'Do the floors on ward two clean themselves?' Biddy said to Branna as she made for the door. 'Is that all you do all day, drink tea?'

'Right, I'm off then,' said Branna. 'You shan't be seeing me in here again for a while. There are better places than here I can go to be insulted.'

Biddy ran, as fast as someone her age and weight and with an incontinence pessary fitted could, in response to Emily's shout. She could count on one hand the number of times Emily had called her with any degree of urgency. The cause was usually a rat, a mouse or a cheeky spider that had made itself at home on the ceiling above her head. But this was not an animal emergency. Biddy could tell.

'Have you heard from your friend at St Dunstan's?'

Emily asked, even before Biddy had reached her desk.

'We haven't. She's been in hospital with her fibroids. Suffered from them since the last child, I hear. But her sister says she's back home now, so we should hear in a day or two.'

'OK, well, in that case, could I come to your mafia meeting, do you think, Biddy? Assuming you're having one? I can avoid the Guinness no longer. Can I take you up on your offer? We need to work together on the Bone Grinder. It's serious, Biddy, but don't tell anyone that yet. I'm someone who wants to embrace a more modern way of running the hospital, but Miss Van Gilder has proposals that are a step way too far. Oh, and by the way, Miss Van Gilder has just informed us that representatives from the Acme cleaning agency will be visiting every ward in the hospital. Can Dessie come to the meeting too? Her changes will affect him.'

'Oh yes, try and keep him away, Miss Haycock. We are all ready. The more heads on this one, the better.'

Down in the porter's lodge, Dessie sat at his desk running his fingers through his hair.

Miss Van Gilder had asked him to justify why he needed twenty-four lads. He had responded with a detailed list of the jobs the boys carried out on a regular basis. As he'd read it back to himself, he'd wondered how they managed with only twenty-four. His heart had swelled with pride. His lads worked damned hard and they earned every penny.

Miss Van Gilder had read his notes and had just passed him her own.

'Here is my proposal as to how we can reduce that number from twenty-four to twelve.'

Dessie turned to the last sheet and the last column and blinked. 'But, Miss Van Gilder, you have increased their hours to twelve a day, fourteen at weekends, and with no additional pay.'

'Quite. You told me only the other day that when the hospital was busy, they quite often worked on into their own time. You told me they would never abandon the hospital when it was busy. All I am proposing is that we transfer that goodwill on to an official footing.'

'But, Miss Van Gilder, if you do that, it is no longer goodwill. It becomes an obligation.'

'We are all obligated. Why should the porter's lads be any different?'

Later that morning, Jake sat opposite him nursing a mug of tea. Both were equally disturbed by the news.

'Jesus, Dessie, what will we do? They are laying off down on the docks. Where will these lads find work? And besides, they are the hospital. It only functions because of the lads. This place is one big family. You can't sack your family.'

'I know, Jake. But if we tell the board that the building is near falling down, I reckon they might even close us down. It's the lads that do the repair jobs to keep this place going half of the time. To think, I only told her the lads worked overtime with no pay to make a case to keep them, not to make it official.'

'She'll be after the cleaners next and then Matron's job. Why is Matron letting her get away with all of this?'

'Because Matron is being asked to attend all sorts of committees and meetings all over the place to do with the hospital and the new NHS. If you ask me, she's out of her depth and that's why she hands things over to Miss Van Gilder.' He sighed. 'There is talk of a new hospital being built, a bigger, modern one with state-of-the-art operating theatres. I hear it could be five years away or fifty, depending on whether the government stumps up the cash. It means our hospital will close. That would be the end of us. We need to keep going as long as we can and look after our lads.'

The phone on Dessie's desk rang and made Jake jump and spill his tea on his sleeve. He watched as Dessie's face creased into a frown of concentration.

'Right. This Sunday at yours? I'll be there. Seven o'clock as usual? I'll pick up some beers. Does Miss Haycock drink sherry, do you think?'

A smile spread across Dessie's face as he put the telephone down.

'You do realize that you and Miss Haycock are

the only people who don't know that you are sweet on her, don't you, Dessie?'

Dessie picked up an oil rag off the side and threw it at Jake. 'Well, you and the lads are wrong. I like her very much. She is a very nice woman and I have the greatest respect for her, but I am not sweet on her.'

'Yeah, right, and my mam, she's the next Miss World, don't you know, as long as she remembers to put her teeth in. Look at the state of you – you can't stop smiling! Jesus, Dessie, you were suicidal a minute ago and now you can't keep the grin from your face.'

'Don't talk such nonsense,' said Dessie testily. 'As it happens, there's a meeting on Sunday. Biddy says Miss Haycock has asked to come along. Both me and Miss Haycock have our minds on the likes of you and the good of this hospital, not daft romance rubbish like you lot. She came back from the management meeting this morning in a right tizz, says Biddy. My mind is now on wondering what this is all going to be about. Not Sister Haycock.'

'Of course it is, Dessie.' Jake was grinning from ear to ear.

Dessie shot out of his seat and stormed out of the porter's lodge. He knew Jake would be scrutinizing his every expression. There was a new bounce to his step and it wasn't just the prospect of finding out information about Miss Van Gilder that had put it there.

CHAPTER 23

Dana was ready to collapse on to her bed when she got back to Lovely Lane. She was even more exhausted now that she was back on days – though for how long, she didn't know. But before she got to bed, she knew there was something she had to do first. Tomorrow night, she was meeting Teddy, and the question of the summer holidays would be brought up. She needed to phone home and see whether they were expecting her back in Belmullet. Dropping her cape in the hall, she went straight to the laundry room, where the telephone was kept.

Not one of the girls bothered to do her personal laundry at the end of a shift. They were all too worn out, and besides, if they left out their laundry in a prominent place, it was almost certain that Mrs Duffy would put it through the twin tub for them and their clean clothes would be hanging on the overhead airer when they came home. Dana imagined what her mammy would say if she ever even saw a twin tub. 'You would go mad with the jealousy if you saw it,' she'd said to her the last time she'd called. Sure enough, as she opened the laundry-room door, her nostrils were assailed by the smell of clean cotton and washing powder. The room was steamy and damp in a comforting way that reminded her of the kitchen back home.

Dana sat herself on the edge of the wooden table that stood against the wall and was piled high with dried laundry waiting to be ironed. For a brief moment she collapsed back on to the pile and laid her head on the clean clothes.

'Oh, how much do I need a holiday?' she said. Her time at St Angelus had been the hardest period of her life. The episode with Patrick, who'd followed her from back home to Liverpool, had been draining. Her new affair with Teddy was exhilarating, despite their earlier misunderstandings. With her eyes closed, she imagined herself in Teddy's car, motoring along country lanes, as free as birds. Going wherever and doing whatever they liked. 'God, wouldn't that be just grand,' she whispered to the ceiling.

Sitting upright, she heard Mrs Duffy approach and open the door.

'Dana, it's you. I had a mad moment there and thought someone might be doing some ironing. But not a bit of it. You girls, you wash your clothes, but nothing gets ironed. It seems to me that your clothes must only ever get worn once.'

Mrs Duffy was standing with her hands on her hips, surveying the mountain of ironing on the table. Dana smiled. They both knew that Mrs Duffy liked to protest, but really she loved doing

400

the ironing. Over the following week, the mountain would diminish and the ironed clothes would quietly arrive on the end of their beds, neatly folded.

Dana smiled at the pile on the table. 'Has the day finally come when you're going to tell us all off? Tell you what, I'm going to phone Mammy and as soon as I've finished, I'll make a start.'

'No you will not,' said Mrs Duffy. 'You are exhausted. Get away, I'll be doing it tomorrow when you're all on the wards.'

'Mrs Duffy, we can't win!' Dana exclaimed with mock indignation.

'Oh, get away, having a moan is my only pleasure in life. Don't deny an old woman that, will you.'

Dana grinned as the door closed behind Mrs Duffy and then she heard her shouting at Scamp. 'Get yourself down off that sofa! How many times do I have to tell you?' Then came the patter of Scamp's feet down the corridor.

Dana waited and, sure enough, a moment later she heard him sneak up the stairs, then the creak of Victoria's door as it pushed open and the sigh of the bed springs above her. Scamp's favourite place was on the end of Victoria's bed.

Dana dialled the number to the post office in Belmullet. She should just catch Mrs Brock, the postmistress, before she shut. The shops in Liverpool had closed two hours since, but that wasn't the way in Mayo. The shops were open as long as the owners were awake, given that almost everyone lived either above or at the back of their business.

The number rang out only twice before it was answered. 'Dana, 'tis you,' Mrs Brock sang down the line to her. Normally, Dana couldn't stand the woman. Today, unbidden, tears sprang to her eyes at the sound of the familiar voice. Mrs Brock was known for her nosey ways, her spreading of the news received in a telegram around the shop almost before her post boy had leant his bicycle against the wall of whatever cottage or farm he was delivering it to.

'Oh God, what will I do now. Mr Joyce is in his shop, shall I send him in the van to fetch yer mammy, will ye ring back in ten minutes, will ye now?'

It was as if she had never left. Listening to the voice of Mrs Brock brought so much back. The smell of the peat and the sound of the cows. Nostalgia washed over her like the breeze off the Atlantic, not half an hour's walk away from her own front door. It had been so long. The months appeared to have been erased from her memory the continuous rain, the never-ending hard work, the expectation of a life of drudgery.

Dana agreed that she would call back in ten minutes. As she waited, she sat on the table and swung her legs backwards and forwards, picturing what she knew would be taking place right at that moment in her village. One of the boys playing football in the street would have been called over by Mrs Brock and told to fetch Mr Joyce from his shop. 'Come here now, would ye, 'tis an emergency, I have a message for the Brogans.'

This was a public service that each child carried out, without resentment or question. Everyone mucked in. 'Tell Mr Joyce I have urgent news,' she would say, and the boy would run as fast as his legs would carry him the full hundred yards to Joyce's shop, holding on to his cap, dust and stones flying as he went.

Mr Joyce would take off his coat, lay it down on the counter, lift his jacket down from the peg and hurry out of the door as fast as his rheumatism would let him. 'I have left the boy in charge of the shop,' he would pant to Mrs Brock as the bell jangled above the post-office door. It had happened to all of them on more than one occasion, even Dana, running messages and watching the shop.

'No helping yourself to anything now, just guard the door and tell anyone who happens to call that I'm with Mrs Brock and will be back presently.' This was indisputable – no one hung around with Mrs Brock any longer than was necessary.

As soon as Mr Joyce's back disappeared through the post-office door, whichever boy it was would have run around his counter and stuffed a liquorice lace or two in his pocket. Dana remembered when she and Patrick were guarding the shop and Mr Joyce had caught Patrick red-handed as the liquorice lace slid through the hole in his shorts pocket and down his leg.

Mr Joyce would have hurried back out of the post office in a flash and jumped into his van to go and pick up Dana's mammy and transport her back to the telephone. It will make her day, all the excitement, thought Dana. She will be talking about her phone call for a week. 'Did ye hear, Dana telephoned all the way from Liverpool, did ye?'

They all loved receiving a telephone call. Dana could see her mammy gabbing away excitedly to Mr Joyce, deliberating on what the urgency of the call could be. Her thoughts travelled the road with them. Her mammy would be sitting on the bench, her feet nestling in cabbage leaves and pig feed, her chatter veering between elation and panic that something was wrong. Mr Joyce would respond with either 'That would be grand now,' or 'Sure, why would ye be getting yerself all worked up, 'twill be nothing but a nice surprise.'

Dana remembered the conversation she had had with her mammy. 'No sex before marriage, Dana, will ye promise me that?' And Dana, always keen to please her mammy, had indeed promised her that. But that was in rural Ireland. Life was very different over there. Here in Liverpool, Dana was amazed at how bold Victoria was with the girls. Completely open about the fact that she and Roland were at it every five minutes. Granted, Victoria was the only one who was, but she was also the only nurse in a serious relationship, just like Dana. Or at least she thought hers was serious.

Maybe she should have promised her mammy that she'd have no sex 'in Ireland' before marriage, but her mammy wasn't daft.

'I know the ways of men, Dana,' she'd said before Dana had left for Liverpool, 'and I don't want ye making the mistakes I have made.' There'd been no explanation of what her mistakes had been or how, if she had her time again, she would avoid them. Dana did know, though, that somewhere in the foothills of her mother's youth stood Mr Joyce. It had taken her a year as a nurse to understand that her mother valued her maternal role more than any other. She had come to realize that her sole aim was to keep Dana safe from the vagaries of everyday life, out of the hands of lustful men, and to help fulfil the dream she'd never quite managed to live herself. In order to do that, she had to maintain her authority and keep her own indiscretions to herself. Dana hoped that one day she would pass a mark in the sand – maybe when she was married and had her own children – and that then her mother would be open and honest with her.

She looked up at the clock on the laundry-room wall. She could practically hear the handbrake being yanked up on Mr Joyce's van. She heard the van door slam and the bell over the door of the post office jangle. She picked up the telephone and dialled.

Within seconds, she could hear her mother's voice crackling down the line.

'Dana, 'tis you, oh God, Mr Joyce said it was and I said, no, she wouldn't waste the money on a long-distance telephone call. Is everything all right, is it? Are ye coming home? What boat will ye be on? Mr Joyce has said he will be waiting there for ye if ye are; he'll shut the shop if he has to and he said he would drive all the way to Dublin if ye get the later boat. He would have ye home by midnight and now don't ye be worrying about all that business with Patrick. He's never set foot back home since he went to Liverpool.'

Dana now knew for sure that people back home didn't know that Patrick had been arrested as a peeping Tom and had served time in Walton Gaol. He probably assumed she would have told everyone and was now too ashamed to return and face the music. As it was, she hadn't told anyone. It was at least a relief to know that if she did go home, she wouldn't have to face him.

'Did ye know that Siobhan has had a baby, yes, she did, such a beautiful baby boy. Wait until I tell her you will be home for yer holidays. God, the town will be out to meet ye.'

Dana could barely slip a word in sideways other than to confirm that yes, she was going home, as expected, and that Mr Joyce would be meeting her from the train in Galway and would transport her back home. As her mother babbled on about the kids, the farm, her father, every one of their neighbours, her friends, the doctor's new wife, the priest's housekeeper's stay in hospital and the failings of the new farmhand, it became obvious that there was nothing on the planet, alive or dead, that could stop the momentum of Dana's visit home and her mother's expectations. Mammy had decided it was happening and that was that.

As she made her way up to her room she felt deflated. She would have to tell Teddy. There was no way she could take him home. He would hate it. The rain, the mud, the smell, the cows, the kids in the streets, in the town, the bog, the peat, the men who drank too much and fought with fists and boots and then talked after. The priest. The smallness of it all. Mass.

Her mother's world would be thrown into orbit if she took Teddy home. The absolute assumption from such a visit would be that they were to be married. Her mother would have a conversation arranged with the priest and the village hall booked before they had even unpacked their suitcases.

There was also the worry that Teddy would look at her through new eyes when he saw her life as it had been before she had arrived in Liverpool. Her family and friends were country people, but not like country people from England. They lived their life slightly closer to the earth. To each other. To God. And no matter how many people Dana met and mixed with, how many of their airs and manners she adopted as her own, she would always be Dana from the farm at heart.

She assumed that Teddy would return to Bolton for his holidays, to his late parents' house. He would stay with Roland and kick his heels at home. Precious time they could have spent together would be wasted as she met her family obligations.

Dana decided she needed a bath to make herself feel better. I'll wash my hair and put it in curlers for the evening and then it will look nice for tomorrow, she thought. It was always Dana's way to make herself busy and to look for a positive. There's nothing for it, I will have to make sure Teddy can see what he's going to be missing when I'm back home in Ireland for the two weeks.

As she sat in front of her mirror, she heard the footsteps of nurses returning from their shift pounding up the stairs. The voice of Mrs Duffy followed them. 'I've bacon and boiled potatoes with a grilled tomato for each of you for supper. I've covered the potatoes in salt and butter and the bacon's almost ready, so don't dally up there now.'

Dana saw a face she barely recognized in the mirror. It was her face, but not the eighteen-year-old face that had arrived in Lovely Lane over a year ago. That had been the face of a child. The eyes that looked back at her were almost the eyes of a woman, but not quite.

While Dana was running the bath, unbeknown to her, Teddy was in a travel agent's on Dunhill Street.

'I'm looking for a nice hotel in the Lake District, for two weeks. Starting at the end of June. Or in

Scotland maybe? Somewhere nice and remote. Where we can take long walks, eat nice food, enjoy romantic views. You get the gist?'

'Oh, certainly, sir,' said the travel agent. 'We have a number of hotels on our books. Is this a special surprise for your wife?'

'Yes,' said Teddy, brimming with confidence. 'She has no idea, but she will be totally delighted when she finds out. It is a very special surprise.'

CHAPTER 24

The following evening, Teddy parked his car a hundred yards down the road from the nurses' home, just as he always did when he was waiting for Dana to check out with Mrs Duffy. This process invariably took some time.

'We used to have the late-pass system here, you know, but I said to Matron, what is the point? They are always back before I leave and besides, if they weren't, I would wait, and not one of them would make me miss my bus home.'

Mrs Duffy repeated the conversation she'd had with Matron on VE Day every time Dana went out for the evening.

'She had partaken of a few, had Matron, and I have cursed meself ever since that I didn't ask her for a pay rise too. She would have given me anything I asked for on that day. As it was, I got her to scrap the late passes, increase the jam ration and promise me that as soon as we could get our hands on fabric again, the rooms could have new curtains.'

Dana never displayed a shred of impatience as she listened and then, giving Mrs Duffy a peck on the cheek and a reassuring 'I will be back before the last bus,' she escaped.

The sight of Teddy waiting in his pale blue shiny Humber made her heart skip a beat. As always, the thought that it couldn't last flitted through her mind before she placed her hand on the door.

'Wow, get you,' said Teddy, leaning over to give her a peck on the cheek as she slipped into the pale tan leather front seat. 'You look amazing and you smell delicious.'

He buried his face in Dana's neck and inhaled noisily. Dana pushed him away with her hand, giggling as she did so.

She wanted to tell him there and then that they would not be able to spend the holidays together as she knew he had hoped. The words were on the tip of her tongue, but something held her back. Teddy had made it clear to Dana that he thought the importance of their relationship cancelled out any prior obligations she might have had to her mammy and her family. That her life had changed and they could not expect her to honour promises she had made before she had even set foot in Liverpool. They had so little off-duty time together that they could not waste the chance to spend two whole weeks in each other's company.

'I've booked us a table in the restaurant on Bold Street,' said Teddy. 'My girl is a princess and she should be treated like one.'

'A princess, me? You wouldn't think that if you

411

saw me helping with the milking on the farm back home. I look about as far from a princess as anyone could imagine.'

Dana thought this might be her opportunity, but as always he failed to grasp the chance to talk about her home or the farm. Sitting up straight, he took in the empty road ahead, turned over the engine, looked in the side mirror and, slipping the car into gear, pulled out and motored on up Lovely Lane.

Dana loosened her headscarf and resolved to tell him the news over dinner. As they passed the park, she stole a look at his side profile and thought that it was a sight she would never tire of. She loved to watch him when he was preoccupied with driving, when he couldn't look at her. She had often watched him from a distance on the wards, talking to a patient or in conference with the consultant and other doctors. Observing him from the periphery of his life was where she felt most comfortable.

'To think, I had never even been inside a restaurant until you took me,' she said as she turned slightly in her seat to face him. 'Get me now, acting as though I've been doing it all me life. Shall I light you a ciggie?'

'Please. I'm getting in the holiday mood. Thought I would give you a taste of what's to come every night for the two weeks we are on holiday,' Teddy said as he reached out his hand to take the lit cigarette from Dana.

She lowered her eyes and inhaled deeply on her cigarette as she felt her heart sink.

Beth Harper was on her ward, working a split shift. From the window of the dayroom, she saw Teddy's distinctive blue car as it sped along the road below. The dayroom had the most enormous bay windows and faced south, giving patients maximum light when they were recovering. The walking patients liked to sit and enjoy a cigarette in front of the fireplace, where an array of chairs were placed in a semi-circle with a small table between them. Beth surveyed the room and judged it to be spotless and tidy after the hustle and bustle of the day. The ward was settling down for the evening and Beth was pleased that they had completed all their jobs with almost five minutes to go. Backs and beds, doctors' visits, bottles and pans, lockers and tables, samples, drugs, drips, and dressing rounds all over and done with. Finished. Patients were sitting upright against starched and plumped pillows in pristine beds with eighteen-inch turndowns, glancing nervously towards the ward doors. All eyes were fixed on the giant clock. The atmosphere in the ward was shot through with anticipation.

'The longest five minutes ever,' said Mr Trimble to Beth, who had stopped at the end of his bed to check his charts. 'I swear to God, when the big finger on that clock gets to five to seven, it takes a rest. It does, you know. You watch.'

'Ah, well, I think it does that at twenty-five past eight as well, five minutes before I am due to go back to Lovely Lane and put my feet up,' said Beth. 'You haven't got long now, Mr Trimble, see, it's just moved. Only four minutes left.'

It was the same every day. Visitors would be arriving in less than five minutes and Sister Crawford would not let a single one through the door until every corner of the ward was spotless. She was far from idle with her threats and patients and nurses alike felt tense and nervous as the minutes ticked by. The patients feared Sister's pre-visitor inspection as much as the nurses. Concern that she might find something untoward caused everyone to hold their breath as she walked up and then back down the ward. If just one locker top was untidy, one jug of water unfilled, one urine bottle not emptied, one dirty ashtray not replaced, she would make all the visitors wait, herded like cattle outside the ward doors as they watched their precious sixty minutes tick by.

'Here she comes,' said Beth to Mr Trimble as, through the glass screen, she saw Sister leave her desk and stride purposefully out on to the ward to begin her inspection.

Mr Trimble gave a sharp whistle through his teeth. 'She doesn't look like she's in a good mood, does she? Eh, look, see that big hooter pressed up against the window on the ward doors, that's John's wife. First through, she is, every night. He says it's because she misses nagging him and can't wait to get to his bed to give him his full hour's worth. She's always hopping mad if visiting is cut short and he must be the only man on the ward to breathe a sigh of relief if it is.'

Beth stifled a giggle.

They both looked down towards John's bed. Seeming to guess that he had their attention, he glanced at them and grinned, nodding at the clock. 'It'll be late tonight,' he mouthed and winked.

Betty Hutch, the ward domestic on duty that night, had spotted a dirty ashtray on the last locker that Sister was yet to reach and was hurriedly removing the offending object and replacing it with a clean one from her trolley. Seeing Sister Crawford heading in her direction, she almost dropped the dirty ashtray as she hurriedly made the exchange. Kicking the brake off the trolley wheel, she pushed the squeaky contraption hurriedly towards the ward doors.

'You will be home tomorrow, Mr Trimble. You won't have to go through any more of this,' said Beth as she filled in his intake and output chart. 'Is that your fourth jug of water today?'

'No, it's my twentieth.'

'What?' asked Beth, her brow furrowed.

'What does it matter, Nurse Harper? I'm going home tomorrow. There will be no one filling in any charts for me there, I can tell you.'

Beth marked his fluids correctly and as she placed the chart back on the end of his bed, said,

'You must be sick of it, having been in here for so long.'

'I've forgotten what home looks like. Came in here in '51, I did. They collapsed my left lung twice, you know. It's going to be very strange. Was trying to remember what pattern the wallpaper is in the parlour, and, do you know, even though I put it up, I can't. Isn't that a funny thing? I can't complain though. I'm one of the lucky ones – I'm going home. The doctor thought I would never recover. The new streptomycin, that made all the difference.'

'For you and a lot of people,' said Beth. 'The difference on the children's ward is unbelievable, even just in the past year. They have three TB cases up there now and they all tested clear in such a short space of time. Everyone is talking about it.'

Beth had lost count of how many tales of success on children's Dana had brought back to Lovely Lane. She was secretly jealous that she hadn't been placed on children's. She relished the prospect of the responsibility. 'Those of us who were interested were told we could go up to the children's wards and study the notes. One little girl, she responded within twenty-four hours. It's just incredible. An exciting time to be a nurse.'

They both looked down the ward as they heard John shouting to Betty Hutch as she made her way to open the doors. 'Take your time, Betty. No hurry.'

His comment was met by an avalanche of jeers from the men who were eagerly awaiting their visitors. The tension had been broken and the clock hand was now very nearly on the hour.

One of the braver men looked as though, if it hadn't been for the catheter bottle at the side of his bed and the drip stand anchoring him down, he would have dived across and opened the doors himself. 'Come on, Sister Crawford,' he pleaded. 'Give us poor fellas a break. I've run out of ciggies. Me missus is out there with me supplies. You know how strict you are about ringing the bell at eight.'

Sister Crawford looked as though she might have been about to object. Instead, she walked over to the highly polished table that ran down the centre of the ward and slowly picked up the brass hand-bell. All eyes upon her, she said, 'Mrs Hutch, unlock the doors.'

Betty pushed her trolley to the side of the wall and slammed on the brake. She opened first one ward door and then the next and then stood to the side as though on parade. Before her, like a delivery of mannequins waiting to be arranged in a shop window, stood the visitors. They dared not cross the line into the ward until they knew it was safe to do so. The ward was silent, the visitors' faces keen with anticipation. Sister Crawford walked to the table, raised the brass bell by its wooden handle and rang four times.

Clutching various bouquets of flowers, the visitors flooded into the ward like a brightly coloured tide. It surged in with force, then dwindled to a trickle as visitors peeled off to the bedsides of their loved ones.

'For goodness' sake, has anyone seen the probationer, Nurse Moran?' Sister Crawford said, heading straight towards Beth. They were words she had become heartily sick of uttering.

'I haven't. Sorry, Sister.'

The telephone in the office began to ring.

'I shall have to answer that. If you see her, send her straight to me.' Sister Crawford strode back down the ward and Beth instantly pitied Bridget Moran, who was most definitely about to become the recipient of Sister's wrath.

'Blimey, you were saved by the bell there, Nurse Harper,' said Mr Trimble. 'You must have nine lives. She was about to tear you off a strip. As if it's your fault that daft girl has gone missing again.'

'I will come back soon,' said Beth, 'and help pack your case ready for home in the morning. As soon as Doctor gives you the free pass on the ward round tomorrow, you can be ready for the off.'

'Bless you, you're an angel. Look, here's the wife. I'm going to get out of bed and take her down the dayroom. Sister Crawford has made me lie still here for three days, just in case I relapsed. I'm feeling rebellious.'

Beth walked across to the other side of the ward

to her friend and housemate at Lovely Lane, Victoria, who was stuffing pillows into cases.

'Where's the probationer?' Beth whispered as she picked up the last pillow and case.

'Time for a quick cuppa in the kitchen,' said Victoria, ignoring her question. 'Visitors are here, we can ease up for a minute. Betty is putting the kettle on and she's got some biscuits.'

Visiting was always a good time to catch a sneaky cuppa, but both Beth and Victoria knew it would be only a matter of minutes before a visitor came looking for one of them.

'You know something, don't you?' Beth said to Victoria. 'Avoiding the question will get you nowhere with me. Where is Nurse Moran, have you seen her? What have you done with her?'

'I haven't done anything, but I do know where she is. One of the doctors asked her to help him put up a drip. She was so excited to be asked and then he sent her down to the stores for a long stand.'

'Oh, the poor girl,' said Beth. 'How many times must Jake have had a probationer turn up and ask him for one of those!'

'I know, but she has been gone a very long time. One of us had better sneak down and rescue her if she isn't back up soon.'

'I'm going to pack up Mr Trimble's belongings after visiting,' said Beth. 'He is finally on his way home tomorrow. Must be wonderful to be TB-free. The poor man was on the isolation ward for over a year. He's breathing like a good 'un now.'

'I can't imagine what it must be like, stuck on the ward for so long,' said Victoria. 'He must have forgotten what his kids look like. He told me Sister Crawford let them come to the ward door at Christmas and wave to him. Seems a bit mean when his sputum samples were clear by then. At least we get to go back to Lovely Lane each night.'

Victoria thumped the last pillow and smoothed the cover into place, then they headed towards the kitchen. Betty Hutch would have the tea waiting for them and Beth's mouth was watering at the prospect of a gypsy cream to have with it.

'I've just seen Dana and Teddy disappearing into town,' said Beth. 'The lucky pair. I wish I was taller, didn't wear glasses and was prettier. Just about everything I'm not, really. I never thought I would be one to want a boyfriend. Always thought it would be a single life for me, but do you know what, I'm actually jealous of you both.'

'Don't feel bad about that, we should all be jealous of Dana. She doesn't know it yet, but Teddy has booked them both into a gorgeous hotel in the Lake District. He's going to surprise her tonight over supper, the lucky girl.'

'Has he booked separate rooms?' Beth asked, then blushed furiously, embarrassed at having even asked the question.

'Oh, Beth, not you too. No, of course he hasn't. Sweetie, the war is over. Life is changing. The world is moving on.'

'Not that fast, it isn't, Nurse Baker. And

anyway, what about, you know . . . What if she got pregnant?' There was an urgency to Beth's whispered words. 'Everyone knows that pregnancy for an unmarried woman means the end of just about everything. Life. Job. Reputation. And a big hello to a future of grind and poverty. Dana is Irish, for God's sake. Surely she must understand what that means.'

Victoria rolled her eyes and bit into her biscuit. But Beth wasn't finished.

'Believe me, Victoria, some single girls who get pregnant in Ireland are never heard of again. The priests rule with the hand of God. Dana doesn't want to risk that, especially not where she comes from. It's even worse in the west of Ireland. It's OK for you, Victoria. You have money behind you. But what the hell would Dana do? Who is to say Teddy would stand by her?'

Before she could say any more she was interrupted by Mr Trimble and his wife, who waved to her as they passed the kitchen door on their way to the dayroom.

'I'll just have a quick word with his wife. Back in a moment,' she said to Victoria.

'Hello, Mrs Trimble, are you looking forward to having him home?'

Mrs Trimble was fastening the waist cord on her husband's dressing gown. 'We're off for a ciggie, Nurse,' she said. 'I don't think the kids are going to sleep tonight. Beside themselves, they are, that their dad is coming home. I'm just worried he will get exhausted because, honest to God, before he's even had his dinner, half of the street will be in to see him.'

Beth looked anxiously towards the kitchen door. Her tea was calling.

'My next-door neighbour, she's making a cake tonight with me mam while I'm here, and the kids are decorating the house and everything.'

'It's like when I came back from the war, Nurse! I'll have to act all surprised, won't I, love?' Mr Trimble looked at his wife and Beth noticed the affection that passed between the two of them. 'Do you know what I'm looking forward to the most? A bit of the old exercise. I've barely moved in more than two years. And me mother-in-law's rock cakes. Now, I must have been sick, because no well man would say he was looking forward to that, would he, Nurse?'

'Mr Trimble, are you sure you should be smoking?' said Beth as his wife took his cigarettes out of his dressing-gown pocket. 'Really, give yourself a chance. Doctor has told you, and you read it in the papers yourself, that a senior committee looking into this thinks that there may be a link between smoking and chest problems like yours.'

'Oh, I will, Nurse. But, you know, it said they only think that. Don't have any actual proof, do they? If we did what everyone thinks, we'd tie ourselves up in knots, wouldn't we? No, I'm sorry, Nurse Harper, but I won't believe a word that committee says until the papers say that they can prove beyond all reasonable doubt that smoking is detrimental. They must be wrong. The ciggies keep it all loose and coming up. I cough better with them. It's terrible without. Me chest gets all tight. I'd be as sick as a dog without these ciggies. And what you don't know is that Doctor gave me the wink and told me I'd be fine. Jesus, the man smokes thirty a day himself.'

Beth shook her head. It was true that the committee didn't have any proof and that the report in the papers had been shot down in flames. Most notably by the nurses who smoked at Lovely Lane.

She didn't have time to respond as Sister Crawford finished her phone call and rushed out of the office. 'Nurses!' she called down the ward.

'I've got to go,' said Beth as Sister's voice rang out.

Victoria shot out of the kitchen with a guilty look in her eyes and biscuit crumbs on her lips.

'Ward eight is full. We have an emergency on the way, nurses.'

'But we aren't on take, Sister Crawford,' stammered Victoria, already sensing that their eight-thirty home-time was in danger of being missed.

'No, I am well aware of that. Ward eight is on take, but as I have just explained, they are full. Would you like me to suggest to Matron that you now assume responsibility for bed allocation, Nurse Baker?'

'Er . . . no, Sister. Sorry, Sister.'

'I am relieved to hear it. Please prepare bed one nearest to the office. It's an oesophageal varices and it's a bad one. This will take both of you. Has Nurse Moran not arrived back yet? Where on earth is she?' Sister saw the glance that passed between Beth and Victoria and the penny dropped. 'Oh, seriously, not another one? Do those doctors not realize how much they inconvenience the ward when they pick on probationers? This is not the time to have a nurse missing.'

They were saved yet again by the ring of the office telephone piercing the air.

Victoria and Beth set about their tasks. The atmosphere on the ward had changed, from tea and biscuits to saving lives. Victoria flew as fast as she could to the linen room.

Within minutes, Jake arrived through the door of the ward, pushing a trolley. Victoria had washed the rubber mattress with diluted Dettol and dried it down and it took her and Beth less than two minutes to make up the bed.

'I'll see to the patient, you see to his wife,' Beth said to Victoria as she nodded to a woman standing looking nervous at the door to the ward.

Victoria raised her eyebrows. Victoria was a competent nurse at exactly the same level as Beth and yet bossy Beth always took charge. Before she could argue, Beth had sprung into action. She met the trolley and picked up the notes from the end.

'This is Mr O'Leary, Nurse Harper,' said Jake.

'Lovely. Thank you,' said Beth. Then she whispered under her breath, 'Sister is going mad looking for Nurse Moran, is she in the stores?'

'She was,' said Jake. 'I completely forgot about her. Casualty is mad busy and when I got back for me break, she was still stood there. Honest to God, the lads are still laughing.'

Beth shook her head in dismay.

'Can you manage the poles with me?' asked Jake. 'Dessie is busy.'

'Of course,' said Beth.

'Right, you get to the bottom then.'

Jake stood at the head of the bed and Beth at the bottom and together they lifted the wooden poles that were slotted through the canvas sheet on the casualty trolley and transferred Mr O'Leary to the bed.

Beth rushed to one side of the bed. 'Just going to roll you over to face me, Mr O'Leary,' she said.

Jake gently rolled him over and as he did so, gathered the canvas sheet into a thin roll along the length of Mr O'Leary's body. 'Now back to me, old fella,' he said as they rolled Mr O'Leary back across the small bump to face Jake.

Beth whipped away the canvas roll with a flourish. 'There you go,' she said as she handed it to Jake. Then she pulled the bed covers neatly over Mr O'Leary and tucked them in around the sides.

'I'm putting the cot sides up on this one,' she said to Jake with a wink. They could both smell the alcohol fumes.

'Are you comfortable there, Mr O'Leary?' she asked.

'My name is Seamus O'Leary, Nurse,' he said. 'Seamus from Cork, pleased to meet ye.'

Beth could tell he had struggled to speak. 'You sound like you've been having a tipple, Mr O'Leary,' she said. 'Did you come here straight from the pub?'

'Holy Mother of God, how did you know that? Did you hear that?' he said to Jake as he turned his head towards him. 'This nurse, she has a gift. She knows where I've come from and I haven't said a word to her yet. Now is that not just remarkable?'

Beth read his notes quickly as he spoke. He had vomited blood twice during the day and the doctor had written in the notes that he had oesophageal varices.

'I'm off,' said Jake. 'Casualty is mad busy, Dessie will be looking for me.'

'How's Martha?' asked Victoria, who had arrived back at the bed.

'She's just fine, Nurse Baker. Not long to go now and I'll be dashing in here meself.'

As Jake left, Victoria turned her attention to Mr O'Leary. 'Hello,' she said as she placed her hand gently on his arm.

'He's got oesophageal varices,' said Beth. 'Like varicose veins, but in the oesophagus.'

Victoria looked none the wiser. 'His wife has gone to the bathroom and will be back in a minute,' she said. 'Shall I make out a name card for the wall?'

'No, it's all right, I'll do it.'

'How does oesophageal varices happen, then?' Victoria was almost irritated that Beth seemed to know what it was without having to dash to the office and ask Sister Crawford, as she would have done. And it was also annoying that Beth seemed to look upon her as someone who was there to assist, not as her equal.

'It's most common in alcoholics.' Beth whispered so that Mr O'Leary couldn't hear her.

'He doesn't look like an alcoholic,' said Victoria. 'They're usually screaming for a drink. Mr O'Leary looks too pale and sick to scream for anything.' His complexion was deathly white and when she'd touched his arm, it had felt unnaturally cold.

Beth put down the notes on the locker. 'I think he's already had a skinful today. He's very merry for a man who's been vomiting blood and has just been hospitalized. I'll do his obs and his charts. Could you fetch a urine bottle, please?'

Victoria felt another flash of irritation. 'Beth . . .' she began.

But Beth cut her off. 'Well, would you look at that. Here comes Nurse Moran.'

They both turned as she came into view, pushing a perfectly normal drip stand. The stands were heavy; their ornate, cast-iron bases were moulded with filigree leaf patterns travelling down the four legs, and though they were on castors, it took two hands to push them. The cream paint was chipped in places, revealing rusting iron beneath.

Victoria breathed slowly and deeply. She was about to say to Beth that, actually, she would do the observations and Beth could fetch the urine bottle.

'God, you would not believe it. The porter made me wait for ever for this stand,' Bridget Moran said as she approached the bed.

'Did he now?' said Victoria. 'Made you "take-a-long-stand", did he?' She pronounced the words very slowly and carefully and both she and Beth watched as the penny dropped.

'Was that another joke?' Nurse Moran demanded.

'It really was, I'm afraid, you poor love. I wouldn't worry, though. You can't expect to complete your probationary months without being totally done over at least half a dozen times,' said Victoria. 'Now, can you fetch Mr O'Leary a urine bottle, please?'

Nurse Moran abandoned her stand with a scowl and headed for the kitchen in the nearest thing to a strop she could manage. As she passed the dayroom doors, she let out a scream.

Seconds later, Beth and Victoria were at her side. They were met by the sight of Mr Trimble laid out flat on the dayroom floor. His face was blue and a horrible gurgling sound came from his mouth and then suddenly stopped. His cigarette lay burning into the wooden floor at his side and his wife stood nearby, frozen in shock.

Beth dropped to her knees and took his pulse. She shook her head. 'Nothing there. Mr Trimble! Mr Trimble!' she yelled as she rolled him over on to his front and turned his head to the side.

'Here, let me help,' said Victoria. 'Go and fetch

Sister,' she said sharply to Nurse Moran, 'and take Mrs Trimble out of here to the visitors' seats outside.'

She led the stupefied Mrs Trimble to the door and placed the probationer's arm around her. 'Just give us five minutes with him, please, Mrs Trimble,' she said.

Turning her attention back to Beth and Mr Trimble, she fell to her knees on the floor as she pulled one of Mr Trimble's arms up and tried to tuck it under his chest. 'His lips are cyanosed,' she said. 'His whole face is becoming cyanosed.'

They both tried again and managed to slide Mr Trimble's hands underneath to elevate him slightly. Beth began to push down on his back, as they'd been taught by Sister Ryan in the school.

Victoria's heart was beating wildly. They had all been taught how to deal with a patient who collapsed, but being taught in the school was one thing, having to deal with the situation in real life was quite another. Whenever something like that happened to one of the nurses at Lovely Lane, they would all sit around at supper wanting to know every little detail, glad it hadn't been on their shift. But now Victoria was in the middle of it. She swallowed hard. Pull yourself together, she thought as she secured Mr Trimble's hands. Her heart continued to beat like a runaway train, pounding against her chest wall.

They both heard the sound of rapid footsteps as Sister Crawford appeared at their sides.

'Well done, Nurse, that is the correct position. Continue depressing his back at five depressions per minute. And you, you stupid girl,' she said, addressing Nurse Moran, 'you have tried my patience to the end today.'

Nurse Moran was standing behind Sister Crawford with her mouth open and her eyes fixed on Beth and Victoria.

'I have already called for the doctors and the oxygen,' said Sister. 'Keep on doing what you are doing and stay calm. You, girl,' she said to the terrified Nurse Moran, 'help Mrs Hutch to make up a tea trolley and take it around the ward. Don't let any of the patients into the dayroom, close the ward doors and fob them off with a story. Say it's being cleaned. Is there any way you can manage that without getting something wrong? Tell Mr O'Leary and his wife that we will be with him in two minutes.'

The probationer looked as though she was about to burst into tears. 'Yes, Sister,' she whispered and made her way to the kitchen.

The thought crossed Victoria's mind that Nurse Moran would simply not be able to remember so many instructions at once.

Within seconds they could hear the rattle of cups and saucers being laid on the drinks trolley and the murmur of voices as Betty Hutch asked Nurse Moran what was going on.

The sound of boots pounding up the stairs at speed intensified the atmosphere and the dayroom doors burst open to reveal the casualty doctors with Jake running behind them and wheeling a cylinder of oxygen into the room.

'God, can you not manage without me? I only left five minutes ago,' said Jake as he swung the oxygen bottle round on its wheels and connected the rubber tubing to the outlet valve.

The fact that the doctors were running brought home to Victoria and Beth the seriousness of the situation. Sister Crawford would as good as shoot any nurse if she caught them running anywhere, even in an emergency. Mr Trimble's face was purple. His body was a dead weight. It felt to Victoria as though all hell had broken loose. She jumped to her feet as Dr Mackintosh took her place at Mr Trimble's side.

'Good work, Nurse,' he said to Beth as he took out his stethoscope. 'Keep depressing.'

Again, Victoria was irritated by this. They had both been attending to Mr Trimble and yet no one thought to say 'Good work' to her. Just because Beth always assumed responsibility didn't mean that Victoria, or anyone else for that matter, was less capable.

The second doctor had brought up a brown canvas bag from casualty. It looked similar to the ones used in field hospitals during the war. He crouched on the floor, undid the leather straps and took out a large wooden box. 'Does he have a blood pressure?' he asked as he unwound the rubber cuff.

431

'I doubt if he does any more,' said Dr Mackintosh. 'But here, I'm going to try something.'

To everyone's amazement, he grabbed Mr Trimble's hands and pulled them out from under his chest.

Beth slipped to the side and everyone stared at Dr Mackintosh in amazement.

'There's this fellow in America, he's been trying this new method and I'm going to give it a go. We have nothing to lose here.'

There was a sharp intake of breath from Sister and the nurses as, with little ceremony or dignity, Dr Mackintosh flipped Mr Trimble over on to his back. Lifting his fist high in the air, he let it come down with a bang on Mr Trimble's sternum and then, lifting the patient's chin, he opened the airway and breathed hard into his lungs.

'Gosh, his chest rose,' said the junior doctor.

'Aye,' said Dr Mackintosh. 'It's supposed to. Do you think you could push down from the front, Nurse Harper, just like you were doing from the back, while I respirate him? While I do that, Doctor, could you please quickly draw up some Coramine. With a bit of luck, if we keep depressing and respirating, we might get some flow through and the Coramine may have half a chance.'

Beth's eyes were wide with alarm.

'You too, Nurse Baker,' he said to Victoria. 'It is extremely hard work.'

Beth didn't respond. She just stared at Dr Mackintosh. It was as though she was in shock.

In a flash, Victoria rushed round to the side of Mr Trimble and fell to her knees. 'Like this?' she asked as she pushed down on his sternum.

'Exactly, Nurse. Sister Crawford, can you hold the oxygen mask here, please.' He indicated Mr Trimble's mouth. 'Doctor, can you keep trying for a pulse or a blood pressure once you have the Coramine ready to inject.'

It felt to Victoria like she had been pressing up and down on Mr Trimble's sternum for ever. Her arms were weakening, the force of her depressions lessening each time, and she could see that Dr Mackintosh had gone puce in the face.

Suddenly, the junior doctor shouted out, 'We have a pulse, by Jove! We have a pulse.'

'Sister, turn up that oxygen to the maximum the outlet valve will allow, please,' said Dr Mackintosh. His face was flushed, his eyes alight. He had just tried something no one at St Angelus had ever done before. And it had worked.

The sudden hiss of the oxygen as it moved from a gentle flow to a loud rush filled the room as all eyes fixed on Mr Trimble. Much to Victoria's amazement, he took a large and loud breath.

'We have a blood pressure,' said the junior doctor, who was almost lying on the floor, having managed to secure his cuff round Mr Trimble's arm and pump up his sphygmomanometer.

'Well done, everyone,' said Dr Mackintosh. 'If Jake is still here, perhaps he could help us get Mr Trimble back into a bed? He will need specialling, Sister. A drip, the usual. He'll need more Coramine.'

Sister Crawford, who was holding the oxygen mask over Mr Trimble's face, said, 'Nurse Baker, you wouldn't mind moving that burning cigarette from the floor, would you? I fear we may all be about to get blown up.'

A visitor had slipped past Betty Hutch and Nurse Moran on the ward. Opening the dayroom door and appearing not to notice Mr Trimble, she said, 'Nurse, could my old man have a bottle, please? He's desperate, he is.'

As Victoria got to her feet to remove the cigarette, the office phone began ringing and the porter's lads arrived outside with the linen delivery.

Within minutes, a very sick-looking Mr Trimble was back in his bed with a drip in place.

Dr Mackintosh sat in front of the fireplace in Sister Crawford's office and wrote up his notes. 'I've put some morphine in Mr Trimble's drip, Sister. I am going to prescribe him a sleeping sedative too. Six weeks' full bed rest. Keep his bowels regular. No stress, and small, frequent meals rather than three large ones. Oxygen every time he looks as though his lips are cyanosed or he is having trouble breathing. All this will be confirmed in the morning by the cardiac team, I'm sure.'

'Very well, Doctor. It looks as though Mr Trimble is never going to go home at this rate. He has gone from being a TB patient to a cardiac patient with no effort whatsoever.'

'Well, Sister, that's not so unusual. However, I am delighted with our results. As soon as I've finished these notes, I'm going back to my room to write a letter to my friend at the Johns Hopkins University in America telling him about our results in using cardiac compression combined with artificial resuscitation. He is leading the field in this research.' He paused and smiled. 'Today was a great day. Not only has Mr Trimble benefited from my friend's research, but this experience will help to inform the whole programme. They are way ahead on this in America.'

He sounded so enthused that even Sister Crawford managed a smile. Dr Mackintosh was such an earnest young man. 'We are lucky to have doctors like you here in Liverpool,' she said. 'So many of the bright ones want to go to London and yet all the experience in the world is here in Liverpool. We have it all: poverty, smog and every disease known to man.'

'Well, Glasgow would see you there, Sister, but you are right, it is a very exciting city.'

Mrs Hutch, without being asked, shuffled into the office and placed a cup of tea in front of Dr Mackintosh. 'Tea, three sugars, Doctor. Good job,' she said, and shuffled back out.

For a moment, as they watched her retreating back, laughter threatened to fill the office.

Sister Crawford took the notes from Dr

Mackintosh. 'Drink your tea, specially made by your secret admirer. Still no sign of a Mrs Mackintosh on the horizon then?'

Dr Mackintosh blushed. 'Not at all, Sister. What is the point? What woman would understand my job or my hours? And besides, we doctors have a terrible reputation for playing fast and loose with the hearts of young ladies, you know, even though I am not of that nature myself. What self-respecting young woman would trust any doctor?'

'Nonsense, you aren't all Casanovas. Some might say that you work the hours you do precisely because there is no Mrs Mackintosh to stop you,' said Sister, probing in her motherly way.

She waited for a reply. There was none. A moment's silence fell when she and Dr Mackintosh locked eyes. Both looked out towards the ward. Both sensed that something was wrong. Both moved as if in slow motion towards the door as the air was pierced by a chilling scream, which Sister recognized as coming from Nurse Moran.

'So help me God, I am going to string that girl up by her boot straps,' snapped Sister as she flung open the office door and strode out towards the sound of the scream with Dr Mackintosh at her heels.

They stopped dead in their tracks. The sight that greeted them would have made anyone scream, and besides, it hadn't actually been the probationer nurse who'd screamed but the newly widowed Mrs O'Leary. While all the commotion had been going on with Mr Trimble, Mrs O'Leary had slipped across to the bedside of her husband, removed the bottle of gin from her handbag and given Mr O'Leary a sip or two, or probably much more. They were each one as big an alcoholic as the other, but only one of them suffered from oesophageal varices. And only one of them had just died as a result.

While Dr Mackintosh had been talking to Sister, Beth and Victoria were in the linen room. They were loading the shelves with the clean sheets the porter's lads had delivered in the middle of Mr Trimble's collapse.

'What happened to you, why didn't you want to do the chest depressions?' asked Victoria.

Beth frowned as she clutched the clean sheets to her own chest, as though to protect herself from Victoria's questions. 'I know it sounds odd, but it was because it wasn't what we'd been taught. I didn't think it was proper. I didn't know how to do the chest depressions, but well done to you, Victoria, because you just got on with it. I am cross with myself. I panicked. Froze.'

At the sound of the scream, they both left the linen room and risked being told off for running.

Beth placed her hand across her mouth at the sight that greeted them. It was truly horrifying. Blood ran down the wall, dripped from the bedside locker and puddled on the floor. It dripped from Mrs O'Leary's hat, and her hair and hands and arms were covered. Her dress was soaked and was slowly turning from bright red to brown.

Mr O'Leary was as white as the pillow he lay against. Blood pooled in the dip of his chest and his counterpane was a now a blanket of blood.

It had all happened so quickly. The patient in the next bed had been talking to his visitors. They were reading the newspaper and had failed to notice. The visitors' chatter and general cacophony that usually filled the ward between seven and eight in the evening had ceased as suddenly as if they had been halted with a conductor's baton.

No one spoke as the ward staff took in the sight before them.

'Jesus wept,' whispered Dr Mackintosh.

The scream came again, followed by pitiful sobbing from Mr O'Leary's wife. 'I only gave him a little sip,' she cried.

The footsteps of the junior doctor returning up the stairs in response to Beth having chased after him filled the ward. The clock ticked. A visitor coughed. The more delicate ladies sniffed into their handkerchiefs.

'His varices must have ruptured,' said Dr Mackintosh as he walked over to the bed and took Mr O'Leary's pulse.

'Clear the ward of all visitors,' snapped Sister Crawford to Nurse Moran, adding, 'There's a good girl,' in a gentler tone.

'It would have been over in ten seconds.' Dr Mackintosh turned to Mrs O'Leary and spoke to her gently. His Edinburgh burr, soft, reassuring and authoritative, worked its own magic at moments

438

like this. 'He would have thought he was having a bit of a cough, that's all. Instead, it was a fatal haemorrhage as the varices ruptured. He wouldn't have known a thing. I am so sorry, Mrs O'Leary.'

Beth led a sobbing Mrs O'Leary away as Victoria, paddling in rapidly congealing blood, drew the screens around the bed. Nurse Moran rang the brass hand-bell instructing the visitors to leave. There was not a single murmur of protest.

An hour later, Beth and Victoria met in the ward kitchen. The death had happened on their watch and so it was their responsibility to carry out last offices. Victoria had volunteered to do it while Beth special-nursed Mr Trimble. Matron had sent two additional nurses from other wards to plough on with backs, beds and obs.

'Sister said Nurse Moran helped you with last offices,' said Beth.

'She did, poor kid. She almost fainted twice. For once, I actually felt sorry for her. If anything was going to make her grow up a bit, tonight should have done it.'

'It was the suddenness of it,' said Beth. 'One minute he was chatting away, the next, gone. Over in a flash. Dr Mackintosh said some people just ignore the fact that they are coughing up blood and die at home. It's always the heavy drinkers, he said. Apparently, the post-mortems always show extensive cirrhosis of the liver as a pre-disposing factor.'

439

'It's just so sad that there's no treatment. Just awful.' Victoria stirred sugar into a cup of tea and handed it to Beth.

'What do we have treatment for anyway? Seems to me that the answer to everything is bed rest. People come in here, we make them lie in a bed for weeks, and so many don't get to go out again. That's the fourth death in here in two days.'

The girls were silent while they drank their tea. Both remained that way until Beth finally spoke.

'If I'd seen him in the street, I would never have guessed he was an alcoholic.'

'They don't all sleep in doorways,' said Victoria, who was convinced her father had been verging on alcoholism when he took his own life. She based this theory on the fact that he had drunk a large whisky with his kippers every morning at breakfast. 'To dissolve the bones,' he used to say when she gave him a disapproving look. He also partook of a bottle of wine and a couple of brandies at lunch and trebled that at dinner, continuing until her mother, or, later, her Aunt Minnie, dragged him to bed.

'People seem to accept alcoholism in the poor and yet turn a blind eye to it in the wealthy,' Victoria said thoughtfully.

The junior doctor crept into the kitchen. 'There isn't a spare cup in that pot is there, by any chance?'

Victoria smiled. 'There is for you. What did you think of that thing Dr Mackintosh did, banging on Mr Trimble's chest? I heard a rib crack, you know.'

The junior doctor picked up the cup Victoria proffered. 'I've never seen it done before, but I have heard about it,' he said.

'He seemed to know what he was doing though,' said Victoria. 'And it worked.'

'Ah, well, that would have been just luck, because, frankly, we don't know what we're doing half of the time. There is very little in our armoury, you know, though antibiotics are changing everything and some of the new drug research they're talking about is almost beyond belief. Dr Mackintosh did well. My job now is to keep the patient going.'

When the junior doctor had drunk his tea and left, Beth sighed as she began washing up the cups. 'I'm jealous of Dana,' she said. She had been thinking about seeing the blue Humber earlier, and about the obvious happiness of Dana and Teddy. 'I think I need a holiday. She is so lucky to have Teddy to spoil her so. On my nurse's wage, I'll be lucky to have enough for the train fare back to Germany, to see my family on the base. In fact, I shall have to write and ask Daddy because I know I won't.'

Victoria put her arm around Beth's shoulder and gave her a hug. All the irritation she had felt earlier at her bossiness had disappeared into thin air. 'There is someone for you, Beth. There is for everyone. Just don't let your devotion to the job mean you don't notice him when he pops into your life.'

Beth responded with the weakest smile. They both knew that, for Beth, that was a very real danger.

'I can't lie. I love this restaurant,' said Dana. 'Although I think 'tis a cheek, the price they charge for oysters. We pick them ourselves at Blacksod Bay and God, they are so cold and fresh and salty. You should see it. You could eat oysters every day.'

Teddy grinned from ear to ear as the salty water from his oyster slipped down his chin. Crashing the shell on the plate, he leant forward. 'You know what they say about oysters, don't you?'

Dana looked at him with big eyes, mouth parted. 'No, what? What do they say? We eat them all the time in Ireland. I have no notion what all the fuss is about. What?'

'They say they are an aphrodisiac,' he whispered.

Dana looked around the restaurant and cast a glance at the waiter. 'Does he think that is why I have eaten all mine?' she asked as the blood rushed to her face. 'Oh my God, Teddy. Are you kidding me? You are, aren't you?' She was now blushing furiously and was convinced that the waiter had winked at her.

Teddy picked up another shell and prised it open. 'Well, he might be wondering, seeing as you ate all ten in as many seconds.'

'That was because I haven't eaten all day and

I'm starving, not because I want any flaming aphrodisiac.'

Teddy laughed out loud. 'Don't worry, Dana, you are safe tonight. I shall return you to Mrs Duffy safe and sound by ten o'clock, as always, and I shall even give the old dear a lift home, to save her from having to get the bus. But in a few weeks' time it will be an entirely different story.'

Without another word, Teddy produced a black-and-white picture of a handsome country house against a backdrop of open water and placed it next to her.

'What's this?' She picked it up and studied it.

The picture was dark, but it was impossible not to be impressed by the size of the building, the beautiful, ivy-covered walls and the expanse of calm water in front of it.

'It's a hotel in the Lake District and you and I have the premier suite for two weeks, beginning the first day of our holidays. I thought we could drive to my house in Bolton, see Roland, spend a night or two at home and then continue up to the Lakes. We can do the same on the way back, to break up the journey. Do you like it?' Teddy nodded enthusiastically at the card in her hand.

Dana gulped. 'It's beautiful,' she said. 'But, Teddy . . .'

He placed his hand over hers. 'Come on, Dana, it's been a year now. We know that you and I are the real thing. I wouldn't dream of asking you to cut short your training, and I have another four years to go myself yet, but that doesn't mean we have to behave like a monk and a nun. As long as we are careful. You do love me, don't you?'

Dana looked across the table into his smiling eyes as, with one flick of his head, he repositioned his floppy fringe back over to the side. It seemed to her as though Teddy never stopped smiling.

Her mother's words rang in her ears. 'God, the whole town will be out to meet ye, as God is true, and now I just won't sleep for the excitement until Mr Joyce fetches ye back from the train. Noel, will ye clean out the turf cuts from the van, our Dana's coming home.'

She swallowed hard. 'I can't wait,' she said as she avoided Teddy's eyes, picked up his oyster and downed it in one.

'That's my girl,' said Teddy, just as she coughed and spluttered.

He was the happiest and most optimistic man she knew, and yet she didn't really know him. With Teddy, the conversation was always about today and the future, never the past. In a whole year he had never once talked to Dana about his mother or her death.

Dana knew that now was the moment. Tell him. Tell him. Tell him. Now. The words pounded her brain. But when she opened her mouth, she said instead, 'Teddy, I'm a virgin and I've never done anything like this before. I've never been in a bedroom with a man, never mind slept in the same bed. I've never been on a holiday even. No one who lives on a farm goes on holidays. They just don't.'

'All the more reason why you will enjoy yourself then. And don't worry about the virgin thing.' He reached across the table and took her hands into his. 'It will all be fine and dandy. There's no rush. We have two weeks to relax and enjoy ourselves. Don't worry about anything. You can trust me, Dana. I'm a doctor.'

CHAPTER 25

Biddy was in a flap. She had opened up the old tea chest, undone the crumpled newspaper wrappings, taken out the Belleek shamrock tea service her family in Ireland had clubbed together for and sent as a wedding present, and washed it piece by piece. Then, convinced that one wash could not possibly remove forty years of dust, she'd washed it again.

'Why on earth are you bothering getting the china out? I have never seen you use those plates before, not once.'

'Because I have . . .'

Biddy didn't get the chance to finish as Elsie powered on. 'No, I tell a lie, I haven't seen it as such, since your Mick disappeared. Before then, it passed by my window every week, in and out of the pawn shop. I'm surprised he didn't take it with him when he went.'

'He did,' said Biddy. 'Or at least he tried. I thought he was back off down the pawn shop and I saw him from the bus. I jumped off and shouted to him and when he saw me, he dropped it on the pavement and ran. The bastard. Broke two plates and a cup, he did. That was the last time I ever laid eyes on him. And, God willing, it will stay that way for ever, unless of course I see him first and if I do, he won't stand a chance. I've kept the broken plates to hit him with.'

Elsie watched as her friend furiously polished the sugar bowl. 'If there's one quality no one can deny you have, Biddy, 'tis that you bear a marvellous grudge. I've never met anyone who can bear one as well as you, and I've know a few in me time.'

'I've no time for grudges now, Emily Haycock is coming around to my house, and you, get your coat off, you're making the place look untidy.'

Affronted, Elsie hung her coat up on the nail on the back of the kitchen door. 'I don't think you have to go to all this bother, Biddy, because Sister Haycock is calling round, 'tis all I'm saying. Dessie is in a fine tizzy though. God, if he asked me once, he asked me a dozen times, what should he bring for her to drink.'

'Well, I thought we would have a sandwich. I've made a nice currant slice and then we can give her a drink and show her the letter,' said Biddy, nodding towards the food she'd prepared, which was hiding in mounds under damp tea cloths on the Formica-topped table.

'He's got sherry. He thought that would be the best thing for a lady, he said. Guinness for us, as usual. Us not being ladies.' Elsie pulled out a chair and sat down.

'What are we then, if we aren't ladies?' Biddy looked put out.

'I don't know, I'm sure, but I'll tell you this, I can feel a bit of bravery coming on in our Dessie. Don't be surprised if he asks her out. He was coming across to me as being quite bold, and I do think I know a bit about these things, Biddy. As you well know, I had my share of admirers after the war. He was all interested, like, in Sister Haycock. I think his sap must be up, Biddy.'

Biddy nearly dropped the Belleek teapot. 'All this talk of Sister Haycock and Dessie, it makes me feel, well, I don't know, a bit odd.'

'It's making you feel jealous, Biddy, that's what it is and there's no point in you denying it. It's written all over your face. Dessie, he's too young for you, Biddy. We've reached the age when the ship has sailed and we never even knew it was docked. We let kids and life pass us by while we sat at the bingo. We got it wrong, you and me, Bid. All we have left is me with my veins and haemorrhoids and you with your incontinence pessary. If you have any affection for that woman at all, you will push her to meet Dessie half way and do her a favour. Can you imagine Dessie as a dad? They might just have a chance if she's quick.'

'Elsie, you are way ahead of me. Why would you think I was ever attracted to Dessie? But you're right, I would like to see Sister Haycock with someone. I'll think of something. Getting a couple to go a bit soft on each other, that's easy for me and you, eh? We've faced tougher than that.'

They both heard the back gate close with a clatter and the unfamiliar sound of heels clipping across the back yard.

'Quick, she's here,' said Biddy as she removed the ashtray from the table and straightened the cloth with her hand. 'Move that, will you,' she hissed, nodding to the open *Liverpool Echo* perched on the chair.

Elsie lifted the cushion up quickly and stuffed it underneath, just as they heard a tap on the back door.

'Come in,' shouted Biddy as she opened the door. 'What are you knocking for? No one knocks when they come in here.'

Sister Haycock stepped into the kitchen and looked around. It was no surprise to her that the place was spotless. She handed Biddy a bunch of bluebells. 'For you,' she said.

Biddy took an empty jam jar out of the cupboard. 'Well now, aren't they lovely. Can't remember the last time anyone brought me flowers. Sit down, Sister Haycock.'

Before Emily had the chance to take up Biddy's invitation, Dessie burst through the back door. 'I thought I'd get here early and open the sherry and check the glasses before she arrives. What time is she due?' he said, before he turned around and saw Emily standing near the table.

'Oh, hello. Damn, I thought I might beat you to it. We aren't used to sherry around here.' Dessie blushed.

Biddy looked at Sister Haycock. Biddy had no idea why, but she was blushing too.

The arrival of Madge and then Branna made the meeting complete and Biddy savoured her moment of triumph by letting everyone else speak first.

Dessie shared his news. 'Well, I managed to speak to the man from the cleaning agency who was writing down all the details in each ward. How many windows, sills, beds, sinks; he was even measuring the length of the skirting boards. I took him a mug of tea and told him I was leaving the job of head porter and moving on.'

A loud gasp came from Elsie. 'Dessie, you're not! You can't.'

'No, I'm not, Elsie. I said it so that he would open up to me and spill the beans, and it worked a treat, he fell for it and told me everything.'

'What did he say?' Biddy, Elsie and Branna had eyes on stalks and Dessie took the opportunity to fill their glasses.

'He said he'd been asked by the Bone Grinder to provide an annual price for the cleaning of the hospital wards using the new mechanical floor cleaners.'

'What, like electric ones that plug into the wall?' asked Elsie, her mouth wide open in amazement.

'Unless you know another way, Elsie? He told

me that with one of these machines you can do the work of three to four cleaners, so, instead of having twelve of our ladies overnight on the main corridor, we would only need three or four at the most.'

There was an audible gasp from around the table.

'Matron won't stand for it,' said Madge.

They all turned to look at her. Biddy noted that there was not a flaw in her make-up. Must have taken her hours, she thought, her eyes glued to Madge's full, shimmery-pink lips as they moved.

'I heard her on the telephone to Dr Gaskell,' Madge continued. 'Talking about Miss Van Gilder. Dr Gaskell's wife is just lovely, you know. Whenever Matron telephones him at home, it's always her who answers the phone. "Darling!" she shouts. I've never been called "Darling" by anyone. Funny how people actually talk like that, isn't it? When Fred was alive, I was "Missus"; that's about as romantic as it got for me.'

'So, when "Darling" came to the phone . . .' Even saying the word darling felt odd to Biddy. '. . . what did Matron say?'

'She told him that they had made a terrible mistake with Miss Van Gilder and that she was upsetting far too many people. That she wanted him to find a way to remove her. Quite agitated she was.'

'And what did Dr Gaskell say?'

All eyes were fixed on Madge. She sipped her

sherry, having declared that she was very definitely a lady. She wriggled in her chair and straightened her skirt beneath her. It felt as though the air had left the room as they waited.

'He said no.'

'Oh, for goodness' sake,' said Branna. 'I got meself all hopeful there.'

Silence fell for a moment while they all took a sip of their drinks, Biddy, Elsie and Dessie from the bottled Guinness, Madge and Sister Haycock from their sherry glasses.

'Did the letter from St Dunstan's arrive, Biddy?' asked Emily. That was really what she had come for. She was trying to absorb the fact that Madge listened in to telephone calls. This was new to her and she wasn't sure what to make of it. But she had been invited to join the St Angelus mafia and she'd been sworn to secrecy by Biddy.

'It did, yes. It did. I was saving it until last,' said Biddy solemnly. She slowly extracted the letter from the pocket of her apron. 'Shall I read it out loud?'

They all nodded.

'Currant slice, anyone?' asked Elsie as she pushed the plate towards Emily.

It looked delicious and Emily politely took a slice. Dessie studied her delicate fingers as she did. He had never been this close to Emily for any length of time before. He had admired her from afar in the workplace, chatted at the doctors' ball and had a dance with her. That must have been when it had begun, the thoughts that drove him mad. They often had brief conversations, passing the time of day, discussing the weather, and now here she was in his friend and neighbour's kitchen. He was feeling bolder than he ever had before because he had seen a light in her eyes and felt the answering beat of his own heart. It was a light he hadn't seen for many years. He doubted himself, wondered if he was being fanciful, but as she lifted her head from biting into the currant slice, she smiled. When the crumbs fell down on to her chest and she flicked them away with her hand, he looked and there it was again, the smile. But it was more than a smile, it was a smile that said something. It said, try me, if you dare.

'Dessie, are you listening?'

Dessie snapped himself back into the room and looked at Biddy. 'Of course I am.'

'Why didn't you answer me then? Ouch!'

Dessie noticed that Elsie had just kicked Biddy under the table and that Branna was filling Emily's glass, which was nowhere near empty. His face flushed and he wanted to die with shame. Had he been staring at her? Had he? Before he had time to melt from the heat in his cheeks, Biddy coughed and began to read once more.

'There were problems wherever Miss Van Gilder went. She didn't have a friend in the hospital. She was cautioned by Matron for ordering one of the doctors around. She sacked half of the domestic staff in the hospital and took on a cleaning agency.

Had a stand-up row with Matron and is just an awful, unpleasant woman. Some say she was dismissed, some say she walked. There were even rumours that the police might have been called in. Matron has been here since the Ark and she's very fretful about the reputation of St Dunstan's, so not one of us got to know all the details, but it was something to do with the cleaning agency she took on. Once Miss Van Gilder had gone, Matron put the domestics straight back on to their old contracts and we never saw the cleaning agency again.'

Biddy looked up from the piece of paper. 'Cathy's sister finishes by saying that we should be on the lookout because Miss Van Gilder has a nasty temper.'

She folded the letter with such care, it could have been made from gold leaf, then placed it back into the warmth of her apron pocket. Inflated by her moment of huge importance, she glanced around the table and said, 'Well then, what do you suppose we do about that?'

She addressed the question to them all and was met by silence as they absorbed the shattering news. Not only was Miss Van Gilder threatening their jobs, she might have been in trouble with the law.

'Well, I don't know. It tells us that if we resist her changes, that might bring out the worst in her, but it also tells us that our assistant matron is potentially corrupt.' This was Dessie, who spoke his thoughts out loud.

'I'm going to have to start listening in on all her conversations,' said Madge. 'Maybe I can find out what really happened at her other hospital. I've only ever listened to the odd one so far. It's getting so busy on the switchboard, feels like everyone in Liverpool is buying a phone. It's amazing, with them being so expensive and all. Even I don't have one. The waiting list is more than six months.'

'Why would you want one?' asked Branna. 'You're on a phone all day long.'

'What you find out is going to be very important, Madge,' said Biddy. 'You, Elsie, you are on the inside in Matron's rooms. You are going to have to up your efforts a bit. And, Sister Haycock, her room is next door to yours.' She raised her eyebrows at Emily.

'What?' Emily looked around the table, slightly confused.

'Well, you can get into her room, can't you?'

'Biddy!' Emily's voice was almost a screech. 'You want me to snoop around her room? I can't do that. I am the director of nurse training.' She glanced at the others, hoping that Madge or Dessie would agree with her.

'It's for the good of the hospital,' said Dessie quietly. 'And for all the women who lost their men in the war and who need the cleaning jobs for themselves and the portering jobs for their young sons. If Miss Van Gilder gets her way, what will happen to the likes of Bryan and Tommy?'

'Or my son-in-law, Jake,' Elsie added.

Emily knew at that moment that there was no way out. She was being sent on a spying mission. She nodded her head. 'I will then, but only when I know the coast is clear and I am safe.'

Biddy smiled and refilled the glasses. 'There you go then. I'm guessing it is just a matter of time until we have Miss Van Gilder beat and this hospital gets back to normal. In the meantime, I think we all need to start standing up to Miss Van Gilder. You know what they say about bullies, they always back down. And that woman, she is a bully.'

'I will drink to that,' said Dessie.

Almost an hour later and not a little tipsy, Emily was walking back to the hospital accompanied by Dessie. The night sky was the colour of blue ink and shot through with stars. To their left, the river washed gently against the bank. Apart from the odd tram, there was little noise around them. Liverpool was tucked up in its lazy Sunday-night bed, preparing for the morning ahead.

Dessie walked alongside Emily and breathed in deeply. She smelt of woman and gentleness and promise. It was not a scent he was used to. He felt as if his head would burst. Thoughts that had lain dormant for years were racing around his brain, and he had drunk more Guinness than usual, which had loosened his tongue. On the end of a deep breath, the words just jumped straight out of his mouth. 'So, have you never wanted to marry then?'

Immediately he said it, a look of surprise crossed his face. It was something he'd been wondering, but he hadn't meant to say it. It was the Guinness talking.

Emily pulled her camel coat around her, more for comfort than warmth. The air was gentle, the breeze carrying a promise of warmer days ahead. 'Oh, well, it's not choice really, Dessie. I have my stepfather Alf to look after and, you know, after the war life was a bit crazy for a while.'

Dessie did know. Everyone knew about the bomb that had flattened George Street and killed Emily's entire family. 'I know about that,' he said. 'Have you heard? There's talk that when they rebuild that road, they might erect a plaque with the names of those who died, in their honour.'

He glanced sideways as they passed a street light and saw the tears welling in her eyes. He understood. He'd lost his wife in the war, but he hadn't shed a tear since the day he'd heard where his wife was when she died. Down on the docks. There was only ever one reason why a woman was down on the docks at night.

He had married his wife in haste; she'd been pregnant, or so he'd thought. But that had turned out to be a lie too. She was like that, he discovered. A woman who lived in a fantasy world. All Dessie had been to her was a house and an income, one she spent faster than he could bring it home. It seemed that all the while he was away fighting, she had spent the money too fast and become

457

bored. He held no ill-feeling towards her. The war had taught him to be generous-spirited. He had lost too many friends. Too many of his men. His wife had paid a terrible price and he still prayed for her soul at Mass, aware that he was the only living person in the world who would. But tears? No, there were no tears.

He took Emily's hand and slipped it through his arm. Then, patting the top of her hand, he said, 'There, there, don't fret. It must be the most awful thing. No one can imagine what that was like.'

Emily sniffed. 'I'm sorry. I know you lost your wife on the same night. I saw the ship go up . . .' She stopped. She had no idea what Dessie knew. She only knew what Biddy had told her.

'Aye, well, we have something in common then, don't we. Look up into that sky . . .'

Emily lifted her head and followed Dessie's gaze.

'There they all are, every one of them. Your little brothers, your mam. Looking down on you, they are, smiling at you. No, I'm wrong. I can see them, they are waving their fists at you, saying, "Be happy, Emily, so that we can twinkle away with the others."'

A sob caught in Emily's throat. For a brief moment, the fanciful notion that her mother and brothers could see her took her breath away and she was flooded with a feeling of desperate loneliness. She missed them. She missed them so much. It was permanently with her. The boys who in her mind would forever be boys. She carried them around with her every day. A dull ache between her ribs that never let up.

'Oh, I'm sorry,' said Dessie, his face creased with concern. 'I shouldn't have said that, it was bloody thoughtless of me.'

'No, not at all,' said Emily as she extracted a handkerchief from her pocket and wiped her eyes. 'It's a lovely thought that they could be stars, looking down on me. It's not something I've ever imagined, but do you know what, Dessie, I might take some comfort from it. Look at all those stars, each one of them could be a loved one. A very loved one.'

She thrust her hands deep into her pockets and, taking a deep breath, craned her neck backwards and looked up at the sky. She turned slowly. The light from the river reflected off her face and, standing beneath the twinkling stars, she looked stunningly beautiful. As she leant backwards, she lost her balance slightly and Dessie reached out to grab her.

'Oh, I'm sorry,' she said, and giggled, her mood restored. 'I had too much sherry.'

Dessie didn't reply. He couldn't. He was so taken with her beauty and the emotion of the moment. He could only say her name. 'Emily.'

'Yes?' She turned to look at him, a slightly quizzical expression on her face.

He hadn't meant to, he was only thinking it. What would it be like? How soft would her lips be under his? How sweet would she taste? But he did it. He kissed her. He reached out his arms and, folding her into them, he kissed her.

At first she stiffened slightly and Dessie, horrified he had made a terrible faux pas, felt his own back become ramrod straight. But then she leant against him. She melted into his arms, her lips gave way to his, he heard a slight moan and she swayed, lost. Dessie stopped thinking. He kissed her in a way he couldn't remember having kissed any woman before. His hands ran through her hair and hers ran across his back. This was not an ordinary kiss. Dessie knew this was the beginning of something he could only just dare to imagine; he knew that, from this moment on, Emily would be his.

He pulled her back gently and, holding her arms, looked into her half-closed eyes.

She opened them wide. 'What are you doing?' she asked with an almost cheeky edge to her voice.

Dessie had never heard her speak like that before and, unbeknown to him, neither had Emily.

'I just want to make sure that you are OK with this. I don't want you to tell me tomorrow it was all a big mistake.'

Emily smiled and pulled him towards her. 'Dessie, you know that "be happy" thing you were talking about a minute ago, when you were pointing out the stars? I think it's just happened.' She
tilted her head and grinned up at him.

He was about to kiss her again; he wanted

more. He wanted Emily in his bed tonight and for ever more. There was no other woman he had even felt attracted to since the war had ended and yet this one was turning his mind upside down.

'Well, that's a relief then,' he said as he pulled her towards him and kissed her again, this time with even more passion. I can wait, he thought. Not for long, but I can wait. Tonight I must get her back to the hospital.

If it was possible, the second kiss was better than the first. Dessie lost himself. He placed his hands inside her coat and felt the warmth of her skin as his fingers found a gap between the waist of her skirt and her top. His hand brushed against the mound of her breast and he felt her slightly, almost imperceptibly, push herself into his hand. A tug blew on the river, bringing him back to his senses.

'We need to get you home,' he said.

Her answer came without a second's hesitation. 'Dessie, I don't have a home, can we can go to your house instead?'

'Are you sure?' he asked, his voice thick and choked with emotion. 'I'm not sure I can behave like a gentleman if we do that.'

'Good,' she answered. And before he could say another word, she kissed him again.

CHAPTER 26

On Monday, Amy had failed to turn up for work for the third time in two weeks.

'A right grumpy madam, she's been,' Lily heard Mrs Mc Conaghy say as her brother-in-law stood with his cap in his hand, explaining her absence.

'You and me, Jim, all of us, we are getting too old for this. Have you taken her to the doctor's?'

'I've tried. I said I'd call in and get her an appointment. She refuses to go anywhere near the doctor's.'

'Well, he's that old and decrepit, I'd refuse to go to him myself. 'Tis woman's troubles.' Mrs McConaghy lowered her voice to whisper this gem. 'Either way, she has to get sorted. Another year from now and Amy will need to start taking over the reins in this office. I'm not getting any younger and I can't go on paying Lily for ever. I'm finding those front steps harder and harder each day and I daren't go down on to the plant floor, for fear I might not get up again. As for the heat from the furnace, to think, I used to pop down for a warm. Too fierce altogether these days.'

She furtively checked to see if Lily was listening. She was.

Bile rose in Lily's throat as she took a deep breath to calm her panic and anger. She had heard every word. Her time at the plant was almost up. They had put on her for years, using her to cover for their mistakes and inadequacies and to salve their guilty consciences. She had run the business almost singlehandedly and it operated like clockwork too. For years, every ledger, draft and payment and all of the wages had been calculated by Lily and written in her own hand. On the occasional week when she had a holiday, she still came in on the Friday to complete the end-of-week accounts and wages. But all along, all they wanted to do was replace her with their own niece and heir. Lily mused on this until the figures began to blur before her eyes. 'I can't keep on paying Lily for ever,' Mrs McConaghy had said and the words beat against her brain.

Amy finally returned to the plant on the Wednesday.

'You look as white as the nets, Amy,' Lily said as she walked through the office door just before the afternoon tea break. She was of course referring to the nets she'd seen Mrs McGuffy hanging in the summer breeze and not the nets hanging in their windows, which she had washed herself on Saturday but had been too embarrassed to hang out to dry, they had been so grey. 'Is your tummy better now?'

'No, I feel desperate. Where is she?' Amy looked around the office. There was no sign of Mrs McConaghy.

'She's popped to the new café on the Dock Road to meet one of her friends from church. Why? Does she not know you're coming in?'

'No, Lily, she doesn't. I'd love a cup of tea, please. Have we any biscuits?'

Two minutes later, Lily placed a cup of scalding tea and a plate of biscuits down in front of Amy.

'I'm eating so many biscuits just now,' she said. 'Especially in the mornings. Can't move without them first thing.'

'Well, that's a funny cure for a tummy bug, Amy. Are you sure you shouldn't be having a bottle of something from the chemist's?'

'There is no bottle to deal with what I have, Lily. There's no making it better, either, not unless I want to butcher myself.' She sighed, then looked Lily full in the face. 'I've had no monthly for weeks and weeks now. It hasn't come. I'm pregnant.'

Lily shot up from her chair, though she'd only just sat back down. 'Oh God, what are you going to do? Was it that man who came to the office? Does he know? Do your parents know? He will have to listen to you now.'

It was a simple observation, but it made Amy melt into a flood of tears. 'That was why I went to see him. I guessed. I knew. I wanted him to know. I waited outside his house again last night so I could see him.'

Lily pulled her handkerchief out of the sleeve of her cardigan and handed it to Amy. 'There you go. Dry your eyes,' she said. She looked though the door towards the steps leading down to the processing plant. Mr McConaghy was on the floor, as was Amy's father. They would be looking for their tea soon, but Lily didn't feel that she could leave Amy.

'He hit me.' Amy began to wail and this alarmed Lily. 'He said he'd told me not to go anywhere near his house and that he'd meant it. He doesn't give a damn. He said he'll say he's never even met me.'

Amy hadn't answered the second part of Lily's question, but she didn't need to. It was obvious from the way she was unburdening herself that Lily was the first to know. Lily felt sorry for her. Despite all the money and support she had at home, despite the processing plant inheritance that awaited her and all the clothes and make-up, when it came to it, when she was truly desperate, the only person she could talk to and trust was Lily, the charity girl in the office. The girl who had nothing. Lily, from whom Amy had stolen Lockie, her only friend.

Lily laid her hand on Amy's shoulder. She had no answer. All she could do was listen and it seemed that, at this moment in time, Amy needed that more than anything.

'Look.' Amy tilted her head back and Lily could see that on either side of her throat were red marks. Marks that looked like fingerprints.

Lily knew those marks, she had seen them herself. In the days before her stepfather had left them all to struggle on without his wage, and before Lockie had told him to back off, he had often lunged at Lily and grabbed her throat when he was mad for a drink.

'Have you seen Lockie?' asked Amy as she blew her nose.

'No, why, haven't you?' said Lily, startled.

'No, I haven't seen him, but I'm going to have to. My only chance is to tell him it's his,' she said. 'He doesn't know, of course. Let's hope he's the marrying kind, eh, Lily?'

Lily felt the air rush from her body as she looked into Amy's eyes, glistening with intent, still wet from her tears. She made to speak, but the words stuck in her throat. She was sure she couldn't have heard that right. That Amy was about to trick Lockie into marrying her? No, that couldn't be right.

'But how can you do that if it isn't his?' she asked. Amy might have stolen her friend to flirt and play around with, she had almost certainly kissed him, but Lily was convinced that Lockie wouldn't have gone any further with a woman he wasn't married to. Lockie was too careful. He lived his life according to a plan and Lily was quite sure that making Amy pregnant would never have been a part of Lockie's plan. She felt her back stiffen involuntarily. She pulled away and removed her hand from Amy's back.

'Because, Lily, I trapped him. It was easy enough to get him to play along. I made sure he was seen leaving the pub with me and it did happen. I already knew by then. In my heart, I knew.'

She looked up at Lily, aware that whatever sympathy there had been had left the room. 'Don't look at me like that, Lily! It was only the once. It could have been his. It's only a few weeks' difference. He will never know.'

Lily shook her head. I can't have heard her right, she thought. But she knew she had. And she knew what it meant. Lockie was about to be tricked into fathering the baby of another man.

The bell above the door jangled and they both looked up to see Mrs McConaghy arriving.

'Amy, Amy, are you well?' she trilled as she rushed over. 'Would you look at the state of you. What devotion to work you have. Would you look at her, Lily! She looks as though she's at death's door and she still turns up for work. You need to take note, Lily.'

The blood shot to Lily's cheeks. She had never once had a day off sick. She hadn't even taken time off when Joe was ill. She'd come in late that one morning when she'd been at the hospital, but that was all. How dare Mrs McConaghy? And if she knew what Lily knew . . .

The door to the plant opened and Mr McConaghy stood there with his brother-in-law. 'Come on, Lily. Are you slacking today? The tea was due five minutes ago.'

Lily remained silent. She wanted to answer them, make a snappy retort and tell them all where to go. Amy had just told her she was about to trap her best friend, her lost friend, into marriage and that was all that was on her mind. She simply could not think straight. She gave Mr McConaghy a sideways look, which left him in no doubt that his wisest move would be to not say another word, and left Mrs McConaghy to fuss over Amy.

She pulled down the large brown enamel pot, rinsed it out and began to heap in the spoons of loose tea before filling it with boiling water from the urn. I have to find Lockie, she thought. I have to warn him. The baby is not his and he needs to know. Who else will tell him if I don't? The eejit of a boy.

Lily hadn't finished pouring the water into the pot when the front door burst open. It was the eldest of Mrs McGuffy's sons, Sam. Lily knew him well; she had seen him only that morning, passing up the nets to his mam. He looked around the office, trying to locate Lily. The sun shone brightly and threw a beam of yellow light into the darker interior, barely penetrating the grey plume of cigarette smoke. It made it difficult for him to see her at first.

'What do you want?' screeched Mrs McConaghy as she made to fetch the pole she used to close the shutters at night and brandish it at him.

Lily was too stunned to speak. Mrs McConaghy, with the contents of the safe never far from the front of her mind, obviously thought he was a thief.

'Don't you set a foot inside this office or I'll call the police,' she screeched.

'What for, Mrs?' asked Sam, looking confused. 'Me mam has sent me down with a message for Lily. Is she here? She's Lily Lancashire from Clare Cottages.'

Then he spotted her in the corner. 'Lily, Lily, it's your Joe. Sister Therese has had to take him to the hospital. He's in St Angelus right now, really bad. Me mam said you are to go straight there and she will look after your Katie.'

For a second, Lily froze with the shock. She couldn't move and it wasn't until the hot water splashed on to her finger that she jumped and, dropping the teapot into the sink, was aware of what Sam McGuffy had just said. This had never happened before. There was something seriously wrong. Joe's breathing had been bad since yesterday. She had been awake for most of the night with him, but when she'd left that morning, she thought he was feeling and sounding much better.

Lily didn't hesitate. She forgot Amy and her plight, forgot the demands of the McConaghys. All she could think about was little Joe.

CHAPTER 27

'**I**s that it then? I've booked us a lovely romantic hotel and you want to travel back to your parents and I'm not even invited?' Teddy's voice rose. Not in anger, more in exasperation and disappointment. He had been so looking forward to the much-needed break. And to taking his and Dana's relationship on to a new level. Judging by the expression on her face, it was the last thing she wanted.

'Teddy, I have to go home. They are expecting me. I have no choice. And if I took you, well, I swear to God, that would be it. The priest would be over quicker than the pig gives birth and I'm not sure they would let you leave if we weren't married. You know that where I come from no woman is thought to be safe with a man. If you date someone and you're alone, it's assumed you are, well . . . .'

'Chance would be a fine thing,' Teddy snapped. 'Dana, it's 1954, not 1854.' He sounded hurt and confused.

'To you maybe. I'd say at home it was more like 1924, but that doesn't matter. It would just be

470

awful for you if I did that. Maybe if we are still together next year.'

'Next year?' Teddy almost slammed his pewter mug down on to the sawn-off upturned beer barrel. The pub was scattered with the unusual tables and brand-new stools, but the sawdust remained.

With an impatient gesture, Teddy took his cigarettes out of his pocket and lit one. Even though Dana was now a smoker, having been converted by Teddy, she noted that he failed to offer her one. Silence filled the space between them as he blew out a long, steady stream of smoke.

It wasn't the money he was worried about, although he had already paid for the hotel in full. It was the huge disappointment. They were due to leave in three days. Why had she taken so long to tell him?

They heard the sound of an ambulance passing by outside on its way to the hospital and as they waited for the bells to stop they both had the same thought. Teddy was due on casualty in less than an hour. If it was an emergency ambulance, he would need to leave soon. Dana was back on nights in children's again, so she wouldn't be on duty until eight o'clock in the evening.

'I'm still going to go, with or without you.'

He now sounded more sad than angry. Dana could see that he was hurt. He hadn't even tried to understand the position she was in. She had a life at home that was a million miles away from anything Teddy, with his solicitor family and smart suburban house, could ever understand.

She put her hand out to place it on top of his, but he snatched his away. 'How are you getting there?' he asked, forcing his mind away from the pain of rejection as he stubbed his cigarette out.

'I'll walk to the boat and get the train at the other end, although there is a day coach from Dublin. Mammy is beside herself expecting me.'

'Well, good for you.' Teddy finished his drink and stood up.

Dana flinched at the thought of Teddy's own mother, who'd died when he was a boy. Now she felt even worse. How could she have been so crass?

'Anyway, I have to get back to work. That was an emergency and I really should be there. Have a good trip home.' And without even a backward glance, Teddy walked out of the pub and across the road towards St Angelus.

'Nurse Tanner, can you make the paediatric cubicle ready, please. Breathing difficulties, distressed little boy recently turned four on his way in with a nun in tow.'

Pammy threw the cloth and chlorhexidine solution she was using to wash down a trolley into the dirty utility room and pulled back the screens of the paediatric admissions cubicle. She knew if the phone call had said breathing difficulties, they would need oxygen. She spotted one of the porter's lads leaving the unit.

'Bryan!' she almost shouted.

Sister Antrobus almost made to frown at her. 'Keep the noise down, please, Nurse Tanner. This is a hospital, not a football pitch.'

'Yes, Sister. Sorry, Sister.' Pammy felt as though she should curtsey to Sister Antrobus. But even if she did, Sister would still look as though she was chewing a lemon.

'I need a full oxygen bottle for the paediatric cubicle,' she hissed to Bryan, trying her very best not to raise her voice.

'Coming up, Nurse Tanner,' said Bryan. Casting a quick glance towards Sister Antrobus, he moved from a trot to a run.

Within seconds, Pammy had secured a drip stand, a giving-set trolley, a Ryles tube administration pack and an examination set and had them all set up exactly as she had been taught in the practical sessions at the school of nursing. The casualty doors flew open and the ambulance men, with no regard to Sister Antrobus, ran in, pushing a trolley with an anxious-looking nun running right behind.

'Is the paediatric cubicle ready?' said one of the ambulance men.

'It is. Just in here, please,' said Pammy as she guided the trolley through. The cubicle curtains were pale green and covered in pictures of white bunny rabbits and there was a hospital cot against the wall.

'Nurse Makebee, can you find a child-sized gown, please, from the linen cupboard,' Pammy instructed. But before she'd even looked up, Doreen from the clerk's office had handed her one, along with the notes.

'The nun who telephoned from St Chad's convent, she called here first,' Doreen said. 'It was me who called the ambulance. She gave me the boy's name, he's been in before. I thought I would bring over the notes to save you the trouble and some time.'

Pammy smiled and gave Doreen a brief hug. 'Thank you,' she said. 'You are a total star, Doreen.'

For a fraction of a second, both girls had the same thought: how close Miss Van Gilder had come to getting Doreen fired.

The police had turned up at Assistant Matron's office some weeks ago, asking to see Doreen. Miss Van Gilder had suddenly and inexplicably come over all faint, so the officer was obliged to go to Matron for help instead. He explained to Matron that there had been another very similar attack on an innocent girl in Durham and that the perpetrator had been caught. They wanted Doreen to help them with the identity parade.

Everyone at St Angelus was protective of Doreen. Matron knew all of the details and had been full of sympathy, insisting that Doreen return to work only when she was ready. When she did finally come back, even Sister Antrobus looked after her; she became her self-appointed guardian angel on casualty and almost blew up at anyone she saw gossiping. That was until Miss Van Gilder met the police, heard who Doreen was and demanded to know the whole story. She took exception to having a person of such notoriety working at St Angelus and on the day Matron left to attend a big meeting in Manchester with Dr Gaskell, she summoned Sister Antrobus from casualty to her office.

'She is a woman of ill-repute, Sister Antrobus. What was she doing in that entry so late at night? I have read the notes: she was drunk on admission. I feel very strongly that she should not be employed by St Angelus.'

Sister Antrobus was the only member of staff at St Angelus to have the bravery to stand up to Miss Van Gilder and the encounter spread around the hospital like wildfire, thanks to Elsie and Madge.

'This is my casualty unit now. The staff on here are appointed by me, with Matron's consent, and they work for me. I will decide who goes and who stays, thank you very much, Miss Van Gilder.'

'I think you forget who is in charge here, Sister Antrobus,' Miss Van Gilder said. 'I am the assistant matron and I take full responsibility for all personnel issues at the hospital.'

'Not on casualty, you don't. That is my domain and that is how it will stay.' And without another word, Sister Antrobus slammed out of the office.

Pammy recognized little Joe immediately, but he was beyond smiling, or even communicating.

Dr Davenport walked into the cubicle at almost the same time as Dr Mackintosh and Pammy noticed the look that passed between them. Little Joe was rambling, confused. His lips were tinged with blue and he was sitting propped up against the sides of the trolley. Pammy felt so much sympathy for the little boy. She remembered how he'd been so grateful for the smallest thing and how everyone had fallen for him. Even Mrs Duffy, and she hadn't even met him, just heard Dana's stories from her shifts on the children's ward. 'He's just one of those kids,' Dana would say over breakfast at Lovely Lane. 'Leaves your heart in a puddle on the floor at the side of the bed when he falls asleep.'

Pammy looked at little Joe. He was in such a state, he probably wouldn't even recognize Dana today.

'If we try to lie him down, he panics,' said the ambulance man. 'There's not much use trying to speak to him, he can only get three words out at a time.' He folded the blanket he'd wrapped around Joe in half and, throwing it back on to the trolley, quickly made his exit.

Dr Mackintosh got out his stethoscope and breathed on the end of it as he gave Joe the warmest of smiles.

'We have seen this young man before, haven't we, Nurse?' he said to Pammy. As he bent down to listen to Joe's chest, he glanced up at her. 'Ask Doreen to ring for Dr Gaskell or the doctor on children's, they've all gone to a meeting in Manchester about the new children's intensive care. I want to get a line up quickly. Good girl, you have it all ready.'

As Pammy began to undo the autoclave bag, she heard Miss Van Gilder arrive in the unit. You always hear her before you see her, she thought. She was berating Doreen for being on the ward and out of the clerk's cubicle. Doreen tried to explain, but Miss Van Gilder was having none of it.

'Your place is behind the screen, not in front of it. You have no business here, out among the patients. You are not fit to be seen on the ward.'

Pammy looked over and saw that Doreen's eyes had filled with tears. Doreen didn't answer, just opened the wooden door that led to her cubicle. She caught the expression of concern on Pammy's face before she left.

Within seconds, Miss Van Gilder was in Joe's cubicle. Pammy's heart sank.

'May I ask, Doctor, why you are putting up a line on this boy? We all know he recovers fairly well. He has been here before; he was on the children's ward, was he not? I remember him quite well. He is a neglected child, nothing more.'

Dr Mackintosh didn't answer. He looked instead to Sister Therese, who was hovering at the end of the bed. 'How long has he been like this?'

'I don't know, Doctor. I think he's been bad again for a while, though he did seem to take a turn for the better this morning. I saw Lily, his sister, on her way to work and I promised her that I would pop up to the house as soon as the mammy went to, er, went to work. When I got there, I saw the poor boy's lips were blue. I'm afraid I panicked and called the hospital.'

'You did the right thing. Does his sister know?'

'I have sent a message to where she works, Doctor. She will be on her way, I've no doubt.'

Dr Mackintosh looked concerned as Dr Davenport moved to the head of the bed and held little Joe upright.

'Has he had a cold or an illness lately?'

'Oh yes, Doctor. The house is not the warmest and Joe has been none too well.' Sister Therese looked as white as a sheet.

Dr Mackintosh recognized her from some weeks ago on the ward. But she was not the perky, audacious nun he remembered. She was quite right to be worried. He was worried too, but he had to hide it.

Joe's breaths were coming in short sharp spasms and Dr Mackintosh noticed that they'd become even shorter in the last few minutes. Listening to his airways, it was clear that there was an occlusion, probably caused by bronchospasm and the phlegm he could hear rattling in his lungs.

'Get a line up now!' he barked at Dr Davenport. 'Let's try the aminophylline. It worked last time.' He decided not to mention that Joe was now much worse. 'I will give a stat dose through the bung and then we can add some to an IV and administer it slowly over a much longer period. Clear the cubicle, please. If you could sit in the waiting area,' he almost snapped at Sister Therese.

She remembered him as a gentle and kind doctor. His manner told her that something was very wrong. And then she heard Miss Van Gilder's voice.

'Doctor, I do not think that is necessary. You know this boy. You know how he responds. You are wasting good money using a giving set. This hospital does not have a bottomless budget. I insist you wait until Dr Gaskell gets here. He's the chest specialist, after all.'

'We may not have time for him to get here. He's in Manchester and may not even return until tomorrow.'

'That may well be the case, but I do feel you should wait.'

Pammy raised her eyebrows at what Dr Mackintosh said next. She was no fan of Miss Van Gilder, but she almost felt sorry for her.

'Get. Out. Now.' Dr Mackintosh gave his instruction in a very precise and clear manner. To have described his approach as firm would have been an understatement.

Pammy looked away and busied herself by trying to remove Joe's clothes and replace them with a hospital gown, which would make it easier to treat him.

Miss Van Gilder blustered while Dr Davenport listened again to little Joe's chest.

'His airways are definitely obstructed,' he said as he stood with a worried frown. 'He's deteriorating quite rapidly. Let's get a move on, fast.'

Little Joe had become almost totally silent. His short inhalations and then long exhalations could barely be heard. His lips had tuned a dark shade of blue and he flopped back against the pillow.

'Out,' Dr Mackintosh repeated to Miss Van Gilder, who, without another word but with much harrumphing, backed out of the cubicle.

Everyone flinched for the briefest second when a scream cut through the air.

'Joe!' It was unmistakably Lily. 'Joe!' she screamed again.

Pammy heard Sister Therese and then the sound of shuffling feet on the wooden floor followed by muffled voices. Looking at Joe, she saw the briefest sign of recognition in his eyes as they flickered in response to Lily having shouted his name.

In the waiting area, Sister Therese caught Lily in her arms and wrapped them around her. 'Shush, my dear,' she said as she held Lily tightly. 'He is with the best people, it is the same doctor who looked after him last time.'

Lily pulled herself free and, not even noticing the retreating Miss Van Gilder, she pushed in through the curtains. At the sight of little Joe she gasped, clasping her hand over her mouth. 'Joe . . .' Her voice was nothing more than a whisper, giving little indication of the terror she felt inside.

Within seconds and before she could even reach

Joe, Pammy had taken her arm and led her firmly out of the cubicle. 'I'm so sorry, love. I don't know if you remember me?'

Lily nodded her head in acknowledgement. How could she possibly forget someone who had been so kind to Joe? One of the Lovely Lane angels. Although she couldn't say so out loud, she was relieved that it was the same nurse today.

'And Dr Mackintosh, I don't know if you remember him?'

Lily nodded again, the tears spilling out of her eyes and over the back of her hand, which was still clasped across her mouth. She was scared to take it away in case the screams in her head escaped.

'Come on, love, let's sit you down with Sister Therese.' Pammy led Lily back to the chair. 'I was just explaining that Dr Mackintosh is about to give Joe the same injection that he gave him last time. You may not remember, but it did work very well and there is no reason why it won't work just as well this time.' She failed to mention that Joe was in a much worse condition this time and that both doctors were very concerned.

Lily had liked Dr Mackintosh and she trusted him. She knew he would do his best. 'Is it the same as last time, though? Is it his breathing?'

'It is,' said Pammy. 'If you go in to see him now, you'll just hold the doctors up. Best to let them get on with things.'

Lily felt mildly reassured. She had seen Joe have a hundred attacks. He always turned a corner just

481

as they began to get bad; he would do the same again, she was sure. 'Thank you, Nurse,' she whispered.

Sister Therese sat Lily down on the chair and put her arms around her.

Lily turned to face her, a look of alarm on her face. 'What happened? Did Mam call you?'

Sister Therese looked sheepish. 'No, Lily. I got to the house an hour earlier than you'd asked.' She dropped her voice to a whisper. 'I knew she would be gone down the pub by three, so I thought I would get there a bit earlier and try and have a word with her. I had a feeling about little Joe. But by two o'clock she had already gone. He was all by himself. He was so pleased to see me, but I could tell his chest was bad by the noise he was making. He very quickly went from being breathless to being very poorly. He was rambling and not making any sense, so I ran to St Chad's with him in my arms. Mrs McGuffy helped me. She looked after Joe while I called the hospital. She'll take your Katie in for her tea after school, if you're still here, so you don't have to worry, it's all taken care of.'

'I will have to thank her when I get home.' Lily was suddenly overwhelmed by a great wave of tiredness and anxiety. She scrabbled for her handkerchief in her coat pocket. She wanted Katie to be there, so they could all be together in one place and she could see her. She felt she had let Joe down. She was the only person who truly cared for him and the same was true of Katie. She had to look after them both. Had she lost the battle to keep the family together? Would Sister Therese or Dr Mackintosh or someone else insist that Katie and Joe were taken into care?

'Can I see him?'

'Not just yet, love,' said Pammy. 'I have to get back to help, but I will ask Nurse Makebee to fetch you each a cup of tea.'

They watched as Pammy stopped a nurse at the office door and spoke to her. Silence fell between them as Sister Therese kept one arm around Lily's shoulders. She searched for something to say that might wipe the look of despair from Lily's face.

'If they are giving him the same drugs as last time, I think he will be better fairly quickly, don't you? You know, the ones that worked so well last time. Do you remember? He was right as rain not long after he had that, was he not?'

Lily heard the click of a rosary from somewhere beneath her habit and she knew that Sister Therese was praying. And lying.

A young pregnant woman left a cubicle. A man on crutches left another. Slowly the light faded and, apart from the occasional scurrying nurse or doctor, the casualty ward emptied. Sister Therese and Lily were the only two people left on the hard wooden chairs, waiting for news.

They watched Doreen as she put on her coat and hat. Catching Lily's eye, a look of sympathy flooded Doreen's face and she came over to them. 'He's with the best doctor in the hospital. The whole of Liverpool, I would say. You should take comfort from that. He looked after me once when I was sick and look at me now, eh? Chin up, it will all be fine.' And with a squeeze of Lily's hands and a kindly smile to Sister Therese, she left for home.

Earlier, Lily had gratefully accepted the tea from Nurse Makebee and felt revived by the sweet, hot liquid. She'd stopped shaking and her breathing had steadied. The activity around them – the pushing of trolleys, the comings and goings, the murmuring voices, the lack of panic, the sense of calm – it was all reassuring in its own way. They were looking after Joe.

'All the doctors and nurses here are so lovely. Miracle workers, they are,' she heard Sister Therese say.

Lily's eyes were fixed on the feet under the curtained-off area that was Joe's cubicle. She waited patiently for someone to come out and tell her what was going on. She wanted to see Joe's smiling eyes, his cheeky grin. She wanted to bend down and let him play with her hair. She just wanted to see him. She wanted to be anywhere but here. She wanted Joe to be better.

'Well, would you look what the wind has blown in.'

Lily raised her head as Sister Therese left her seat to greet Lockie, who had just walked in through the casualty doors.

'We never see you around Clare Cottages any

more, young man. Doing mighty well for yerself, so I hear now.'

'I came as soon as I heard, Sister,' he said, walking on towards Lily. 'They told me when I went into McConaghy's.'

He removed his cap and sat on the seat next to Lily. 'How is he?'

Lily felt relief wash through her at having Lockie there. 'He's terrible, Lockie,' she said, not holding back. 'I've never seen him so bad.'

'Poor little fella.'

Sister Therese decided to take advantage of Lockie's visit. 'Lockie, have you half an hour while I rush back for the Angelus and check on Katie?'

'You go, Sister. I will stay until everything is sorted. I'll knock at St Chad's on my way back.'

Sister Therese had only just left when Pammy stepped out of the cubicle to have a word with Lily. Spotting Lockie, she said, 'Hello, I'm Nurse Tanner. Look, we are going to have to keep him here again, I'm afraid. The chest doctor isn't even here today, he's at a big meeting in Manchester, so Dr Mackintosh wants Joe to be where he can keep an eye on him. He'll probably go up to the children's ward later, when we know he is going to be stable. Can I get you both some more tea?'

Lockie nodded his head. 'It looks like Lily could do with some. Could I pop out and get her a bite to eat, Nurse?'

'Of course you can,' said Pammy and she gave them both a smile.

On her way back with the tea, she passed Dr Mackintosh, writing up his notes in the office.

'Thought that was for me,' he shouted out as she walked past. 'Who is the second one for?'

'It's for Joe's sister. Her young man has arrived.'

Dr Mackintosh leant back in the chair and looked out of the office into casualty to see who Pammy was referring to.

Lockie had put his arm around Lily's shoulders and her head was resting on him, her eyes closed. Casualty was now empty apart from little Joe and they were the only two people in the waiting area. Sister Antrobus and Miss Van Gilder were long gone.

Dr Mackintosh's heart sank at the sight of Lockie and his throat constricted with disappointment and jealousy. You should have known, he thought to himself. A young woman as dignified and pretty as Lily is never likely to be single.

Teddy Davenport was watching him. As he sat down, he said, 'You can't win them all, and don't I know that for a fact.' He sounded bitter and almost spat the words out.

Nurse Makebee spotted both of the doctors and, stepping into the office, she asked sweetly, 'Would you chaps both like a cup of tea? Sorry there's nothing stronger to put in it. More's the pity.'

Both doctors looked up sharply. Dr Mackintosh was not terribly fond of Nurse Makebee. Her manner was so confident, she acted like a nurse who had been qualified for a very long time, not a probationer. He had seen her in action on casualty, flirting with the medical students. It was blindingly obvious her goal in life was to marry a doctor. One of the students had told him she already had a boyfriend, but you would never have guessed it from the way she behaved. Teddy, however, had no such reservations. Without any encouragement, he said, 'As we're quiet, how about I come and help you?'

As they walked away, they were observed by Pammy, whose face creased in concern, and Dr Mackintosh, who felt deflated, although he wasn't quite sure why. He turned back to his notes.

Lily lifted her head up from Lockie's shoulder and reached for her handkerchief.

'Are you sure you don't want me to fetch you some food? Do you want me to go and tell the McConaghys that you might not be in work tomorrow? I'm here to help. What can I do?' Lockie said.

'I couldn't swallow food, Lockie. Do you think the McConaghys will be mad at me? What can I do? I can't leave Joe here. I'm not just his sister, Lockie, I'm his mam and dad, too.' Her voice filled with bitterness. 'I have to be, because no one else is.'

She was all alone in the world. The responsibility she felt for everyone and everything had weighed her down for so long. She suddenly felt angry with Lockie. She felt so angry that she wanted to shout at him for having forgotten about her while he was cavorting with Amy and for the mess he'd got himself into with Amy. But she remained silent. They were friends, that was all. Lockie had no obligations towards her. It was just that today she had realized how alone in the world she was and she had never felt so frightened in all of her life.

'After the training you've had, you will make a great mam one day,' said Lockie. He could see the expression on her face had altered to one of resentment bordering on anger and he was reminded yet again of what a dreadful life she'd had.

Whether it was because of the surge of anger towards her parents or her terror at how poorly Joe looked, what Lily said next was very out of character. It was none of her business. It was between Amy and Lockie. But her sense of loyalty towards the only person who had ever regarded her as an equal fought down her natural instinct to keep her own counsel. The words beat a tattoo inside her brain, demanding to be expressed. She knew that once they were spoken, they could not be undone.

Lily recalled Amy's confession and knew that before Lockie left her side she would tell him. She would hurt him, but it had to be done. She owed it to him to protect him, even though he didn't know that he was in danger. She would help him in his hour of need, just like he was there for her today. And one day he might thank her. Amy was about to alter the course of his life. He deserved to know.

Once she made up her mind that she was going to tell him, the words just fell out.

'Lockie, Amy is pregnant and she's going to trick you into marrying her.'

Lockie moved away from Lily and looked at her with such horror, it was as if she had suddenly grown an extra head. Confusion flooded his face.

'What in God's name has just made you say that?' he asked.

'Because it's true.' There was not a hint of emotion in Lily's voice. There were so many strong feelings inside her right then, fighting to make her sad or mad, that instead she displayed none.

The legs of the chair scraped along the wooden floor as Lockie leapt up. He turned his back to her, took off his cap, smoothed down his hair and for a split second appeared to study the ground before swivelling round to face her again.

Looking down, he hissed, 'You are only saying that because you don't want to have me and so you don't want anyone else to either.'

Lily felt wounded. It was as though Lockie had slapped her across the face. He was towering over her and she could feel his anger beaming down at her. For the briefest moment, she felt scared. Her stepfather was the only other man who'd ever been angry with her and her heart began to pound in her chest. Her voice had lost all its strength and sounded weak and thready as she answered him.

'Lockie, that's not true. You are like a brother to me. But I know that Amy is pregnant and that is the reason she is showing you so much interest.

The father of her baby is already married and won't have anything to do with her. She needs someone to get hitched to and, Lockie, you are proving mighty easy.'

Lily tried to sound sympathetic, but it was near impossible. She had problems of her own which were much bigger. Would she ever be allowed to return home with Joe? What would happen to her and Katie? She had held it all together by the skin of her teeth, but she knew now that Joe had almost died. A line had been crossed. She was filled with a sense of impending doom. This attack had been by far the worst. She would never be able to leave Joe again for fear of what might happen. Now that her stepfather was gone, her mother was so much worse. Lily had needed to take the rent book to the corporation offices on her way to work yesterday and had paid the rent for two weeks in advance. It had left very little for coal or food. How would she manage if she couldn't return to McConaghy's? She felt as though she was running out of time and life was about to change for ever. As if she was sitting on the precipice of disaster.

Lockie's face was suffused with disbelief and anger. She knew what was about to happen. He could not face the reality of what she had said. He would walk away. He would leave her there.

He was going.

Her chances of seeing Lockie again would be slim if she didn't return to McConaghy's. He never came anywhere near Clare Cottages. Before today, she would have felt apprehensive about revealing what she knew; she would have stammered and stumbled and probably changed her mind. But she had a job to do, and that was to tell him everything. So she did.

She was stunned at Lockie's reaction. Instead of thanking her for saving him from making the biggest mistake of his life, he was turning on her.

'You just don't want me to be happy, do you, Lily? Life has dealt you a rotten hand and because something nice has happened to me, you are determined to stop it.'

Lily looked up into his face. 'Are you mad? I am your friend. I'm not saying this because I want you for myself. How could you think such a thing?'

'Because it's written all over you, Lily. Amy isn't pregnant, there is no other man, and I know that, because I see her every day at McConaghy's. I'm going. Perhaps one day you'll say sorry for all of this.'

And with that he turned and left.

She heard the doors swing shut, but she kept her eyes fixed on the curtains around Joe and didn't once look over to see Lockie go.

As Lockie ran down the steps, he bumped straight into Dr Mackintosh.

'Whoa,' said Dr Mackintosh, reeling slightly, but Lockie didn't reply. He took the stairs two at a time and his footsteps could be heard echoing across the yard as he marched towards the main door.

CHAPTER 28

Another hour passed before Lily could see Joe and he was finally stable enough to be settled on to the ward. The sky was beginning to fade into night. Joe was calm, on a drip and sleeping. Lily felt faint with relief.

'Has your chap left then?' asked Pammy, interrupting Lily's thoughts as she sat on the chair next to her and looked around.

'Oh, he's just a friend, from home and work. He's no one special.'

'Oh right. Well, I just wanted to say that one of my friends, Nurse Brogan, is the night nurse on children's and so Joe will be in great hands. From what I remember from last time he was in, she adored him.'

Dr Mackintosh joined them and spoke to Lily. His heart leapt at the sight of her. She looked vulnerable and her face was tear-stained and strained. As she jumped up from the chair to greet him, she wobbled dizzily. He put out a protective arm to steady her.

'Hey, careful there. Are you OK?'

Lily nodded. 'Sorry, I just jumped up too quickly. How is he? Is he better now?'

Dr Mackintosh slowly removed his hand from her arm and she couldn't help wishing he would put it back. It had felt warm and comforting through the wool of her cardigan.

'He's a better colour, but he isn't back to normal yet. His airway was almost occluded and he went into a further bronchospasm. There is a great deal of mucus. I don't mind saying, he gave me a bit of a scare. Do you know how long his breathing had been bad for?'

Lily furrowed her brow. 'Well, it's always bad to a degree, but the puffing for his breath, that was going on all of yesterday and last night. He told me he thought it was a bit better when I left for work, or I wouldn't have gone. I would have taken him to the doctor's, I would.'

'I know you would,' said Dr Mackintosh, 'and so does Joe. These things can be very unpredictable. This time I'm putting a machine by the side of his bed, just in case. It's known as a respirator, but don't be frightened, we'll only use it if we have to.'

Lily wanted to ask, just in case what? But she didn't.

'We will look after him to the best of our ability, Lily, and we'll use everything we have in our arsenal. We have asked Dr Gaskell, the most senior chest doctor in the region, never mind this hospital, to take a look at him and he is heading back from a meeting in Manchester to do just that. He was due to stay overnight but he's driving back. That's how much of a priority your little Joe is to us.

As soon as I explained the situation to him, he volunteered and told me he was on his way.'

Lily wanted to cry with gratitude. 'I know it's not allowed, but can I stay with Joe for a bit?'

Dr Mackintosh nodded. 'You certainly can.' He knew he would have Miss Van Gilder and the ward sister to answer to, but he had seen too many children die in the arms of strangers. Despite all of the doctoring and treatments at his disposal, he had often sensed that the presence of a mother could have made the difference between life and death. And where death was inevitable, it would have helped calm the child's fear. He hated the visiting restrictions on the children's wards and was determined to fight Lily's corner. 'Come with me,' he said. 'I will take you to the ward myself. They won't argue with me.'

As they walked up the stairs to the ward, he was conscious that he had overstepped his own boundaries. He had never before escorted a relative to the ward. Never curious to know more about their life and background, never inclined to dawdle in their company. He wanted to sit with her. To hold her hand and reassure her.

When he left her sitting by Joe's bed, he felt an acute sense of loss. He could tell she was nervous around him, to the point that she shook when he spoke to her. She was afraid of authority, had something to protect and hide. He had seen it before, so many times.

Lily's could barely take her eyes off Joe. The

strangeness of his pallor, the equipment, the white-
ness of his skin against the large white bed. His
arm protruded from a crisp white sheet and was
strapped up in a wooden splint, a crêpe bandage
wrapped round and round it to stop him bending
his arm. There was a drip stand to one side of his
bed and the respirator Dr Mackintosh had
mentioned on the other. He was propped up on
pillows and his bed was canopied in a tent that
pumped out steam to help his breathing. The
room smelt of camphor oil and something with a
mild antiseptic edge.

Joe, exhausted, now slept. 'Lily,' he had gasped
when he saw her. 'Lily, are you all right?'

Lily's eyes had filled with tears. 'Me all right?
You're the one who's poorly, not me.'

Joe smiled. 'I'm sorry, Lily.'

'Joe, it's not your fault. Why are you saying
sorry? You can't help it if you're sick.'

He lifted his un-splinted hand and, taking the
lock of her hair that had fallen on to the pillow,
grasped it and began to twirl it round in his fingers.
Lily smiled and stroked the side of his face. She
knew what would happen next. Within seconds,
worn out from panic and stress, he fell fast asleep.

As she sat by his side, she slipped her hands
through the metal bars of the white cot and held
on to his limp hand. She focused on keeping
herself together, praying, wondering if her mother
even knew where Joe was, if Katie had been fed
and where she would be sleeping.

There was something the doctor hadn't told her, she was sure of it. He had looked more concerned than he had the last time. She went over and over his words in her mind as she listened to every single breath Joe took. His words felt alien. Like he'd been talking to her about someone else's brother and not little Joe. Her head was swimming as her mind fought against the possibility that Joe could have to go through the rest of his life like this. It seemed that he was getting worse as he got older.

Later, Lily sat there with an empty cup and saucer in her hand and looked out over the city from the large window in Joe's cubicle. She watched the street lights flicker off in the offices and shops and down in the dock buildings and other lights coming on in the houses. She watched people scurrying home, heads bent, long figures in dark coats carrying bags and umbrellas, impatient to be indoors and out of the rain that had drizzled the whole day long.

Ten minutes later, Dr Mackintosh popped his head around the cubicle door to check on Joe. He was carrying a tray, which he laid down on the bedside locker.

'For you,' he said. 'The orderly in the kitchen told me to bring it in for you.'

Lily could smell the food and her mouth watered in response. 'Do you always do that?' she asked, nodding towards the tray.

'Well, not exactly, not me personally, no, but we

do like to look after our visitors when patients are particularly poorly. Especially the pretty ones.'

He wanted to bite his tongue off. How could he be so crass, so stupid? He sounded pathetic. Like he was trying to emulate the flirting of Dr Teddy Davenport with Nurse Makebee. But he had failed badly.

Lily blushed. No one in her entire life had ever called her pretty. She had no idea how to respond. She also doubted that he had ever carried a plate of shepherd's pie and a pot of tea in to a visitor before. She smiled the first proper smile since she'd arrived at the hospital.

Dr Mackintosh decided to revert to a position of professionalism, to save face. Later, he would blame his indiscretion on the darkness of the cubicle, the atmosphere created by the night-light and the drama of the situation.

'I just want to check Joe's breathing and put some more of the drug into his drip,' he said as he placed the ends of the stethoscope into his ears. 'You go ahead and eat. The day staff are handing over to the night staff and, if I'm not mistaken, one of Joe's favourite nurses is on duty tonight.'

Lily smiled again. She stood up and helped the doctor lift up Joe's gown. 'Is he going to be OK?' she asked anxiously.

'He's sleeping peacefully and that's the best thing we can ask for.' They both had their heads bent over Joe in the bed and her hair fell across his hand as he gently turned Joe on to his side so that he could listen to his back. 'I saw your boyfriend leaving the ward. Will he be back?' He tried to sound as though he was distracted and merely being polite. But Lily's reply was like music to his ears.

'Oh, he's not my boyfriend. That's Lockie, I've known him since I was a kid. He's been a good friend to me over the years and I see him often in work.'

His heart danced at the news. Lockie had been the only man to come near her in her hour of need. If there was a boyfriend, he would have been there, he was sure of it. So Lily was not attached to anyone. His spirits soared.

Anthony Mackintosh was well aware that he had fallen into a pattern of behaviour that would turn him into a lonely old man or an alcoholic, whichever came first. His shifts began early and could last until ten o'clock at night, at which point he would call in to the pub and meet whoever happened to be in there from the doctors' residence. It had recently occurred to him that other doctors came and went over time but he was still there, unmarried and unchanged. As he downed his pints, he felt as though the world was moving on around him. At the doctors' dance last year he had even offered to cover casualty so that all the younger doctors could go and have a good time. The way things were looking, he would never have a wife or children. The fear of a permanently empty, lonely life had sharpened his thoughts and opened his eyes, and there was Lily. She was the first female to catch his attention and make him look twice, the first to affect the rate of his pulse just from looking at her.

'He's doing fine,' he said as he stood upright. 'Obviously, I can still hear a slight wheeze, but I'm not sure this little fella will ever be free from that altogether. Otherwise, though, I would say he's doing OK.'

'That's such a relief to hear. Will he be all right if I leave and go home to see to my sister, Katie? Will they let me back in once I've left?'

Dr Mackintosh shook his head. 'I'm afraid that my luck won't last until tomorrow. I had to be very forceful indeed with the assistant matron to let you stay this long. They call her the Bone Grinder, you know, but don't repeat that.'

Lily almost giggled.

'This will be it, I'm afraid, until visiting on Sunday. But the nurse on duty tonight is fantastic and I know she dotes on this little chappie here. I'm knocking off soon, so why don't you let me run you home, then you can see to your sister.'

Lily felt swamped with shame. He was a lovely man, but how could she possibly let him see the conditions she lived in; and not just her but Katie and Joe too. It was impossible. Her chest tightened and she felt tears of self-pity prickle at her eyes. He was looking at her with the most gentle expression she had ever seen on anyone's face.

He instantly knew what was wrong.

'Lily, I know where Clare Cottages are. I've been in Liverpool for some time now. It's not as if you're far from the hospital. You are exhausted, let me give you a lift, please. But eat this food first or the orderly will have my guts for garters. I'll meet you opposite the Lovely Lane entrance in half an hour.' And without another word, he was gone.

It was as if someone had removed the plug at the bottom of a well. The tears she never allowed to reach the surface began to pour out and once they'd started, they would not stop. She couldn't touch the food he had brought for her. Sitting in the chair, she placed her hands over her face and wept.

Joe's little hand brushed against her knee. 'Lily, what's wrong?' he croaked.

Wiping her eyes, Lily smiled and jumped up. 'For goodness' sake, would you look at the state of me! Nothing, Joe. Do you want a drink?'

Joe nodded his head and Lily reached up for the feeding cup on the locker. Ten minutes later he was sound asleep once again. Lily felt torn and could barely bring herself to leave his side. The night nurse, the one Joe called Nurse Dana, came towards her.

'Hello, are you off? Look at you, you've been crying, haven't you?' Dana reached out and put her arm around Lily's shoulders. 'Look, do you know what, I shouldn't say this because I shouldn't really have favourites, but Joe is definitely mine. I am very fond of him, I am, and if you're worried leaving him here with me, don't be. I will look after him as though he were my own.'

Lily believed her. Dana's concern and fondness for Joe were plain to see.

Lily looked down at Joe and gave him one last brief kiss on his soft warm cheek and downy hair. 'Night-night, little fella, I'll be back soon,' she said. And as a gasp of tears grabbed her and threatened to prevent her from leaving, she fled the cubicle.

Minutes later, for the first time in her life, Lily stepped into the front seat of a car. It smelt of leather and wood and something strangely medicinal. She had never sat so close to a man before and the rawness of the male smell was intoxicating.

'Right, let us go and rescue that sister of yours, shall we?' In the light of the street lamp, he saw the tears welling up in her eyes again. 'Now, now,' he said. 'Don't cry. Katie will be looking to you for reassurance, to know that everything is all right and that Joe is going to be fine. If we turn up and you're crying, that's not going to create a very good impression, is it?'

As they walked up the concrete steps of Clare Cottages, Lily noticed for the first time how strong the smell of urine was. She was embarrassed by the piles of dog and human waste on the pavement and the stairs, and the rubbish clustered in piles along the landing, where the kids had kicked it. They approached Mrs McGuffy's house and

Lily could smell Dettol. Mrs McGuffy had obviously already washed down the landing outside her door, as she did every night.

The front door was open and, with the briefest of taps on it, as was the way, Lily walked straight in. Anthony hovered by the threshold.

Lily looked around at the scrubbed children sitting in a row, clean and tidy. The house was spotless. Mrs McGuffy was kneeling on the floor, leaning over a tin tub in front of the fire, bathing the baby in the last of the water.

'Your Katie's not here, love,' she said to Lily as she looked up. 'How's little Joe, are they keeping him in? God, he was in a bad way after you left, Lily. Near scared me to death, he did. He's in the best place, in St Angelus. I thought he was dead.'

Mrs McGuffy was as matter-of-fact as any woman in the cottages. Prickles of fear ran across Lily's skin and she almost shivered. She couldn't even let herself imagine what would have happened if Sister Therese and Mrs McGuffy hadn't got to Joe when they did.

'He's asleep now. They gave him the same injection as last time and it worked. He's so tired. I don't think he's slept properly for nights, so hopefully he'll sleep through tonight now he's breathing better. They'll probably keep him in for a little while, just to make sure.'

'Well, 'tis the best place for him and that's a fact. Sister Therese has taken Katie over to sleep at St Chad's and she said there's a bed over there tonight for you too. Katie loves it in the convent, I think she's going to take the veil, that one, when she's older. The nuns are so kind to her.'

Lily was shocked. Mrs McGuffy had seen something that was right under her nose but had never occurred to her. Katie did love going to the convent. Lily had been fighting to keep her out and yet she had never even thought that Katie might have wanted to be over there, in the home with the other kids, warm and fed.

'I suppose I can't blame her,' she said. 'Compared to our house, it must seem like heaven over there.'

Mrs McGuffy got to her feet and, picking up a very grey but clean towel, swept the baby out of the bath and wrapped him into it. She plonked him on to the lap of one of her daughters, who began to rub him dry. The children were quiet. Reading, well behaved.

Lily couldn't help but comment. 'Your children, they aren't noisy, they're always good and quiet. I never hear them shouting.'

'Oh, they do,' said Mrs McGuffy. She took a cigarette from behind her ear, bent over, pressed it on to one of the hot coals on the fire, put it to her mouth and puffed hard. 'They run around the yard like the rest of them. But each one of them knows what's expected of them, Lily, so they don't mess me about. It's bath time now. Everyone has a job and they know what their job is, don't you, kids?'

Two of the children looked up and said, 'Yes, Mam.'

A cough from the front door made Mrs McGuffy jump. Lily had almost forgotten that she'd left Dr Mackintosh standing on the landing. 'Jesus to Mary, who is that at the door? Is that you, Seamus?'

'No, er, it's one of the doctors from the hospital. He brought me home.'

'Well, God love us and save us, a doctor at me own front door and I don't even need one. Is that not just my luck. Let me see him now.'

Before Lily could say another word, Mrs McGuffy was at the front door. Lily felt like she wanted to die.

Anthony regretted coughing as he saw the toothless Mrs McGuffy sweeping towards him. A smell of cooked cabbage and potatoes wafted over as she walked past the range.

'Well, hello, Doctor. That was very kind of you to bring the girl home. Katie is in the home in St Chad's, and the mother's down the pub, been there all day.' She whispered this, so that Lily didn't hear. She didn't mention that she knew all about families with drink problems. Her sister-in-law back in Mayo had a husband who was barely out of the pub himself.

'Bye, kids,' said Lily. She turned and followed Mrs McGuffy to the front door. Her face was scarlet as she wondered what the doctor in shining armour would make of her neighbour.

'I'll take Lily over to St Chad's then,' he said. 'She's had a rough day today.'

'Thanks for all you did, Mrs McGuffy,' said Lily as she moved quickly along the landing.

Anthony raised his hat and followed her.

When they were back in the car, he placed his hand on the ignition key then turned to look at Lily. His face glowed orange in the sulphur street light, but the rest of him was shrouded in shadow. 'I don't want you to be embarrassed,' he said. 'As a doctor, I have seen people from every walk of life come through the casualty doors, from lords and ladies to street children. Everyone is the same, Lily. I worked in Glasgow and there are plenty of Clare Cottages there. You aren't so special here.'

He smiled and turned the key. The engine fired into life.

Lily couldn't help herself, she smiled back. His physical proximity made her heart race and her breath come faster.

'To St Chad's,' said Dr Mackintosh as he checked his side mirror and swung his car around.

He dropped her off at the gate. They both saw the porch light come on and behind the stained glass on either side of the door Lily recognized the outline of Sister Therese.

'I'll go now,' said Anthony as he opened the car door for her. 'It's late. Please make sure you have something to eat, Lily, before you fall asleep. Promise me.'

She looked up at him and was so filled with gratitude, she could not find the words to thank him.

'I know this probably isn't the right time to ask, but when things settle down a little, could I take you out for lunch, or supper even? Somewhere nice? I think you deserve it.'

Lily nodded. She had no idea what to say. She had no idea what tomorrow would hold, never mind in a few weeks.

Anthony was back in the car and down the road before Sister Therese reached Lily. He decided to call in to the Grapes and have a quick beer with his colleagues, just as he'd done almost every night of the past five years. He walked in and immediately saw Oliver Gaskell at the bar; as was often the case, an adoring young nurse was standing next to him. Anthony tried to place her. Ah yes, the new probationer on men's medical, he thought. Nurse Moran. Irish and pretty, but terrified of her own shadow. Someone needed to warn her. The last probationer who'd fallen under Oliver Gaskell's spell was still nursing her broken heart.

Oliver had seen him come in and had waved to him, but Anthony decided not to disturb them. Over on the bench in the corner sat Teddy Davenport with the new nurse from casualty, Nurse Makebee. She was sitting on Teddy's knee. Seeing this, Anthony raised an eyebrow. He could have sworn that Teddy was about to go on holiday with Nurse Dana Brogan, whom he'd just left on night duty on the children's ward. I'm getting old, he thought; it must be couples' night. He then spotted one of the junior housemen at the bar. At last, a man alone.

'Drink?' the houseman mouthed.

Anthony was about to shout 'A pint, please,' but at the last minute he changed his mind. He wanted to go back to the ward, to check on Joe. He doubted he would sleep tonight if he didn't. 'I'm just going to check on one of the kids on ward four. Get me a pint on the next round. I'll be back in half an hour.'

A couple of hours later, when the bell for last orders rang out, Teddy Davenport, with one arm slung around Nurse Makebee, asked the houseman, 'Who does that full pint belong to? Are you sickening for something?'

'No, not me, it was Mackintosh. He said he would be back in half an hour, but no sign of him.'

'Well, waste not, want not.' Teddy laughed a little too loudly as he picked up the pint and kept drinking until it was finished.

'What an impressive man you are,' purred Nurse Makebee.

Teddy wiped his mouth with the back of his hand. 'Have you ever been to the Lake District?'

CHAPTER 29

Dr Mackintosh saw the headlights of the old Austin as it pulled in through the hospital gates and immediately recognized it as belonging to Dr Gaskell. It came to a halt directly opposite the steps to the main entrance. Anthony broke into a sprint and came alongside it just as Dr Gaskell began slowly extracting himself from the driver's seat. He was stiffer and slower of late and getting in and out of his car following a long drive was something of an ordeal these days.

'Thank you so much for coming back tonight,' Anthony gasped, almost out of breath after his sprint from the back entrance. 'The little boy, Joe Lancashire, is really worrying me. But even so, I didn't expect to see you here tonight. I thought you'd go home to bed first.'

Dr Gaskell turned his key in the lock of the car door and shook his head.

'You can't take chances with little children with such severe breathing difficulties,' he replied. 'When you have been looking after the bronchioles and lungs of the young of Liverpool for as long as I have, there is one thing you learn above all else: a child can deteriorate faster than a sinking stone. I would much rather see him tonight, and tomorrow as well, if possible.'

Dr Mackintosh looked at the much older man in awe. His reputation was well known, right across the country. His efforts to convince the government to introduce the Clean Air Act were unrelenting. Anthony had the hugest respect for the man and not just for his medical knowledge and professionalism but for his dignity and manner as well. However, he was ill prepared for his next question.

'Have you just left the Grapes? Was my son in there?'

Anthony didn't know what to say. He didn't want to lie to a man he respected so much, so he just nodded.

'Thought so. Which young nurse has fallen victim this time?'

'Er, she's the new probationer on men's medical. Young Irish girl by the name of Nurse Moran.'

The car safely locked, the two men walked towards the lamp hanging above the steps to the main hospital entrance. Its pool of light guided their way.

'Do you know, Dr Mackintosh, I don't know whether to be impressed or concerned. I really don't. You young men today, you're very different from how we were in my day. We used to set our cap at a young lady, feel very grateful if she allowed

509

us to court her and then, when a suitable time had passed, we married her.'

He pushed open the heavy, half-wood, half-glass door leading to the corridor and gestured to Anthony to pass. 'After you,' he said, and Anthony felt embarrassed that he hadn't got there first to hold the door open for Dr Gaskell.

'It sometimes seems to me that now the war is over everyone has gone slightly mad. What about you, Dr Mackintosh? By all accounts, you are the complete opposite. I hear you're a workaholic, and you're proving that by being here now.'

Anthony gave a cough and grinned as he looked sideways at Dr Gaskell.

'All right, all right! I know I have the same reputation, and God knows, I have earned it after forty-five years in this place. But I have a wonderful woman at home who keeps my feet on the ground. I don't have to worry about anything at home, other than my roses and catching mice. Whereas you have no one, or so I hear. That is not a good thing for a doctor who works the hours you do.'

Anthony blushed. He had no answer for Dr Gaskell. The truth was, he had become so set in his ways that it felt almost impossible to change. Ten years ago, he wouldn't have thought twice about asking a young lady out; now he had no idea how to go about it.

'Try and sort that out, Dr Mackintosh. We all need a good wife. Mrs Gaskell is marvellous. I'm afraid you will never catch the best, she has been mine for a very long time and there is no equal on this planet, but I am sure you can find someone to run a close second. Someone to make sure your shirts are ironed, your gloves are by the front door ready for when you leave and, most importantly, that you are fed.'

Anthony was consistently underweight and could go days without a proper meal. He lived on slices of toast at the greasy spoon.

'The thing is, if you really want to indulge your workaholism and not end up in the asylum, you can't manage without one.'

'I shall try my best, sir,' said Anthony.

They had now reached the top of the stairs and made to turn towards ward four. Dr Gaskell cast his eyes down ward three and reassured himself that all was calm. The hospital might now belong to the NHS, but when St Angelus was run as a voluntary trust it had been his responsibility, with Matron sharing the burden. Every birth and death in Liverpool's dockside neighbourhoods, and each illness in between, had landed at his door. Now it was all in the hands of the politicians, but old habits died hard. He could not step away from responsibility. If there was a patient in the hospital who needed his care, he would be there. At times like this, the NHS with all its rules and regulations might as well not have existed.

The red night-lights burnt dimly in ward three and the sound of infant snores floated through the door. Dr Gaskell smiled. All was well.

Turning in the direction of ward four, both men startled as they saw Nurse Dana Brogan hurrying towards them at full pelt. When she saw them, she let out a yelp.

'Oh, thank God. I was going for the phone. It's Joe. I can't get any sense out of him and he's as blue as anything. His breathing is bad. I turned the drip up like you said, Dr Mackintosh, but it's not touching him.'

They talked as they hurried down the corridor towards the cubicle. As they approached, Dr Mackintosh saw a nurse from ward three trying to hold Joe and stop him hurting himself against the cot sides. He was obviously struggling to breathe, but in his confusion he was ripping the oxygen mask from his face.

Joe was in two worlds. In one he was panicking and trying to breathe; in the other there were confused images and voices running through his head. It was Christmas morning and he was riding his bike along the half landing and Katie had her hand on the back of the seat and she was yelling, 'Pedal, Joe, pedal!' but he couldn't because the exertion had robbed him of his breath and so instead he lifted his feet up in front of him and Katie ran behind until she fell on the floor laughing. He heard Nurse Dana, she was shouting, and two men were holding his head, one he knew and the other who was kindly and old, but they were trying to put a tube down his throat and it made him panic and he couldn't breathe any more. 'Hold on, Joe,' the one he knew said, 'it's just a tube. Switch on the respirator,' the doctor was shouting to someone, but he couldn't breathe. He just couldn't do what they were asking. He heard the nurse shout, 'Joe, help us, Joe,' but it wasn't the nurse, it was Katie again and she was shouting, 'Pedal Joe, pedal!' and now his legs were suddenly free and he could. He could pedal faster and faster and he could breathe. He took a long, deep pull of the sweet, clear air, not the smoggy damp mist he was used to in Clare Cottages, and he pedalled faster as Katie whooped with laughter and he heard Lily saying to him, 'Night-night, Joe. Night-night, little fella, I'll be back soon.' Lily was coming back. He turned around, he wanted to see Lily, she was coming back, he had to be there. Lily wouldn't know where to find him and she would get upset, and he wondered, should he turn back for Lily? He looked behind him and although he could hear Lily, 'Night-night, Joe,' he couldn't see her anywhere, but he could see Katie, laughing and running after him. 'Pedal, Joe, pedal!' She stopped and clapped her hands in glee, and turning, he saw the sunshine and the light before him and he felt free and overcome with happiness and exhilaration and he shouted, 'Lily, I can ride my bike! Look, Lily!' And he laughed out loud, long and hard, with all the breath he needed for the first time ever as he pedalled faster and faster towards the light.

★　★　★

Mrs Duffy stood in the kitchen, watching the bacon sizzle in the pan. Scamp lay at her feet. He had won the battle of wills and he had her wrapped around his front paw.

'No, you can't have the bacon from the pan. You will get the leftovers and nothing more. A bit of rind if you're lucky.'

Scamp dropped his ears flat against his head, laid his chin on his front legs and looked up at her imploringly. It was a technique he'd perfected in his first week.

'Oh, for God's sake, how do you do that?' she scolded. Taking the end of a slice out of the pan, she threw it into his bowl. 'Now go away, do you hear? Don't you be bothering me again, this is for my nurses.'

She heard the click of the front door as it opened and closed. 'Aha,' she said, 'there you go, Scamp, the first one back off nights. Bacon's nearly ready, come and get your tea!' she shouted.

There was no reply, but she heard footsteps in the morning room. Leaving the kitchen, she came out to see Dana pulling out one of the high-backed chairs and sitting down. Glancing at the wall, Mrs Duffy checked her chart to see who was off duty today. She had already dispatched the girls who were on day or split shifts, giggling and chatting, out into the sunshine.

The off-duty rotas were placed on the noticeboard outside every ward each Thursday and the nurses in Lovely Lane were under strict instructions to fill in the chart in the morning room with their off-duty days by Friday. That way Mrs Duffy always knew who to expect for breakfast and when.

'Ah,' she said to Dana, 'the terrible three will be missing you today. They're off duty, they'll all be down in a minute. I know they're going into town to do a bit of shopping today. Is there anything you would be wanting?'

There was no reply from Dana and Mrs Duffy turned round.

'Oh my, you look shattered,' she said. 'So much responsibility for you on the children's ward. Here's your tea, and your bacon sandwich is coming up. Give me two minutes to fill your hot-water bottle and then we can pack you straight into bed, miss.'

She heard the thunder of footsteps charging down the stairs. 'Would you listen to that lot! I kid you not, they arrive a minute off the bacon being ready, not one before or after. Would you credit it!'

Pammy, Victoria and Beth piled into the morning room. 'Morning,' said Pammy. 'Would you look at that sunshine. And Dana off on her holidays the day after tomorrow, Mrs Duffy. Aren't you the lucky one?' she said to Dana.

'Can I help, Mrs Duffy?' said Beth as she filled up the milk jug, not waiting to be answered.

Victoria was tipping cornflakes into a bowl and Pammy stood at the fireplace finishing off her make-up in the mirror over the mantelpiece.

'We are off into town, Dana, is there anything you want?' Victoria asked.

She was met by silence. Mrs Duffy laid a plate with a bacon sandwich in front of her and her brow creased with concern.

At the exact same moment, they all became aware that something was wrong. It wasn't just because Scamp walked over to Dana and laid his head on her lap. It wasn't because Dana failed to answer Mrs Duffy when she asked her was there something wrong and would she like an egg on her bacon sandwich. Nor was it the fact that she failed to join in with the chatter. It was the tears that poured down Dana's cheeks and the pain in her voice that made them all hold their breath for a fraction of a second while they realized in horror that Dana had done what they all dreaded and had been warned against. She had become involved and something dreadful had happened. She couldn't speak, and for the longest time just sobbed and sobbed.

CHAPTER 30

L ily was woken by the sound of the police knocking on the door of St Chad's. The entire convent was roused as they raised and lowered the large brass knocker three times. St Chad's wasn't used to early-morning visitors and Lily could hear the flustered scurry of a postulant's footsteps along the stone flagstones. As she sat up in bed, her blood ran cold.

She and Sister Therese travelled to St Angelus in a cab. Before yesterday, she'd never even sat in a car; now she was taking her second ride in one within a matter of hours. As they sped along Lovely Lane, Lily spotted Nurse Brogan. She was walking with her head bent low and she looked deflated and sad. Desperately worried, Lily sat back in the seat of the cab. All the police had said was that she needed to hurry.

Once they reached the hospital, Lily ran down the corridor from the main entrance to the ward. There was no one around to chastise the poorly dressed girl and the nun, habit flying, who was holding up her skirts as she chased after her. The lights were dim, the corridor empty. The morning light was still too weak to chase the shadows from the corners and alcoves. The sound of her footsteps rang out through the hospital.

'I'm coming, Joe. I'm coming,' said Lily as she began to mount the stairs, not knowing she was too late.

They were escorted by a nurse to Matron's office. Matron had said that she would deal with them herself. She was now at the stage of trying to steer almost everyone out of the path of Miss Van Gilder. She did not want to prolong Lily's agony so she got straight to the point. 'We have lost Joe, Miss Lancashire. I am sorry to tell you, he has passed away. He had a further attack and it was too soon after the first. I am so sorry.'

Lily's anguished screams could be heard throughout the hospital.

'Joe had the most experienced chest doctor in the region looking after him,' Matron said. She had waited patiently for Lily's sobs to subside so that Lily could focus on what she was saying. It was at times like this that her professionalism was tested to the limit and her years of experience stood her in good stead. 'He went into respiratory arrest following a further bronchospasm and Dr Gaskell and Dr Mackintosh worked very hard throughout the night to try and save him. They did all they could to help Joe, using some very special equipment to assist his breathing.'

Lily remembered the respirator at the side of the bed. Dr Mackintosh must have known.

'His chest was very bad, but you know that, don't you? Dr Mackintosh told me you took very good care of him.'

Lily's head shot up. 'But, I wasn't with him, he died alone,' she whispered.

'Oh no he didn't, my dear. He died in a nurse's arms. Joe had quite stolen Nurse Brogan's heart, I can tell you that. And Dr Mackintosh carried him to the mortuary himself, wrapped in a blanket, not on a trolley. By all accounts, your little brother was a very special person. Would you like me to take you to the mortuary now so that you can see him? I always think it is a good thing to do. Helps you to cope with the days ahead.'

Lily nodded. This was the moment she had been waiting for since Matron had told her he was dead. She wanted to see him. But now it was here, she began to shake so violently she could barely stand.

Twenty minutes later, in the chilly, forbidding mortuary, she kissed Joe goodbye. She ran the back of her fingers across his cold face and hair and hands. She took in his wayward curls and angelic face and burnt them on to her memory. 'I will never forget you. Never,' she whispered. Through her tears she saw that someone had laid the teddy that had brought him comfort on the children's ward and the book the nurse had read to him by his side.

She stood and ran her cold hands down the front of her skirt. Then she jumped as the mortuary attendant slammed the refrigerated drawer shut.

Silence fell. It was the end of Joe's life. The end of her own as she'd known it.

'Nothing will ever be the same again, will it?' she said to Sister Therese, who laid a comforting arm across her shoulders. 'I will never love another person in my life as much as I have loved Joe, and I will never stop missing him. I swear to God, I shall pray for him every day for as long as I live.'

'Hush now, hush.' Sister Therese rubbed her back and guided her towards the door.

Lily hadn't noticed, but the mortuary attendant had made an inconspicuous little cough and when Lily hadn't responded, he'd thrown Sister Therese a knowing look. It was time for his break; he was hurrying her along. Life was continuing as normal around Lily, but from the depths of her grief, she was oblivious.

As Lily and Sister Therese walked back through the hospital corridors, they were passed by Miss Van Gilder. She liked to make an impression and had made it a rule to be in her office and at her desk more than an hour before Matron was at hers. Today was an exception: Matron had clearly made a special effort to start early.

Miss Van Gilder recognized Lily as the young woman who'd been on the children's ward the previous evening. Lily was difficult to miss with the nun flapping alongside her as they staggered towards the main exit. If the nun hadn't been present, she would have torn the girl off a strip. She didn't allow visiting on the children's wards other than on Sundays. That was the rule and Dr Mackintosh had violated it last evening. He had dared to defy her authority and she would not normally have tolerated it, but the warning bells had rung. That was how she had almost been caught out last time. She needed to get on with the job and avoid drawing attention to herself or her conduct. So she had given in, albeit reluctantly.

'Excuse me, young lady,' she called out. 'I do hope you are aware that there will be no further visiting now until Sunday.' Fancy her having stayed through the night, she thought. Nun or no nun, that doctor has taken a liberty. 'The doctor said you would only be staying for a few hours. We have standards to uphold here, you know. Rules to obey. Your little brother is no different from any other child on the children's ward. We don't make exceptions.'

Lily stopped and stared at her. She shook her head, unable to speak. Sister Therese crossed herself, glared at Miss Van Gilder meaningfully for a good few seconds, then hurried Lily towards the door without saying a word.

Two minutes later, when Miss Van Gilder entered her office and looked down at her desk, she saw the first report of the day waiting for her on the blotter. It was the morning bed report. One new bed available on the children's ward. 'Well, how was I to know?' she muttered as she picked up the phone.

'Switchboard, get me the Acme cleaning agency on the phone.'

'Yes, Miss Van Gilder,' replied Madge in her smart telephone voice. 'Would you like to hold or shall I call you back?'

'Call me back,' she snapped as she laid the Bakelite telephone back on its cradle with a loud ping. Miss Van Gilder thought people said thank you and please far more often than was necessary. A waste of good words.

While she waited, she sat down, opened her desk drawer and once again pored over the details of the contract. He had missed out ward seven. How could he have done that? She wanted and needed that quote finalized for the next LDHB meeting. Then they would have a decision. She could see no good reason why it would take more than a month to go through the process of laying off the domestics and orderlies and putting the new contract in place. Then they could move on to the porters and, as quickly as possible, the laundry services.

She extracted a photograph from the drawer and gazed at the whitewashed cottage by the sea. It had always been her wish to retire to a nice little cottage in Cornwall. Just like the one she and James had honeymooned in. For a brief moment, she was lost in thought as she dreamt about waking up to the sound of the sea lapping against the shore. The telephone rang out and made her jump as she hurriedly stuffed the photograph back in its place and slammed the desk drawer shut.

'I have the Acme cleaning agency on the telephone, Miss Van Gilder,' said Madge.

'That will be all,' she replied and then waited for the telltale click indicating that Madge had moved on to her next call.

Madge sat back and took in the large frame of her switchboard. She did indeed pull her own plug out, but then she slipped the jack plug and long wire out from the board, pulled it down and slowly reinserted it into the light marked *Asst Mat.* Miss Van Gilder was entirely unaware that the click could only be heard when Madge left the conversation, not when she joined it.

Madge moved her headphones into a more comfortable position and turned down the volume on the bells. There were only three lights on and no requests to page doctors; the switchboard activity this morning was light. She picked up a pen and paper and prepared to write. But even she was shocked by what she heard next.

'Mother? Mother, are you there?'

Madge sat upright. For a moment she thought she had inserted the jack into the wrong point. She bent her head and stared. No, she was right, it was the assistant matron's office. She heard the irritated response.

'For goodness' sake, Luuk, stop that at once! Do not call me "Mother" on the telephone.'

'Why not? No one can hear us. I heard the operator go and there is no one in my office. Is there anyone in yours?'

Miss Van Gilder, forever suspicious, glanced around her. Luuk was right. They were alone; she could relax.

'Luuk, you missed out ward seven in your proposal. How could you have been so stupid? I want to take this to Matron, convince her it's the right thing to do, and I can only do that if the numbers are correct. Then I have to take it to the board to have the money approved. Do it this morning, please, and get it over to me right away.'

'Darn, sorry, Mother. I tried to get on to ward seven, but I remember now, it was chaos. I planned to measure up, but all hell had broken loose – there was blood everywhere, doctors running, people crying, a young nurse asking me did I know where she should take a drip stand to – and so I left it. Look, I will hazard a guess, does it have the same number of beds as ward four?'

'It does. There is no need for you to come back, just get on with it, please, and have it with me as soon as possible. I need my twenty per cent. The NHS is throwing money at contracts like this one. There's no one checking and they are leaving it to the matrons to decide whether or not they are value for money. And the boards have even less of an idea, most of them having hardly set foot inside a hospital, which means the contracts are getting passed unchallenged. So, please, I don't want any raised eyebrows. Just get on with it.'

'Yes, Mother, right away. I will bring it over myself.'

Miss Van Gilder hesitated. She wanted to tell him not to bother and to just pop it in the post. But maybe he was right. That way, there was no danger of it getting into the wrong hands, and they both knew the consequences of that happening. She had been forced to pack up her belongings at St Dunstan's and flee before the police arrived to question her. She would not let Luuk be so careless again.

As she put the phone down, a headline in her copy of the *Nursing Times*, which had been delivered to her desk along with the post, caught her eye.

Matrons Do Not Have the Commercial Skills Required to Run New NHS, Say Whitehall Mandarins.

She read further.

Whitehall officials are expressing concern that hospital matrons are not capable of negotiating hospital contracts with the efficacy needed in complex commercial dealings. NHS budgets are rapidly being depleted because of poor decision-making by nursing staff who have been given responsibilities way beyond their capabilities.

'How dare they?' she muttered.

Concerns have been raised regarding the power of hospital matrons over all things commercial. When interviewed, Mr Thornton said, 'Hospital matrons have been trained to make sick people better, not negotiate contracts. Over the next two years we will allocate regional managers to each cluster of hospitals across the UK. Matrons will then be able to concentrate on what they do best, which is nursing and organizing the day-to-day care of patients. There will of course be no threat to their role. Matrons are here to stay.

Miss Van Gilder frowned. Time is running out for us, she thought. It had all been so simple. Luuk had set up an office in Liverpool and was drawing up a proposal that overcharged by sixty per cent. The two of them would buy the machines, cut the number of staff and re-employ some of the sacked domestics at wages of thirty per cent less than what they'd previously earned. She and Luuk would cream a handsome profit off the top.

I might have time to get one more hospital in after this one, before they cotton on, she thought. She opened the jobs section of the *Nursing Times* to see what was available. And then I shall have enough to buy this house.

She picked up the phone again. 'Switch, get me this number.'

A few minutes later, Madge called her back.

Again, Miss Van Gilder waited to hear the click from the board.

'Mr Walton from Walton and Ramsbottom estate agents speaking.'

'Ah, yes, good morning. I am enquiring about the cottage you have for sale.'

Madge scribbled like mad. She now had the information she needed to take to the meeting, but what to do with it? What did she mean by her twenty per cent? It was enough of a shocker that Miss Van Gilder had a son. Where had he been hiding? It looked as though between them they were about to rob the hospital blind.

Folding her paper carefully, Madge leant sideways, retrieved her handbag from under her chair, opened the clasp, dropped the paper inside and snapped the clasp shut.

'Right, meeting time,' she said and dialled the school of nursing to summon Biddy.

CHAPTER 31

Emily lay in bed and gazed through the window at the blue sky. The top of a sycamore tree waved in the breeze. It was a perfect Sunday morning. Before Dessie went downstairs to make the tea, she'd asked him to open the curtains. There was nothing she loved more than the sunlight pouring into the bedroom, but she knew it made Dessie nervous. Even though they'd now spent many nights together, he was terrified that a neighbour might glance up and catch sight of her. Whenever she needed to use the outhouse, he first stepped into the yard and looked up to check that none of his neighbours were at their upstairs bedroom windows. Emily would hover in the kitchen doorway until Dessie said, 'Right! Now!' and she would dash across the yard. Before she left the outhouse, she checked through the small window on the side wall.

'This is hardly romantic, is it?' she would say as she slammed the kitchen door behind her. But there was little discussion about it because Dessie could never refrain from kissing her before she reached the end of a sentence.

Dessie carried the tea into the bedroom and she smiled up at him. She could not believe what was happening to her or how she felt. The kindest man in the world was looking after her, loving her and she felt like a new woman. A different woman. She was no longer Emily Haycock, unwilling spinster of St Angelus. She was Dessie's lover and just the thought of the nights they had spent together was enough to flood her cheeks with colour.

'Here you go, Sister Haycock,' said Dessie as he placed the cup in her hands and sat himself down on the edge of the bed.

She was naked and the covers were dishevelled, kicked down to the bottom of the bed only half an hour since, when they had woken and made love.

He looked down at Emily and blinked. 'I keep thinking I am dreaming,' he said. 'How did this gorgeous woman end up in my bed? Did you get the wrong house? Take the wrong turn?'

Emily began to giggle under his gaze and pulled the sheet up to cover herself.

He took a sip from his tea as he assembled his thoughts. 'Here was me thinking all this time that that was it. I would work until retirement, save enough money to be comfortable, help out a few others on the way and that would be me done. Apart from tending to my pots and the football, I couldn't think that there was anything else in store for me. But look, here you are, lying in my bed, drinking the tea I made for you and you haven't run away.'

Emily cheekily set her chin at him. 'If the second cup isn't as good as the first, I will be off in a flash. Don't go taking me for granted already.' She wagged her finger and Dessie, having placed his cup on the floor, lay down next to her and gathered her into his arms.

'Don't say that, not even if you're joking. I couldn't bear it and I've only known you for a bit.'

'Well, that's not quite true, is it? We've actually known each other for years.'

Dessie kissed the top of her head. 'Strictly speaking, I've known you for longer than you've known me.'

Emily lifted her head off the bed and looked at Dessie, startled. 'How is that then? We've both worked at the hospital for the same length of time.'

Dessie held her tighter. He told himself it was to stop her from slipping off the edge of the bed, but really he couldn't hold her tight enough. He was more afraid of her slipping out of his life. 'Well, you forget, don't you, that I'm almost ten years older than you and when you were six, I was already sixteen. I knew your stepfather, Alf. We signed up together. You won't remember, but all the lads around these parts were in the same regiment.'

Emily didn't answer, she let the knowledge settle.

'I was sorry to hear he was in the home for veterans. I have been to see him once or twice, but by the time I was demobbed, he was not too good and didn't know who I was. I think he thought I was one of the doctors.'

'That was you!' Emily's head shot up from the pillow then sank back down again just as quickly.

'Yes, it was me. And do you know, I have always known where you go every night when you visit him.'

Again, there was no response. Emily's love for her family, the mother and brothers she had lost in the bomb, burnt in her heart and she never spoke of it. There was a time when she'd thought the pain of her loss would kill her, when she didn't dare recall the memories of Richard and Henry, so their voices had haunted her sleep instead. She'd thought she would go mad with grief, but then Alf beat her to it and she had to look after him and as a matter of necessity she'd had to lock her own sadness away in her heart.

'I never knew that,' she whispered.

'I know. That was how I intended it to be. I didn't want to mention it and rake up the past for you.'

'Do you miss your wife?' Emily had seen the sky burning red with the flames on the night the docks were hit.

'No, not at all. She was down at the docks. Everyone thinks I have no idea what she was up to while I was away. But I was under no illusions. I'm not sure we ever really loved each other, you know. She just needed someone at the time.'

Emily breathed in deeply. The room smelt

musky, of sex and Darjeeling. It was an unfamiliar smell to her and one she liked. They had spent almost every night together since the first – not wanting to be apart, and carefully evading Miss Van Gilder's watchful gaze – and she could not imagine sleeping alone ever again.

It started as it always did. They didn't need words. The silence that sat between them was calming and natural, allowing both of them to deal with the past and reconcile the present. He lay on his side and began to trace the outline of her breasts with his finger. Looking into her eyes, he moved down over her thighs.

'Don't close your eyes,' he whispered. 'Look at me.'

She turned her head to the side, embarrassed. 'I can't, I'm still new at this.' She half giggled and then turned to face him. 'I don't really know what to do.'

'Yes, you do,' he said. 'You know very well because you have been the best lover any man could wish for.'

She was smitten. They were delirious with their love for each other and she did not hesitate even for a second. As she wrapped her arms around his neck and pulled him down towards her, she was filled with the confidence of a woman who knew she was loved.

Hattie Lloyd was one of the first to arrive at Mass. Popping her head inside the church, she could see that neither Biddy nor Elsie had turned up yet, so she lit a cigarette and waited by the railings in front of the soot-stained building.

St Angelus was not the most attractive church in Liverpool, but it was one of the best attended. Biddy had once commented that the churches in the smarter parts of Liverpool were so much nicer. 'The poor go to church to pray for help, the rich forget to go and say thank you, but for that they are rewarded by visits from the bishop and a golden eagle for the Bible to rest on. At St Angelus we have a bit of old wood. How is that right?'

Elsie of course had no answer. She just loved her church even more and dedicated an extra hour a week to making the flowers on the altar look that little bit nicer.

When Biddy passed through the gate, she saw Hattie raise her hand, drop her cigarette on the path and grind it out with the toe of her shoe. 'What's got into you?' said Biddy. 'You look like you've won on the pools. Either that or you've got a moth trapped in your knickers.'

'Don't be so vulgar, Biddy,' reprimanded Elsie. 'Not outside the church door, for God's sake.'

'Don't you blaspheme then,' said Biddy.

'Oh for goodness' sake, you two, shut up bickering, will you?' Hattie interjected. 'Sometimes it's more like you two are sisters than friends. Well, listen up now, will you, I have a bit of news for you, I do.'

The bells pealed out loud and clear and the chattering stopped briefly.

For Biddy and Elsie, whose lives were dominated by hard work and routine, hearing the words 'a bit of news' was like receiving a mild electric shock.

Biddy's eyes narrowed; she was instantly suspicious. 'News, what news could you have?' she asked, her voice loaded with disbelief. Hattie Lloyd was not part of the mafia and Biddy wanted to make sure it stayed that way. She didn't want Hattie thinking that a bit of gossip would automatically qualify her for inclusion.

Out of the corner of her eye, Biddy caught a flash of red, and for a second, Hattie's impending news was overshadowed by a moment of wonder at the fashion statement that was Madge, walking in through the church gate.

'Where in God's name did you get that coat?' asked Elsie. It was long and red and it even had a fur-lined hood. 'It's a sunny summer's day, it looks ridiculous.'

'Stop it now, Elsie. I can wear a red coat if I want to. I got it in George Henry Lee's. It was on sale for less than half price. How else am I going to get a fella at my age? I need to wear something eye-catching.'

'No, you don't,' said Hattie. 'You can wear any old cast-offs to bag a fella. Ask Emily Haycock.'

Biddy almost dropped her handbag on the pebbled path and it was just as well, because her first instinct was to whack Hattie with it. 'What do you mean?' she asked. 'Why would you say that?'

The bells stopped ringing for a moment as one of the younger priests walked past. 'Morning, ladies. God be with you,' he said as he disappeared through the door. He was totally ignored. All eyes were on Hattie Lloyd.

'Well,' said Biddy, 'what do you mean?'

'What? You actually don't know? Am I really and truly the first? Well, well, fancy that. I will say, though, you can't deny that she needs a bit of fun, can you? Or him, for that matter. I reckon they are very suited, I do, but I do wish they would come clean and tell you ladies. I can see it's a secret I'm going to have to bear. If they don't want the world to know, then it can't be my place to do it. Mind you, I hope they get a move on, I'm sick to death of hiding behind my bedroom curtains, I am.'

The penny dropped with a clang. Hattie lived next door to Dessie. But that couldn't be right. Emily would have told Biddy. But even as Hattie spoke, Biddy knew it was true. Emily had been unable to wipe the grin from her face for days now and Biddy had guessed something was different, though she'd assumed it was related to work. Everything with Emily always was.

Hattie looked as though she could have bitten her own tongue off. 'How could I be so stupid?' she said out loud. 'You knew, didn't you?' She had let the cat out of the bag and lost her moment of glory.

'Hattie Lloyd, you have been practising for fifty-four years. After a while and with so much practice, it's easy.' Biddy tried to make up ground. 'Of course I knew. I will be honest with you now, obviously I knew. And I had my suspicions it was Dessie, but as you know, she's my boss and I didn't want it spreading around on the gossip mill. But now you know, Hattie, we aren't going to be able to stop that, are we?'

'Oh no, Biddy,' said Hattie earnestly. 'You can depend on me for that.'

CHAPTER 32

Lily sat on a long wooden bench in the hallway of the convent, holding her mother's hand. Sister Therese had told her that morning that the police had been unable to locate her stepfather. 'He's probably dead too,' she'd replied, her voice low with grief. Lily no longer cared.

Her mother was sobbing next to her. She'd followed Lily around all morning like a child. 'Hold your mother's hand,' Sister Therese had instructed, and Lily had, even though it did not feel like the right thing to do. It was an unfamiliar gesture. She tried to recall a time when her mother had held hers, or, much more painfully, Joe's, but the memories failed her; there were none. It was she who had fed Joe his bottles when he was a baby. She who had carried him around on one hip for months on end. Lily had loved her little brother with all of her heart, whereas this woman sitting next to her, her mother, would struggle to recall Joe's smiling eyes, the touch of his fingers on her face, the expression on Christmas morning when Sister Therese had bought him the tricycle, the giggle that made him cough. All of those memories belonged to Lily and were hers to hold and keep for ever. Her mother had nothing. She would miss nothing and, Lily knew, in the shortest time would remember nothing.

The nuns had bathed her mother in attention and she had revelled in it. Lily slowly turned her face sideways and gave her a long look. Her expression was vacant. She tried to feel pity, something, anything, but there was nothing. Her heart was full of pain for Joe and worry for Katie, but for her mother, nothing.

She turned from her mother to Katie, who was enveloped in Sister Therese's habit while they waited for the hearse to arrive at the end of the drive. They had both slept at the convent every night since little Joe had died and in a strange way it hurt Lily to see Katie now looking so well because she was living proof that Lily, in her struggle to hold her family together, had been selfish and wrong. Joe was dead and that was her fault. If she had allowed Sister Therese to take them both into the St Chad's home, he might still be alive. She had never been able to get over the humiliation that her siblings were not orphans and so should not be taken in. She had been determined that while she was there to love and care for them, they should remain at home. She had been so wrong. She had struggled for too long. Her heart felt like lead in her chest. Guilt, sorrow, recriminations, they were all waiting to add their weight, but not today. Today there was room only for pain and grief and Joe.

Her mother sobbed again. Lily ignored her. She had nothing to give. If Lily was at fault, this woman, who spent twice as much time in a public house as she did in her own home, was even more to blame. It had taken her mother almost twelve hours to sober up before she could fully take in the facts, and her reaction had been to head straight back to the pub, to share her news with her wastrel friends and to be bought drinks of pity. Lily knew that after the sorrow and the pain would come hatred and anger towards the woman sitting next to her. Tomorrow, that would come.

'Here it comes now, here's the hearse. I can hear the horses' hooves. Look after your mother now, Lily. You go at the head, I will walk with Katie.'

Lily eased herself up from the bench and pulled her mother up with her.

'Is he here, Lily?' she asked in a pathetic, pleading voice that Lily had never before heard.

Lily nodded. An unexpected wave of pity washed over her for the wretched woman at her side. She took a deep breath as she squeezed her hand reassuringly.

She forced her legs to move towards the door. She could hear the rolling of the cart and the fluster of the horses as they stopped outside. Her heart beat wildly in her chest. She looked down at the mosaic-tiled floor and for a moment studied it as she composed herself and calmed her breathing. She had wanted to open the door, to see him, but now that the moment had arrived, the panic that was threatening to swamp her almost won. Lifting her head, the black-painted door with the two arched stained-glass windows stood before her and through the intricate patterns she could see movement on the drive.

'Wait a minute, Lily.' Sister Therese stepped forward and pulled the black mantilla veil down over her face. Lily had no idea where the clothes she was wearing had come from; she was sure Sister Therese had told her, but like everything else over the past few days, it had gone.

Her mother bent her head, weighed down by shame or fear of the sight that was to greet them as Lily opened the door. There were footsteps on the gravel drive. Someone was walking towards them. Lily thought of Joe, outside, waiting for her, and it was all she needed to give her the courage to make the next move. She put her hand on the large brass handle, turned it and in a second swung open the door.

Father Brennan stopped in his tracks in the middle of the drive. He was a priest, but he was a man and uncomfortable in the presence of a woman's tears. He looked over Lily's head towards Sister Therese. A question passed between their eyes. 'Are they ready, can we leave?' Then he turned his back on Lily, ready to lead the funeral procession.

Lily's eyes were now fixed beyond him, on the tiny coffin. It lay on the back of the flat, open hearse and her heart collapsed at the sight of it.

'He has no flowers,' she whispered. 'There's no flowers,' she said as she half turned towards Sister Therese, expecting her to magic flowers in the wave of a hand. Of course he wouldn't have flowers. Where would the money come from to buy flowers good enough for an angel? For the sweetest, most loving of all little boys.

She had never seen a hearse that wasn't adorned with flowers and she almost screamed out. She wanted Joe to have the best, to be dressed in the most beautiful flowers, to be taken through the streets like the finest of them all, but there were no flowers because there was no money. She wondered who had paid for the hearse. No one had mentioned money to her, or at least not that she could remember. She turned to her mother, wanting to wound her. 'There are no flowers. He may as well be on the rag-and-bone man's cart.'

A gentle shuffling came from behind, one Lily had become used to. The sound of robes rustling and soft shoes gliding along tiled floors.

'Look at the nuns, Lily,' whispered Katie.

Lily dragged her eyes away from Joe's coffin and, turning, saw the nuns lining up behind them, in two rows, heads bent. Without anyone saying a word, they began to chant in prayer. It was haunting. As the sound reached Lily's ears, she was touched by something that had come among them, carried on the wings of the prayers. Lily could feel it; it was heavy and sad and joyous all at the same time. It was the Holy Ghost and it was all around her. She felt as though she could reach out and touch it, take it in her hand and hold it. It had come for Joe, to carry him to the church, to the place where he would rest in peaceful, uninterrupted sleep.

Unlike her mother, Lily didn't cry. Still she held her tears. Father Brennan gestured to Sister Therese to walk down the path and, giving Lily the slightest push, she nudged her onwards. Lily's legs worked and one foot did move in front of the other. It wasn't until she reached the gate, to within touching distance of Joe, that she began to tremble and shake. Her beloved Joe, the little boy she had worried about since the moment he was born, was only feet away from her and all that prevented her from touching him was the wooden casket. But still she did not cry.

She felt Sister Therese reach out and hold on to her coat. Sister was telling her to wait. She remembered that now. She had to stop at the end of the path and wait for the crack of the whip and the horses to move, and she did. Her eyes were fixed on the smallest coffin as Joe began to roll away from her, and as he did, the scream almost escaped. The sudden lurch of the hearse was Joe leaving her and her instinct was to reach out and hold on to it, knowing that if she lifted the lid of the coffin, she could lift him out and hold him in her arms one last time, just one last time. But he was rolling further away and this time it was her mother who squeezed her hand. Turning sharply to look at her, her mother whispered, 'Hold on, Lily,' and the only other sound was of the horses' hooves on the cobbles and the turning of the wheels and the chanting of the nuns. Another faint push in her back and she began to walk once again.

It was as they turned the corner and Clare Cottages came into sight that she saw them. Her neighbours, good and bad, young and old, were standing there, along with their hundred and more children, all of them silent, every last one of them. Mrs McGuffy blessed herself, stepped forward to the slowly moving hearse and laid alongside the coffin a wreath of green and white blossom and rose stems. As she stepped back, another woman held a child up, a friend of Joe's, and he laid down a bunch of daisies. Lily's eyes blurred with tears and all she could see was the outline of men, women and children covering Joe's coffin with armfuls of blossom, wildflowers and variegated leaves. She knew that the blossom had come from the park and the cut flowers were fallen strays scooped off the dockside while the ships were being unloaded.

The women blessed themselves and bent their heads as the hearse passed them, and the men raised their caps in respect to the little boy who had not long ago turned four. Their children looked sad and Lily could hear their tears; children who had played with Joe on his beloved bike, until his mother had finally sold it. His source of pride, pleasure and dignity exchanged for a night in the pub. 'Bye, bye, Joe,' she heard one little boy cry, and then another, 'Bye, bye, Joe.' The air became filled with the low moan of women crying as the tiny coffin passed.

'We don't deserve this,' said Lily's mother. Her crying had stopped, her eyes now dry as she stood in wonder at the actions of her neighbours.

'He deserved it. It's for him, not us. He was better than us.' Lily almost spat at her as she spoke, her anger quickly bubbling to the surface before she took control and it disappeared once again.

The hearse had stopped to allow the women to arrange the flowers. When they'd finished, the sound of the whip cut through the air and the horses continued on their way to the church.

As they moved on, Lily heard footsteps. Turning her head, she saw through the black grid of her veil the residents of Clare Cottages, the children she couldn't bear to hear playing, the women she thought despised her, and even the men, who had today not turned up for work, falling in behind the nuns to walk the hundred yards to the church. They were with Joe, escorting him on his final journey. But it wasn't until the hearse stopped at the church that Lily's tears began to fall. Waiting at the gates were Lockie and the McConaghys and Mrs McConaghy's brother-in-law and the men from the plant and Amy, who also looked tearful. Without a word, Lockie stepped forward and, nodding to Mr McConaghy, they lifted the coffin into their arms and carried Joe down the path to the church. Mrs McConaghy held the largest wreath that Lily had ever seen, tied up with yards of blue satin ribbon.

As Lily turned to look at the crowd of people behind her, she said to her mother, 'All this, it's for Joe. All these people, they're here for him. Imagine if he could see this.'

'He can, Lily,' said Katie. 'He's here. He can see it. Lockie is carrying him. Did you not see him? He was on Lockie's shoulders. I saw him, he waved to me.'

And that was the moment when Lily broke because she knew that Joe truly was being carried, on a wave of affection. People had turned out to mourn him; he was covered in flowers. Joe was loved.

After the service, as the mourners dispersed, Sister Therese gently steered Lily out of the church. 'Mr and Mrs McConaghy have put on a spread for everyone at the Irish Centre,' she said. 'I'll take Katie and your mother with me. I think there's someone who wants to have a word with you.'

Lily thought it must be Lockie and lifted her head to scan the graveyard. But it was Joe's doctor from St Angelus, Dr Mackintosh. He raised his hand and it struck her that he was nervous as he walked towards her. His head was bent and it was obvious from the paleness of his skin and the redness of his eyes that he had shed his own tears too. Her heart reached out to him, across the gravestones.

CHAPTER 33

A my felt faint. She pressed the flat of her hand against the wall to steady herself while she waited for Lockie at the bottom of the steps to the processing plant. Auntie had allowed her to leave a few minutes earlier than usual, but not without a raised eyebrow and a grumble.

'I cannot even recall an occasion when Lily asked to leave early,' she said. 'Have you finished today's order sheets, Amy?'

'Of course I have,' Amy replied as she pushed the pin though her hat, making a mental note to get on to it tomorrow. She had done the same thing the day before and unfinished work was piling high in the drawer, away from prying eyes. It will all get done once Lily comes back, Amy thought to herself, although now even she was beginning to worry that, just maybe, it might not.

'Do you think Lily will be back soon?' she asked her auntie. She was desperate for Lily to return. Amy was nowhere near as competent as Lily and Mrs McConaghy was plainly unimpressed. Her special status as niece and heir was wearing thin now that she was the only person helping.

'How will you manage, Amy,' Mrs McConaghy had asked when Amy had taken herself off for a walk at lunch time, 'when all this is yours?'

Amy had looked around her. I'll sell it, was what she thought, but not what she said.

Mrs McConaghy didn't wait for an answer. 'Lily never took a lunch break,' she said. 'She ate as she worked, although, God knows, she barely ate. I gave her lunch every day. She thought I didn't know, but she used to slip most of it into that basket of hers as soon as my back was turned.'

'She must come back to work soon,' said Amy. 'She can't manage without the money. I'd give her another week and then she'll just turn up.'

'Let's hope so, Amy, because I am very concerned that you are just not cut out for this work. I blame your mother, of course. She has never been a worker herself, but still . . .' She could barely suppress the disappointment in her voice.

When Amy asked to leave early, Mrs McConaghy knew it was to meet Lockie and so she allowed it. She trusted Lockie above all the other traders. 'No one asked him to carry that coffin, nor your uncle; they just did it. That's the measure of them,' she'd said to Amy a hundred times since Joe's funeral.

Standing on the steps, Amy sensed Lockie was near. Turning, she saw him in the distance as he walked up from the docks, the moving cranes his backdrop, the silver strip of the Mersey glinting in the sunshine. She shielded her eyes with her hand to see him better. He was bent forward against the incline of the rise, his cap pulled forward, hands thrust deeply into his pockets. No matter how hard she tried, she could not make her heart flip at the sight of this man. He was too good, too pure, too willing to accommodate her every tantrum.

She put her hand in the air and waved, expecting him to wave back as he usually did. There was no response. He must have other things on his mind, she thought. His own business was growing faster than he could accommodate it and he had told Amy he was thinking of taking on two lads to help, and another horse and cart. 'There's talk of motorized wagons to do the horses' job, but no one around here could afford one of those,' he said. He was always thinking, thinking: how could he stay ahead of the game?

'Hello, how are you? How's your day been?' she asked with enthusiasm.

Time was moving on. She had taken to wearing looser clothes; underneath them, she was showing. She wore her scarf long and over her dress and more than one person had passed comment and made the connection between her size and the amount of cakes her auntie bought. Very soon people would become suspicious and start talking. If she didn't persuade Lockie to marry her, there would be no way out. She might as well kill herself there and then. Her life would become a purgatory, one she could not bear. She would be sent to a mother and baby home as soon as the words 'I'm pregnant' left her mouth. She would be banished from society, her home, her life. The baby would be given up for adoption and she would be sent to Ireland, to an old-fashioned, judgemental relative and she would live out her days incarcerated, expected to help out on one of her uncle's farms. Her parents would never forgive her. Her mammy and daddy would near die with the shame. Her aunt and uncle would disown and disinherit her.

She had no one to turn to for help. Doreen's father had slammed the door in her face when she'd called round to see her weeks ago. Lily had not returned to work since Joe had died and was apparently living in St Chad's with her sister.

Her heart began to beat faster as panic set in yet again, just as it had every day for weeks now, each time her skirt failed to fasten and her hand wandered down over the firm bump in her belly. Lockie had to be her salvation. He was her only way out, but it had to be quick. She had to tie him down and there was no more time. It had to be tonight.

'I'm just the same as I was when you saw me this morning in the office,' Lockie replied.

Amy was about to mention that he'd been as miserable as hell that morning and had barely spoken a word. She'd hoped he would be in a better frame of mind by the evening. 'You weren't too happy then, Lockie. Has the day not got any better? What's wrong?'

Lockie didn't answer her, just looked down towards the river.

'What shall we do?' he asked. 'Shall we get a bite at the café and then go for a drink?' His mind was working overtime and he was struggling to put on a good face. Lily's words had been running round and round in his mind since the night in the hospital.

Lily is jealous, he reasoned. Wants me for herself. She's trying to turn me away from Amy. She can't believe anyone else would want me. He had said those words over and over to himself and yet the more he said them, the less they rang true. He had been unable to let her words go: 'She needs someone to get hitched to and, Lockie, you are proving mighty easy.'

If Joe hadn't died so suddenly, he would have gone to St Chad's and demanded that she explain herself and stop badmouthing Amy. But he had lost his temper instead, on the worst night of Lily's life, and the shame of it haunted him. Still the thought plagued him: did Lily want me for herself? Could that be the case, the reason why she's telling such awful lies? Is she that desperate? Was she hoping I would be the one to give her a hand up out of her miserable life at Clare Cottages? Did Lily want me to save her?

'That'll be great,' Amy answered. She suppressed a shiver. She hated the café. She loved the Grand, but when she'd suggested to Lockie that they walk up town to the Grand for a drink, Lockie had almost laughed out loud. 'The Grand? That place is for nobs. You won't catch me going in there.'

And so they made their way to the café on the side of the docks, where the men with no wives and the shop-girls on their way out for the night called in for a burnt, fat-blackened double egg and chips.

Even the thought of egg and chips had made Amy want to heave, and now, as they walked towards the Grapes, the food sat like a congealed lump in her belly.

Before they reached the pub, Lockie changed his plans.

'Amy, I have to go and see a man about a horse.'

'Since when?' Amy spluttered.

'Since now. Can you make your own way home?' Before she had a chance to reply, Lockie was off and running down the road.

He found Lily's mother, sitting alone in her home at Clare Cottages with the lights off. She was asleep in the chair, drunk, and it was not yet seven o'clock. On his way back down the landing, he saw Mrs McGuffy, standing in her front door, smoking a cigarette with three other women. It looked decidedly like they were gossiping. Throngs of children ran around in the yard, screaming and playing. Some were laughing, some were crying and on the landings little girls were carrying around even smaller babies on one hip.

'You looking for Lily?' shouted Mrs McGuffy.

'You won't find her here, Lockie. She's not been back, she hasn't. Sister Therese has been looking after her since little Joe died.'

Lockie walked over towards the women.

'What about Mrs Lancashire? She's on her own in there, looks like she's already had a skinful.'

'Aye, she has. They took her to St Chad's as well, tried to dry her out, they did, but she kept escaping. Didn't want to be there, she said. You know what she's like for the drink, Lockie. Can't keep the woman out of the pub. You'd have to lock her up to do that.'

Lockie looked back at the door to Lily's house. 'I think it might come to that,' he said. 'Either that, or there'll be another death.'

'I'll make sure that doesn't happen, lad,' said Mrs McGuffy, her voice full of kindness. 'I'll pop in and put her to bed later, just like I did last night and the night before. We look after our own around here. We have to, no bugger else does.'

Lockie doffed his cap and then ran down the stairs. Two minutes later, he was at the door of St Chad's.

Sister Therese wasted no time in telling Lockie that he could not come in. 'I will be getting a bad name,' she joked. 'Our Lily is having that many visitors.'

Lockie raised his eyebrows. Visitors? Who? He decided it must be the McConaghys, although Amy hadn't mentioned anything.

'You can't see her today, Lockie. But come back

on Sunday and I'll make sure she's here for you.' And without another word, Sister Therese closed the door.

Sunday! Lockie paced up and down anxiously. He was desperate to see her. How could he wait that long?

Leaning against the moss-covered wall of the convent, he rolled himself a cigarette and thought about Lily. He thought about everything she'd been through. How she never complained, always put those she cared about first. Then he thought about Amy. He stubbed out his cigarette. He knew exactly what he had to do now.

CHAPTER 34

Dessie stood on the inside of his front door and kissed Emily. He was heading off to the mafia meeting at Biddy's house.

'I feel like a right fraud,' he said as, taking a deep breath, he wrapped his arms around her. 'Something like this isn't supposed to happen to a normal fella like me from the Dock Road.'

Emily's arms encircled his waist and she buried her face in his chest. She loved the way he smelt. The closeness, the mustiness, the maleness. She had grieved for her family for so long, had given all of her time to Alf and hadn't taken seriously the attention of any man, until now.

The wool of his Fair Isle tank-top began to itch her face as she pulled away and looked up at him. Although the evening was warm, Dessie would never dream of stepping outdoors in his shirt sleeves alone.

'So, how do I get out of here then?' she asked with a grin. 'Will I hear the back gate bang?'

She had arrived under the cover of darkness the previous evening and they had spent the day indoors, revelling in the time and space in which to enjoy each other's company.

'Now, I have thought about that one long and hard,' said Dessie, 'and I have a plan.'

'That sounds intriguing.' Emily raised her face for yet another kiss. 'Are you going to share this plan with me?'

'I'm going to have to. Otherwise you'll be incarcerated here for ever. I suggest, my beautiful angel,' Dessie kissed Emily again, 'that we come clean and we go to the meeting at Biddy's house together. I mean, why are we even hiding? Either that or you exit the back way, once you hear Hattie next door leave for the bingo.'

Emily stood back and took both of his hands in hers. 'I think the Hattie to the bingo option, because we don't want to be gossiped about, do we? We don't know what is going to happen.'

A frown crossed Dessie's face. 'I thought you would jump at the chance for us not to have to sneak around. All this cloak-and-dagger stuff, it's hardly normal, is it?'

'I know, Dessie, but we work in the same place and will probably be working together for a long time. It's complicated, isn't it. We don't know what is going to happen to us.'

Dessie took a long deep breath and as he did so he pushed back a tendril of her hair that had fallen across her forehead. He wanted to see all of her face. He wasn't sure if Emily was batting him away or if what she was saying made complete sense. Everything she had said was correct; it was true, but . . .

He looked down at her. Beautiful, innocent eyes and the face of a woman who should by now be a mother. If that was ever to happen for Emily, it would have to be soon. He had nicknamed her his angel because she was just that, and he was afraid that, like an angel, she would one day fly away and leave him to the loneliness and sadness of his former life.

'I find myself trying to imagine what life was like before you, and I just can't,' he said. 'And yet you've only been in my life for the shortest time. I was lonely. My bed was always neat and tidy, but it was cold. I know these things now, but I wasn't really aware of them before.'

'Me too,' said Emily. 'I've spent so much of my life sleeping alone that I thought it would be impossible to actually sleep with someone. No one told me that what happens is you fall asleep in someone's arms last thing at night and wake up in them the next morning. I should have read more books. I might have made more of an effort to meet a nice man; to marry, even. I was clueless, Dessie. So wrapped up in my love of nursing and poor Alf, I forgot about me.'

Dessie pulled her to him and kissed the top of her head. He allowed himself to imagine what it would be like if he woke tomorrow morning and this had all been a dream. The thought filled him with horror. He revelled in Emily's company. Their conversation, the small talk, the lovemaking. The waking up with her in his arms.

'Emily, we aren't a courting couple. We are a couple who have made love, well, I've lost count of the number of times.'

'More than twenty,' Emily chirped.

Dessie roared with laughter. 'Are you really counting?'

Emily blushed and nodded. He blushed too. How could he explain that he simply just couldn't get enough of her? That he was hungry to make up for the time he had lost.

He didn't even think about what he was about to say, the words just fell out of his mouth. They didn't need thought or agonizing consideration. He loved her. It was as easy as that. The most natural thing in the world to say and, yes, to do. He would do it tomorrow if he could.

'It's so wrong,' said Emily. 'But I can't help myself.'

He only half heard her words as an impulsive thought ran through his brain. He knew immediately that it was absolutely the right thing to do, and he couldn't help himself, he just blurted it out.

'Emily, will you marry me? As quickly as possible, so we can stop hiding and tell the world right away.'

Emily felt her heart flip. The tears rushed unbidden to her eyes, faster than she could stop them. She was swamped with an immediate sense of elation. And then it left her, as quickly as it had arrived.

'Oh no,' she said as a look of desolation crossed her face.

'Oh no, what?' Dessie laughed. 'That's not my answer, is it?'

Emily shook her head. She loved Dessie and she already knew that. She couldn't even remember life without him, but there was one glaring and obvious fact that she had momentarily forgotten. St Angelus did not allow married nurses and if she said yes, her career would be over. She would not see her nurses through to the end. Her life's work would be finished. Her school of nursing, her office, her nurses, Biddy. The framework of her life would disappear overnight.

She sobbed. 'Dessie, I can't. I can't marry you. I don't know how. I just can't do it.'

Biddy shrieked at the sight of her cat running out of the kitchen with a salmon-paste sandwich in his mouth.

'You bleedin' little thief,' she shouted as she ran after him, grabbing the mop as she passed the back door. She raced across the back yard, brandishing it as she went and missing Madge and Elsie by a whisker.

'Oh, put that filthy thing down, Biddy, you nearly hit the sponge cake.'

Branna was following close behind and came through the back gate before Elsie had a chance to close it. 'Are we all here then?' she asked, looking down the entry behind her.

'No, Dessie and Sister Haycock have to arrive yet,' said Biddy.

'Ah, well, I'm guessing they will only be along if they can drag themselves out of the bed for long enough.'

Biddy had placed the mop against the yard wall and taken the sponge cake out of Elsie's hands. Now she wished she hadn't as she almost dropped it. 'What bed? Whose? What are you talking about? Why would you say a thing like that?' she shrieked.

'Because it's true,' Branna replied. 'Bryan had to drop the time sheets at Dessie's house and he saw her. She didn't know he saw her though. Bryan took the sheets to the back door and Dessie was acting a bit strange, so he hovered around to see what was going on and not even a minute later they were both there, in the kitchen, kissing. Hattie Lloyd says there's been some funny noises coming from the bedroom too.'

'Well, if a single word of any of that is true, we will know it the minute he arrives. If Dessie is getting his leg over, he'll be like the cat who's found the cream, the lucky bugger,' said Madge.

'Oh, what is wrong with all of you? You are sex mad, you lot. First Hattie spreading rumours and now you, Branna. Is poor Sister Haycock not entitled to a private life? You are a gang of witches, all of you.'

They had shuffled into the kitchen through the back door, Madge's heels wobbling on the cobbles of the yard and Branna's arms folded in indignation. Elsie was in the process of carefully untying her headscarf from over her tightly curled hair when Dessie walked in.

'Evening, ladies,' he said in exactly the same way he always did.

As he turned his back on the group to hang his jacket on the nail protruding from the back of Biddy's kitchen door, Biddy silently mouthed, 'Told you so,' to a baffled-looking Branna.

Branna pulled back a chair and sat down. 'Does anyone know if Sister Haycock is joining us?' she asked with as much nonchalance as she could muster.

Dessie grabbed the chair next to her and, swinging it around, straddled his legs across the seat cowboy-style and folded his arms across the top. He studied the marks etched into the backs of his hands and didn't say a word.

Silence filled the room as, without any awareness that they were doing so, the four ladies stared at Dessie.

'Lovely cake. Can I have a slice?' asked Dessie, leaning forward and turning his gaze on the sugar drizzle. 'I've got such a massive appetite, I could eat the ragman's donkey.'

Biddy cut him a slice and slipped the plate across the table towards him. 'I'll make the tea. Would you like a cup, Dessie?'

'I would,' said Dessie. 'I'm dying of thirst. Am I being greedy if I ask for another slice of that cake? Even though it looks almost too good to eat.'

Elsie swelled with pride. 'You eat as much as you want, Dessie, go on. I'm watching me figure.'

'Hungry, are you, Dessie?' asked Madge.

'I am that,' said Dessie, as, in an ungentlemanly way, he licked the back of his fork.

While Dessie tucked in, a quartet of quizzical eyebrows were raised. Confused looks darted between the ladies as tea was poured and sugar stirred. Branna mouthed to Biddy, 'I'm bloody right.'

The day was fading and the light in the kitchen had dimmed. Biddy flicked the switch on as she walked past with the kettle. The stark lone light bulb was above Dessie's head. All the better to interrogate him by, thought Madge, who until now had been silent. If there was anything going on between Dessie and Sister Haycock, Biddy would get to the bottom of it, that much Madge knew.

Biddy sat down opposite Dessie and cut him another slice of cake. It was Elsie's cake, but it was Biddy's kitchen. Rules were rules. Biddy was a feeder. Dessie was an eater. They worked well together.

'So, what have you been up to on your day off?' she asked him pointedly.

Elsie poured the tea. She was allowed to do that. In the background, the kettle simmered on a low heat as the whistle struggled to burst into song. The clock on the wall ticked down the seconds while the women waited for Dessie's reply. The kettle sang an introduction, the icon of the Holy Mother hanging on the wall strained to hear, and they all waited while he swallowed.

'This and that,' he said before he shovelled in another mouthful. 'Out and about, you know.'

'Hattie Lloyd says she's hardly seen you move beyond the front door recently. Says you've had your curtains closed a lot. She's worried about you. Not been feeling well then, Dessie?'

'She said she's heard a lot of banging on the bedroom wall,' Branna blurted out.

Biddy felt a strong inclination to pick up the teapot and pour it over Branna's head.

Madge only just about suppressed her smile, for fear of Biddy biting her head off.

'I'm decorating the bedroom,' said Dessie. 'Stripping the old wallpaper off. I'm done with peonies on the walls.'

Not one of them failed to notice that Dessie was now bright red.

You're stripping something, but it's not the walls, thought Madge.

Dessie forked another portion of cake into his mouth quickly, before anyone else could ask him another question.

Madge, who thought she had the most to say at the meeting and was now getting twitchy, broke the silence first. She could tell they were not going to get anything out of Dessie, so it was a waste of time trying.

'Can we carry on with the meeting now?' she said. 'I have some very important information, ladies.'

Dessie threw her an appreciative look. She gave him the faintest smile back. Her meaning was clear: your secret is safe with me, Dessie.

Dessie's furtive movements and new-found appetite were all but forgotten as chair legs scraped, bottoms shuffled and three voices chimed in tandem, 'What? What have you got?'

'Well, now, let me tell you.' Madge extracted her notes from her bag. 'There have been some interesting telephone conversations between our Miss Van Gilder and her son.'

'Her son?' The loud and sudden shout could be heard as far as the entry. Even the cat, now perched on the windowsill, stood and arched its back in astonishment.

Madge grinned from ear to ear. She was enjoying her moment. 'Yes, her son. And he isn't just her son, he is also the owner of the Acme cleaning agency. Does that ring any bells?'

'That's the man who's been on the wards with a clipboard and a pen, getting in everyone's way,' said Branna.

'That's right, Branna, and whatever the two of them are planning, she is taking twenty per cent. It's all about money. She was as dragon-like with him on the phone as she is with everyone else.'

'Oh my giddy aunt,' said Branna. 'Would you credit it. The woman's a thief.'

'No, no, surely not. I can't believe she would do anything illegal,' said Elsie. 'You couldn't meet a woman more proper, like. She has a son?' Her brow furrowed in disbelief.

'I can hardly believe this is true. What do you think, Dessie?' asked Branna.

Dessie had put down his cake and was about to reply when Madge added, 'And there's more.'

'Wait!' screeched Elsie, keen to savour the moment. 'Let's have top-ups. We don't want no one jumping up and down now when we all need to concentrate. There is good news here and a plan to be made, just wait.'

Elsie whacked Biddy's gas up full, while Branna busied about taking the steri milk down from the press Biddy had found in the flea market and now loved. It reminded her of home and she would never let it go, no matter how many new-fangled kitchen appliances came on to the market.

'Can I use fresh leaves, Biddy?' asked Elsie.

'I think the occasion demands it, don't you?'

Elsie washed the pot out in the kitchen, humming to herself as the tap ran. When she looked up, the back gate opened and a nervous-looking Emily Haycock stepped into the yard from the entry. Elsie grinned her toothless best effort and waved furiously. A hand raised in response.

'Biddy, get another cup down, Sister Haycock is here.'

Dessie picked up his almost empty cup and pretended to drink. He needn't have worried. The others were more interested in the fact that Emily was about to walk through the door and ruin Madge's news.

Biddy joined Elsie at the sink and rinsed out a cup. 'See, I told you all that was nonsense. If there was anything going on, she wouldn't be turning up here now, would she?'

'Sister Haycock, here, come and sit down.' Branna stood and pulled over a seat from under the window to squash into the now almost crowded table. She threw a look towards Dessie, who appeared to be drinking from an empty cup. It wasn't like him not to be a true gentleman. He would normally have broken his leg trying to be the first to fetch a chair, for any of them. It was his way.

'Something is wrong,' whispered Elsie to Biddy. 'Those two aren't having a fling, nothing like it. They're barely speaking. He hasn't even looked at her yet.'

'That's because he can't, Elsie. Something is wrong, but having seen them both now, I would say 'tis definite that they are. As much as it pains me to say it, Hattie Lloyd was right. Only people who are in love don't speak to each other. They aren't just at it, those two, it's more than that.'

Branna was chatting away to Madge and Emily had sat down and was being almost overly bright and breezy.

'In love? Are you sure?' Elsie almost wobbled as she poured the water into the pot.

'Be careful, you daft bat, you nearly burnt us both there. Yes, I am absolutely sure. And do you know, I'm happy for them. They both deserve a bit of love.'

'Biddy, are you going mad?' Elsie almost hissed. 'She has just said hello to everyone and not a word to Dessie.'

'Of course I saw that. Do you think I'm deaf or what? That, Elsie, is how I know.'

Once the tea had been poured and everyone was seated, Biddy began to explain to Emily what was happening. 'Right, it's the Miss Van Gilder problem. Madge here appears to have made quite a discovery, don't you Madge?'

'I do,' said Madge. 'I was just telling the others that I overheard a telephone conversation . . .'

'Overheard, my arse,' said Biddy.

Madge blushed furiously and shot Biddy a venomous look. 'Anyway, it turns out that Miss Van Gilder's son runs the Acme cleaning agency . . .'

'Her son?' repeated Emily. 'But she is *Miss* Van Gilder. There was no mention of a son at her interview.' She put down her cup and her face went pale. 'She didn't mention her son to us at any time. And to think, she is so against abolishing the married nurses ban. That makes me more cross than anything.'

'Well that's just a part of it, so it appears, Sister Haycock,' Madge said. 'The two of them run the Acme cleaning agency together, it seems. I overheard Miss Van Gilder tell her son that he had made an error on the quotation, that he had to put it right and that she was going to Matron with the quote and then to the board for approval for the funds. She also said that she was taking twenty per cent.'

There was a stunned silence around the table. If it had been any other day, Emily would have felt gleeful at there being so much ammunition against Miss Van Gilder.

'And there is more.'

'Goodness me. More?' said Emily, who was already about to suggest that they telephoned the police.

'She also made a telephone call to a man in Cornwall, making enquiries about a cottage that he had for sale. She told him that she would have half of the money available to put down in about a month and the rest in another three months.'

Everyone began to speak at once.

'A right pair of thieves we have in our midst,' said Biddy.

'We can't just let her go ahead. Shall we tell Matron?' asked Branna. 'Call the police ourselves and be done with it. Throw them in the nick, both of them.'

'No!' Madge almost shouted. 'You cannot tell Matron, I would lose her trust. She would think I was listening in on every conversation. Don't you dare, do you hear? I have a reputation to uphold. I am not a spy and I don't want anyone thinking I am.'

'But what do we do then?' asked Branna. 'That St Dunstan's letter alone isn't enough, is it? It didn't give us any hard facts, and it doesn't prove anything about what she's going to be doing here. Only you have the proof of that, Madge.'

Branna was annoyed that she hadn't been able to bring in any juicy titbits about the Bone Grinder herself. As the domestic on ward two, she was a bit out of the loop. She got all the gossip about her former boss on ward two, Sister Antrobus, and she knew there was no love lost between her and Miss Van Gilder, but that was hardly news – the whole of St Angelus knew that. Now that she wasn't working under her, Branna had come to appreciate the way Sister Antrobus was such a stickler for rules. She wouldn't allow any thieving behaviour, thought Branna. That was for sure. If Sister Antrobus could somehow get to hear the truth about Miss Van Gilder . . .

'I think I can help there, can't I?' said Emily. 'I will be at the forthcoming board meeting. I can question her about what's going on. Probe her until I can trip her up and get the answers we want.'

'What a brilliant idea,' said Biddy. 'Do you think you could catch her out? There is only one way this cleaning agency scam could work and that is if they are overcharging the hospital and laying off the workforce. God alone knows how much hardship that will inflict on everyone.'

'I won't let her leave the boardroom until I have,'

said Emily, smiling for the first time since she had arrived.

While the others digested her proposal, she looked across the table at Dessie. He lifted his head and gave her the saddest smile. Her heart wanted to break in half right there and then. She wanted to run to him and cup his face in her hands and smother him with kisses. She had hurt him. Wounded him. And there was nothing she could do about it. She could not give up her life to marry him. She was Sister Haycock, director of the school of nursing at St Angelus. Confidante of Dr Gaskell. New friend to Matron. Mentor to her student nurses, her girls. She was not a wife. He was the most wonderful man in the world and she had hurt him. The first man she had lain with, given her heart to, and now, only a few hours after they had last been in bed together, they were as good as strangers.

He had not taken her rejection of his proposal well. 'I had forgotten about that,' he said when she'd finished explaining why she had to say no. He was visibly shocked. 'But all women give up working when they get married. That's the normal thing to do. People would think there was something wrong with me, that I couldn't keep my wife, if you carried on working.'

He'd dropped her hands and taken a step past her towards the door, putting distance between them as he ran his fingers though his hair.

'Dessie, it's not about that. It's just that I have

worked for all of my life, no one has ever kept me, and I love my job as much as you love yours. I've knocked down a barrier to get where I am. In many hospitals across the country, Matron is still in charge of nurse training.'

'I must have made a mistake,' said Dessie. 'I thought you were the kind of woman who would want to have a family. To make a home. I thought you would be glad to give up work.'

'Dessie, it's just the opposite. Yes, if I had a family, of course I would want to look after my children and bring them up. But how do we know we will even have children? I can't give up work and sit in a house all day waiting for you to come home. And the rules at St Angelus are that if I get married, I have to give up work, you know that.'

Dessie looked devastated, but he was not a man of words. 'What an idiot I have been, Emily. I am sorry.' And before she could reply, he was out of the door and gone.

And now Emily was sitting across from him, unable to make things better. She clenched her teeth to stop herself from becoming tearful and stood up. 'I have a busy day tomorrow, everyone. I have to go now, but I will do my best at the board meeting. I will trip her up, I don't know how, but I shall.'

She hovered while she put her arms through the sleeves of her coat. She kept glancing towards Dessie, to see if he might follow her. But he sat with his hands resolutely clasped in front of him, leaning on the kitchen table, staring at the crumbs on his empty plate.

'Well, bye then, everyone,' said Emily.

'See you in work tomorrow,' said Biddy.

'Bye, Sister Haycock, and good luck. We're depending on you,' said Branna.

'If I hear anything else, I will let you know,' said Madge, tapping the side of her nose with her forefinger.

Never in her life had Emily taken so long to depart from someone's house. She willed Dessie to stand, to make an excuse, to say he would walk her home. His back remained rigid.

Two minutes later, Emily was standing out in the entry, feeling desolate, lost, and all alone once again. It was worse now than it had been for all those years, because before she hadn't known what she was missing. Now the loneliness took her breath away. She was almost panting; her heart was racing and burnt hot with the pain of it. As she made her way down the entry, the tears blinded her and she stumbled as she ran. Then she heard a voice shout out, a voice she hadn't heard for many years, since the night the bomb fell.

'Emily, is that you, love? Emily, come here, love! It is you, isn't it?'

Maisie Tanner ran towards Emily, her arms loaded with fish and chips wrapped in newspaper.

'I'd put me arms around you, but I'd drop the chips. Come on, no answering me back, follow me. Come on, put your arm through mine. Here.' Maisie slipped Emily's arm through her own. 'You remember the way, don't you?'

Emily did, although it was a long time since she'd last walked down Arthur Street.

An hour later, she was sitting in the Tanners' front room, a teacup and saucer in her lap and a plate of chips next to her on the side table. The house was full of the noise of children, who Emily could tell were keeping their voices down as a result of the firmness in Maisie's whisper.

'Is that Sister Haycock who teaches our Pammy up at the hospital?' she heard Lorraine ask.

Emily wondered how Maisie would answer. Would she say, 'Yes, and she was with me in the air-raid shelter on the night I gave birth to you. She held my hand all the way through until you popped out.' She didn't say that. All she said was, 'Yes, it is. Now go and take your chips next door and eat them there, I'm busy for a while.'

Emily smiled. It was a long time since she had lived on these streets. She remembered how everyone ran in and out of each other's houses and it seemed as though nothing had changed.

Five minutes later, the house emptied of all the Tanner children. Maisie sat down with her own tea in the chair opposite Emily.

'It's lovely to see you, Maisie.' Emily smiled through her embarrassment.

'And you too, love. Eat your chips, go on, don't let them go cold. I've often thought about you. I knew it was you at the hospital, when our Pammy got through on to the SRN course. Me and Stan, we didn't think she had a chance, you know. I said to our Stan, no one from round here ever gets to be one of the nurses. Us lot, we do the cleaning and the laundry. I can't tell you how proud we were.'

'Well, she got in on her own merits,' said Emily. 'Though I can't deny she is one of my favourites.' She looked around the room she had once known well. It was much the same as their own had been. 'Your mam's not here,' she said.

'Me mam? God love her, no. She died ten years ago. She always loved you, me mam, felt dead sorry for you, she did, after that night. She never got over it, you know, Emily. Just couldn't accept why the people she had known all her life weren't around any more or why we had the bombs dropped on us. I kept telling her, it's because we are so close to the docks, Mam, but she didn't hear me. Just kept talking as though everyone was still here and then crying when she realized they weren't. It was awful, just awful. No one really likes to talk about it, you know. Still a bit raw, like. And for people like you more than most. Do you want more tea? Come on, eat those chips up, I said.'

'I can't, Maisie. I'd love to, but I can't.'

'Well, that's because you're upset. Come on now,

I'm going to pour you another cup of tea and you're going to tell me all about it. Our Stan won't be home for ages. It's his pub night tonight. All the men who were in the same regiment in the war, those from these streets anyway, they meet at the same time every week in the Irish Centre. Stan says that's because they don't like to talk about the war when they're at home. Not in front of the kids. And they don't want their wives to know how close they came to being widows. Besides, I wouldn't have a clue what he was talking about, not really. And it was bad enough here as it was.'

Maisie refilled Emily's teacup and launched straight in. 'Right, I know this is man trouble and that is one thing I am good at. I fix everyone's problems around here, me. I'm known for it. No one will disturb us. Our Pammy, she lives in Lovely Lane, but you know all that, you see her there often enough. So go on, tell Maisie what's up.'

Stan was met by his sons at the bottom of the street. They were waiting for him. Maisie was right, it was his veterans' night, but he always went home first to have a wash down in the tin bath and change his clothes. Stan and his mates, they were very particular about standards.

'All right, lads, what are you doing here? Why aren't you in the house having your tea with your mam?'

'Mam says you can't come home for your wash tonight. You have to have your tea an' all down the pub. She's got a crying visitor and she said to tell you you are barred from home.'

'I'm barred, am I?' Stan began to laugh. 'And who's the crying visitor then?'

It was not unusual for there to be someone with a problem in Stan's house. Maisie had become the agony aunt for miles around. 'It's because you're married to the perfect man,' he'd joke. 'They want to know how they can catch a fella just like me. Tell you what, Maisie, it must make you realize how lucky you are to have found me.' Stan usually received a thump at this point or at the very least a slap around his legs with the tea towel.

'It's not funny this one, Da. It's serious. It's the sister from the hospital who teaches Pammy.'

Stan removed his cap, scratched his head and put it back on again. He gazed down the street towards the house. 'Well, well. Emily Haycock. I knew we would see her back in our house one day.'

Little Stan was hopping on one leg from one paving stone to the next, avoiding the lines and cracks.

'Right, I'm off to the pub. Tell your mam I won't be back late.'

Ten minutes later, Stan walked into the Irish Centre and headed to the bar. One of the veterans had already beaten him to it. He had returned from the war with more medals than Stan and seen more action than anyone on the streets. He was a good man. A man Stan liked.

'Evening, Dessie. I thought I would be the first here tonight. We haven't see you for a while.'

Dessie turned around to face Stan, his pint in one hand, his arm leaning on the bar. 'No, I've been, er, a bit busy recently.' He scrunched his eyes. Busy falling in love, that's where he'd been. And now here he was, back on the treadmill of his life. Back to the routine.

'What's up, mate? You look like you've lost the crown jewels. Is it woman trouble? It looks like it to me. Right, let me buy you another pint and you can tell me all about it before the others arrive.'

CHAPTER 35

The residents of Belmullet could count on one hand the number of sunny days they had enjoyed that year. Sadly, not one of them had coincided with Dana's two-week visit home. Diving out of bed, she peered through the curtains and sighed at the bright sky.

'Have you done that deliberately?' she said out loud. The room was cold and slightly damp. She thought of the Lovely Lane home, with its pretty curtains, huge fire in the hallway and bathroom just along the landing. Her room there was never damp. She pulled on the trousers and arran sweater she'd worn almost every day since she'd arrived and drew the curtains back.

Today was the day she would start the long journey back to Liverpool and she would strip the bed and clean the room before she left. Her mother's workload was great; Dana did not want to add to it.

Looking down towards the milking shed, Dana saw her mammy walking up the slight incline towards the house. She carried a pail of milk in one hand and with the other fanned away the midges which swarmed around her face. Dana tapped on the window, but she was so busy saving her skin from being eaten alive, she didn't hear. Dana ran down the stairs, through the kitchen door and along the path to greet her.

'Here, let me take that pail. What's the point of me coming home to give you a break?'

'Oh, get away with you,' said her mammy. 'You'll be gone after lunch. How is it you think I can manage when you aren't here but can't when you are?'

The milk spilled over on to Dana's sneakers. 'Oh God,' she wailed, 'now I'll turn up in Liverpool smelling of stale milk.'

'Aye, stale Irish milk at that. What a lovely smell that will be,' said her mother.

Eyes met and both women burst into spontaneous laughter.

'I don't need your help, Dana, but I'll miss you when you're gone,' said Nancy in a tone of voice she normally reserved for when she was attending a requiem Mass.

Dana stopped and set the pail of milk on the ground so she could swap hands. The metal handle had dug into her palm and, not for the first time, she wondered how her mother had put up with the rain, the toil and Dana's father for so long.

'Will we be seeing you again?' Nancy asked the question as lightly as possible, but her words were loaded.

'Mammy!' Dana tried to appear affronted, but there was one person in the world she could never deceive and she was standing right in front of her. 'Are you seriously asking me would I be ever visiting my own home again?'

Nancy swept up the pail of milk and, with the ease of a woman who had done it every day of her life, set off up the path with Dana hurrying in her wake. 'Well, why not. 'Tis a perfectly sensible question. There's many that leave Mayo and don't ever return. You have hardly said a word about this boyfriend of yours. Is it ashamed of us you are?'

'God, no, Mammy, not at all,' Dana lied. But, as always, her mother had hit the nail bang on the head. That was part of the problem, but by no means all of it. It was also the weight of expectation, that if she turned up at home with a doctor on her arm, one as charming and lovely and funny as Teddy, her mammy would have the banns read the next day and Mrs Kennan would be baking the cake without having even being asked.

'He wanted to come, he really did,' she almost whispered. 'It was me, not him. I wanted to be sure about bringing him back home.'

'Well, what was stopping you then?' Dana's mammy took a look at her daughter's face and knew instantly what she was thinking.

'Dana, you cannot change your past. You are who you are. A girl from a farm on the bogs who has done very well for herself, being a nurse and all. But I will tell you this, if he is a man worthy of you, that won't bother him one little bit. It's who you are when you're with him that will matter, not where you were born. And yes, I know what's going on in that head of yours. The talk of a wedding would have been wild, it would have got as far as Sligo, but so what? He might even have liked it. Found it good craic an' all. Unless of course 'tis us ye are ashamed of?'

In a few words, Nancy had made Dana feel truly foolish. She had voiced her fears and made them sound ridiculous. She felt stupid and elated all at the same time. 'Mammy, I could never be ashamed of you. Shall I bring him home at Christmas? Would you like that?'

'Christmas? Do you have the time off?'

'Not exactly. The week after. And if Teddy can get it, I can invite him and you can meet him then.'

Her mammy's eyes filled with tears. 'Well, fancy that, our Dana bringing a doctor home. I'll have to invite Father Michael round for tea and let Mrs Kennan know to stock up.'

And once again, both women were laughing, this time in each other's arms.

Teddy signed the cheque at reception and scanned the bill once more before he handed it over.

'That all seems to be in order,' he said as the hotel manager handed him the receipt.

'Thank you, Dr Davenport. Is Mrs Davenport packing?'

'Yes, she is having one last check around the room.'

'Ah, yes, the ladies always do. What would we do without our efficient wives.'

Teddy felt himself begin to blush and, turning, looked out of the large bay window and pretended to admire the flowers and the fountain on the front lawn. 'Your gardener does an excellent job,' he said, changing the subject.

'I shall tell him you said so, Dr Davenport. He does enjoy hearing feedback from the guests.'

Teddy was saved from any further attempt at small talk by the sound of Sarah Makebee coming up behind him.

'I'm here, darling,' she said breathlessly as she crossed her perfectly gloved hands in front of him. 'Are the bags in the car?'

'They are,' said Teddy as he took out a cigarette and lit it.

'Oh, Dr Davenport, here is the gardener himself, perhaps you would like to pass on your comments. It is a great morale booster for the staff.'

Teddy hesitated. The one thing he'd noticed about being a doctor was that people treated you as though you were royalty. It was not an aspect of the job that he disliked, in fact he liked it a great deal. It was just that at this moment he was feeling very uncomfortable. A woman with red hair had walked across the car park and for a split second he had thought it was Dana. It was a reminder of his other life. His real life in Liverpool with Dana and at St Angelus. His having cheated on Dana for the very sophisticated Nurse Sarah Makebee would be frowned on by almost everyone. He would not be forgiven for a very long time. Dana was popular. He was popular, but that was all about to change.

While Sarah slid elegantly into the leather upholstered front seat of the car, Teddy walked over to the gardener, who almost dropped his wheelbarrow as he approached.

'Lovely garden. The flowers are a delight. Must be a lifetime's work to maintain all this.' Teddy swept his hand to take in the huge borders and immaculate topiary.

'Thank you, Dr Davenport. I'm from Liverpool, you know.' The news that a doctor was staying at the hotel had obviously spread.

'Yes, I did detect the accent,' said Teddy with a twinkle in his eye.

'I moved here after the war, when I was demobbed. I like the quieter way of life up here, couldn't stand all that noise and bustle in Liverpool. It looked worse after the bombs than some of the battlefields I had been on. Mind you, I'm off to visit the sister and her husband tomorrow. I'm to help clear the rubble away from one of the churches. My old church, as it happens. All this time and there's still bomb rubble all over the place. Unbelievable. I visit twice a year, always glad to get back here though. Anyways, I hope I don't bump into you. St Angelus is the last place I want to find myself.'

'I don't want to see you either,' Teddy said, shaking his hand. He was back in his car and down the drive within minutes.

'You seemed keen to get away,' said Sarah as she applied her lipstick. She almost made Teddy slam on the brakes in shock at her next sentence.

'Teddy, darling, these past few days, it's been lovely and everything, but do you mind terribly if we don't tell anyone?'

'Well, no, no,' Teddy spluttered. 'Why?'

Sarah opened the clasp of her handbag, slipped her compact inside and clicked it shut.

'Well, it's just that my boyfriend is starting at the hospital next week. He's a registrar in London and if he knew, well, he wouldn't be very happy.'

It was a few seconds before Teddy could speak. 'And here was I, the big I am, thinking you would be telling everyone and I would be the most unpopular man in the hospital for cheating on Dana.'

Sarah laughed. 'Oh heavens, no, why would I do that?'

Teddy felt hurt. He was confused. Had he wanted her to do that? 'Well, I'm not sure. Girls generally do.'

'Really? Not in my experience. Not my sort of girl.'

Silence fell between them as things began to fit into place. To Teddy's surprise, Sarah had turned out to be far from a virgin and had in fact taught him a thing or two between the sheets. It was news to Teddy that women actually had orgasms. He had rather stupidly thought that sex was something women endured. He had arrived in the Lake District with the vestiges of youthful naïveté still clinging to him, and now he left it well and truly a man.

'Well, if that's what's happening, I take it you won't mind if I pick up where I left off with Dana?'

'Oh God, no,' said Sarah. 'Suits me fine.'

Teddy thought he should feel better than he did. He had enjoyed a fortnight like none he had ever known. He'd lost count of the number of times he'd made love to Sarah, but it hadn't been love-making. Not really. It was nothing more than sex and a polite regard for each other and a few shared meals. 'Oh, and the walk,' Teddy said out loud.

'What, sweetie?' asked Sarah.

'Oh, nothing, I was just thinking aloud. Sorry.'

In his mind's eye, Teddy saw Dana's face. She was laughing and lifting her face up to him to be kissed. As he slammed down through the gears to turn a corner, he realized he had just nearly lost the thing in the world that was most precious to him. He had almost thrown away his happy future and the perfect wife. But somehow, because he wasn't the catch he thought he was, Sarah was more interested in her present boyfriend than him. What a lucky break, Teddy thought.

He had already decided that when Dana's boat docked he would be waiting for her. And next time she went home to Ireland, no matter what she said, he would be with her.

CHAPTER 36

'Can we have an X-ray for this wee lass, please,' Dr Mackintosh said to Pammy. 'Bilateral tib and fibs.' As Pammy turned to go and collect an X-ray request form from Doreen, he whispered, 'Dad is fine, the car is fine, but this little lass will be lucky to walk straight ever again. Father said he braked to miss a dog and she slammed bang into the dashboard. Her nose is broken to smithereens and her legs don't look great.'

The screams of pain from the young girl had filled the casualty department. The sight of her own blood-covered body had terrified her as much as the inability to move her legs. She had fought against having the diamorphine so Dr Mackintosh had tried to personally calm the fear away. He held her hand and spoke to her in soothing tones in the hope that if she was pacified, the drug could take hold. He couldn't inject any more and feel safe doing so. Finally, the screams had subsided, replaced with pathetic sobs, and as a result the department was quieter once more.

When Pammy reached the clerk's hatch, Doreen's

face was full of concern. 'Is that little girl going to be all right?' she asked as she handed the form to Pammy along with some carbon paper. 'Don't forget to put the carbon paper between both sheets. We need three copies.'

'The poor kid, only five years old. Have you got a pen, Doreen? I've lost mine somewhere, again.'

'Nurse Tanner, I don't believe you have ever had one! No one can lose as many pens as you do.'

'Oh, I have! Honestly, I nearly bandaged one inside a broken arm yesterday.' Pammy shot an anxious look towards the cubicle where the little girl was now dozing. 'I do it all the time. Thank God I always notice, or the patient does, just in time.'

Doreen shook her head and smiled. Having worked on casualty for so long, she knew just how much happened more by luck than good management.

'The little girl will live, but Dr Mackintosh says it will be a miracle if she ever walks straight again. These new cars, they are so fast and dangerous,' said Pammy. 'Me own dad wants one. Me mam says never. She wants a telly first, but they can't even afford that. Me dad says that when a telly can reach fifty miles an hour with no trouble at all, like the cars do now, she can have one.'

'Well, at least the little girl will live, that's the main thing,' said Doreen.

Dr Mackintosh handed the girl's distraught

father a cup of tea and sat down on the hard wooden chair next to him. 'Your wee lass is going to be fine once we've operated. But we won't do that just yet. First job is getting on top of her pain and I want some clear X-rays.'

The girl's father, smartly dressed and well spoken, could barely hold back his tears. 'I don't know how it happened, Doctor. I wasn't even driving very fast.'

'You drink your tea. We will take her straight up to the children's ward from X-ray and we can have a proper chat just as soon as I know the extent of the damage. I know it wasn't your fault and no one is blaming you.'

Anthony patted the smart man gently on the shoulder then looked up as a woman ran through the casualty doors carrying a child in her arms. She headed straight for Pammy.

'Nurse, Nurse, he pulled the chip pan down on top of himself!' She was screaming and casualty flew into action, just as it always did when a burns case came in, which it did about once a day.

'I told him the chips weren't done, but he's always hungry, he couldn't wait. Help him! Help him quick!' the mother screamed.

Anthony looked at the clock on the wall. He had arranged with Sister Therese to visit Lily at St Chad's in less than an hour. To see how she was, nothing more. The memory of her tear-stained face in the graveyard after her brother's funeral haunted him. Her paleness accentuated by the black mourning clothes, her vulnerability as she'd waited quietly while he came over to talk to her. He'd wanted to take her in his arms and comfort her, but of course he hadn't. Today he would be able to see how she was. But unless someone came to relieve him on casualty, it was never going to happen.

Lily didn't hear Sister Therese enter the room or see her approaching. She heard and saw very little. Her mind was preoccupied with memories and pain and she lived almost in her own world. A world where the nuns woke her and Katie, where they fed the two of them, sent Katie to school and allowed Lily to sit in the chapel or her spartan room. She spoke, but not often. Ate, but not much. Cried, all day every day at first, and then with periods of quiet, anguished guilt and regret in between.

'Lily, you have a visitor.' Sister Therese left a moment of silence for Lily to reply. There was none and so she continued. 'It's Lockie. He came by the other day and I told him to come back today. He'll be waiting over the road, I imagine.'

She took Lily's cardigan down from the wardrobe and held out the sleeves for her to slip her arms into.

'Come on, up you get. 'Twill be nice to have a chat. He can tell you what's going on down at the processing plant. Give you all the gossip. There is a world out there, Lily, and it's still turning round and round.'

Lily looked up in surprise. Sister Therese had shown her nothing but sympathy and kindness, but now there was an edge to her voice. Lily didn't want to see Lockie. The thought of walking as far as the church gate was exhausting. She had nothing to say. No interest in the McConaghys or the plant or the gossip or anything else. Did Sister Therese not understand? Joe was dead and buried. The world had stopped. Sweet, brave and so-grown-up-beyond-his-years little Joe, with his fair hair and bright blue eyes and all his trusting innocence and unquestioning, perfect love, was dead. The sob came before the tears; it always did.

'There, there. Come on now, stop the tears. You are worrying us all sick and making yourself ill, you know that, don't you? And do you think Joe will be happy up above, looking down on you with your crying all the time?'

Sister Therese had wrapped her arms around Lily's shoulders. She pulled her in towards her and hugged her tight, like she always did. The tears soaked right through her habit. Always a nun and never a birth mother, she felt that God had put her there, in that place, to absorb Lily's pain. To carry it into church, damp on her own heart. To lift it up to God and hand it over into his care. 'Take the weight of this sadness, it is too much for her to bear alone,' was the prayer she said five times a day as she knelt, her shoulder still cold and wet with Lily's tears. 'Take away her guilt, oh Lord,' was the second prayer Sister Therese uttered, for Lily could not stop blaming herself for Joe's death.

She waited for Lily's sobbing to subside, then gently pressed her. 'Lockie has come to see you. Now that's a friendly thing for him to do, is it not? And that nice Dr Mackintosh is coming to see you today too. Did you remember that?'

Lily nodded. She had. He was a kind man. As she recalled his words in the graveyard after the funeral, she felt a lifting of the heaviness.

'I will come and see you at St Chad's, if that would not be intruding. Just to check up on you. To see if you are well.'

'But I'm not sick,' she'd replied.

'Well then, maybe I could just come and visit. To reassure myself that you are well. Could you bear that, do you think?'

Lockie watched Lily's every step as she walked towards him. Her hands were thrust into the pockets of her cardigan. Her head was bent and the wind lifted her hair and blew it about her, all but obscuring her face. Her feet barely left the floor as she went, as though the effort was too much. The air of dejection she carried about her brought a lump to his throat. This was not the Lily he had known for all of his life. Lily with her jaunty step and bobbing ponytail and the wide, welcoming smile that he'd become used to each time he opened the door at McConaghy's. This cowed figure was so low, so troubled, so full of pain. He had expected that, but not this stumbling ghost of the Lily he had once known.

His heart stopped as a tram came trundling into view and she appeared not to notice. 'Lily!' he shouted. She failed to hear him. 'Lily!' he shouted, louder still. There was no recognition.

He looked over at the face of the tram driver, but the driver wasn't looking back.

'Lily!' Lockie roared. And this time, without waiting for a reply, he ran. There was no time to think, not a moment to consider his actions. Lily was walking into the path of the tram and he had to act.

He screamed her name as he covered the ground between them, running faster than he had ever done in his life. He kept his eyes focused on her stumbling form, on her windswept hair, and thanked God her pace was slow. With his lungs fit to burst from the exertion and his heart pounding in his chest, he heard the bell of the tram ring furiously in protest. But he had no time to look. He had to reach Lily, he had to be by her side. Everything now made perfect sense. He had been the worst kind of fool not to have known it earlier. The heartache he could have saved her from, the love he wanted to give her, the home he was desperate to provide for her.

'Lily!'

This time she looked up. The tram bells rang again and she saw Lockie on the tracks. Her hands flew to her mouth in disbelief as, with one leap, he was beside her, hands on her shoulders, both of them staggering backwards. People in the tram stared out of the window in amazement. The driver waved his fist. Passengers shook their heads in disbelief.

Lockie placed both of his hands on his knees and bent over, pulling in long gulps of air. 'Lily, I thought you was done for there, I did.' Aware of the insensitivity of this remark, he quickly added, 'Oh, no, I'm sorry, I didn't mean that. That was a stupid thing to say, Lily. I'm sorry.'

He expected her to turn and walk away, but instead she said, 'Lockie, your cap, it's on the track.'

He spun round, checked that the tracks were clear and ran back to retrieve it. With a quicker step, Lily followed.

'How ar' ye?' he asked as she drew near. He reverted to the safety of the greeting used by the Irish community he had lived among for all of his life. 'Are ye well?' Again, he could have bitten out his tongue. 'I'm sorry, I'm a stupid eejit, but you already know that, eh, Lily?'

Lily nodded. She almost smiled at the ridiculousness of his question. How was she? She had never been worse.

'People always say when they're feeling grand, don't they?' Lockie filled the silence with impulsive words. 'But they don't like to say when they are the other way, you know, not so grand. It's all right to say, "I'm top of the morning," but you never hear anyone say, "It's the worst day of me life." Why do you think that is then?'

He snapped a twig off the privet hedge and began pulling the leaves off one by one.

'Thanks for coming.' It was all Lily could manage in response.

'You don't have to thank me, I wanted to come. How long are you staying at the convent? I went to Clare Cottages, to your house. Mrs McGuffy, she's taking care of yer mam. She was asleep in the chair when I went. There won't be anything you can do about your mam, Lily. It's you and Katie you have to think of now. Mrs McConaghy, she's paid the rent man.'

Lily opened her eyes wide in surprise. 'How?'

'Well, Sister Therese went down to the plant and she told them and they said they would be glad to pay it until you were back on your feet. Sister Therese said it was the easiest arm she had ever twisted.'

Lily was aware that at the very least she should feel grateful, but she could feel nothing. She nodded her head. Despite the anger she harboured towards her unkind, alcoholic mother, she was relieved to know she was OK. Maybe somewhere inside her there was a shred of love for her mother, but it was hard to locate and even harder to show.

'I can't go back home, Lockie.' The sob came and then the tears. Lockie's arms opened and just as she did with Sister Therese, she fell into them.

He tightened his arms around her. He wanted to kiss her tears away, but now was not the time. He wanted her to melt into him and he into her. She was so thin, he could feel her heart beating against his chest. And then he couldn't help himself. He placed his fingers under her chin and, lifting it towards him, he looked into her eyes for a long moment then bent his head to kiss her gently.

There was only the faintest response. Not wanting to move things too quickly, to scare her away, he stopped and pulled her into him once more. Taking each side of his donkey jacket, he wrapped it around her.

Only her head popped out of the opening and she felt his warmth seep into her bones. She wanted to stay there for ever.

'I'm sorry, Lily,' he said.

From deep inside his jacket, she could barely hear him, but she didn't need to. She pressed her cheek harder against him.

'I was a stupid, vain eejit to think that you were saying all those things just to stop me from being with Amy. I've never heard you say a bad word about anyone, so why would you have started when little Joe was sick? You wouldn't. It was me. You were just worried about me. You are always worrying about someone and I couldn't see it. Will you forgive me, Lily?'

Lockie spoke into her hair. 'Will you?'

Lily had no words; it took such effort to speak.

She had to dig down deep inside to find anything to say and it was just all so exhausting. She nodded.

He was happy with that. It was enough for now.

'You don't have to worry no more, Lily. You and Katie, I am going to look after you both and we will find a way to take care of your mam too. We will get our own house. I'm ready now, to take on extra lads, and this time next year it's my own plant I'll have. And, Lily, we will be working for ourselves. Us. You, me, Katie and our own children. One day soon, Lily, all this will feel better and you will be happy again.'

Lily made no response. How could she tell Lockie that she would never be happy again? How could he understand that?

Anthony Mackintosh urged his car up the hill with the accelerator pedal flat to the floor. One of the housemen had arrived and had taken over the chip-pan casualty. He had trained during the war and was no stranger to burns. The little girl with the broken nose and the legs smashed in four places was resting, awaiting her X-ray results. Anthony had arranged a time with Sister Therese and he didn't want to be late. He was a man of his word and it was important to him that he made a good impression on the nun.

As it was, he didn't have to knock at the convent because Lily was already standing at the gate. His heart lifted. That must mean she was keen to see him. That she was feeling lighter in her mood, less sad and tearful. At first he didn't notice Lockie, but then he saw the flash of the dark coat behind her. Something made Anthony depress the brake and bring the car to a stop. He switched off the ignition. Lily hadn't seen him and neither had Lockie, who appeared to have eyes only for Lily. He heard the faintest of goodbyes brought on the breeze into the car. Lockie was leaving. He was smiling. He turned to Lily, put his arm around her shoulders, pulled her to him and kissed the top of her head.

Friends kiss each other, Anthony told himself. Friends do that. Lily had told him she and Lockie were just friends, hadn't she? Friends from a long way back, at work and home. But Anthony's stomach had turned to jelly and it was telling him something else entirely.

Anthony watched as Lily half smiled back up at Lockie. It was faint, but it was a smile. If she would just look over at him in the car, give him a fraction of that smile, he would be a happy man. She appeared to be comfortable with Lockie's arms around her, buried in his coat, as though it was a place she was used to.

And then Lockie bent his head, kissed her lightly on the lips and took his leave. Friends don't kiss each other on the lips. He needed to tell himself that only once. He was too late. Lockie had beaten him.

As she watched Lockie walk away down the hill, the smile fell from Lily's face. She did not return his wave, but nor did her gaze falter.

Anthony placed his hand on the chrome handle of his car door, ready to pull it down, hear the click, open the door. Ready to step out of the car and walk across the road to the convent. He would raise his hand in greeting, ask her how she was, tell her he'd been worried about her since the funeral. No, he would tell her the truth. That he'd not been able to think about anyone or anything else since the funeral. That she lived in his heart and his head and that he was sick for her.

But his hand didn't move. It trembled slightly as it rested on the handle. Lily didn't turn. She thrust her own hands into her pockets, flicked her head to let the wind push the hair out of her face, and stared at the road that Lockie had walked down only a moment before.

Anthony's hand pressed down harder. The handle gave way. 'Look over, look over, see me,' he whispered. He willed himself to get out of the car, but he couldn't. He had spent so much of his life alone, this stepping out towards something else altogether, it was too much. His heart told him to cross the road, but his head told him to drive away. He had lost and he knew it. He lifted his hand from the handle and, turning the key, started the engine and drove away, back to safety and the lonely life he knew.

Lily turned towards the convent. She had watched Lockie walk away and as he did, it occurred to her that she loved him too. She didn't have the energy to feel exhilarated, her stomach didn't flutter at the thought, but he made her feel safe, as if all her cares had slipped from her shoulders. Her and Katie, they would survive. Lockie would look after them. She would never have to return to McConaghy's. She could take time to heal and to learn to love Lockie back. One day, she would wake up and her life could begin again and when that day arrived, Lockie would be there.

She heard the car and turned to look. She recognized the driver, the side of his face, even though he was wearing a hat. It was Dr Mackintosh. Sister Therese had told her he was coming and she had known why. There would always be a special place in her heart for the man who had been with Joe at the moment he died. For the man who had tried to save him. But it was not the love she could one day have for Lockie. Dr Mackintosh was not of her world. A lifetime would pass before he could understand the pain she had known. But Lockie did understand. He had known and protected her since she was a child and her future was with him. It was something she knew, and with that knowledge, the first layer of sadness fell away.

CHAPTER 37

Within minutes of seeing Lily with Lockie, Anthony walked back into casualty. He'd been away from the unit for less than an hour. Nurse Tanner waved at him from the office, where she was talking to Dr Gaskell. As Anthony made his way over to the hatch to talk to Doreen, he saw Dr Gaskell leave the office and slip behind a set of curtains with a pack of case notes in his hand.

Doreen was typing out case notes.

'Anything in for me?' he asked her.

'No, Dr Mackintosh. We thought you were done for the afternoon. It's all easing off now.'

His heart sank. He preferred it when it was busy.

'Nurse Tanner is helping Dr Gaskell, you could see if they need anything.'

He walked over to the office. As soon as he got there, Pammy began speaking at the speed of a train.

'We weren't expecting you back so soon, Doctor. Being a workaholic, that's a disease, you know. I'll see if I can get someone round here to treat you, shall I?'

Any other day, Anthony would have smiled. There was something about Nurse Tanner. She spoke to everyone she met as though she had known them for all of her life. He liked that. Many of the nurses treated him as though he were God himself, which he did not like. It made him feel isolated, enhanced his loneliness.

'You know what you need, don't you?' said Pammy.

Anthony looked surprised. 'Who says I need anything?'

'I do,' she said. 'Look at your face, you can't even crack a smile any more. What you need is one of me mam's roast dinners. Usually served at three o'clock, but because I'm working, it's later today. Now I know you aren't supposed to be here, so come on. Come round to our house for a roast. Honest to God, Maisie Tanner's roasts are famous. I bet anything you like, you'll be prescribing them after you've tasted one.'

Anthony was speechless.

'Great, that's a yes then. We leave in twenty minutes, but be prepared, when the street knows there's a doctor in our house, they'll be queuing up outside.'

An image of Lily flashed into his mind. Pammy Tanner was nothing like Lily Lancashire; maybe that was just what was needed. Pammy was offering to be his friend and, for a man like him, that was a good place to start.

'Lovely, thanks. I'll bring the car round to the

601

front,' he said. 'Are you sure your parents won't mind?'

'Mind?' said Pammy. 'Mind? They'll be talking about it for weeks. I wouldn't be surprised if me mam puts a notice in the *Echo*. A car, eh? God, fancy that! Me mam'll have a heart attack. Not just a doctor, a doctor in a car.'

Anthony grinned for the first time in a long time. 'Well, I hope she doesn't have a heart attack, but if she does, I might be able to help.'

'Oh, right, yeah, of course. Look at you, smiling now. See, it suits you. Right, I'm off to hand these notes to Doreen. See you at the front in twenty.'

On her way over to Doreen, Pammy slipped behind the curtains to where Dr Gaskell senior was sitting on a trolley and, given his age, looking rather silly.

'First time I've sat on one of these,' he said. 'Jolly uncomfortable.' 'You did well there,' said Pammy, 'getting out of the office before Dr Mackintosh came in. We might have known – you know what they say, talk of an angel and hear the flutter of its wings. As soon as you started taking to me about him, I might have guessed he would walk in and catch us. I'm superstitious like that, me. Anyway, all done! It was easy really. He's coming to ours for a roast tonight. Me mam, she'll sort him out. He just needs a bit of home cooking and a good talking to by me mam.'

Dr Gaskell smiled. 'Good girl! That's just the ticket, a smashing idea. You did well there. Give your mother my best when you see her, Nurse Tanner.'

Pammy was on her way back out through the curtains. She swung around. 'Me mam? You know her?'

'In a manner of speaking. I looked after your grandmother when she had pneumonia.'

'Of course you did,' said Pammy. 'That was the old days, wasn't it? You looked after everyone and everyone loved you for it. You're a hero on our street. You are, you know.' She smiled a smile well beyond her years and without another word stepped through the curtains.

Maisie Tanner paced her kitchen, waiting for Stan to return. On the range sat a pan filled to the brim with carrots and swede. At the side was another full of spring greens.

'Where the hell is your father?' she snapped as Lorraine walked into the kitchen, a book hanging from one hand and a bemused look on her face.

'He was down the Irish Centre with his old soldiers as far as I know. What time is our Pammy coming? I'm starving. I hate having to wait for me dinner on Sundays. Is little Stan in the outhouse?'

'Lorraine, I've never known anyone ask as many questions as you do. Little Stan is in the outhouse, yes. He gets more like your father every day. Went in there an hour ago with a copy of *The Beano*.'

Lorraine flung open the kitchen door and,

standing framed in the opening, shouted, 'Little Stan, get out! I'm bursting.'

'Lorraine, pipe down. Do you want everyone in Arthur Street to know our business?'

No sooner had Maisie finished speaking than Stan opened the back gate. 'You bursting, are you, love?' he said to Lorraine. 'They all heard that down in the pub. Someone's running up with a pot for you.'

'Dad!' squealed Lorraine. 'Stop it! No, they didn't. Get little Stan out of the toilet then.'

'My pleasure, love. Stanley!' Big Stan opened the toilet door wide, revealing little Stan sitting in contemplation, his trousers around his ankles, his face buried in *The Beano*.

'Daaad, stop it!' Little Stan threw *The Beano* to the floor and in one leap left the toilet seat and made to close the outhouse door again.

A fight between little Stan and Lorraine broke out in the yard. Big Stan stepped into the kitchen just as *The Beano* flew across his path. He kissed the cheek his wife offered to him.

'Them two, what are they like, eh?' Stan removed his cap and in one carefully aimed throw sent it sailing through the air to land squarely on the nail in the door. 'Yes!' he exclaimed and punched the air. 'The day I miss is the day you will know I'm going gaga.'

Maisie was not in the least impressed. 'Where have you been, Stan? I thought the dinner was going to burn.'

'Oh, that looks as good as it smells,' said Stan. 'My favourite, brisket. Shall I make the gravy?'

'No, you won't. I know you, you just want to take all the credit when all you've done is swan in in the last few minutes. I'm going to plate up, though, for Mrs Cunliffe. I'll do that first and then you can run down the road with it in a bowl wrapped in a tea towel while I serve out the rest. She can have hers while it's nice and hot then.'

'I'm here to please, Maisie.' Stan lifted the cushion on the chair to extract the *Daily Post* he had slipped under it the previous day.

'No, you don't,' said Maisie. 'Put it back. I need you to mash in a minute. Stan, have you had a chat with Dessie? Do you think we can get him round here for his tea and I'll get Emily Haycock. Could we pull that one off, do you think?'

Stan lifted the lid off the potatoes, took a sniff, asked, 'Are they ready?', placed it back down, turned his back on the range and rested on it while he thought.

'We could have a go. Invite them both over, but us not be here. We could take the kids to the pictures and leave their plates on the table with a couple of candles. How does that sound?' He began to giggle. 'Bloody ridiculous, that's how it sounds.'

'What can we do, Stan? They are obviously potty about each other, it's such a shame. They won't even speak to each other now. I saw Biddy down at the bingo and I told her, like, that I had seen

Emily coming out of her house and brought her into mine and she said, well, I wouldn't worry no more, not a word has passed between them. The whole hospital knows now, she said, because they avoid each other like the plague and it's so unlike them both, so unnatural. It's a right mess. How can two people be so stubborn?'

'What are you like, eh, Maisie? A right little Cupid, you are. Always trying to match people up.' Stan wrapped his arms around her and hugged her to him. 'It was so easy for us, wasn't it? Both at school together. Born only houses away from each other. I can't remember a day in my life when you weren't there.'

'Love isn't meant to be difficult. It shouldn't be a hardship or awkward like it is with those two,' said Maisie.

'If every man had someone like you to come home to, there would be no wars. You know that, don't you? We are lucky, but not everyone is.'

A scream from the outhouse filled the kitchen. Lifting her head, Maisie saw Lorraine sitting on the toilet and little Stan running back in from the door he had opened wide.

'Well, speaking of wars, there's always little Stan and our Lorraine to help out,' said Maisie. They both grinned at the antics of their usually well-behaved offspring.

Lorraine screamed as she shook her legs and threw her shoes out of the door, aiming them at her brother. 'Dad! Dad!' she screamed. 'Get him!'

There was no reply from Stan as suddenly neither he nor Maisie could speak. There was a tall, strange man they had never set eyes on before standing in the middle of their kitchen and Pammy was standing next to him, looking as though she wanted the floor to open up and swallow her.

'Mam, Dad, this is Dr Mackintosh, from casualty. I've brought him home for some dinner.'

Maisie's answer was interrupted by an Izal toilet roll flying in through the back door and landing right at her feet.

CHAPTER 38

Emily pulled up the sash window and, unwrapping the greaseproof paper, took out the bread crusts to lay on the outside ledge.

'Where are you, Gully?' she said as she stuck her head out and looked left and right. There was no beak peeking from behind the drainpipe, waiting for her. No cautious staring eyes or padding feet edging closer. He was gone.

Emily smiled as she stared out at the canopy of dense white cloud, over the rooftops of the hospital and across to the grey and cold-looking Mersey.

'Good luck, Gully,' she said. She was about to pull the sash back down when she heard him call. He was standing on the roof of the porter's lodge, a building she had averted her eyes from for days. She had not wanted the embarrassment of having to make eye contact, should Dessie walk in or out of the lodge.

'Go on! Go!' she said to the bird. 'Get lost. Go and find yourself a wife and make gully babies.'

And at that, he flew off the roof of the lodge and soared away, down to the docks. Emily felt close to tears. He had been waiting for her, to show he could fly and to say goodbye.

Emily jumped as Biddy came up behind her. 'Has he finally flown off then, your little seagull?'

'You knew?'

Biddy looked at her with disdain. 'Did I know? Of course I knew. I know everything. That's at least your second one this year, isn't it? They sometimes leave the nest too young and when they do, they have to hang around for a while, scrabble for a bit of food until they're strong enough to fly. You did a good job with him. Mind you, they are bloody everywhere, so don't go doing it too often. It's a hospital we work at, not a bird sanctuary. Are you ready for this board meeting? It's all on your shoulders now, you know. Everyone is depending on you.'

Emily swallowed hard. 'I'm ready, Biddy.'

'Good. What's your plan then?'

'Well, I don't have one.' Emily looked sheepish.

It was a look Biddy was familiar with. 'You don't have one? How are you going to expose her for the thieving con-woman she is then?'

'I don't know, Biddy, but I will.'

'Sister Haycock, the last time you attended one of the board meetings, we ended up with Miss Van Gilder as assistant matron. Is this "I don't know" malarkey a good thing?'

Emily was in no mood for being contradicted. 'It's the only thing we have, Biddy, and if you will excuse me, I am going to be late for the meeting.'

With a flounce, she turned on her heel and headed for the door, only stopping to throw the ball of greaseproof paper in the bin as she passed.

Biddy stared at the closed door as the determined clip of Emily's heels reverberated down the stairs.

She picked up the phone on Emily's desk.

Madge answered within seconds.

'Madge, she's off. I'm going to Elsie's room to listen from the back. I'll ring you with news. Have you got that?' Biddy shouted the last four words.

'Biddy, it's a telephone, not a quiz. Of course I've got it. Fingers crossed, eh. Did she have a good plan up her sleeve?'

'Did she? Of course she did. You know Sister Haycock. A plan a minute, that one.'

Biddy placed the phone back on its cradle and, taking a duster out of her pocket, polished the receiver. Her breakfast sat in her gut like a brick and her heart felt heavy. Digging deep into the pocket of her skirt, she extracted her rosary. 'Please let her pull this off, because if she doesn't, there will be a lot of families wondering where the next meal will be coming from.'

All the LDHB members were there, standing around, drinking Elsie's tea and chattering about the proposed plans for the big new hospital. The beaming, smug-faced Mrs Jolly looked like the cat who had the cream.

'She loves the fact that she's now the chair of the board, that one,' said Emily to Dr Gaskell.

'Now then, Emily, it's better to go with these changes, not resist them. We need to try and find our own way to work alongside them. I'm surprised I'm having to say this to you. You've been chomping at the bit to bring about changes of your own for quite a little while now.'

'Yes, but have you read this?' Emily gestured at the board table. In each place sat a pristine white copy of the agenda for the meeting and a copy of Miss Van Gilder's proposal.

'I have. The first item up today is the structural reorganization of staffing quotas and the second is the hospital cleaning proposal.'

Emily looked impressed.

'See, I haven't only seen it, I've studied it.'

She wanted to tell him what she knew and what the others knew. But that would be impossible without getting Madge into trouble. 'We have to find a way to stop this,' she whispered. 'Can I have your support? I mean, if I try to stop it, will you back me up?'

Dr Gaskell smiled at her over the top of his teacup. 'Emily, I am relieved you have asked. I was depending on you.'

There was a clatter of cups and saucers as members of the board took their seats around the table. Mrs Jolly cast a disapproving look towards Emily as she sat next to Dr Gaskell.

It must kill her that I am on the board, thought

Emily as she reread the agenda. She looked up and Dr Gaskell winked.

'Good morning, Sister Haycock,' Elsie said as she pushed the trolley up behind her. 'More tea?'

'Yes, please.'

'Good girl. You need to keep your strength up.'

As she turned round to take back the cup and saucer, Elsie winked at her. 'Good luck,' she whispered. 'I've put an extra sugar in for you.'

Emily gulped and smiled weakly.

Matron walked into the room with the step of a woman half her age and took her seat.

Did Matron just wink at me too? Emily was bemused. Has Dr Gaskell already told her I'm up to something? She put her head down and continued to read the detailed agenda.

'Shall we begin?' Mrs Jolly's voice boomed out over the large oak table.

Her authority was undermined only by the creaking wheels on Elsie's tea trolley and her 'Oh, sorry, everyone' as she bashed into the kitchen door before leaning forward to open it.

Mrs Jolly frowned. Elsie irritated her. She resented her overfamiliarity. She was one of the pre-NHS dinosaurs who did everything the old way. The wrong way.

'Matron, I am delighted to note from the agenda that there is a proposal to address the staffing levels at the hospital. I gather that Miss Van Gilder is the person to thank for this. It seems to me that some members of staff are way past their time of usefulness to the hospital and may only be here on account of their long service.' She shot a knowing look towards the retreating Elsie, who was struggling to manoeuvre the heavy wooden tea trolley through the kitchenette door.

The look hit the spot. Elsie wilted.

'Are you referring to me, Mrs Jolly?'

The line of bent heads, busy poring over the agenda, shot up at once. The meeting was already becoming interesting and they hadn't even reached item one.

Dr Gaskell had sounded both surprised and hurt.

'I most certainly am not,' said Mrs Jolly, affronted. She blushed with embarrassment.

'Oh, well, maybe you mean Matron then? You see, we have both been here for an awfully long time and, do forgive me, but the longevity of our tenure has, until now, often been regarded as rather an advantage. There have been occasions when our experience has been deemed useful.'

'Well, of course, Dr Gaskell, I entirely agree. But it is the case, is it not, that some members of staff are more useful than others. Obviously, in the case of Matron and yourself, your experience has been invaluable during St Angelus's transition from voluntary trust to NHS hospital. But we all have a shelf life, do we not? Even me, dare I say it.'

'Oh, indeed, Mrs Jolly. Even you.' Dr Gaskell leant forward and folded his arms on the desk.

Mrs Jolly was now obviously uncomfortable.

Mrs Twigg reached down towards the floor, took her handkerchief out of her handbag and coughed into it. Emily gave her the faintest smile. Mrs Twigg was almost squirming in her seat. Emily could tell she was a woman who loathed confrontation. She had presumably agreed to join the board out of duty to her dead husband and her country.

The other members of the LDHB were sitting ramrod straight in their chairs, hats perfectly in place, heads slightly bowed. Emily wasn't sure if she had actually ever heard any of them speak. Mrs Jolly did all the talking. The others were either too weak or too committed to the new plans, happy to abolish everything that had once represented community in a local hospital and follow Mrs Jolly and her political leaders down the road of the universal NHS.

'I think it might be best if we bring Miss Van Gilder in and hear what she has to say,' said Mrs Jolly. 'Don't you agree, Dr Gaskell?' Asking Dr Gaskell as an afterthought was a deliberate slight, thought Emily. This was only the second meeting he hadn't chaired in all the years he could remember.

The room braced itself as Mrs Jolly shouted to Elsie, 'Could you ask Assistant Matron to step inside, please.'

When Elsie opened the door, Miss Van Gilder stopped mid pace on the opposite side and glared at her. Your days are numbered, was the message she wanted to convey.

Elsie didn't speak, she just inclined her head towards the board table and gave Miss Van Gilder a menacing grin. Your days are numbered, was the message she too wanted to convey. Then she turned right along the corridor and headed for the back door of the kitchenette.

A confused expression flitted across Miss Van Gilder's face. Why had Elsie looked at her like that? But she had no time to ponder. The board members were waiting.

'Ah, Miss Van Gilder,' Mrs Jolly said enthusiastically. She was keen to get started. She wanted to get on with lifting St Angelus out of the old ways it had clung to. Here was a woman who was going to make the changes that were needed.

'What a wonderful choice Miss Van Gilder was for assistant matron,' she'd said to Mrs Twigg in the car on the way to the meeting. 'She will not flinch from her duty. She will bring about the changes that are so badly needed at St Angelus. She is a true angel.'

'Miss Van Gilder. We are most impressed to see that you have already produced a very comprehensive report regarding the modernizing of St Angelus and the reorganization of staffing. And in such a short time, too. Matron, what a bonus you have in Miss Van Gilder. Your workload must be so much lighter.'

Matron wished that was the case. In fact, the opposite was true. She had spent the last weeks trying to calm down any number of explosive situations. Miss Van Gilder had such an unfortunate and domineering manner, and Matron could think of barely a single person working at St Angelus whom she had failed to upset.

But she didn't say that. She merely nodded half-heartedly.

Dr Gaskell was certain that he heard a sharp intake of breath from Miss Haycock, and, much to his surprise, from Mrs Twigg as well. He had been studying inhaled and exhaled breath all his working life. He had definitely heard it. If Mrs Twigg was on their side, they might have a chance. However, Mrs Jolly had the casting vote.

He studied Miss Van Gilder as she opened her notes. He had been working with the angels of St Angelus his entire career and yet this one had flown into the boardroom like a winged nemesis. He and Matron would not be able to defeat her or reclaim their beloved hospital. Miss Van Gilder was on a mission and in her eyes was the glint of a woman who would not be stopped.

'Perhaps we should take item two first,' said Mrs Jolly. 'It seems to me that the reduction in staff numbers will come about as a direct consequence of item two. Am I correct in this assumption, Miss Van Gilder?'

Miss Van Gilder removed her spectacles, laid them carefully on the table before her and waited a few seconds before she began to speak.

'That is indeed the case, Mrs Jolly. However, I placed the reorganization of staff as item one as that is the main objective of Matron's endeavour. To ensure that the hospital runs as efficiently and economically as possible.'

Clever move, thought Emily. Passing it over to Matron, protecting your back. They all know it's you. Matron would never want to put people out of work or let the children of fallen soldiers go hungry.

'How that is achieved is of secondary consideration. I have today included a proposal from the Acme agency, but it could be any agency. I have of course diligently examined many quotes and have chosen Acme as my preferred option, although you may have other ideas.'

Miss Van Gilder held her breath and looked around the table, noting the admiring expressions. The last time she had reached this moment, some stupid man on the St Dunstan's board had piped up that he knew a man he had served with who was starting a cleaning business employing the wives of the fallen. She had had to think on her feet and argue for the fiscal responsibility of using an established company as opposed to a fledgling risk. 'After all,' she had chirped, 'it is not our money.' She had made that particular man look like the idiot he was, and she was ready to do the same again today.

'Miss Van Gilder, you have obviously put an enormous amount of effort into producing this report. I doubt that there is one person here who would be able to match the hours you have dedicated to securing the best deal for St Angelus.'

'Why, thank you, Mrs Jolly. Yes, well, it has been a case of not just securing the best agency for the job but finding one that understands modern cleaning methods. One not afraid to substitute machines for inefficient staff and, in the case of this hospital, older women, many of whom have costly health complaints resulting in many hours of absenteeism. I do believe I have found just such a company in the Acme cleaning agency.'

'May I please, Mrs Jolly?' Dr Gaskell had raised his hand and inclined his head, seeking permission to speak.

'Of course.' Mrs Jolly was a stickler for protocol and if anyone attempted to speak without first seeking her permission, she would cut them off with her razor-sharp tongue.

'Just how many of our present workforce will be made redundant if we accept your agency proposal, Miss Van Gilder?'

'All of them, Dr Gaskell.'

'All of them?' Dr Gaskell's voice rose as he spoke. 'You want to make every woman, some of whom have worked here for all of their working lives, remaining loyal to us throughout the war and ever since. All of them?'

Miss Van Gilder did not flinch. 'Dr Gaskell, each one of those women would of course be given priority when the agency recruits. As the owner pointed out to me during our negotiations, they always give preference to the women who know the hospital and its corridors and wards.'

'Really? How very generous of him. And at what price? Do our loyal and trusted staff receive a rise in their wages?'

Miss Van Gilder did not care for Dr Gaskell's tone. The smile had left her face. 'All the costings are listed under item two,' came her crisp reply.

'Please, Mrs Jolly, if I may?' Emily indicated that she would now like to speak.

'Yes, of course,' Mrs Jolly replied, without enthusiasm. She regarded Emily as a junior member of the board and did not value her contribution. She made a mental note to tag an extra item on to the agenda, that Miss Van Gilder replace Miss Haycock on the board at future meetings.

Emily shifted uncomfortably in her chair. 'Miss Van Gilder, I have examined the costings with a fine-tooth comb. Dr Gaskell may be interested to know . . .' She looked up to check that she had Dr Gaskell's attention. 'And I think there must have been a typing error on the part of the agency owner, because, as I see it, the workers he employs will be on only half the wage that the St Angelus cleaners are paid at present.'

Miss Van Gilder picked up her glasses, placed them on the bridge of her nose and looked down at the proposal before her as though checking to see if what Emily had just said was correct.

'Yes, well, the war ended almost nine years ago, Sister Haycock. I am afraid it is time to put the hospital first.'

'I agree.' Emily launched straight in without even bothering to catch Mrs Jolly's eye for permission to speak. 'Putting the hospital first has always been the position of everyone who works here, certainly since I arrived. Our hospital gleams like a new pin. The shine on the corridor floor bedazzles; you could eat your dinner off the ward floors. Our hospital, Miss Van Gilder, is the cleanest hospital I have ever worked in or seen and it is like that because the people who clean it were born here, their children were born here and their loved ones die here, as they themselves may do one day. Our workforce is emotionally invested in the well-being of our hospital. Everyone who works here cares with all their heart how clean and presentable St Angelus is. And, goodness me, this is not some hospital on the south coast. It is positioned on the banks of the Mersey in a dirty city with the filthiest air and the poorest people. How . . . How . . .' Emily's voice cracked. She paused and took a breath. 'How can your new cleaning agency expect those women to work with the same zeal and passion when he is cutting in half the wage they take home to feed their families?'

The room had fallen silent. If Dr Gaskell could, he would have leant over and kissed Emily. Matron thought her heart would burst. And unbeknown to them all, on the other side of the green baize door, Biddy and Elsie held hands while Biddy wiped a tear of pride from her eye.

'Whatever happens today, no one can say she

hasn't fought for us,' Biddy said. 'And if anyone ever tries to say any different, my God, they will have me to answer to.' And with that, they both placed their ears back on the upturned brandy glasses Elsie had taken out of Matron's sideboard for the purpose of more efficient eavesdropping.

'May I speak, please, Mrs Jolly?' Matron interjected. 'Miss Van Gilder,' she continued hurriedly, without waiting for permission, 'have you ever noticed the little competitions that take place between our ward sisters?'

A look of confusion crossed Miss Van Gilder's face.

'Do forgive me, I know it is difficult for a newcomer such as yourself to take in everything in such a short space of time,' Matron said pointedly. 'I have to admit, it was a few years before I cottoned on.' She laughed. 'I had always felt proud at how immaculate the hospital was, Mrs Jolly, but then it dawned on me that it was nothing to do with anything I said or did; it was all down to the ward sisters. Each sister wanted to be known for having the cleanest ward. They endeavoured to achieve the highest standards and the lowest number of post-operative infections and they drove their poor cleaners and probationer nurses to the limit in order to attain just that. That is why each ward has its own allocated domestics and orderlies. Because not only do the ward sisters and nurses take pride in the cleanliness of the wards, so do the cleaners themselves. And you know, that's why we make our nurses do their share of the cleaning too, especially the probationers. They begin by being taught that very important sense of pride in cleanliness. Now my question is, Miss Van Gilder, will your agency honour this system? Will each ward sister have her own dedicated cleaners?'

Miss Van Gilder was ready for this question, although the meeting was not going as well as she would have liked.

'The new cleaners will be machines, Matron. There will be no more mops and buckets, but floor cleaners and polishers. Cleaners will no longer be expected to have the same involvement as they did before; they will be sent to wherever in the hospital they are needed.'

Emily decided it was time to administer the killer blow. 'Miss Van Gilder . . .'

Mrs Jolly coughed her disapproval.

'I am sorry. Mrs Jolly, chairman, through yourself, just one last question.' Emily stormed on without waiting for a reply. 'Miss Van Gilder, do you know the owner of the Acme cleaning agency?'

Elsie squeezed Biddy's arm. Biddy almost yelped with the pressure.

'Ouch, will ye stop! I want to hear the answer.'

'Oh God, Biddy, I've almost wet meself. Rita Hayworth herself couldn't have done any better than that.' Elsie was almost jumping up and down on the spot.

'Matron, is there someone in the kitchen?'

Mrs Jolly peered towards the baize door in puzzlement.

'Only the domestic staff, preparing your lunch,' Matron answered.

Unbeknown to Elsie, she had given Miss Van Gilder time to compose her response.

'Obviously I know the owner. I have met him on a number of occasions. He spent time in the hospital and on the wards. He had to tell me what could be achieved and for what price.'

Clever reply, thought Emily.

Dr Gaskell furrowed his brow and looked directly at Emily. Her question had been loaded. He knew that there was something behind it, but he didn't know what.

'Is that the only capacity in which you know the owner, Miss Van Gilder? You had never met him before you came to St Angelus?'

'Sister Haycock!' Mrs Jolly's voice boomed down the table. 'That is the second time you have spoken without having the courtesy to seek the permission of the chair. You shall not speak again.'

Dr Gaskell coughed. Mrs Jolly took the hint.

'Miss Van Gilder, please answer that question. But, Sister Haycock, do not ask a supplementary question again. I am chairing this meeting, it is not a free-for-all.'

Miss Van Gilder averted her gaze. She would now have to tell a direct lie.

Before Miss Van Gilder had a chance to reply, they were all slightly startled to hear the most timid

623

of voices piping up. 'Mrs Jolly, may I be permitted to help Miss Van Gilder with this question?'

It was Mrs Twigg. A lady who rarely spoke, though Emily had always felt that she was on her side. She had squeezed Emily's hand in sympathy the day Miss Van Gilder had been appointed and Emily had been grateful.

'Why, of course, Mrs Twigg. Poor Miss Van Gilder is being bombarded with questions. I am quite ashamed, I have to say, that someone who has put so much work into this should receive such a hostile reception.' Mrs Jolly beamed encouragingly at Mrs Twigg.

Mrs Twigg picked up the proposal as though examining a fact. The board members fell silent. All eyes were upon her. They knew very little about her other than that she had lost both her husband and her only son. Her husband in the Great War, her son in the Second World War. Dr Gaskell had talked to her a few times over their pre-meeting coffee and she'd told him that she now tried to dedicate her time to causes that would make the world a better place. 'There must never be another war,' she had said.

Emily thought the air in the room felt heavy. Biddy and Elsie lifted their glasses off the door and checked to see if anything was wrong. Biddy shrugged and placed hers back again.

Miss Twigg lifted her head and looked directly at Miss Van Gilder. The sweet smile left her face and her expression hardened. Emily thought the feather sticking out of her hat looked totally ridiculous and wondered when women would stop wearing hats indoors.

Dr Gaskell thought, what a sweetie, she is trying to help.

Matron was suspicious. This woman was one of Mrs Jolly's acolytes. She had been directly nominated to the board by Mrs Jolly; her intervention could not possibly be helpful to the hospital.

'Miss Van Gilder . . .' Mrs Twigg's voice warbled with age and carried no authority. 'Is it not the case that the owner of the Acme cleaning agency is your son and that you left your last hospital just as you were about to be exposed for your dishonesty?'

The sound of breaking glass filtered through into the boardroom from the kitchenette.

CHAPTER 39

Matron and Dr Gaskell both stood in front of the window in Matron's sitting room while they waited for Emily to join them. Matron produced a decanter of sherry and Dr Gaskell did the honours. When Emily entered, she thought what a cosy room it was. The old burgundy leather chairs. The huge fireplace. Soon it would all disappear and be replaced by a new emergency-care unit. Sad, but a reality of booming, post-war Liverpool, she thought, as she walked across the acreage of carpet to join them.

Dr Gaskell handed Emily a glass. 'We have a few things to celebrate and while we're once again on the front foot, even if for the shortest time, we also have a few changes to implement.'

'Not all entirely with my approval,' said Matron.

Dr Gaskell smiled broadly. 'Margaret, I have never known you to approve of everything I say. Never! However, I credit the better running of this hospital to your difficult nature.'

He raised his glass. 'Emily.'

'As you can see,' said Matron, 'we are all on

first-name terms now, but I'm afraid it will always be "Dr Gaskell" for me.'

'And me,' said Emily as she took the glass and grinned at Dr Gaskell. He was up to something, she could tell.

'Emily, I wanted to say well done. If you had not opened up that line of questioning, I have no idea where that meeting would have ended up. I am not going to ask you how or why you travelled down that particular road or how you colluded with Mrs Twigg – I am not sure I want to know the details – but you were a class double-act.'

Emily took a large gulp of her sherry. She too would have liked to know how and why Mrs Twigg had taken up her line of questioning. She had never said more than half a dozen words to the woman. If there was any colluding with Mrs Twigg, she hadn't been involved.

'Have the police gone now?' she asked.

'Yes, thank goodness. I really do not like it when the police are in any part of the hospital other than casualty. Before you know it, a reporter from the *Echo* will be here. I don't know how they do it. When that factory burnt down, they were here before the patients, all over the place. I found one in the kitchens.'

'Ah well, they say that money is at the root of all evil, do they not.' Dr Gaskell raised his glass to his lips and sipped his sherry.

'It would appear so in the case of Miss Van

Gilder,' Emily said. Despite the excitement of the day, she looked downcast and deflated. Her usual sparkle had all but disappeared.

Matron looked at Emily and Dr Gaskell coughed. 'Go on,' he said. 'Or would you like me to do it?'

'Oh for heaven's sake!' said Matron. 'Really, I don't know what has got into you lately. Emily, Dr Gaskell and I have something to say.'

'Only Matron is the one about to do the talking.' Dr Gaskell grinned at Emily.

'We have decided that, while we have an advantage over Mrs Jolly and the LDHB, there is one change we would like to bring about. I concede that it is time. I may have stuck to my guns a little too long over this and as it is a rule I introduced a very long time ago, it is one I would like to be personally responsible for removing. I would rather that than have Mrs Jolly do it some day in the future as a means of imposing new rules from above. As from now, the no married nurses rule is to be abolished.'

For a few seconds Emily could hardly believe what she was hearing. It was as though she had stepped on to an alien planet.

'Am I about to wake up?' she asked. 'Matron, you have just called me Emily. And you've said that you're abolishing the married nurses rule. I absolutely have to be dreaming, don't I?'

Dr Gaskell reassured her otherwise. 'If you had not done what you did today . . . And, goodness me, it was a brainwave to enlist the help of Mrs Twigg, the most timid member on the panel. You deserve to be rewarded and this has been your pet project for some time.'

'You do understand that we will be leading the way?' said Emily. 'Even most of the London hospitals don't allow married nurses yet.'

'Exactly – not yet, they don't,' said Dr Gaskell. 'But, as you know, I sit on a number of committees in London and the universal abolition of the no married nurses rule as an NHS initiative is very much on the agenda. So why shouldn't we be the first? St Angelus should very definitely lead the way.'

Matron held out her hand to take Emily's glass. 'Finish your sherry, Emily. I think there may be something you have to go and do.'

Emily's eyes filled with tears at the prospect of trying to patch things up with Dessie. Which was clearly what Matron had in mind. Emily suspected Biddy's chattering tongue, but she couldn't think about that now. Matron's decision would change everything, but would Dessie see it that way? Had she put him off for ever? She handed Matron her glass. Today was certainly a day of huge surprises.

'I can't,' she whispered.

'Oh yes you can. You have already done a lot more today than say you're sorry. Do you really want to end up like me and all the other spinster matrons who have given their lives to nursing? To live out your days in a home for retired matrons or a hovel of a bedsit on Scotland Road because it is all the pension will stretch to?' Matron sighed and moved across to the window. 'Your support for a change in the rules has forced me to think about all this, Emily. There's a reason that nursing is a profession of the middle classes. I'm one of the lucky ones, I shall inherit from my mother, so when the day comes for me to leave here, I will manage well enough. But how will you survive alone, Emily? Who and what will you have? As you know only too well, nursing is one of the worst-paid jobs in the country. And the sad truth is, however careful you are, even if you are frugal, live in and save every spare penny throughout your working life, it's still unlikely you'll have enough for an even remotely comfortable old age.'

Everything Matron had said was true. Emily had no one and nothing.

'How do you know about . . .?' she asked.

'Never mind that. Did I ask you how you knew Mrs Twigg?'

'But . . .'

'Emily, no ifs or buts. He's waiting in my office. He thinks I have called him up here for a meeting. Go to him now, go on.'

Once Elsie and Biddy had cleared up the shattered brandy glass Elise had dropped behind the boardroom doors, they wasted no time in spreading the news of Miss Van Gilder's demise. By lunch time the mafia had their plans in place. There would

630

be a celebration in the hospital social club that night for all the domestics and everyone on Dessie's team.

While Matron, Dr Gaskell and Emily were drinking sherry, Branna was buttering bread and spreading paste on sandwiches down in the social club. Taking a break, she picked up the phone to Madge.

'Are they sending the keg here, Madge?'

'They are, Branna. Dessie organized it. He's sent four of the lads over with a trolley to collect it and some bottles of Guinness too for the ladies, in case we run out. They sent a Black Maria for Miss Van Gilder, did you see it?'

'I did. Good riddance. This will be the best party this hospital has ever known. We live to fight another day, eh, Madge? Have you seen Biddy and Elsie?'

'The last I saw of them was half an hour ago. They had Nurse Tanner with them and they were on their way to see Matron. I heard Matron telling Dr Gaskell on the phone to hurry to her rooms. She told him that if Sister Haycock came to the front door, Biddy and Elsie and Nurse Tanner would leave out the back. Fingers crossed that we'll have something else to celebrate tonight as well, Branna! Wouldn't that be lovely.'

'Well, well, it's all going on! Me, I'll just keep making the butties.'

'You do that, Branna.' Madge was laughing. 'But lay off the Guinness until tonight, would you.' She

631

pulled out the plug to the social club. 'Right, who's next to know the old bat's gone and the jobs are saved? Ah, the mortuary . . .'

Branna returned to the tower of unbuttered bread and hummed contentedly. She picked up her knife as Tom came in through the back door, carrying yet another tray of provisions from the main hospital kitchen.

'More bread, Branna. And cook sent over a slab of cheese. She said not to do all paste. People might think she did them. She said to make some cheese as well.'

'I'll grate it, Tom. It will go further that way. How many of the lads do you think will be coming tonight? I'm doing two rounds for each of them. Is that enough?'

Tom's eyes hadn't left the pile of sandwiches while Branna was talking.

'Here you go, take this one,' she said as she spread fish paste on two slices of bread.

Tom almost slammed the bread tray on the counter as he reached out to take it. He would never have asked Branna, he was too polite, but Branna could spot a hungry boy a mile away.

'Did you see the Black Maria, Branna? The police took old Bone Grinder. Can you imagine? What did she do?' He spoke between mouthfuls.

'She was a bad woman, Tom. She tried to take money from the hospital that wasn't hers and she tried to lose us all our jobs.'

632

Tom didn't know enough to know what question to ask next.

'Wait there,' said Branna and she filled him a mug of tea. 'There you go. Wash that down before you get back to work. How's your mam?'

Tom didn't reply until he had finished his tea and wiped his mouth with the back of his hand.

'Ta, Branna, that was grand, that. Mam's not well. She's had to give up her cleaning job at the school. She is coming in to St Angelus for an operation soon. She said she doesn't mind because she'll be able to see me every day at work.'

'Ah, did she, lad? Well isn't that lovely. And I bet she's jealous because I get to see you all the time. You're a good boy, Tom.'

Tom grinned from ear to ear as he picked up the tray to return it to the kitchen.

'See you for the craic later,' said Branna. 'With a bit of luck the hospital will be quiet tonight.'

As Branna watched Tom head to the door, she felt vindicated. She had let Biddy, Elsie and Madge gather their various bits of information about Miss Van Gilder, but, unbeknown to them, she had decided to make her own intervention. The notion that Sister Antrobus could be a useful ally had stayed with her since the last mafia meeting. She knew everyone thought Sister Antrobus was a tyrant, and goodness knows, Branna had had her run-ins with her when she was in charge of ward two. But Branna thought they might use her formidable reputation to their advantage. Everyone knew that Sister Antrobus was at loggerheads with Miss Van Gilder – it was the talk of the hospital every time they met and the sparks flew – so Branna had sought her out.

'We have a problem with Miss Van Gilder,' she'd said to her. 'I can't tell you how I know what I do and it has to be kept confidential, because I don't want to be getting anyone into trouble, but is there a way you could help?' Then Branna described everything they had uncovered about Miss Van Gilder and her son.

'Leave it with me,' Sister Antrobus said, her eyes gleaming. 'I think I have an idea, but I cannot tell you what. Don't mention to anyone that you've spoken to me.'

'Leave no stone unturned when dealing with a worm,' Branna muttered now, as she buttered yet more bread. 'No stone unturned.'

She would bide her time before telling the others that she had enlisted the help of Sister Antrobus. That day would come. Branna understood that in St Angelus knowledge was power and she now fancied a bit of that power for herself. 'Next time Madge comes the big I am . . .' she said to herself, slapping marge on another slice.

CHAPTER 40

At first, Amy ignored the pains. Bad stomach, she told herself. She ploughed on through the jam roly-poly the lady who did had left for pudding, but as a wave of nausea swept over her, she laid down her spoon and pushed the bowl away.

'Are you leaving good food?' her mother asked. 'Mind you, just as well. I'm sure you've noticed yourself, Amy, but you are putting on a few pounds there, my girl. Won't find yourself a husband looking more like that pudding than eating it.'

'I couldn't eat another thing. I'm full,' said Amy. 'I'm off to bed.' She pushed back her chair and stood up.

'Have you forgotten your manners? Since when did you think you could leave the table without asking?'

Amy ignored her mother and walked to the door, leaving her parents at the dining table. She knew that an argument would begin the moment she left.

'It's your fault, spoiling her so much. She doesn't even pretend to have any manners any more.'. Amy's faults were always laid at her father's door.

'You won't be wanting to get to bed so early soon,' said her father to Amy's back. 'I'm buying us a telly.'

'Well, I won't be able to watch it, not much anyway,' her mother piped up between mouthfuls. 'I can't sit in one place that long. Not with sciatica like mine.' She eyed Amy's bowl to see whether she'd left enough to be worth finishing off.

'You manage to do that most of the week when I'm at work,' her husband shot back. 'You've got a woman coming in every day now, what else do you do if you don't sit? You can't even remember how to cook a potato. The range is a stranger to you.'

Amy was almost glad they had launched into one of their arguments because she was seized by a horrendous pain. It felt as though someone had slipped a vice around her belly and was beginning to tighten the screws. She placed her hand on the doorframe for support and only just checked herself before she screamed out in agony. She gripped on tight. Stay up, stay up, were the words beating through her brain. She felt faint. Then, as fast as it had arrived, the pain began to fade.

Her parents, now in the full swing of what was becoming a major row, failed to notice her as they focused on inflicting their own wounds on each other. Her father berating her mother for her laziness. Her mother accusing her father of cruelty and indifference. All done across the safe barrier of a dark-oak Stag dining table, newly purchased from George Henry Lee's.

The pain had been debilitating, but as it began to ease, Amy pushed herself to the other side of the door and closed it before they noticed. Panting, exhausted and terrified, her first thought was that she was going to die. This can't be happening to me, she thought. It can't be. Panic almost broke through and she very nearly screamed out loud. All of her life, Amy had been given everything she wanted. But now Lockie had abandoned her and she had no idea who to turn to. 'I don't want this, I don't want it,' she sobbed. As the agony subsided, the questions screamed in her brain. Where to go? What to do? But no answers came back.

A soothing orange light crept into the hallway as the sulphur street lamp outside the front door ignited and filtered through the stained glass in the circular window of the front door. On the coat stand, Amy's black church coat and hat called out to her. Lifting the coat, she smelt the perfume on the collar. She slipped it on and wrapped herself in it. The familiar comfort of the satin lining soothed her burning skin. It took only a few steps to reach the door. Her parents' shouting was by now so ferocious, she didn't even have to worry about them hearing the gentle click of the Yale as it dropped.

Dana dropped her case on the pavement by the pier head and sat on it as she waited for Teddy to arrive in his car. She had telephoned Lovely Lane from the post office before she'd left

Belmullet, just as she'd promised she would, and Victoria had answered. 'When you get off the boat, you're not to move until Teddy gets there. He's given me explicit instructions for you to wait for him. He's longing to see you. Very excited he was. If you ask me, you should go away more often!'

Dana had laughed off Victoria's comment, but the fact that Teddy had obviously missed her so much brought with it a warm feeling on a chilly evening. She was happy to move no further than the pier head. It had been a choppy crossing and she had vomited twice. She was looking forward to being back in the Lovely Lane home with Mrs Duffy fussing over her.

She had toyed with the idea of stepping into the famous wooden-hut café to grab a cup of sweet tea, to settle her stomach, but she stopped short just before she reached the door. Sitting behind the gingham-curtained windows was Sister Antrobus and opposite her was a woman wearing a hat with a ridiculous feather sticking out of the top.

Dana decided to turn around and plonk herself back down on her suitcase. Even though she was off duty and not within the environs of St Angelus, she was sure that Sister Antrobus would find some reason to have a go at her. And besides, given that Teddy was working on casualty, Sister Antrobus would be the last person he would want to see.

She looked up the road and shielded her eyes as she heard what she thought was the sound of his engine. A smile crossed her face and her heart flipped. The speck on the horizon was indeed her Teddy's distinctive pale blue car and he was coming just for her.

Sister Antrobus had ordered tea and an Eccles cake. Mrs Twigg was having tea with white bread and butter and a sprinkling of salt.

'I don't think you should underestimate how many families you have helped,' said Sister Antrobus. 'As soon as I heard what was happening, I knew I had to speak to you. I was honour-bound not to reveal the source of my information, so I simply could not take this to Matron.' She poured the tea as she spoke.

'If you had taken your information to Matron, you would have earned yourself a great deal of praise. Indeed, you would most likely have found yourself back in charge of ward two as your reward.' Mrs Twigg stirred in her sugar, keeping her gaze fixed on Sister Antrobus as she did so.

Mrs Twigg had been sorry to hear that Sister Antrobus had been moved from ward two to casualty. Even so, she'd often thought her manner rather too military for the women's ward.

'I am aware that would have been a possibility. However, one has to do the right thing.'

Sister Antrobus had been surprised when Branna had confided in her. They had rubbed along well, she and Branna. Very few words had ever passed between them, but there was an implicit understanding that ward two had to be the cleanest in the hospital. Both women were happy to make that their goal and so there had been very little need for conversation. When Branna had told her about Miss Van Gilder, Sister Antrobus had known exactly whom to contact. She had no idea how Branna knew that the new assistant matron was a con-woman, but she was prepared to believe her without question.

Mrs Twigg sipped her tea. It had been quite a dilemma for her, when Sister Antrobus had asked her to speak out. However, she had a lot of respect for Sister Antrobus, who had once looked after her son. In fact, Sister Antrobus was one of the reasons Mrs Twigg had agreed to accept a position on the board of St Angelus when the LDHB had approached her. Her late son had been hospitalized during the early days of the war and Sister Antrobus had taken very good care of him. She would always be in the sister's debt. She didn't ask how Sister Antrobus had acquired the facts about Miss Van Gilder; she had simply asked herself the question, if my son or my husband had come to me with this information, what would I have done? She knew what they would have expected of her. It was her duty. As much as she disliked having to speak up at the board meetings, it had fallen to her to do the right thing.

'The police asked to speak to me after the meeting. I told them I had received an anonymous tip-off and that the rest was down to Miss Van

Gilder. She really put up very little defence. They arrested her son, Luuk, within the hour, so I heard.'

'You were a heroine, Mrs Twigg. A heroine,' said Sister Antrobus.

'Not a bit of it. Sister Haycock's questioning of Miss Van Gilder set me up beautifully. It seems likely she may have had the same information. Be that as it may, I was very flattered that the LDHB has invited me to chair the board at future meetings. I'm not sure what has happened to Mrs Jolly. Another cup of tea, Sister?'

Teddy drove faster than usual. He was in a hurry to reach Dana. He felt as though he had been granted a second chance. He had asked himself the question over and over again: how could he have been so stupid? To have fallen for the charms of Nurse Makebee, to have turned his back on Dana as he had? 'You stupid, stupid man,' he said as he banged the polished wooden dashboard with his fist. He could see her up ahead, sitting on the edge of the pier head, perched on her suitcase, her chin in her hands, her red hair blowing in the wind. He looked up to check it was safe before he crossed the tram lines and, seeing that it was clear to go, he slipped the car up a gear, put pressure on the accelerator and made to cross the wide expanse of road.

He didn't see where she had come from, the pregnant girl in the black coat. It was as though she loomed up from nowhere as she staggered across the road. He shouted out a warning, put his foot to the floor of the car and heard the brakes screech in response. He saw her face seconds before she hit his windscreen and then there was nothing but silence.

Sister Antrobus saw it happen through the café window. She watched the girl move out from the side of one of the dockside buildings and then observed with amazement as, without looking, she staggered across the tram tracks in the direction of St Angelus.

Sister Antrobus did not hesitate. She jumped up, sending her fresh cup of tea flying, and strode hurriedly outside. She was surprised to find Nurse Brogan there and even more surprised to discover that the driver of the car was Dr Davenport. From the poor nurse's distress, it quickly became apparent that this was no coincidence. Nurse Brogan had obviously been waiting for Dr Davenport. Sister Antrobus immediately took control of the situation and gave instructions to Mrs Twigg and the café owner. 'Tell them to send two ambulances,' she shouted, 'and on the double.'

'Here, you take this,' she said to the rather surprised driver of the first ambulance to arrive. She threw Dana's case on to the front seat. 'Nurse Brogan is coming with you in the back. Put your light on and your foot down.'

'You take Dr Davenport,' Sister Antrobus said

to Dana as she helped her up the rear steps of the ambulance. 'I will travel with the girl. She is still alive, but only just, and she's very pregnant. She will need an emergency caesarean as soon as we get there, in which case the baby may still have a chance. Dr Davenport looks to me like he might come round. Keep talking to him.' And with that, she was gone. There were two lives that needed saving inside her own ambulance.

Seconds later, the sound of two-tone sirens filled the air as both ambulances screeched up towards St Angelus.

'Teddy, can you hear me?' Dana fell to her knees beside him in the back of the ambulance.

He was strapped into the trolley bed as though it were a straitjacket. Both legs were very obviously broken and there were a multitude of injuries to be attended to. His eyes were swollen to the size of purple eggs and impossible to open, but he could speak.

'Dana, is that you?'

'Yes, it's me, my darling. I'm here with you. We are both in an ambulance. You've had an accident, but you are going to be just fine.'

'Are you sure?' His lips were dry and bloodstained and he had difficulty speaking.

Dana opened the last packet of gauze she could find among the ambulance supplies and applied more pressure to the wound on his forehead.

'Yes. I'm not going to lie to you. You are pretty

beaten up, and it was a nasty accident, but you are alive and kicking, my darling.' Her voice broke on the last words as relief swamped her.

Her tears dropped on to his face and she quickly wiped them away. 'Please hurry,' she whispered as he seemed to leave her again. She felt the ambulance take a corner virtually on two wheels, and then came the sound of brakes and a sudden jolt as they stopped.

Dana leant forward. 'We have arrived now, Teddy. We'll be out in a second. I will be here for every single second and I shall beg Matron for a transfer to male orthopaedic. I will be with you all the way, my love, and we will get you right.'

Teddy had come to as the ambulance jolted. He squeezed the hand Dana was holding in response. 'The pain,' he muttered. And then, 'Sorry, Dana, I'm so sorry.'

'Oh God, why are you saying sorry?' she sobbed. 'It's not your fault, my love. You couldn't help it, she just walked . . .'

The rear ambulance doors flew open and Dr Mackintosh stood framed in the back light of the fading day. 'Right, let's not waste time. Straight to theatre,' he shouted to Jake and Bryan who had raced over with a trolley.

Dana couldn't move. She didn't want to leave Teddy's side.

Anthony Mackintosh didn't bother with the steps; in one leap he was alongside Dana, and with both hands under her elbows he propelled her towards Jake. 'You take Nurse Brogan inside, Jake,' he said. 'Bryan and I will see to Dr Davenport.'

Dana couldn't see through her tears but allowed herself to be led inside casualty.

'Can you take Nurse Brogan off me, Doreen?' asked Jake.

'Of course,' Doreen replied. 'You get on.'

Mr Mabbutt, the orthopaedic surgeon, hurried past them both. 'Take him straight to theatre,' he shouted out of the open doors as he headed for the back stairs to theatre.

'They are doing exactly that,' said Sister Antrobus. She was already wheeling a trolley into the clean utility room, dressed in her day clothes. Twenty minutes had passed and she had organized casualty to run in the manner of a field hospital and with the same degree of precision.

Oliver Gaskell had been working on maternity when the news of the RTA came through. He raced through the front door of casualty as Mr Mabbutt left for theatre. 'Mother? Baby?' he barked at Sister Antrobus as he came alongside her.

'We have both, Mr Gaskell, but we also have no operating theatre available,' said Sister Antrobus. 'Today's list hasn't yet finished, they are mid way through an appendix and the emergency theatre will be busy for some considerable time with Dr Davenport. He is in a very bad way, I'm afraid. It was first come, first in, and his ambulance got here first.'

'God, no! Not Teddy. How bad is he?'

'I have no idea, Mr Gaskell. I am a nursing sister, not a doctor. Now, with regards to the mother, I have set up the clean utility room with a cubicle bed and a delivery pack. There is no need for a caesarean, the baby is making its own forcible entrance. Forceps will be required. Everything is in there ready for you. Nurse Tanner will assist you. Mother had no external injuries or bleeding. The houseman already has her on a ventilator and he is working wonders at keeping her alive.' She lowered her voice. 'But not for long, we fear.'

Oliver Gaskell nodded. 'Head injury?' he enquired.

'Yes. Severe. Dr Mackintosh has already performed a neurological examination. There's nothing. No pupil reaction, no response to stimuli, nothing. No other physical injuries, but . . .'

'Righty oh, I had better get cracking before we run out of time. Do we know who her husband is?'

'We don't have a clue. No handbag with her, nothing in her coat pocket other than a receipt from a hairdresser. The police will follow that one through.'

Oliver Gaskell disappeared through the door of the clean utility room. Sister Antrobus saw Nurse Tanner and Dr Mackintosh in the process of gowning up. She was content. Nurse Tanner had come a long way in a very short time. She hadn't asked her to gown up; Nurse Tanner had obviously done so on her own initiative. There was a time when she would have reprimanded a nurse for such presumption, but not today. And besides, she could honestly say that Nurse Tanner would do a good job. Instead, she turned towards the desk.

'Doreen, please ring the Lovely Lane home and tell Mrs Duffy we need Nurse Baker up here. I believe her fiancé is related to Dr Davenport. Ask her to come and look after Nurse Brogan and to let her fiancé know what is happening as he is obviously Dr Davenport's next of kin. Could you then ring Matron and ask her to let Dr Gaskell know that one of the hospital doctors is in a serious condition in theatre, but I have no prognosis if she asks. Please tell the sister on duty in the operating theatre to telephone with regular updates in order that we can reassure Nurse Brogan, Nurse Baker, his family and the rest of us. He is one of our own; it matters,' she added. 'When you have done that, could you please just pop your head in the door of the clean utility and see if Nurse Tanner needs any help with the baby when it's delivered. Ask someone on children's to bring a nappy and a shawl down.'

'I will do all that now, Sister,' Doreen replied. 'Could you check on cubicle two? There's a gardener in there from the Lake District. He is visiting his sister, says she has given him tinnitus. I have no one else to ask, everyone is busy.'

'I will. Thank goodness Dr Gaskell's son was still on duty,' said Sister Antrobus as she headed for cubicle two. She was not the only one who continued to refer to Oliver Gaskell as his father's son.

'Sister . . .'

Sister Antrobus turned back to answer Doreen's question.

'Do we know who the young woman is? Should I be ringing someone other than the police?'

'We don't. She wasn't carrying a handbag, which is very odd. It's almost as though she wanted to walk in front of a car. Or a tram, maybe. But no, there is no one to call. I wish there were because that is one prognosis I am very sure of.'

Nurse Tanner hurried out of the clean utility room and placed a gurgling baby into Doreen's arms. It was tiny, but it was wriggling. It was alive. 'Here, Doreen, take the baby, would you?' she said. 'We have nothing in there to lay a baby down on even, and the mother needs me.'

Pammy could just about see through the river of tears that had filled her eyes. Doreen's response was equally emotional as the tiny bundle looked up at her with wide and knowing eyes.

'It's a little girl,' Pammy said. 'Can you carry her up to ward three? I know it's not in the rules to carry a baby, but we've only two porters on tonight. They are all at a big party over in the club. I need to see to Dana.'

'Of course I can, but don't worry about Nurse Brogan. Nurse Baker, Nurse Harper and Mrs Duffy are with her and she is being well looked after. Sister

Antrobus has put them in her office and closed the door. Jake took a tray of tea in a minute ago.'

Pammy's mascara had streaked and dried on her cheeks in black rivulets. 'I look a sight, don't I?' she said as she rubbed at her cheek.

'It's the least of your troubles tonight,' said Doreen as she hugged the baby to her.

Pammy made her way back to the clean utility room. She had been due to go off duty hours ago, but she refused to go home. Casualty had never been so busy before.

'Go!' Dr Mackintosh had told her. 'The night staff are arriving, we can manage.'

They had been standing outside the door to the clean utility, out of view of the main casualty unit.

'Are you kidding me?' she said. 'That's my friend out there. I'm not leaving while Dana's in such a state.'

And that's mine in the operating theatre, Anthony had thought to himself.

'Oh, I'm sorry,' said Pammy. 'I didn't mean that. Dr Davenport and you are good friends too.'

'I know you didn't,' he replied, and without thinking he held out his arms and Pammy fell into them. For a moment he held her tight and they took some comfort from each other's warmth.

'Right, back to work,' he said. 'Let's see if we can do anything for the mother. But you have already worked fourteen hours straight.' He stood back slightly and with both hands held her upright. He blamed his tiredness, emotional stress and all manner of hypothetical circumstances, but really he had no idea where his next words came from. 'Nurse Tanner, when this is all over, would you come out with me? I love your mam.'

Pammy half giggled and her tears began again. 'You want to go out with me because you love my mam?'

Anthony grimaced. 'Agghh, I didn't mean it to come out like that . . .'

'I know you didn't. Don't worry, I know what you mean. She works miracles, my mam. She sent me into Matron's office today. Wanted to work one of her miracles through me. You won't believe what I had to talk to Matron about. I'd love to go out with you. But first, we have to get through all of this. When will we hear from theatre?'

'Oh, it will be ages yet.' He took a deep breath. 'Teddy will take a great deal of repairing and putting back together, and then there's the shock. He has to survive that and that's his biggest obstacle. Mr Mabbutt and the anaesthetist will be having a very difficult time up there.'

Within minutes Nurse Tanner and Dr Mackintosh were out on the unit again.

'Has she gone?' Sister Antrobus asked.

Pammy removed her handkerchief from her apron and wiped her eyes. 'It was almost as if she was holding on, waiting for the baby to be safe before she went,' she said. 'And the shock of the delivery of course,' she added as Sister Antrobus frowned.

'Far more likely,' replied Sister Antrobus. 'No

room for sentimentality on a good casualty unit, Nurse Tanner, although there's a lot of it about today. However, well done. You coped well. Are you taking the baby up to ward three?' she said, addressing Doreen. She looked down at the bundle in her arms. 'What a tiny scrap of a thing. They will weigh it upstairs.'

Doreen stopped outside clean utility and peered in. The houseman was writing out the death certificate and had pulled a sheet up over the mother's face. 'Has she gone?' she asked. 'The police have arrived. It's mad out there,' she said.

The bundle began to whimper, as though it could sense its mother was nearby. Doreen's gaze lingered on the young woman's hands as they lay uncovered by her side. They were delicate, elegantly manicured. Almost familiar. The room felt different to Doreen, although she could not say why. A shiver ran through her.

'I'm not an expert in this stuff, but it might be best to take the baby away,' said Dr Mackintosh as he came in behind her. 'Some think a baby can smell its mother.'

'You all right, Doreen?' asked Pammy as she wiped down the dressings trolley.

'I am. I feel as though someone just walked over my grave. What a shame she never got to hold her baby,' said Doreen, indicating the young woman on the trolley. 'She is such a beautiful little thing.'

'Did you not hear me say? There's no room for

651

sentimentality on a good casualty unit. Off with you. Take her to ward three, where I sincerely hope they have a cot ready.'

'Yes, Sister, right away.' Doreen slipped past with the baby nestled in her arms.

But Sister Antrobus hadn't finished. 'Nurse Tanner, are you wearing make-up?' Casualty may have felt like a battlefield, but nothing slipped past the beady eye of Sister Antrobus.

As Doreen walked up the stairs, she couldn't help feeling that she knew this little girl already. She never took her eyes off her. Big, blue, staring eyes. 'Don't worry, there will be a bottle coming in a minute,' she said as the baby sucked furiously on her fist.

She turned into the ward and the staff nurse indicated a cot. 'Just put her in there for now. I swear I will get a feed down her as soon as I have a moment.'

Doreen took in the vast, lonely cot and the bottle that stood waiting in a jug on the locker. The ward was busy to the point of mayhem. Looking around her to ensure that no one was watching, she picked up the bottle and, settling into the nursing chair, she fed the tiny girl. The baby guzzled greedily, her eyes never leaving Doreen's. Doreen had no idea why, but for the first time in a long while, as she stroked the tiny, perfectly formed fingers topped with papery thin fingernails, she thought of her old friend Amy. She missed Amy. Time had passed and the hurt had subsided. It wasn't

Amy's fault she'd been attacked, but Doreen lived at home and her father's order that she must never speak to Amy again had been unequivocal.

She lowered her head and breathed in the smell of the newborn. 'Oh, you have just stolen my heart,' she whispered to the feeding baby. 'I'm going to have to keep my eye on you.' Something told her that the little girl would become a part of her life.

Half an hour later, the staff nurse returned, ready to take over from Doreen. 'I wonder what we should name her,' she said absent-mindedly. 'I have to put something in the notes. Any ideas? How about Doreen?' The nurse smiled down at Doreen as she lifted the baby on to her chest to wind her after the feed.

'Oh, God, no, don't inflict that on her,' said Doreen and then she surprised herself when she added, 'Why don't you call her Amy? That's a lovely name.'

The nurse had no time to argue as the child in the next cot began to whimper. 'Smashing. Amy it is then. You are right, it is a lovely name.'

Dr Mackintosh headed off to see to a patient he had left in the last cubicle and Pammy made her way to join Dana and the others.

'Over here, everyone,' said Sister Antrobus. 'Into my sitting room. Nurse Brogan, Nurse Tanner. Mrs Duffy. It's all yours until we know what's happening. Nurse Baker, bring your fiancé in too, of course.'

Doreen was now back behind her desk, having reluctantly left little Amy on ward three. She was typing out the patient notes for the gardener who'd been discharged by Dr Mackintosh. She'd nearly finished when the telephone rang.

'Hello. Casualty,' she said when she picked up. Thank God it's not the red phone, she thought. That was the one that linked directly through to the emergency ambulance service. Her relief did not last long.

'Hello, it's Sister here from the operating theatre. Mr Mabbutt would like to speak to Dr Mackintosh urgently please. Now.'

Stunned, Doreen laid the receiver on the desk.

Dr Mackintosh was tending to an elderly lady who had been admitted with a broken hip right in the middle of the RTA. There was also a child who had been hit in the face with a stone. His family were distraught, sobbing in the waiting area, convinced he had lost his eye. They had all that to deal with, the busiest time she had ever known on casualty.

To her relief, right then Dr Mackintosh appeared on the outside of the curtained cubicle he'd been working in. 'Dr Mackintosh!' she said. 'Quick, it's the phone for you. Sister from the operating theatre. She says it's urgent.'

She held up the receiver to him and watched, her heart pounding, as the blood drained from his face.

'It's too soon,' Anthony said almost to himself

as he glanced at the huge clock on the wall above Doreen's head and took the phone.

Just at that moment, Matron walked in, much to Doreen's surprise. Doreen walked over to meet her, thankful to leave Dr Mackintosh to his call.

'Hello, Doreen, I have come to help,' Matron said.

Doreen couldn't concentrate. She had worked in casualty for long enough to sense when something not good was about to happen. It was as if the air left the room and time stood still. Without a word of explanation, Dr Mackintosh threw down the phone and ran towards the stairs leading to theatre. Through the open door to the sitting room, Doreen saw Nurse Brogan, white as a sheet, staring after him in a daze, her hand gripped tightly in Nurse Tanner's. Nurse Baker was in there too, with her fiancé, and Mrs Duffy as well. Doreen heard a desperate, anguished sob from the room as Mrs Duffy rose from her seat and, giving Doreen the faintest smile, closed the door.

Hours later, Doreen's desk stood empty and tidy. Everyone was now long gone. Dispatched to the safety of a ward, to Lovely Lane, or home.

Matron allowed herself a small smile as she saw Dr Mackintosh slip his arm around Pammy's waist when she passed through the door he was holding open for her. It was almost morning and they were the last to leave. It was a gesture of familiarity she guessed could only lead to greater intimacy. The thought occurred to her that the abolition of the no married nurses rule meant that Nurse Tanner could be working at St Angelus for a very long time to come.

Betty Hutch hummed to herself as she mopped the floor. 'Oh, sorry, Matron,' she said as she wiped right over the toe-caps of Matron's shoes.

'That's all right, Betty,' said Matron, 'they needed a good clean.' Matron knew the name of every single domestic at the hospital and always made a point of speaking to them when she passed them in the corridor on her way back to her rooms.

The two night nurses were washing down the walls of the clean utility room. Satisfied that all was in order, Matron walked over to Sister Antrobus's sitting room.

Sister Antrobus was clearing up the discarded tear-soaked handkerchiefs and empty teacups. 'What a night,' she said as she straightened her back. 'You really don't ever know on casualty what is going to happen next, do you?'

'No, you certainly don't. And that is more true now than ever before. If you think what casualty was like only this time last year, it's almost frightening how fast things are changing. One road accident can dominate the casualty unit for many hours. And who'd have thought it would be one of our own.' Matron sighed heavily.

'Yes indeed. Well, Matron, there has been a lot of tea drunk tonight, but now seems the time for something stronger. I keep some whisky in the medicine cupboard for those patients who need it. Would you like some?'

'I think that's a jolly good idea, Sister Antrobus.'

Matron raised her glass and took a warming sip. She felt overcome with gratitude towards the woman who, on her day off and in her own clothes, not even in uniform, had held casualty together on the busiest night they had ever known.

'Sister Antrobus, I think you should know that Mrs Twigg telephoned me to see if you and Nurse Brogan were all right. She also enquired after Dr Davenport. She told me that you were both having afternoon tea at the time of the accident.'

Sister Antrobus blushed and took a much larger sip from her own glass.

'So, you see, I can only guess at the connection between yourself and Mrs Twigg. I have worked here long enough and I am sufficiently familiar with this old building to know that, indeed, I should not ask.'

She waited for Sister Antrobus to fill the gap. She did not hold her breath.

As she'd expected, Sister Antrobus made no reply. Instead, she looked down into what was left of the amber liquid in her glass and swirled it around.

'Well, I had better be getting back. Blackie will think it most odd that I have left him in the middle of the night.' She placed her glass on the table with painstaking care, giving Sister Antrobus an extra few seconds, should she change her mind.

657

She knew that this conversation would never be referred to again.

As she opened the door, she turned and said, 'Sister Antrobus, I want to thank you. Not just for tonight, but because of whatever it was you did. I am sure I will never know exactly who did what, but I am sure of this, that because of Sister Haycock and yourself, St Angelus lives to fight another day.'

Teddy lay on the trolley in the anaesthetic room in theatre. His heart had stopped beating twice and both times Dr Mackintosh had successfully used his new technique to bring him back. 'Amazing work,' said Mr Mabbutt. 'I think you are going to have to teach that method to everyone in the hospital, Dr Mackintosh.'

It was just before dawn when Dana, Victoria and Roland were allowed into the theatre block. 'I have done what I can for now,' Mr Mabbutt told them. Victoria stood in the middle, holding both Dana's and Roland's hands. 'I can't do any more yet. He needs to stabilize before I dare touch him again. The good news is, if he makes it through the next twenty-four hours, we will be in with a fighting chance. His legs were broken and his spleen was ripped. All we can do now is pray.'

Dana tried to speak, but the words stuck in her throat.

Roland made a better job of it. 'How do you feel about it all, Mr Mabbutt? Do you think he will pull through?' Roland looked as though he was terrified of hearing the answer. His face almost flinched in anticipation of the verdict.

'I have to say, Mr Davenport, I do. He is a young man, strong and fit. We have stopped the internal bleeding, got four units of blood straight into him and his blood pressure is climbing. His pulse is stronger. We have a good chance here.'

Dana's sob caught on her breath. 'Oh, God, thank you, Mr Mabbutt!' she cried.

'Now, now, Nurse Brogan, there is no need to thank me. You have a long road ahead of you. Dr Davenport is looking at six months of healing, at the very least. And, as I said, we aren't out of the woods yet. However, he is going to need a great deal of looking after. I'm not entirely sure how those legs are going to heal, never mind anything else.'

'They will heal,' said Dana with determination in her voice. 'They will heal because I will look after him every day. I will give up nursing and take him back to Mammy's if I have to. He will heal, Mr Mabbutt.'

Roland and Victoria left Dana with Teddy while they went to fetch the car. 'You are coming back to Lovely Lane to sleep, Dana,' Victoria had said sternly. 'There is no argument about it. We can all come back later, but without sleep we will be no use to anyone.'

Dana stroked Teddy's hair back from his face and kissed the back of his hand. She watched the drip and took his pulse, did all the things she would have done if she was specialling her own patient. She noticed the eerie quiet of the hospital, as she often did when she sat with a patient at night. The dark corridors, night-lit wards and silence gave St Angelus a very special feel in the early hours. Soon, the bustle would begin again. The bright overhead lights would flick on and the sound of water running into bowls and bedpans clanging on to metal trolleys would fill the air.

'I have to go, my love,' she whispered into Teddy's hair.

The smell of anaesthetic was strong on his breath and the houseman who had been told not to leave his side hovered nearby. But she didn't care. She had nearly lost her Teddy and that alone made everything else seem so trivial. She felt the slightest squeeze on her hand and his eyes half fluttered.

'That's a good sign,' whispered the houseman.

'It is. It's a very good sign,' Dana said as her eyes filled with tears. 'You sleep, my love,' she whispered, 'because from tomorrow we start work to get you better and I will be with you all the way. I won't leave your side.'

'I'm sorry.' Teddy spoke. He tried to twist his head and yanked at the giving set in his hand. The words came out as a whisper, through dry and cracked lips, but they were unmistakeable the second time. 'Dana, I'm sorry.'

'Teddy, I don't want you to say those words again, you eejit.'

Teddy tried to lift his head.

'No, Teddy. Please, just stay still, will you. I don't know what it is you are trying to say sorry for and I don't care. We have months of healing ahead of us and you can talk all you like then. Only the future matters from now on. Do you understand? It's all that matters. Only the future. I'm sorry too, Teddy. I'm sorry too. I should never have left you to be alone.'

Five minutes later, Victoria crept into the room to collect Dana. She smiled at the sight before her: Dana, asleep, her head resting on Teddy's hand. Teddy, already looking more rested.

'I'd say he has improved in the last half hour alone,' said the houseman as he finished taking Teddy's blood pressure.

'Good,' said Victoria, 'because Dana won't be happy with anything less than that rate of recovery.'

Betty Hutch wheeled her bucket into the mop cupboard. She had stopped humming some minutes back. Her coat was on and fastened and her headscarf tied under her chin. She held her hand on the door to let the catch slip down without the usual clatter. She would call in at the dairy at the end of Arthur Street on her way home for a pint of warm milk, but first she had news to pass on. Matron and Sister Antrobus had made up. And they had Sister Antrobus to thank for saving the hospital as well as Emily Haycock. Betty had heard every word. They hadn't even noticed her as she mopped right outside the sitting-room door. If she was quick enough, she might just catch her neighbour, Biddy, before she left for work and pass on the news. She might catch Elsie too, on her way to the bus stop. There was nothing Betty Hutch liked more than passing on a bit of news.